The Barefoot Billionaires

A Barefoot Bay Collection

Roxanne St. Claire

Author's Note:

Welcome to Barefoot Bay, a slice of paradise on tropical Mimosa Key, tucked into the Gulf Coast of Florida. Here you'll find a small but upscale resort called Casa Blanca, where love is always in the air.

In the following novellas, you'll meet a trio of sexy, flirtatious, irresistible billionaires and the unlikely heroines who steal their hearts. I hope you love these stories of redemption and romance!

Secrets on the Sand: Our first hero is Zeke Nicholas, who has turned his mathematical genius skills into a mountain of money. But Zeke sits on that mountain all alone, longing for the one thing money cannot buy: a lifelong partner and true love. That's about to change in the most unexpected way.

Seduction on the Sand: Lucky, charming, and blessed with every gift, Elliott Becker expects his simple purchase of rural land in Barefoot Bay will go the way everything does for him in life…easy. Until he meets the woman who currently owns that land and suddenly everything is…hard.

Scandal on the Sand: Nathaniel Ivory, billionaire bad boy and part of an American dynasty. Nate's got his hands full with his plans to prove to his family that there won't be any more trouble, headlines, or scandals. Until he comes face to face with a woman who promises all of those and more.

Pull up a beach chair, kick off your shoes, and fall in love with three unforgettable Barefoot Billionaires!

—Roxanne St. Claire

Contents

Secrets on the Sand

Dedication

Dedicated to reader, friend and fan Tonya Loose Dawson
in appreciation for her constant support and cheerleading!

Chapter One

"Oh, how the mighty have fallen."

Amanda froze at the sound of Tori Drake's sneer, refusing to react even though the cold porcelain of the toilet rim pressed against her forearm as she brushed the bowl.

"Mandy Mitchell's up to her elbows in someone else's shit."

Of all the other housekeepers to be assigned to the same floor, she had to get Tori. "As you know, I go by Amanda Lockhart now."

"Ah, you'll always be Mandy Mitchell to me, hon. Homecoming queen. Head cheerleader. Runner-up for Miss Teen Florida. Junior housekeeper." She choked softly. "What's wrong with this résumé, kids?"

Breathing slowly, holding it together, Amanda sat straight, the move pressing the hard tile into her knees with the same force that Tori's insults hit her heart. But not as much force as she'd like her fist to hit the other housekeeper's face.

"Do you need anything to finish your rooms?" Amanda asked, faking nice as much as she possibly could. She was too far behind this morning to get into it with Tori. Besides, if the universe decided it hated Amanda enough, she could very well be calling this woman "boss" soon. The thought made her almost want to hurl into the toilet instead of clean it.

"Oh, I don't need a thing," Tori said.

"You sure? Because my supply cart is right there, and I've got plenty of Pine-Sol and Clorox." *In case you want to drink a little.*

"Nah, I've cleaned all my rooms, of course. That's why they call me the fastest maid in Barefoot Bay. Possibly on all of the Gulf Coast. Maybe the entire state of Florida."

"Why not the world?"

"Why not?" Tori snorted with self-satisfaction and stepped further into the bathroom, which was sizable, being in a high-end resort hotel, but no room was big enough for the two of them. Uninvited, Tori leaned lazily on the granite vanity, sliding a judgmental finger over the surface. "You didn't use the Magic Eraser on this."

"I'm not done yet."

"Oh, you're just about done, my friend."

At the smug tone and the subtle warning, Amanda twisted from the toilet to look up at the other housekeeper, narrowing her eyes. "What does that mean?"

Tori crossed arms well-toned from hard work and deeply tanned from years of baby-oil-and-iodine-infused sunbathing. Her gray eyes danced with a secret, and derision pulled at her lips. "We are very close to a done deal."

Amanda's heart dropped. This was the worst possible news. "I'll believe it when I see it," she said.

Tori arched a penciled brow, forming lines on her forehead. More lines than Amanda had, considering they were the same age of thirty. The thought gave Amanda small consolation since beauty and lines now took a back seat to money and survival.

"Then you better believe it, sister." Tori pushed her butt onto the counter. "My man Jared has nearly closed financing and has made an offer on office space right in downtown Mimosa Key, not ten minutes down the beach. J&T Housekeeping, LLC, is about to be a reality, and guess what that means?"

The end of the world. Well, not quite. But most likely the end of this job. Once Casa Blanca Resort & Spa outsourced housekeeping to one company, then Amanda would have to work for that company or leave the resort. If "J&T Housekeeping" got the business…unemployment loomed.

"It means congratulations are in order," Amanda said, barely keeping the bitter out of her voice. But it was hard not to be bitter. Amanda had made the huge mistake of nursing the fantasy of opening that housekeeping firm herself when resort management announced the outsourcing plan. The taste of independence, of owning a business, of never having to clean a toilet again, had been sweet…for about two weeks.

She'd even met with the resort owner to talk about it. Then she'd done enough research to learn that the venture would require about five grand in starting capital. Which would be about $4,900 more than Amanda had to her name.

"You bet congrats are in order." Tori crossed her ankles and swung her feet. "The first thing Jared's going to do is put me in the office and out of other people's toilets."

Envy wormed its ugly way up Amanda's chest, even though she knew that jealousy was exactly what Tori wanted.

"What will *you* do?" Tori asked, as if they didn't both know that the first order of "office" business would be to fire Amanda. Or give her the worst shifts imaginable. "I mean, what are you trained to do? Not too many beauty contest options around these days. Maybe you could go coach the cheering staff down at Mimosa High. Still have your old uniform, Mandy the Magnificent?"

Oh, Tori loved to pull out that old high school nickname, didn't she? "I have to work," Amanda said.

"You sure do. And that's a stunner for you, isn't it? Thought you'd be some rich guy's wife and give parties and have tea. But that didn't work out for you so well, did it?"

No, it hadn't worked out at all. She stabbed the toilet brush harder, biting back a response.

In Tori's pocket, her cell buzzed, offering a reprieve. She pulled it out and read a text. "Oh, boy. That guy who checked into Bay Laurel yesterday is going out for lunch and wants the villa cleaned ASAP."

Amanda looked up. "I'm not scheduled to do any of the villas until after three o'clock today."

Tori lifted a tough-shit shoulder. "Sucks to suck."

"I can't—"

"Hey, hey, hey." She waved a warning finger back and forth. "You know the company motto. Can't is a four-letter word at Casa Blanca Resort & Spa."

Amanda had heard Lacey and Clay Walker, the resort owners, make the statement enough times at all-staff meetings that she swallowed her argument.

"Anyway." Tori pushed off the counter and slapped her work sneakers on the floor. "Management's watching. Dude's some kind of big-ass deal, and they are giving him the royal treatment. You better get over there and clean your sweet cheeks off, babycakes."

"Me?" She sputtered the syllable. "I've got three more rooms to do here in the hotel before I can start the villas. These have to be done before noon."

Tori smoothed her uniform, the same peach and brown as Amanda's, but much tighter. "Sorry, darling, I have a date with Jared for lunch." She gave an evil grin. "Business planning and then…my reward for getting my work done early." She turned to smooth stick-straight blonde hair in the mirror.

There was no way Amanda could clean that villa *and* finish this floor by noon. "Come on, Tori. It's one guy in a huge villa. Can't you run over there and do a quick job before you go to lunch? Or maybe pick up one of my rooms?"

Tori never looked away from the mirror, dabbing at her mascara. "You know what your problem is, Mandy?"

She had a feeling she was about to find out.

"You're not driven enough. You think you can get by on your good looks, but, honey girl, have you *looked* at yourself lately?" She turned from the mirror to stare down at Amanda, tsking softly. "It's like you forgot who you once were." Very slowly, Tori crouched down, getting face to face with her. "But the rest of the nothings and nobodies in your royal court haven't forgotten a thing."

Despite the assault of sour breath and mean spirit, Amanda refused to cower. "You better go, Tori. Jared's waiting. It's time for you and your husband…oh, I mean fiancé. Oh, wait." She couldn't resist. "He hasn't given you a ring yet, has he?"

Tori stood quickly. "At least I didn't get dumped and end up living with my parents. And, oh, I'm not four rooms behind on my morning work." She lifted her foot and tapped the side of the toilet with her sneaker's toe. "You missed a spot, angel."

The fastest way to the beachfront villas was via a golf cart up the stone walkway that led from the main resort through the entire Casa Blanca property, but, of course, no carts were available when Amanda needed one. She didn't relish walking the path, but not because of the hot sun or tropical heat. In January, the Florida barrier island's humidity was tempered with lovely Gulf breezes, and the view of Barefoot Bay usually lifted her mood. But walking the path generally meant rubbing elbows with the well-heeled resort guests, as they meandered from the exclusive villas to the private beach.

Not so long ago, Amanda had at least felt at home with the beautiful people strolling through resorts like this one, wondering which four-hundred-dollar cover-up to wear to the beach or whether she should have champagne or chilled vodka after her oxygen facial. Now? She couldn't remember the last time she tasted champagne or did more than wash her face before falling into bed, bone-tired from cleaning toilets and scrubbing showers.

Honey girl, have you looked *at yourself lately?*

Tori's words stung, even though Amanda didn't need to worry about how she looked. She needed to worry about how to pay debts on a maid's income without depending on...on *anyone*. Amanda Lockhart would never again depend on a man, a friend, a parent, or a gift.

Shouldering the weight of a bucket full of supplies in one hand and a long work mop in the other, she held on to that unwavering objective. To erase the ugly conversation she'd had with Tori, she peered through palm fronds and over sea oats to the turquoise Gulf of Mexico sparkling in the sun. But even the splash of yellow beach umbrellas and the squawks of seagulls and terns didn't cheer her.

If J&T Housekeeping became a reality and got the business to provide all of the cleaning services for this small but upscale resort, she'd have to leave this slice of paradise. And she'd have to find something to do for work, because she wasn't going to be able to stay at her parents' house much longer. Their round-the-country RV adventure would be ending soon, and she wasn't going to live with them. It was too humiliating and suffocating.

Although, she should have been used to humiliation and suffocation. Doug Lockhart had been quite adept at putting her through both.

She arrived at the two-story vacation villa only slightly damp and out of breath. Setting her bucket down, but still holding the mop, she pulled out her master card key from the lanyard around her neck and tapped on the mahogany door.

"Housekeeping!" she called automatically before sliding the key in the lock.

She waited a beat, then tapped again and started to turn the knob, but the door whipped open from the other side, practically yanking her arm with it.

"You're here now?" A man loomed in silhouette, backlit from the patio well behind him.

"You asked for..." She blinked as he took a step closer and she could see him clearly, losing her train of thought as she met Gulf-blue eyes fringed with dark lashes. Straight ebony hair brushed the collar of an expensive shirt. He was all black and blue...which was probably the shape this man left every heart he encountered. "I'm here to clean."

But he seemed speechless, too, holding her gaze for a heartbeat or two, a frown pulling at his thick brows as he studied her—hard—then glanced at her mop. "I see that." His eyes back on her face again, he searched every inch, from brow to chin and back again.

The scrutiny lasted one second too long, so she lifted the card key, flipping it to show her ID. "I'm with the resort." Because he looked like he didn't believe her. Or at least he didn't believe...something. "You asked for your villa to be cleaned?"

"Uh, yeah, but later."

Damn it! Tori had lied to her to throw off her schedule. Now she'd have to trudge all the way back down to the hotel. "All right, sorry for the incon—"

"No, wait." He almost reached for her, then caught himself. "Stay and...clean." He nearly swallowed the last word, as if it didn't sound right to him.

"I don't have—"

"Who are you?" he asked, still staring at her face.

Oh, jeez. Just her luck to get the nutcase. Great-looking, but a guest didn't care what the maid's name was unless he had a screw loose.

"I'm Amanda Lockhart from housekeeping." She bent to scoop up the bucket as if that could prove it. "I was informed the Bay Laurel villa was ready for cleaning, but I can come back at a better time."

"No, it's just that..." His voice trailed off. Easily six-two with broad shoulders in a crisp white shirt tucked into pleated khaki pants, he wasn't simply gorgeous, he oozed that indefinable something that came with money, class, and power. On most men, that revolted her. On him? Had to admit, nothing was revolting. "I have a guest," he finally said.

She stepped back quickly, imagining some sultry brunette stripping down in his bedroom. Maybe two of them, by the looks of this guy. "I'll come back. Say, three o'clock?"

Laser-blue eyes sliced her. "Do I know you?" His voice was tinged with something she couldn't pinpoint in that split second. Hope? Expectation? *Something.*

"Doubtful." She croaked the word, probably because there was no way anyone who had a single female hormone floating in her bloodstream would forget him. "Sorry to bother you, sir."

"No," he said quickly, opening the door even wider. "No, please. Come in…" That frown pulled again. "Amanda, did you say?"

She hesitated a second longer. "Not if you're in the middle of something with a…a friend."

The hint of a smile pulled at full lips, his eyes crinkling with a flicker of humor. "Not a friend." He leaned a little closer and whispered, "But if I tell you who it is, you have to promise not to laugh."

She didn't move, her senses slammed by a clean, masculine scent and the low timbre of secret in his voice.

"It's my mother," he said, the smile widening. "And if you're not careful, she'll want to help you clean."

She let out a quick laugh, the nerves receding but not the toe-curling impact of him. "I don't need any help, but if you're entertaining…"

"I'm afraid she's not. Entertaining, that is." He backed up to clear the doorway for her. "We're on the patio."

With a little uncertainty, she stepped into the cool air and rich comfort of the Moroccan-inspired decor. He fit in a place like this, as though the high-end designer had planned the dark wood and plush furnishings around someone with his size and command.

Deep inside, a familiar warning bell rang with a reminder that she'd sworn off men. All men in general. This kind of man in particular. Especially one who continued to look at her too intensely.

"Why don't I start upstairs so I can stay out of your way?" Without waiting for a response, she walked toward the wrought iron banister, gripping her bucket and mop so they didn't slip out of damp palms. Still, she could feel him looking at her, those gas-flame blues burning a hole in her back. Tensing, she put one foot on a step before sneaking a peek over her shoulder.

Sure enough, he was staring. With so much intensity it stole her breath.

"Is something wrong?" she asked.

"I…I have the strangest question," he said, coming closer.

"Yes?" She braced herself for whatever it might be. A cleaning suggestion? A proposition? Maybe something as innocent as his favorite beer in the fridge? Guests could be strange. Not usually this drop-dead delicious, but strange.

He let out a self-conscious chuckle, shaking his head, a little color rising. Good heavens, was he *nervous*? Did this tall, dark, imposing master of the universe even know what insecurity was?

"Are you..." He angled his head, frowning hard, looking almost apologetic. "Are you Mandy Mitchell?"

Oh. Her knees buckled a little. Maybe with relief, maybe with that same shame that threatened her when Tori taunted with "senior adjectives" ripped from the pages of a yearbook.

"Not anymore," she said softly, the weight of the bucket becoming too much at that moment. As she set it on the step, she nodded with resignation. "But, yes, I was. Do I know you?" Because, whoa and damn, how was it possible she didn't remember meeting him?

"It is you." He broke into a slow, glorious smile that was like someone had switched on a spotlight, blinding and white, that softened the sharp angles of his face and shadow of whiskers in hollow cheeks.

"Zeke Nicholas." He took a few steps closer, reaching out his hand. "Mimosa High? Class of '02?"

She'd gone to high school with this guy? And hadn't dated him? Impossible. Without thinking, she lifted her free hand to his, getting another shock to the system when his fingers closed over hers, large and warm and strong and...tender. "I'm sorry...Zeke." *Zeke*? She'd never met a man with that name.

"Don't be sorry," he said, reluctantly releasing her hand. "We didn't exactly run in the same circles."

And why the heck not? "Are you sure?"

He laughed, the rumble in his chest a little too hearty and sincere. "Yes, I'm sure."

"I'm sorry, I don't remember..." Anyone or anything that looked like him. "A Zeke."

"I went by my full name then." He gave her the most endearing smile that reached right into her chest and twisted her heart. "You're going to make me say it, aren't you?"

"To help me out?"

He looked down for a split second, then back to her face, the gesture shockingly humble for a man who couldn't be too familiar with humility. "Ezekiel Nicholas."

Her jaw dropped as a memory snapped into place. "Ezekiel the Geekiel?" The second she said it, she gasped softly and lifted her hands to her mouth. "I'm sorry." God, she was as bad as Tori throwing kids' nicknames around.

"No, no." He turned his hands up in surrender. "Guilty as charged by the dreaded senior adjectives." Then he leaned a little closer and lowered his voice, his face close enough for her to count individual lashes. "Mandy the Magnificent."

This time the words didn't sound ugly, spiteful, or laden with jealousy. On his lips, the words were a sexy, sweet whisper of admiration that made every nerve in her body dance.

Ezekiel Nicholas. How was this possible? How had that nerdy, skinny, four-eyed freak who could do Einstein-level math but couldn't make eye contact with a classmate turned into...a god?

"You've changed," she managed.

"You haven't." There was a softness to the words that nearly did her in, especially coming as an echo to the ones that had haunted her on the way up here.

Honey girl, have you looked *at yourself lately*?

Certainly not the way he was looking at her right now. A slow flush rose up from her chest and probably gave her cheeks some much-needed color. "Yes, I have changed," she said simply. "But clearly the years have been good to you."

"You work here." It was a statement of painful fact, but not the way he said it. "That's great." He actually sounded like he meant that, unlike others, who couldn't hide their amusement at the irony of Mandy Mitchell's fall from magnificent to maid. "Really, that's great."

"And you're staying here," she said after an uncomfortable few seconds passed. "With...your family?" He did say his mother was on the patio. Was there a Mrs. Nicholas? A Zeke Junior?

"I'm alone. My parents still live in the same house off Harbor Avenue, but I came back for a surprise party for my dad, so I decided to stay here."

For a long, awkward beat, they looked at each other through completely different eyes than the ones that met five minutes ago. Now, they had a history—or at least a shared past.

"Yeah, wow, Mandy." He shifted from one foot to the other, still kind of shaking his head like he couldn't believe what he was looking at. And who could blame him? She was a maid. He was a guy who rented thousand-dollar-a-night villas when he came to his hometown.

"Well, I..." She gestured toward the stairs. "I better get to work."

He gave her a slow smile, the kind that took long enough for a woman's heart to rise to her throat and fall to her feet.

"I'll be here for a week," he said.

"Oh, really?" Great, she'd have to see him every damn day. Him in his custom shirt over granite muscles and she in her housekeeping uniform and mop.

"Yeah, I was able to combine this trip with some business on the mainland, so..."

So...what? She nodded, unsure if she could simply walk away. Not that he was magnetic or anything. It would have been rude. And, dang, he *was* magnetic.

"Any chance we can get together?" he asked.

Was he asking her on a date? "Oh, I don't..." *Date. Ever. Remember, Amanda? Ever.* "I don't know..."

His gaze dropped over her uniform, lingering on the lanyard hanging around her neck, zeroing in on her name. "Oh, of course, you work here. Sorry." And no doubt her last name made him assume she was married.

"Yes, I work here," she said, hoping that would be enough excuse and explanation.

"Ezekiel?" A woman's voice interrupted Amanda, calling loudly from the patio. "I've got another one! Susan Fox confirmed for her and Jennifer. You remember Jennifer Fox, right? Really lovely and still single." Her voice rose with the last word, and Zeke looked skyward with an eye roll of complete frustration.

"'Kay," he called back. "Be right there." He leaned on the newel of the banister. "My mother is on a mission."

"Then you better go help her."

He puffed out a breath. "She doesn't need help, trust me. But..." He seemed entirely reluctant to move. "It's nice to see you," he finally said. "I always remembered you, Mandy."

She couldn't return the sentiment because, to be fair, she hadn't thought about Ezekiel Nicholas since... No, she'd never actually given him a moment's consideration. Ever. Until now, when she absolutely couldn't and shouldn't give him anything.

"I haven't been Mandy Mitchell for a long, long time," she said. That woman had died years ago, stomped out by a man not entirely unlike the one in front of her. "And, you know, judging from how I must have treated people in high school..." People like him. "That's probably a good thing."

His blue eyes widened in surprise. "How you treated people?"

"I was, you know, probably a little bit of an entitled bitch, but..." She made a self-deprecating gesture to her supplies. "What do they say? What goes around comes around?"

He gave her a look of sheer incredulity. "You weren't a bitch. You were beautiful."

The words nearly melted her. She opened her mouth to reply, but he lifted a hand and brushed his knuckles against her cheek. She almost shivered with the bolt of electricity that shot through her.

"Still are," he said softly.

"Ezekiel!"

Her throat closed too much to even dream of saying a word as he walked away. Silently, she trudged up the stairs, a mop in one hand, a bucket in the other, and the most unwanted longing pressing on her heart.

Ezekiel Nicholas was a dream, but he'd never be hers. She'd learned the hard way that dream men brought nightmares.

Chapter Two

It took Zeke a minute to force his teenage pathetic self back into the hole where he'd shoved him somewhere between MIT and Harvard Business School. He took slow steps to the open French doors, still processing what had just happened.

Since Zeke had been living in New York and amassing his wealth through hedge funds, Ezekiel the Geekiel had rarely emerged. Zeke often forgot that deep inside him lived a kid who squirmed at the thought of eye contact with any girl and turned positively pitiable when breathing the same air as Mandy Mitchell.

Who now worked as…a maid? What the hell was that all about?

Didn't matter what she was, because some things never changed. Holy hell, he was thirty years old, had a net worth that a small country would envy, and made speculative investments before his morning coffee that were so risky that failure meant professional—or real—suicide.

And then he morphed into a fucking schoolboy at the sight of an angel who'd once picked up his whole spilled backpack after some idiot tried to plow him down in the hall. That day freshman year, when he'd finally managed to look at her and choke out his awkward thanks, she'd smiled, and the sun came out and birds chirped and he fell head over heels in love.

He'd forgotten her, of course, over the years. But seeing her today brought back so many old feelings, he—

"Ezekiel, what is taking you so long?" On the pool patio, Mom stood with one hand on a narrow hip, tapping a cell phone impatiently against her cheek. She used the phone to point to the lists, notes, and papers she'd spread over the patio dining table. "I can't plan this whole event alone. I need your help."

"You're doing fine, Mom." He attempted to focus on his mother and her issues, not the housekeeper and her...grass-green eyes. "And the event's planned."

"We still have to round out the final table arrangements," she said. "And I'm having some good luck getting more young ladies to attend." She leaned to the side to peek around him through the French doors. She wore her sixty-eight years well, he had to admit, keeping trim and making sure not a single gray hair showed among the black. Her forehead crinkled mightily when she raised her brows in question. "Who were you talking to?"

"Just..." A memory. "The maid."

Why was she a housekeeper? The incongruity of that hit him like a two-by-four.

"Well, you didn't have to give her your life history."

He bit back a laugh at the irony of the statement. For a time, Mandy *was* his life history. At least, she was the object of a boyhood crush that had sure come crashing back at the sight of her. "I was giving her instructions."

"Why do you need a maid when you've barely slept in this place for one night? And so big, Ezekiel. Why do you need all this space?" She waved the phone at the villa, her dark eyes leveled at him in accusation. "Why spend all this money?"

"Because I have it."

"Pfft." She blew out a breath. "Money isn't everything, young man."

"Tell me about it." It sure hadn't impressed Mandy Mitchell enough to say yes to a date.

Okay, she had a different last name and so she was married. He had to give points to her for not taking his offer anyway, like plenty of women who could have rationalized a drink with an old high school classmate. Still, the rejection stung.

His mother was looking at him with so much pity, he could have sworn she was reading his mind. And with Violet Nicholas, the world's most intuitive mother, that was entirely possible.

"Oh, honey," she said, coming around the table to reach for him. "You see? I'm right. You're miserable."

He had to laugh. "I'm not miserable." At least he hadn't been until ten minutes ago. Would it have been so hard to have a drink with him? Okay, married, definitely. But he hadn't seen a ring.

"But are you happy?"

Happy? How should he answer that? Honestly, of course, and not only because he and his brother had decided years ago that Mom had "liedar." Her secret superpower had made an über-honest man out of him, which was both a blessing and a curse.

"I'm quite satisfied with my life," he said, adept at giving her a non-answer. And that wasn't a lie. He *was* satisfied. Like he was satisfied with a good massage, or a great haircut, or even some mindless sex.

Satisfied wasn't...fulfilled.

No surprise, she wasn't buying it. "What does that mean, satisfied?"

"It means exactly what I've said. I'm content. Life is good." He pulled out a chair, scraping the paved patio noisily. "Really good." Grabbing the water bottle he'd left out here, he tipped it back and doused a throat that had been dry since he'd opened the door and seen...her.

He hadn't been sure at first. She'd looked different. Natural. Plain, even, if that was possible. A tad older, but not a bit less perfect in his eyes. Even if she was a—

"I asked you a question, Ezekiel."

She had? "Sorry."

Exasperated, she dropped into a chair across the table. "What makes your life so good? That...that two-hundred-foot boat you have?"

"One hundred. And it's technically a yacht."

She rolled her eyes. "Oh, maybe it's one of the six houses you pay for in all those different countries."

"Four, and they're all paid off. And not that many countries, Mom. Two are in the U.S." And one in St. Barts and another in the south of France. Why *wasn't* he happy?

"Then is it all that autographed old baseball equipment you're always buying?"

He laughed at her description of one of the world's most expensive and extensive sports memorabilia collections. "Babe Ruth's 1920 Yankees jersey? Mark McGwire's seventieth home-run baseball? You know I love that stuff."

"Fifty million dollars' worth?"

"Sixty," he corrected. "I did a little shopping last month."

"And that's all you want out of life?"

No. He wanted laughter in his quiet houses and a family on his empty yacht and a partner in his massive bed. He wanted wholeness in a life that should have been overflowing but felt utterly...hollow.

"Ezekiel?" she urged.

He opened his mouth to answer, but of course no lie would come out. "I can't, Mom."

"You can." She leaned closer. Love and concern etched lines on her face as she lowered her voice. "You can try again."

He shook off the advice. "I mean I can't lie."

"Of course not. So these baseballs and boats and houses don't make you happy?"

He tipped the nearly empty water bottle in a fake toast, silent.

She nodded. "I thought as much. Your father is turning seventy, Ezekiel."

"I know, that's why I'm here, remember?" He pointed toward the list, happy for the change of subject. "Are you finished with the table...organizing?" He really had no idea what she was doing and couldn't care less, but he got to Florida so rarely, he owed her some attention.

She lifted a shoulder. "I thought of a few more last-minute additions. You know, some friends of mine—*and their daughters*—who I think I should add."

"Please don't do that, Mom. I do not want this party to turn into an army of eligible bachelorettes."

She waved a hand and leaned forward. "I hope it doesn't give your father a heart attack to walk into a restaurant and see a hundred people all there for him."

Zeke eyed her, trying to gauge if that was a particularly adept subject change or a hint at information he hadn't yet been able to get out of her. "Something wrong with his heart?" Last year, it had been the hip replacement. The year before, cataract surgery.

She trained her eyes on him. "Ezekiel, we're not exactly spring chickens, you know. We want to see the Nicholas name continue."

Guilt and grandchildren. Man, she was in her element now. "Aaaand we're back to the subject of the missing grandchildren." He let his head drop forward like he'd been clocked.

"Don't you smart-mouth me, young man. They are missing! Your brother had to marry that woman who refuses to give up one minute of her job at a bank so I could have a grandchild."

He chuckled at how she made Laura sound like a teller. "Mom,

Jerry's wife is the CEO of one of the largest credit unions in the world. And they're happy without children."

"Are you?" she demanded.

"Happy without children or a CEO of a credit union?"

She glared at him. "Stop with the disrespectful mouth. I'm not one of your lackeys. You know what I mean. How long are you going to live this…" She flung a hand at the world in general. "Devil-may-care lifestyle of yours?"

Sometimes he was so lonely he wondered if even the devil did care about him. "Until I find the right person," he admitted. Maybe he'd choose better next time.

Mom sat back and crossed her arms, flattening him with the same look he'd get when she'd find him awake in his room until three AM doing partial differential equations for fun. She knew what had happened; hell, she'd been there. Only, she didn't know the gory details. Still, she never stopped hoping that next time it could be different, even if she refused to even say the name of his—

"Well, you're going to be happy to know that I'm doing something about this situation."

He wasn't happy about anything in that sentence. Not the tone, not the fact that she was doing something, not even the reality that there was a *situation*. "What are you doing or shouldn't I ask?"

"I'm…" She let her voice drift off and looked down at the pages. "I've really got some terrific prospects picked out to come to the party."

"Mom, please. I really don't want you meddling—"

"Meddling! I'm your mother. I'm helping, not meddling."

She didn't know the difference between the two. "There's nothing to do, Mom. Honestly, I'm hap…" The lie stuck like dirt in his mouth. "I'm fine."

"Oh, you're fine all right." She stood suddenly, as if the chair couldn't contain her any longer. "You're so fine you are going to spend every day and night alone, and I am never going to rock a grandbaby." She loosened her arms to make a cradle. "You know, Ezra is a very popular name now."

This from a woman who'd named her sons Jeremiah and Ezekiel. "Mom." He stood slowly. "I date a lot."

"Dating isn't love!"

"No shit." He regretted the words the minute he'd mumbled them.

"Because you've dated the wrong women!" She came around the table, falling into the chair next to him so she could grab his arms and squeeze. "We're going to find you a nice girl. Not one of these skinny supermodels I see on those society pages with you. I'm going to find you a good, sweet, nurturing woman to be the mother of your children."

"Mom, honestly, I'm okay without turning Dad's party into *The Bachelor*."

"I don't think you're okay. Look at you."

Inching back, he gave her a shocked look. "What about me?"

"All you do is make money and go to that gym and keep getting..." She grabbed his bicep and tried to close her hand around it, which of course was impossible. "Is it necessary to be this muscular? Are you trying to kill people with these arms?"

He laughed and shook her off. "Just staying in shape."

"You know what keeps you in shape? Babies keep you in shape! A family keeps your heart in shape." She slapped a palm over her chest, smacking it loudly. "I know this is right, Ezekiel. That party will be like Cinderella's Ball, and you'll be the prince with his pick of the finest."

He didn't know whether to hoot or howl.

"Now, don't you give me that face, young man. I've been giving this a lot of thought. You'll have your choice of the loveliest girls on this island, in Naples, Fort Myers, oh, heck, I know people with eligible daughters in Miami Beach!"

He rearranged the look of shock and horror into a serious scowl. "Mom, I do *not* want to be hounded by a bunch of gold-digging females who are trying to snag a husband. That's not why I'm here. I'm here for you, and Dad."

"And your business meetings."

"Yes, I have a few things scheduled with clients while I'm here, but honestly, I'm not here to..." He stood up, corralling his frustration. As he did, he caught the sound of something from the balcony above, outside one of the upstairs bedrooms.

The doors were open up there. How much had she heard?

"That's just the maid," his mother said.

He looked up and caught a flash of honey-colored hair inside the upstairs sliding glass door. Even in a maid's uniform, with no makeup, and clunky sneakers, she was sheer perfection. But, then, Mandy Mitchell could wear a burlap sack, and he'd want to get in it with her.

"Are you even looking, Ezekiel?"

"I am." And looking at her was still one of his favorite pastimes on Earth. He'd sat in the same classroom with Mandy Mitchell exactly twice in four years—not that she remembered—and the tilt of her nose, the angle of her jaw, and even the arches of her eyebrows over jade-green eyes were burned into his every synapse.

"You're not looking in the right places, then," his mother said pointedly.

"Yes, I am."

When his mother didn't answer, he caught her following his gaze, and then she sighed. "Such a sad story, that Mandy Mitchell."

"What's the story?" He tried to sound disinterested, but hated how much he needed to know.

"You remember her from Mimosa High, right? The beauty queen, head cheerleader, prom princess, you know."

He knew. "Yeah."

She shook her head, tsking softly. "She got married right after college. Married quite well, too, they say."

He snorted. "Not well enough."

"Oh, he left her with *nothing*."

"She's divorced?" He had to work not to keep the elation out of his voice.

His mom tsked loudly but kept her voice at a whisper. "Dumped, more like. She probably cheated on him because what woman leaves a marriage with nothing?"

Plenty of women did—if a man did a prenup properly. His lawyer had mentioned it on more than one occasion.

But his mother was still relaying Mandy's story. "One day, she was a socialite in Tampa and the next, she was back in Mimosa Key, living in her parents' house on Sea Breeze Drive, while they gallivant all over the country in an RV."

Mandy wasn't married. The words ricocheted through his head.

"And have you seen her up close?" his mother asked. "Maybe it's me, but she sure doesn't look like the stunner she once was. It's like she stopped caring."

Maybe her skin didn't glow like polished porcelain and her eyes didn't have an artist's palette painted on them, and maybe she wasn't wearing a miniskirt that made his teenage boy's body take over every thought. But none of that was what made Mandy Mitchell beautiful to him.

His mother's attention was back on the lists. "You're going to like Elizabeth MacMann. Her father is a dentist, you know, in Naples. They belong to our club."

The country club in Naples. The dentists. The daughters. It all sounded like hell right now. Overhead, he heard the vacuum start up.

His mother stood. "Let's go have lunch so that girl can do the downstairs."

"I'm not that hungry, Mom." Not as long as he'd have a chance to talk to Mandy.

She eyed him harshly. "Why are you lying?"

"I'm not lying," he denied hotly.

"Well, something has you looking...hungry. Yes, I know that look in your eyes, son. You need some nourishment. I want to go before your father calls me to pick him up at his physical therapy. Let's go."

"All right." Reluctantly, he got up, realizing he was hungry. But not for food.

The question was, how was he going to satisfy that hunger?

Chapter Three

When she heard the front door close, Amanda hustled to the window to see Zeke let his mother in the passenger side of the car, then go round to get behind the wheel and drive away.

Only then did she let out the breath she'd been holding all the while she'd cleaned…and listened.

Hey, the sliders were open right over the patio. The conversation had drifted up. And…

He had a *fifty-million-dollar sports memorabilia collection*? A yacht? Four homes? And…he wasn't happy?

No, he hadn't said that, not once. But anyone with a brain, heart, and an ounce of knowledge about human nature could hear that between the lines. Well, shoot, what did it take to make someone happy, then?

She knew what his mother's answer would be. It was all Amanda could do not to break into a chorus of "Matchmaker, Matchmaker" after listening to that.

Well, at least he hadn't married one of his supermodel actress tabloid ladies and tried to bend, fold, and mutilate her into a woman he thought was perfect. Not like some powerful men she knew.

But a guy who looked like that and had cash out the wazoo? "Spare me," she whispered to herself as she lugged her bucket and mop downstairs. "Trouble with a capital T. So he's rich, big deal. Money doesn't buy you happiness."

It could, however, buy the business that would save her from having to work for Tori.

The thought meandered around her head as she walked down the hall to the master bedroom. Shame she'd been too shortsighted and status-conscious to have become friends with Ezekiel the Geekiel. Now she could have asked him for a loan.

She paused and got down on her knees, spying some dust along the baseboard. A guy with four houses and millions in "old sports equipment"—he wouldn't miss five grand. Pushing up, she headed into the master, where the plantation shutters remained closed, keeping the oversized room dim and cool.

The bed was unmade, a single leather duffle bag open at the bottom to reveal neat piles of clothes still packed inside. As she stripped the bed, the soft, masculine scent of him drifted up. Unable to resist, she pressed the empty pillowcase to her nose and sniffed, closing her eyes and remembering how he'd looked when he'd admitted his real name.

Shy. Humble. Hot as freaking hell.

She tossed the case onto the pile of sheets and went to the linen closet for a fresh set. Too bad she wasn't a woman without morals. She could...do him for five grand. The thought made her laugh out loud, but, damn, after it got planted, she couldn't help thinking about it.

She smoothed the fitted sheet, pulling the fine Egyptian cotton taut over the mattress. She took a second to let her finger caress the creamy linen, closing her eyes to imagine that man in this bed, naked, ready, hard... A completely unexpected and lusty thrill wended through her, giving a sharp jolt of desire she hadn't felt in a very, very long time.

Nice to know her bastard husband hadn't wrung *everything* out of her.

Finishing the bed, she turned to the bathroom, which should surely cool her inappropriate thoughts. Passing a two-person marble Jacuzzi, she stepped into the massive shower, looking along the wall at the six jets on either side—to accommodate two people, of course—all the way eight or ten feet high where, oh, damn it. Really?

A tiny little dragonfly clung to the tile, fluttering translucent wings. She let out a soft grunt. How did that get up there?

It didn't matter. Amanda had to get him down. Aiming carefully, she tried tossing her sponge at him and nearly grazed his wing, but he flew around the top of the shower and perched on the rain-shower nozzle in the ceiling.

"Oh, you're going to be sorry you didn't cooperate, buddy," she whispered to him. "This shower ain't big enough for the two of us."

She didn't have her step stool, so Amanda glanced around and spied the bucket she'd brought in. "That'll work." Turning it over, she checked the stability, which was good enough for a quick swipe, and placed a sneaker on it to hoist herself higher. "Hey, little guy." She waved at the dragonfly, hoping that would get him to fly down. "Come here. Come down to Mama."

On her tiptoes, she reached, but the dragonfly leaped from the wall and buzzed her. Amanda let out a soft cry and nearly toppled, grabbing hold of the wall to prevent a fall.

And DragonBastard flew back to the very top of the shower, ten feet in the air, his buzzy wings laughing at her.

"And now you die," she said, unhooking the faucet hose that was meant to make showering easy and luxurious but was about to drown an insect. Climbing up on the bucket again, she took aim with one hand, twisted the water on with the other, making the spray shoot forward with so much force it shook her whole body, wobbled the bucket, and all hope of balance.

Like it was happening in slow motion, Amanda felt herself suspended in midair for a split second, then down she went, slamming onto marble and losing hold of the spray hose that danced and twirled and soaked her from head to toe.

Slipping on the wet marble, she reached up to twist off the faucet, accidentally hitting the other knob, and instantly all twelve jets spewed ice-cold water.

"Holy, holy crap!"

"You need some help?"

She squeezed her eyes shut against the water and the horrible possibility that she'd heard a real voice, a human voice, a man's voice. Unless that flipping dragonfly could talk.

The water stopped. Shit. No dragonfly could do that.

"I call this above and beyond the call of cleaning duty."

She let out a soft sigh and finally opened her eyes, looking up at the silhouette of a man looming over her. Even blinded by water in her eyes, Amanda recognized the width of his shoulders and the soft lock of black hair that fell near a blue eye. And, of course, a sly smile he couldn't fight.

As she opened her mouth to reply, the dragonfly buzzed down, right in front of Zeke's face. He snagged the insect with one quick snap of his wrist, careful not to crush him.

"Normally, I'd take this outside to live another day, but from the sound of things, you have a personal beef with him. Want me to squeeze the life out of him?"

Like the sight of this man was squeezing the life out of her lungs? Nothing—not even the DragonBastard—should suffer like that. She shook her head. "He may live."

"How about you?" With his other hand, he reached down.

"I may die of embarrassment." She pushed up on one knee, but he closed his hand over her elbow to help her up.

"Don't die until you dry off." His gaze dropped over her uniform, slowly enough that she couldn't help imagining the soaking wet cotton clinging like a second skin to her body. He lingered for a second on her breasts, definitely not reading her name tag this time. Under his gaze, she felt her nipples bud like little traitors.

"I call it a sign you throw yourself into your work. Literally."

Despite the chill of cold water trickling over every inch, heat rose to her cheeks. "I try," she said, attempting a smile.

He returned it as he helped her stand, backing up with the dragonfly fluttering madly in his other hand. "Let me take him out."

When he disappeared, Amanda nearly folded right back down on the wet marble. What was she going to do now? She glanced down at the thin, wet, nearly see-through fabric and swore softly. Wouldn't that be a nice sight for resort guests as she walked back down the path! No doubt, that would get back to her boss.

She stepped out of the shower stall, unable to avoid a glance in the mirror. Her heart dropped like she just had from the upside-down bucket.

Tori's words echoed. *Have you looked at yourself lately?*

Sopping hair, soaked face, drenched uniform, and...oh, nothing about the woman gazing back from the mirror was *magnificent*.

Hearing his footsteps, she stepped away from the depressing sight and inhaled, digging deep for cool and composure.

"Would you like something dry to wear?" he asked, filling the bathroom doorway.

The question threw her, so unexpected and kind. Any other guest would have been furious at the intrusion and insisted she leave, right after they reported her to management.

"I'm..." She ran her hands over her torso. "I'll be out of here in a minute and send a...better maid."

"That's crazy. There's a clothes dryer here, right?"

Her pulse kicked, and not just because the offer was so damn thoughtful and the man delivering it was as handsome as he was sincere. It was so…unexpected. "In the laundry room, but I—"

"Then we'll have those dry in ten minutes." He reached for the knob to close the door. "There's a robe in the closet, but I'm sure you know that."

Without another word, he closed the door and left her standing in stunned shock. Really? No chastisement for her incredible clumsiness and stupidity? No derisive look that he didn't get better service for all this money?

Grateful to the point of shaking, she slowly undressed, trying not to think about the fact that she could—no, she would—get fired if she got caught undressing in a guest's bathroom.

She slipped off her ID lanyard and set it on the counter, then unbuttoned the shirt, peeling the wet fabric from her body. Kicking off her sneakers, she did the same to the slacks, opting to keep her underwear but tossing in her water-logged bra.

She stepped into the robe and pulled out her ponytail, toweling her hair in the mirror, where things weren't that much better than they'd been a minute ago. Touching her pale cheeks, she leaned closer, seeing her face through his eyes.

Mandy the Mess.

She pinched her cheeks to return some color and licked her finger, blinking in an attempt to darken her pale lashes. But that didn't work. Then she remembered that inches from her hand, in the top drawer, was the complimentary makeup kit that management supplied in every bathroom in Casa Blanca. One of the perks of a resort owned by a woman, she'd often thought.

Very slowly, she tugged at the handle and pulled out the drawer, seeing the makeup, sunscreen, and some personal items.

It had been a long time since Amanda had bothered to put on makeup for a man. So why start now? She closed the drawer harder than necessary. What was she doing, anyway? Trying to impress a rich man? Hadn't she learned her lesson about men like that the hard way?

Scooping up her wet clothes, she opened the door, wearing a bathrobe and no mask.

Amanda found Zeke in the laundry room, the dryer wide open and waiting. He was staring straight ahead, his thoughts so far off and intense that he didn't hear her behind him. She paused for a second, taking him in, from the soft black hairs that brushed his collar to the strong, muscular back that pulled an expensive white shirt tight across his shoulders. His waist was narrow, the shirt tucked into crisp khaki pants, and his ass...

She let out a sigh. That right there ought to be illegal.

He spun around and caught her, sending a rush of shame to her cheeks. "Sorry, I..." Flustered, she walked to the dryer. "I can do this."

"No, please, give them to me." He reached for the ball of wet uniform, his hands closing over hers. She caught his gaze, locked on her, and they stood for the span of two, three, four strong heartbeats.

"I can do it, Zeke," she said quietly. Almost reluctantly, he lifted his hands from hers but didn't look away. "My guess is you don't run a lot of the dryers in your house...houses. Four, is it?"

His gaze flickered away. "You were listening."

"No, no. I did catch a little of your conversation, though." She shouldered him to the side and leaned over to toss her clothes in the dryer. "Your mom is..."

"Relentless," he supplied with a laugh, crossing his arms as he leaned on the granite folding counter next to the dryer. "It's a family trait."

"Is that how you account for your success?" she asked, bending over to unhook a button that had gotten caught inside the dryer.

"Might be, yeah. I get what I go after."

The smokiness in his voice made her turn in time to see his gaze on the gap in her robe. Slowly, she stood, tightening the robe, her stomach plummeting like she was on a roller coaster.

"And apparently you have a fondness for...sports equipment." She attempted a lightness despite the blood singing in her head.

"I have my weaknesses."

"Like most rich men," she muttered, turning away.

"Excuse me?"

She froze in midstep on her way out of the tiny laundry room, already feeling breathless from the lack of space and the growing heat from the dryer. "Never mind, I'm...I guess I'll..."

"What? Clean in your bathrobe?" He stayed leaning against the counter, his arms still crossed, amusement tugging at the corners of his eyes. "What did that comment mean, exactly?"

"It was me being a little bitchy," she admitted. "Which is totally out of line considering how easily you could get me fired for this."

His face softened. "I would never do that."

"Thank you. And, anyway, I seem to be well on my way to doing that all by myself."

"Because you had a little run-in with the shower hose? You don't give yourself enough credit, Mandy."

She smiled at the sound of her name on his lips, so sweet it actually made her next breath come out shakily. Or maybe that was the size and closeness of him and the way his whole face shifted from handsome to heartbreaking when he smiled.

"I give myself plenty of credit," she said. "In fact," she added with a dry laugh, "I'm basically living on the stuff now."

He lifted an eyebrow in interest.

"Not that someone like you could appreciate that, but..." Why had she told him this? Because she wanted pity? Help? A loan? A little disgusted with herself, she started to turn, but he reached out and snagged her elbow.

"Don't leave."

"I...can't really, well, go anywhere," she said. "But maybe I could dust."

He laughed, still holding her elbow and inching her closer. "There's no dust. Tell me about how you are getting yourself fired."

"You really want to know?"

"Yes." He let go and propped his hands on the counter at his back, the knuckles nearly white, she noticed, as if he were forcing himself to hang on and not touch her.

Oh, Amanda Lockhart, what an imagination you have.

"Well, it looks like we're having a management change, and I'm not going to make the first staffing cut when we do."

His features shifted to a concerned frown. "Really? Are you sure?"

"Positive."

"I'll give you a good recommendation. Will that help?"

She let out a breath of surprise and gratitude at the offer. "That's so sweet. I'd love to read that letter, too. 'Amanda's strengths include pest control, eavesdropping, and water management.'"

He laughed. "But she looks damn fine in my bathrobe."

She opened her mouth to reply, but whatever she was going to say got stuck in her throat. Because...that wasn't true. "I thought I heard you tell your mother you don't lie."

"I don't." His eyes grew darker blue, all mirth disappearing as his expression shifted to dead serious. "I really never lie. I deal in numbers and facts for a living, and numbers and facts never lie."

She waited for him to continue, lost in the way he spoke with authority and the shape of his mouth every time it moved. His lips were...perfect. Under the soft velveteen of the robe, she burned with a slow, tingling heat that was definitely not caused by the dryer.

"Well, you're lying now," she said, her voice surprisingly gruff. "Because I don't look fine. I look wet and...tired. And..." *Broken.* "I've had some tough years."

"They don't show," he said, as factually as if he'd added two plus two. "In fact, I can't take my eyes off you."

For a long moment, she didn't say anything, but tried to swallow, her throat tight and dry. Was he being honest, this man who claimed to never lie? It sure seemed that way, but—

"And there was a time," he said, slowly taking his hands off the counter as though he trusted himself to be steady now, "when I couldn't look right at you."

She blinked at him.

"It was like looking at the sun," he whispered, taking one step closer. "So bright and so blinding that it hurt." In front of her, he gently put his hands on her shoulders, holding her perfectly still in the doorway. "And you know how when you look at the sun, you can't see straight for an hour? You have spots in your eyes and everything else in the world is gray?"

It sounded honest. It sounded...lovely. Somehow, she managed to nod, any hope of a reply trapped in her hammering chest.

"Looking right at you used to do that to me." His thumbs grazed her collarbone, the touch so light she almost had to close her eyes and let the electrical impulses rock her. "It still does."

"Now I know you're..." *Lying.* He had to be lying. Saying whatever he thought he had to say to get this robe off. "Different."

"From high school?" He lifted a brow. "Yeah. I'm different. Back then I couldn't talk to you without wanting to fold in half. Now I can't talk to you without..." He lowered his head, inches from her face. "Mandy."

She closed her eyes then, the sound of her name on those beautiful lips like music and rainfall and thunder and…

Softness. His kiss was so soft, it shocked her. His grip grew tighter, his lips hungrier, and a low, masculine catch in his throat was as seductive as a stroke of his fingertips.

He flicked his tongue, she angled her head. He eased her closer, she bowed her back. He pressed against her, and she—

Shoved him away with a grunt. "Don't!" Fury and fear clutched at her, twisting with way more force than desire had. What the hell was *wrong* with her?

He blinked, jerking his hands in the air like a caught criminal. "I'm…shit, Mandy, I'm…" He swallowed, shaking his head. "I'm not sorry, but I really didn't mean to…"

"To what? Kiss me? Undress me? Sweet-talk me with some…some bullshit about the sun?"

His eyes darkened. "I told you I don't lie."

"Well, I don't generally make out with the guests." *Except the ones who make me lose my mind.* "I feel like some kind of…I don't know." But she did know. There was a word for women who did what she'd been thinking about since she'd laid eyes on him. An ugly word.

"God, I'm so sorry." And he looked it, too. His brows drawn together, his eyes raw with self-disgust, his hands dropping to his sides.

"That's what you guys do," she said, old but certainly not dead emotions bubbling up inside. "You make a woman think she's special and then you want to…destroy her."

His eyes widened. "Mandy—"

She held up both hands. "Nobody calls me that anymore." She pivoted and marched out, not sure where she was going, but she couldn't take that tiny space and giant man anymore. Everything vibrated—her head, her body, her heart, her memories.

He wasn't like Doug—or was he?

She crossed the living room, heading to the other side of the house. She'd hide in the bedroom until her clothes were—

"Amanda." He snagged the robe sleeve. "Please, let me talk to—"

She jerked her arm so hard she slipped right out of the sleeve, but he held on and the robe fell open, revealing her nakedness and pulling a soft shriek from her mouth.

The click of the front door reverberated, like a bullet shot underwater.

In slow, shocked motion, they both turned, speechless as the door flew open and hit the wall.

"Housekeep—" Tori froze in the doorway, her eyes wide. "Well, would you look at that?"

Before Amanda could scramble back into the robe, a bald head appeared behind Tori and JT's eyes damn near sprang out of his head, too. "Whoa, Amanda. That's probably a little more customer service than we generally offer."

Chapter Four

In one lightning-fast move, Zeke slipped Mandy back into her robe, getting close enough to feel her whole body trembling. What an idiot he was! He couldn't keep his hands off her for five minutes? Now she was as white as that robe.

"Who the hell are you?" he demanded of the morons who'd just barged in. "Can't a guest expect privacy?"

The woman sauntered in, appraising him up and down like some kind of hungry hooker. "We're with housekeeping doing a room check. You're supposed to be at lunch."

"Guess Amanda's dessert." The meathead behind her loped in and grinned. "Sorry for the inter—"

Zeke took two steps and had the guy's collar before he could take his next breath. "What did you say?"

"Hey, hey, sorry, sir." He held up his hands and shook his head, fear in his eyes. He should have been afraid for that comment. "We were told to check on this villa because Amanda isn't exactly the best house—"

Zeke tightened his grip and lifted the guy a half inch off the ground.

"Zeke, please." Mandy's voice cracked with the plea.

Slowly, he let the guy drop but continued to slice him with a look that he knew communicated exactly how much pleasure he'd get from throwing him against the wall. "You can leave now."

The other woman put her hands on her hips and shook her head at Mandy. "Honey, you know we gotta tell Lacey about this."

"It's not what it looks like," Mandy said.

The woman gave a sharp laugh. "Well, it sure doesn't look like cleaning to me."

Zeke whipped around and glared at her, but she looked up and smiled. "Not that I can blame the girl."

"Hey," the other man said harshly. "Let's go, T."

"And leave her here?" She tsked. "I am certain there are legal ramifications and employee guidelines and every other manner of professional misbehavior being displayed. Amanda, dear, why don't you find your clothes from wherever you dropped them, and we'll ride you back to the management office?"

Zeke was in her face in one second. "Why don't you shut your mouth and get your skinny ass out of this villa before I call the cops?"

She flinched a little, then shot a look at Mandy. "Got yourself a hothead, darlin' I heard you like them with a little fire in the belly."

Zeke inhaled so hard he felt his nostrils quiver, and the woman had the good sense to slink away.

"We'll see you in Lacey's office," she said, backing out of the door just before Zeke slammed it in her face and flipped the deadbolt and guest lock. Only then did he turn to survey the damage.

But Mandy was gone.

He shot through the kitchen and stopped cold at the laundry room door at the sight of her back to him, naked but for pink underpants, as she tried to hook her bra.

"Go away," she said.

He stepped into the kitchen to give her privacy. "I feel like shit," he said.

"You got Tori to leave."

Tori? "Tori Drake?" He knew she looked vaguely familiar.

"The one and only. And she's made a career out of getting back at me for being on the homecoming court when she was the one servicing the football players."

Damn, it was like a high school reunion around here. "I shouldn't have…I shouldn't have touched you."

She didn't answer, and he banged his head against the wall behind him, squeezing his eyes shut. *Son of a bitch!* "I don't suppose I could make this up to you."

"Five thousand would do the trick."

His eyes popped open. "*What?*"

"Never mind, I'm making a joke in a very unfunny situation." He heard a zipper slide and the rustle of more clothes. "I told you I was on the way out of this job anyway."

He stepped into the doorway as she buttoned the top button. "That may or may not be true, but I'll be damned if you are going to lose your job because I acted like an asshole."

"You weren't an asshole," she said softly. "You're just a man."

Which was obviously one and the same to her. Damn it, he was such a moron. "Mandy."

She looked up from the button, adding a punch to his gut when he saw the dampness of her eyes. "Sorry, I'm a little bitter. I left my sneakers in the bathroom. Excuse me." She brushed by him and left him standing like a helpless, hopeless idiot.

He heard her in the living room and pushed off the wall, refusing to let her leave without saying goodbye. She was sitting on the sofa, tying her shoes, her blonde hair, dry now, hanging like corn silk in front of her face.

He took a slow step closer. "I told you I am honest, probably to a fault."

She didn't look up.

"So you should know that what I'm about to say is true and not some asshole guy spouting bullshit because he wants to get laid."

She knotted the lace, silent.

"I had a crush on you in high school that pretty much crippled me at the sound of your name."

Her hands stilled.

"I couldn't..." He gave a dry laugh. "I couldn't breathe when you were in the room."

Very slowly, she lifted her face to him.

"I know you were...like royalty. And I was not. And I know now, as a man, that none of that matters. But I want to tell you this."

She stared at him, waiting as he walked up to her and got down on one knee so they were face to face.

"Once, when we were freshmen, some kid mowed me down in the hall and knocked all my books and my sixteen different calculators and protractors to the floor. You stopped and got down, like this, and helped me pick up every single thing. And when that kid laughed at you, do you know what you said?"

Her green eyes still swam in tears as she shook her head.

"You stood up and flattened him with a look and said, 'Get to class because you obviously have none.'"

She started to smile. "I could be a real—"

He held up a hand, silencing her. "Angel. I thought you were an angel. I thought you were…" He swallowed. "Obviously too good for me."

"Zeke, I…"

He looked down and took the laces of the other shoe, slowly tying them for her. When he'd knotted them, he looked into her eyes again. "You told me a few minutes ago that I was relentless."

She nodded.

"Wait until you see the power of that."

He heard her suck in a quiet breath. That was good. He wanted to take her breath away. And he would. She just didn't know that yet.

The sun spilled into the Gulf that evening, turning the water a thousand shades of gold and pink, tinged with violet, topped with twilight. As Zeke walked barefoot over the sand of Barefoot Bay, he barely noticed nature's artwork. His head down, he turned the hard piece of plastic hanging on a yellow lanyard over in his hand and read the name for the hundredth time.

Amanda Lockhart.

She'd left her ID and master key in his bathroom, which would probably be yet another transgression against her. His trip to the management offices found them closed for the evening, but he wasn't about to give this key up to some lackey at the front desk. Whoever "Lacey" was, he was going to find her, and finally, he'd bumped into a talkative, friendly, and quite attractive young woman who'd identified herself as the owner of the resort's hot-air-balloon business.

Zoe Bradbury had had an enchanting personality, and when she'd found out he was the guest staying in Bay Laurel, she'd made one call, and sent him up the beach to the owners' house. He appreciated people who could get things done and had told her so.

The Walkers, who evidently designed, built, owned, and managed the resort, lived in a two-story stucco home covered with ivy and facing the water at the very northernmost end of the bay. A stroller was parked next to a truck and a golf cart in the circular drive, and as he reached the property, the front door opened and a red-haired woman in a crisp white shirt and jeans stepped out to greet him.

"Mr. Nicholas?" Concern tinged her voice, and her brows pulled over amber eyes, confirming that most resort guests weren't typically given this kind of access to the owners. Good. He wasn't most resort guests.

"Mrs. Walker?" Holding the badge in his left hand, he reached out his right and they shook. "Please call me Zeke."

"I'm Lacey. I understand we had an incident in your villa today. Would you like to come in?"

He heard the playful squeal of a baby behind her and shook his head. "I don't need to invade your home, ma'am. I merely want to clear a few things up, and I can do that right here."

She crossed her arms and nodded, the breeze picking up a strawberry-colored curl from her shoulder. "Please do."

"Mand...Amanda left this." He handed her the ID and card key, and she closed her eyes, obviously not happy. "After she nearly killed herself trying to get a dragonfly out of the shower and accidentally turned on the water and got soaked through to the bone."

She looked up, a question in her eyes.

"I don't lie."

A smile flickered. "I believe you."

"I hope you do and not the two people who stormed my rented villa—without announcing themselves, I might add—and assumed the worst, which was completely wrong."

She swallowed, processing this. "You have to admit it was an extremely awkward situation."

"Awkward, but not what it appeared."

She nodded slowly. "I've talked to Amanda."

"And?"

"I had to let her go," she said unapologetically. "No matter how or why her uniform was wet, wearing a guest's robe and staying in the villa is unacceptable behavior for a housekeeper." Her eyes tapered, and he caught the accusation.

"I persuaded her to stay. We knew each other at Mimosa High."

"You went to Mimosa High?"

"Class of '02."

A warm smile, the first he'd seen, lit her face. "Well, I'm a few years older than you, but I'm a Scorpion, too." Then she frowned, shaking her head. "I didn't know Amanda was an alum, but then, I really have only talked to her at length one other time."

"Then you don't know that she's not at all like what those other employees assumed."

She toyed with the card key, sighing. "They're not only employees," she said. "They are actually the winners of a bid I put out a few months ago. I'm planning to outsource my housekeeping function to one company, and they've got the job. I need to trust them."

Realization dawned. "So that's why Amanda told me she'd be fired shortly."

Lacey's eyes flashed. "Why would she assume…really?" She tapped the plastic key against her hand, thinking. "I didn't know this situation was brewing," she admitted. "And it makes me all the sorrier I couldn't help Amanda when she came to me."

"Instead, you fired her."

"No, no. Not today. Awhile back. She wanted the outsourcing business," she said. "And she seems to have the brains and ambition, so I told her she'd be in the running if she could get a business off the ground. But, sadly, it does take working capital to start something like that, and she couldn't—"

"How much?"

She lifted her brows and gave a shrug. "I'm not sure, but the proposal she'd put together looked like she'd need a cash infusion of about five thousand dollars, so more than she has, I'm afraid."

Five thousand would do the trick.

Her words played on his memory. "Can't she get a small-business loan?" he asked.

"I'm sorry, Zeke, I really don't know her personal situation, but—"

"Don't you think you ought to know an employee's personal situation before you fire her?"

She drew back, her shoulders square. "She was found in a villa undressed with a guest. I'm running a first-class, five-star resort, and I make no apologies for my business decisions or employee relations."

In the entryway behind her, a man appeared, holding a baby who couldn't have been a year old. "Everything okay out here?"

"Yes," she said, indicating him. "This is Zeke Nicholas, our guest in Bay Laurel. Zeke, this is my husband, Clay Walker."

"The architect?" Zeke asked.

He nodded. "I designed the resort."

"I'm a fan of your work. I…I thought you were older."

Clay smiled, his blue eyes glinting with understanding. "My father's an architect, as well, and much better known than I am." He gave the baby a little pat. "And this is Elijah. We're hoping he picks up a drafting pencil soon, too."

Lacey laughed. "Not that soon."

Zeke gave the little guy a wink when he turned big blue eyes exactly like his daddy's on him. "Cute kid. And, look, about today? My side of the story is the truth."

"Thank you," Lacey said. "I appreciate you stopping by and returning the card key."

"I'm sorry to have interrupted your family time."

"I'm always available for guests," she said.

He started to leave, but stopped midstep. "Can I ask you one more question?"

The couple nodded in unison.

"Is your decision about the outsourcing of that business final?"

They shared a look, the kind that told him they talked about everything and didn't make any decisions in a vacuum.

"We've made a verbal agreement," Lacey said. "But nothing's signed. Why?"

"If Amanda were able to finance that business, would you give her a shot, in spite of what happened today?"

Lacey sighed, slowly shaking her head, but her eyes said she knew what he was suggesting. "Oh, I don't know. That would be—"

"Oh, Strawberry." Her husband shifted the baby to his other arm to get even closer to her. "How soon we forget."

"What?" she asked him.

He gave her a half smile and swiped a hand through near-shoulder-length, sun-streaked hair, an earring twinkling in his lobe. "I seem to recall a young woman who, not so long ago, had to do some pretty creative maneuvering to get her own business, and there were plenty of people who thought her track record didn't merit a second chance. Not to mention her relationship with one of her business partners."

Her face softened as she smiled at him, the connection between them palpable. After a second, she turned back to Zeke, her eyes shining. "Everyone deserves her shot, I suppose."

Zeke nodded. "That's all we'd ask."

A few minutes later, he was halfway down the beach on his way to his next stop before he realized he'd said "we."

Chapter Five

Amanda had a good shower cry. Ugly, hard, and stinging, even though she didn't get soap in her eyes.

When the water heater gave out, she finally dried off, slipped on a tank top and sleep pants and poured a glass—okay, a vat—of wine before heading into her room. Her *old* room, not the master she'd slept in for her year of free rent in exchange for house-sitting. Mom had long ago turned Amanda's teenage-girl room into a den/guest/catch-all combo, which had turned dusty and musty from lack of use. In every corner, the fading light left shadows...and memories.

This room might look different than it had when it was a teenager's sanctuary, but Amanda had left plenty of herself in here. Sleepovers, studying, and hours of...admiration. The closet doors were sliding full-length mirrors, trimmed in brass.

How many hours had Mandy Mitchell spent in front of her own reflection? God, she'd been self-absorbed. No wonder Tori hated her. Along with everyone else she'd probably treated like second-class citizens.

Except Ezekiel Nicholas. Had she really thrown that "class" comment at a bully? She didn't remember having a caring bone in her body back then. But that's not how he saw her. And she didn't even remember the book-bag and bully incident.

Without taking even a glance at her reflection in the mirrored door, Amanda rolled it, searching the floor for the plastic container Mom had used to store what had been on the bookshelves.

Spotting the box, Amanda slid to the floor, taking a deep drink of wine before setting the glass on the nightstand. She had to find that yearbook.

As she dug through pieces of her life packed into a bin, she refused to let the nostalgia get to her. They were things from her bookshelves, that's all. Not *her*. A tiara from homecoming, a framed picture of her in her cheerleading uniform, a dried corsage from prom, the program from the Miss Teen Florida pageant—they were distant, ancient memories of a girl who no longer existed.

She should probably thank Doug for humbling her in their marriage, for years of put-downs and insults and reminders that he had the power and she was nothing but a wife. It hadn't taken long for Amanda's confidence to crumble. Now she was building it back up, but this time, she would leave the arrogance behind.

When she lifted the graduation cap, her fingers hit the hard edge of a book cover.

Mimosa High Yearbook 2002...A New Day Has Come

The edition was more serious than most years, less emphasis on partying at the beach and more emphasis on making a difference in the world. Of course, the first month of their senior year had been September of 2001, a time in history marred by events that had changed every heart in the world.

Amanda leaned back against the bed, reaching for another sip of wine before opening the book. Then she flipped to the seniors, and the pages automatically opened to the middle of the alphabet, with her picture on the left-hand side.

She ignored it and skimmed straight to the N's, stunned to see Ezekiel Nicholas directly underneath her.

"Holy crap," she whispered to herself. She didn't know what was more amazing—the fact that he'd gone from zero to a dime since they'd graduated or that she had never even noticed his picture under hers.

He was right under her on the same page, and she'd never even known he existed beyond a cutting nickname.

I thought you were an angel.

His confession still rang in her ears. After one of the most difficult, harrowing days of her life, when she'd actually been told: "I'm sorry, Amanda, but we have to let you go"—yet the only words that she wanted to think about from today were...*I thought you were an angel.*

She stared at his picture, able to see the early lines of what would become a handsome male jaw and those piercing blue eyes hidden by thick glasses. He wasn't smiling. Had anyone even talked to him? Had she ever again been nice to him?

The doorbell made her jump, pulling her from her reverie. That was Jocelyn Palmer, of course. Her neighbor who ran the Casa Blanca Spa hadn't been at the resort today when Amanda got fired, but no doubt she knew about everything, since she was very close friends with Lacey Walker.

She waited a minute, staring at Ezekiel the Geekiel a minute longer. She didn't really want to face her neighbor right now. She didn't want to admit she'd gotten herself in such a sticky situation with a resort guest that it had cost the job Jocelyn had helped her get.

The bell rang a second time, followed by a loud knock. On a sigh, Amanda pushed herself up, still holding the yearbook. She snagged the wine glass, as though that would prove just how bad she felt about losing her job.

At the end of the hall, she turned toward the living room, glancing out through the white sheers just as a figure walked away from the door.

A male figure. Frozen, Amanda stared at Zeke Nicholas. What was—

He turned at that instant and caught her looking before she could duck out of the way.

For a second, time froze as they stared at each other, then a slow, easy smile broke over his face that was as real and warm as the setting sun behind him. He pointed to the front door, and she let out the breath she'd been holding.

Oh, God. There was no reasonable way out of this, she supposed. She tucked the yearbook under her arm and opened the front door. He stayed on the walk, down two steps, so they were at eye level, but he was no less gorgeous and intimidating than when he had her by a good five or six inches.

For a moment, they stared at each other, and all she could think of was how much he'd changed since...

His eyes dropped, and she realized her tank top was just this side of see-through. She angled the yearbook over her chest. "I looked you up," she said, hoping that explained why she suddenly felt the need to shield herself with it.

"And I see I've driven you to drink."

She raised the glass. "Clearly, I'm having my own little pity party."

"No one should do that alone."

No one...should look that damn good after being positively invisible in high school. How had he done that?

She could practically feel his desire to move forward, like a horse held at the starting gate. "Can I come in?"

No. She could hear the word in her head, imagine how easy it would be to say, and how effective and right and smart and safe it would sound. Just…no. Simple. Two letters. One syllable.

"Of course you can." Or that.

He strode forward and up the steps, making her clutch the yearbook, determined to hold her ground and not back up. Except, now he was too close and too tall and too…much.

"You're under me," she said softly.

His eyes glinted with surprise. "Not at the moment."

"Right under me on the senior picture page. The L's, M's, and N's are on the same page and we…lined up."

"Really? I've never seen that yearbook." He reached for it. "May I?"

Well, he had seen her boobs for a flash already today. She relinquished the book and tried not to feel self-conscious about the thin material covering her. "You've never looked at our yearbook?"

"I didn't have great memories of high school."

She gestured toward the sofa. "Well, have yourself a stroll down memory lane then. Would you like a glass of wine?"

She watched him walk past her to sit down, placing the book on the table without opening it. "I'm all right, thanks."

That was an understatement. He still wore the same crisp khakis and five-hundred-dollar shirt he'd had on today, and he still looked perfect. He still smelled like summer in the woods. He still oozed power and control and testosterone, all those things she was determined to avoid.

She folded into a chair across the coffee table, crossing her arms and curling her legs under her, not asking the obvious question of why he was here but wanting to see how he'd open this conversation.

Sitting down, he leaned his elbows on his knees, steepling his long fingers right under his chin. "I understand you lost your job."

"Good news travels fast on Mimosa Key, as always."

He didn't say anything, looking directly at her. But why *was* he here? To apologize? To finish what he'd started? A slow heat traveled up her body. She damn well better get acquainted with the word "no" or she could qualify as the world's stupidest woman.

"You and I both know that's not good news. I feel really bad about what happened."

Yes, he was there to apologize. She could let her poor hormones rest now. "Thanks, but, honestly, it was inevitable. You—that, um, situation—forced me to move faster to find another job."

"What are you going to do?"

She lifted a shoulder. "I heard the Toasted Pelican is hiring waitresses. All the peanuts you can eat and rotgut you can drink."

He didn't smile at the local humor. "You need to start your own business."

She let out a soft laugh. "Yeah. That'd be nice." So would robbing a bank.

"I mean it."

"I know it," she replied, unnerved by more than his intense gaze. She couldn't breathe. How did he know this, anyway?

"I have a check for five thousand dollars in my pocket."

She stared at him, the words nearly doubling her over with their impact. "*What?*"

"I have a check for—"

"I heard you." She shot to her feet, indignation and fury and shock rocking through her body. "How? Why? What...why?"

He stood, too, instantly gaining the advantage of height. "Because you need it to start your business, and I'm the reason you don't have a job."

Her jaw hung open as she tried to piece together the puzzle and came up with...nothing that looked like a picture.

"I spoke to Lacey Walker," he said, obviously reading her confusion.

"*What?*"

"I spoke to—"

She swiped her hand through the air to silence him. "I heard you," she repeated through gritted teeth. "I don't believe what I heard, but...why would you do that?"

"You left your employee badge and master key in my bathroom."

The sting of embarrassment mixed with fury, tingling her skin and sparking her nerves. "So you took it to the owner of the resort?"

He nodded, crossing his arms. "At her house. I met her husband, too, and their baby."

He'd gone to Lacey's house? "I'm dreaming, right?" She choked the words. "Tell me this is a nightmare. Any minute I'm going to wake up and realize this isn't happening, that I had a horrible day that has spilled into a really...bad..."

Her words faded as he reached out and brushed his knuckles along her jaw, sending a thousand goose bumps to join the chills of fury she already had. "Not a dream. I know what you want, and I have a check in my—"

"I don't want your damn money!" Jerking back from his touch, she practically spit the words at him.

"Mandy, I want to help you."

"In exchange for what?" She slammed her hands on her hips. "You want to buy sex? I'm sure there's plenty of places you can do that on the Internet or over on the mainland."

"Sex?" She had to give him credit, he looked pretty horrified. "I'm not here to buy sex."

"I admit," she said, anger still rolling through her veins like lightning. "You don't look like you need to do that, but, whoa, buddy. I know…people…guys…men like you have—"

"You don't know men like me." Now *he* sounded mad. Oh, that was rich.

"I do—"

"You think you know men like me. But I guarantee you, Mandy, you have never met anyone like me."

She opened her mouth to argue, then shut it, only because of the raw sincerity in his voice and eyes. Maybe she *didn't* know a guy like him.

"I am not here to buy anything." He tunneled his fingers into his hair and slowly swiped it back, leaving it a little tussled and messy. And sexy as hell.

She closed her eyes, trying to look disgusted but really forcing her brain to cooperate and stop thinking of him that way. She *couldn't.*

"I feel incredibly responsible for your losing your job and…I told you this afternoon, you did me a favor a long time ago and I never forgot it. I know you need this money to get started and, hell, Mandy, I'll never miss it."

Lucky bastard. With a little grunt, she turned and headed into the kitchen to get away from the overwhelming sight of him. But of course he followed her. She stood at the sink, her fingers splayed on the porcelain, staring out at her mother's tiny backyard.

"I don't mean to sound so cavalier about money."

Judging from his voice he was about a foot behind her. Maybe two. Too close. She gripped the sink until her arms shook.

"But I give to charity and—"

She turned slowly, a rueful smile on her lips. "Charity? I guess that's not quite as bad as what I thought."

"Mandy." His eyes softened, and he lifted his hands in supplication. "I'm trying to help you."

And just like that, she felt everything melting. Her heart. Her fury. Her complete inability to trust anything with a Y chromosome. "I know," she whispered, hating that her voice cracked and her eyes stung. "I have…issues."

He managed a smile. "I noticed."

"I had a bad…marriage."

"I figured."

"He hurt me."

His eyes flashed. "I'm sorry."

"I kind of hate men."

He fought a smile. "I'm getting that."

"Especially men with money and power and…all that entails."

"I don't know what that entails, Mandy. I'm just a guy who's done really well in business, and that's turned into a lot of money."

"A *lot*," she repeated.

"A whole hell of a lot," he agreed. "I'm not going to apologize for that or for every asshole who doesn't know how to treat a woman." He reached into his pocket and pulled out a piece of paper—his check, no doubt. She didn't have the nerve to look at it or the wherewithal to take her eyes off his. "I have absolutely zero expectations from this and, if it will make you happy, we can consider it a loan with no interest and no due date."

"Which makes it a gift, not a loan."

His lips curved. "Semantics. Is that a yes?"

"No." She inched back, hitting the sink, her gaze slipping to his hand before returning to his face.

Five thousand dollars… from a drop-dead god of a man who could wield that power…

"You're thinking about it," he said, fluttering the check.

On a sigh, she looked again. "I could get bonded and buy equipment and rent the office and hire…oh." Disappointment thudded again. "Never mind. This is a waste of time."

"Why?" He stepped closer. "I can help you do all that stuff. I've started dozens of businesses."

The offer slayed her, it was so genuine. "I mean it's a waste of time because I need customers. Lacey will never give me the outsourcing business now, even if I could put the whole package together. She was so mad this afternoon, she was spitting nails. I'm done at Casa Blanca."

"I don't know about that," he said. "Her husband seemed reasonable, and she believed me when I told her what happened."

She searched his face, daring to hope, daring to dream. "Really? What did they say?"

"I wasn't quite sure, but I get the impression she's been in your shoes before, having to take a risk." He paused and gave her a meaningful look. "I get the impression her husband helped her."

"Oh, yeah. I've heard stories about how they met on the beach and fell in…" Her voice grew tight. They fell in love, got married, had a baby, and lived happily ever after.

Fairy tales that sure didn't happen to every woman.

"Anyway." Amanda waved off the thought. "I have to think about this."

"Bad idea." She could have sworn he took a step closer but didn't actually seem to move. Somehow, he was…trapping her. And, damn it, she liked it.

"Why?" she asked. "I have to think about it. I have to sleep on you, I mean, on it."

He grinned and pointed to her with the check. "You've got sex on the brain."

She had to laugh. "No, it was a slip of the tongue."

"Don't think about it, Mandy. You'll think yourself right out of the offer. Take the money." He took her hand and tried to pry her palm open. "Make a business plan and—"

She kept her fingers squeezed. "I have a business plan."

"Good girl. Then put together a list of every step you have to—"

"I have that list." She was ready. The only thing stopping her was…pride and self-respect and… Her fingers slackened a bit. "It could take me years to pay you back."

"I don't care."

"I do." She let out another sigh, almost opening her hand, but this was…so wrong. "I'm going to feel like I owe you."

"You owe me nothing. I'm here for a week or so. I have some meetings and my dad's party and, other than that, I'll help—"

She snapped her fingers and pointed at him so hard and fast, he drew back an inch. "That's it!"

"What?"

She snapped again, over and over, unable to contain her happiness. "I know what I can do for your five thousand dollars."

"I don't need anything, Mandy."

"Oh, yes, you do." She tapped his chest playfully, already loving this idea. "You need a bodyguard."

"What?" He shook his head. "I'm not in any danger here. I've used bodyguards in certain countries, of course, but I don't need protection on Mimosa Key."

"Wanna bet?" She clapped her hands together, so completely happy with the idea. "You need someone to hold back the legions of single women your mother is prancing past you at that party."

His eyes lit and his jaw unhinged—the look of surprise and delight making him even more handsome, if that was possible. "You're right. I need a girlfriend for that event."

"Or at least a date."

"No, no, it would have to be official to get my mother off my case. But…"

"But she knows me and knows I'm a maid here, and she'd figure out in a New York minute that you're lying," she supplied, reading his expression.

"Except that I don't lie. Ever." He shook his head, his smile tight. "And she knows it. Because she has liedar."

Amanda choked. "Liedar?"

"The ability to smell a lie a mile away." He gave a self-deprecating laugh. "Of course, I am the world's crappiest liar."

"Oh, well. That's a shame because I really… liked the idea."

He was searching her face, thinking. "I love the idea."

The way he said it made her toes ball up on the tile floor. "Then you have to lie."

"Not if… it's true."

More toe-curling. "I'm not your girlfriend, Zeke."

"But what if we make it official? You are my girlfriend, and I am not lying."

Oh, that would be…not good. "Semantics," she echoed. "We obviously just met…" At his look, she conceded with a nod. "Okay, we knew each other in high school, but it's a stretch to say I'm your girlfriend and it not be at least a white lie. Can you tell one? Or can't I just be a really clingy date?"

His eyes narrowed, and he took one step closer. "No. There's a much simpler answer." Tipping her chin with one gentle finger, he lifted her face to his.

"Which is?"

He annihilated her with the intensity of his gaze, crazy-sky blue looking right through to her soul. "Mandy Mitchell, will you be my girlfriend?"

"Zeke...I..."

"Don't say no."

No, no, *no*. But not a word came out as he lowered his face and covered her mouth with the sweetest, softest, sexiest kiss she could ever remember.

Chapter Six

Zeke angled his head but purposely kept the kiss air-light, no more than a brush of a promise, because Mandy was about as secure in his touch as a wisp of smoke. Everything in him wanted to push her against that counter, crush her open-mouthed, and move his hands up and down the delicious body that was all too visible under the flimsy top.

But then she'd disappear. He knew that. But he lingered one second longer, taking one tingly taste of her lower lip. Only then did he back away. Her eyes were still closed, her lips parted, her chest rising and falling with one strangled breath. She'd flattened her hands on his chest, either ready to push or pull. He didn't know which.

"Now I won't be lying," he said softly. "You're my girlfriend."

She opened her eyes, the green rimmed with a darker emerald, her golden lashes fluttering up to her brows. "You'll...still be lying."

"Nope." He shook his head. "It's official. Sealed with a kiss."

"That's not enough."

He couldn't help smiling. "Oh, well, there's more where that came from."

"No, no...I..." She lifted her hands as if she suddenly realized she'd splayed them across his pecs. "I can't. It would be...wrong."

"Wrong? Why?"

"Because...I'm not..." She closed her eyes for a second, gathering her wits, slowly taking her hands to her sides, being careful not to touch him, as though he might burn her. "This has to be strictly business," she finally said. "Absolutely, unequivocally, no doubt about it...a business deal."

Which was about as sexy as a rock, but okay. Maybe he could get her to change her mind. Or maybe not.

"Strictly," she repeated, pointing a finger at him.

He tried to ignore the punch in his gut, but it was hard. Of course...that's what Mandy Mitchell wanted. She wasn't like most women who saw dollar signs and private jets and a life of luxury with him. She saw...Ezekiel, the kid she'd never noticed in high school.

What was it going to take to erase that lifelong first impression? Trust, first. "Absolutely a straightforward business arrangement," he assured her. "In fact, why don't we draw up a contract?"

Her eyes widened at that, and he could have sworn he saw a glimmer of horror. "A contract?"

"So you know I'm serious." He glanced around, reluctant to walk away and not get this close to her again for a while. His eyes landed on the roll of paper towels. "Here." Reaching over, he snagged one and tore it off.

"That's going to be your contract?"

"Legal and binding." He looked around again, and she jutted her chin to the tiny desk built into the corner.

"There's a pen."

He turned, grabbed a felt-tipped pen from the cup, and laid the paper towel on the counter, smoothing it out as he bit off the pen cap and kept it between his teeth.

"I, Ezekiel Nicholas..." He scribbled the words, the ink bleeding on the soft paper towel. "Do agree to pay five thousand dollars to..." The pen cap garbled his words.

She slid it out from between his teeth. "Amanda Lockhart."

He grimaced. "You'll never be that to me." As he started to write the A, she put her hand over his.

"Okay, Mandy Mitchell. Only for you."

He hated that those words kicked his heart and her hand made him tense, so he nodded and looked down at the paper towel, turning the A into an M. "...Mandy Mitchell in exchange for..."

He hesitated again, and she got a little closer, so he could smell something citrus in her hair and feel the warmth of her. He continued writing. "In exchange for her appearance at social functions as my..." Then he looked at her, waiting for her to provide the descriptor.

"Pseudo? Imitation? Pretend? Fake?" She shrugged. "I don't know how else to say it."

"In math, any number that's the product of a real number and the square root of a negative one is referred to as imaginary. Would that work?"

She smiled. "Imaginary girlfriend it is."

On the contract, he finished the sentence. "…my imaginary girlfriend. Okay?" He searched her face, looking for humor in their little arrangement, but he didn't see anything but seriousness and, hell, a little fear. He hated the bastard who'd put that fear in her.

"No," she said softly. "You have to add that there can't be any…"

Sex. She might as well have spelled it out with her own marker. He turned back to the paper, his brain already seeking…loopholes. "We hereby swear that those services will not include…" His pen stilled as he waited for her to spell it out.

"You know," she said.

"I need a legal term."

"How about 'any activities that require the removal of clothes'?"

He lifted both brows, already seeing the loopholes and how to…get around, through, and under them. "Are you sure?"

"Well, I expect we'll have to, you know, hold hands and act like we're together in public. I mean, at least for the benefit of your mother and the Cinderellas at her ball."

He laughed softly. "You heard every word of what I said to her, didn't you?"

"Not on purpose," she said. "But, yeah, I picked up quite a bit."

He looked at her for a moment, enjoying the close contact, the chance to gaze into her eyes, and the softness he saw when she let her guard down. "Okay, then. Your words, your rules." On the paper, he wrote exactly what she'd said.

Any activities that require the removal of clothes.

"Is that ironclad enough for you?"

She leaned closer to read, her hair brushing his cheek as she did. Above her, he closed his eyes and took a silent breath of lemon and flowers, the desire for her as strong as the first day he'd seen her.

"That's good," she said.

He made two straight lines on the bottom, and then scratched his signature with little more than three strokes of the pen. He handed it to her, and she wrote very slowly, very clearly.

Mandy Mitchell. She smoothed the paper towel again. "I better be careful with this."

"I can put it in the safe in my villa," he said, reaching for it.

"Good idea." She turned, still trapped between him and the sink, and they looked at each other, a heartbeat of awkward followed by both of them laughing softly. "Should we shake?" she asked, holding out her hand.

"As long as our clothes stay on..." He took her hand and gave it a firm shake, then pulled her fingers to his mouth, dying for one more touch of his lips against her skin. "We're legal."

Her eyes shuttered as he pressed his mouth to her knuckles.

"So, when is the party?" she asked.

"The party isn't until Saturday. I'll arrange for a personal shopper from Naples to come here with samples of clothes for you to wear." At her look of surprise, he added, "I mean, if you're forced to keep them on, you might as well like what you're wearing, right?"

"Right. Is that how you shop? They come to you?"

"Now," he admitted with a laugh. But she still looked stunned and about to turn down the offer. "Mandy..." He took her chin and angled her face toward his. "There are some perks to being my girlfriend, even an imaginary one. Oh, I almost forgot." He picked up the check he'd set on the counter. "This is yours."

She eyed the check, then him, then the check again. "Thank you."

He slid it into her fingers, relaxed now. "It's a pleasure doing business with you, Mandy."

"Yeah, Zeke." She slipped away. "I'm sorry if I seem, well, odd to you. I hope you understand."

"You don't seem odd."

He followed her into the living room, getting the clear message she was walking him to the door. There, he added, "You seem like you've been hurt and you're protecting yourself."

She gave him a grateful smile, one that warmed her eyes and made him ache to take her in his arms. "I really appreciate you being so understanding." She stopped at the door and turned the handle to usher him out. "Then, I guess I'll see you Saturday."

Loophole number one. "No, not Saturday. Tomorrow. At six."

"Tomorrow?"

"I'm having dinner with a client." Again, her mouth opened with an "o" of disbelief. He fluttered the paper towel he was holding. "This doesn't specify that we're only going to be together for that party. I'm here for a week, so I've got an imaginary girlfriend for that week."

"But…"

"I'll follow the rules, Mandy," he promised. "And you'll enjoy a trip to Miami."

"Miami? That's a long drive."

"Oh, we're not driving. I have a helicopter chartered for six-thirty. We'll go a little early and swing over the Everglades."

"The Ever…" She let out a breathy laugh, all color draining from her face. "Oh…okay. I guess. I don't really love to fly."

"This is nothing like flying." He brushed her cheek as he walked out. "It'll be amazing. You'll see." It took everything in him not to kiss her, but he managed to get out the door without giving in.

He'd won round one. Mandy Mitchell was his girlfriend. He'd take care of the "imaginary" part in no time.

The day had started dreamy, moved into unbelievable, and right now? A nightmare.

Every bump, jolt, drop, and roll had Amanda holding tighter to Zeke, her gaze out the helicopter window. All the beauty below was lost, though, as Amanda imagined what it would feel like to die.

The burnished gold sunset behind them and the cobalt waters of the Atlantic ahead of them, even the bright strip of land she recognized as Miami Beach, were just a blur right now.

"Don't be scared." Zeke rubbed his thumb along the inside of Amanda's wrist, his finger warm and the pressure welcome, but neither enough to slow a heart that thumped with the same beat as the blades overhead.

She shook her head, and leaned closer to him, giving a quick look to the pilot, who could hear every word they said through the microphones attached to their headsets. Captain Davis already knew she was terrified, and that was embarrassing enough.

"It's not what I expected," she said, her voice muffled in the headsets that pressed around her ears and drowned out the more deafening sounds of the chopper. "Really, nothing today has been that way," she added.

The whole day had been amazing, though. Not at all what one would expect from the day after being fired. She'd met with the bank, an attorney, and even had had lunch with her friend Jenna, who used to work at Casa Blanca but now was second-in-command at a small housekeeping service in Naples. She'd learned so much and gotten so much closer to her dream that it was dizzying.

Not like this ride, however.

Then, when she'd gotten home, a stylist and personal shopper had showed up along with a wardrobe that a movie star would envy, and they'd dressed and made her up for tonight like she...well, like she was a star. Was that how rich people lived, she wondered as she smoothed the tangerine-colored silk of the high-low strapless dress they'd chosen. She crossed her legs to admire the strappy sandals...and caught Zeke admiring, too.

He made no effort to pretend otherwise, leaning closer and threading his fingers through her hair and brushing her bare shoulder. As he did, the helicopter took a fast fall, making Amanda let out a tiny shriek as she clutched his other hand, a damp palm pressed against his dry, cool one.

"Sorry about that, folks," the pilot said. "Getting a little gusty tonight. But on your left, you'll see our destination. So, not much longer now."

Except...they still had to get down. Amanda tamped her growing fear; she'd always hated to fly, hated that she had no control, hated the fact that she simply didn't understand the physics of it...and this was like flying on steroids.

The pilot dropped them lower, giving them a chance to see the twilight glinting off the white sand of Miami Beach.

"That's Fisher Island," Zeke told her, using their joined hands to point to a triangular-shaped island at the lower tip of Miami Beach. "We're going to that house, on the eastern side."

She followed his gaze but didn't see a house, unless... "That's a house? It looks like a hotel."

Zeke laughed. "Garrett Flynn is a little extravagant. And Meredith, his wife, is an incredible hostess, so the estate is lavish."

Lavish was an understatement. Amanda forgot the helicopter horror for a moment, studying the waterfront property consisting of several red-topped Spanish-style structures situated around a center pool the size of a small lake, complete with a waterfall. A yacht and several smaller boats were moored at a long dock.

"Flynn's a venture capitalist," Zeke said, as if that explained the insane luxury.

"From the looks of it, a good one," she added. "Is that how you know him? Through business?"

"And we're in the same club in New York. Also, before he got married last year, he was on my softball team."

She couldn't imagine being young enough to be on a softball team and owning that estate. But then, look at the man next to her.

The chopper took another free fall, and the pilot tipped to the left, making Amanda seize up again. "Whoa," she whispered.

"Sorry again, folks," the pilot said into their ears. "We definitely are hitting some turbulence."

Zeke put a solid arm around her. "No need to worry. Captain Davis is the best in the business."

"Thank you, sir," the pilot said.

He slid Mandy's headset off her ear, pushing his microphone back so he could speak directly, and privately, to her. "We're almost there, Mandy," he whispered, the warmth of his breath and the genuine kindness in his voice sending chills over her. "Just relax."

She threw him a grateful glance, aware that the pilot might not hear Zeke's whispers, but he could hear her response. "I'm trying," she mouthed, her grip on his hand hard enough to dig her nails into his skin.

"Think about how much fun you're going to have tonight. It's a beautiful place, right on the water, and Flynn and Meredith are great people. I know they'll have a good crowd."

Her eyes flashed. "I thought it was a business meeting."

"I mix business and pleasure all the time."

She slid him a look and gave a sly smile of warning. Had he forgotten already that this was "strictly business"?

"Well, not all the time," he added, close enough to her ear that each word tickled. "You do remember that you're there as my girlfriend?"

"Imaginary," she reminded him.

"Folks, we'll be landing in a few minutes," the pilot said. "But it's going to be a bumpy one, so hang on."

"Oh, great." Mandy tried to laugh but failed as her imagination went crazy with how bad "bumpy" could be.

"Stay calm," Zeke whispered, lifting her hand to his mouth to kiss the jitters away. It almost worked.

As they descended lower, the turbulence increased, forcing the pilot to make a wide turn and hover. She leaned over and looked out, the Atlantic Ocean far, far below.

"Helicopters crash," she said softly.

"Not this one," Zeke replied, reminding her that he could hear even her most private whispers. And so could Captain Davis. A strong bump jolted them into each other and elicited a soft cry from her.

The pilot was speaking softly to the Fisher Island helo control tower, the words "rough" and "turbulent" and "wind velocity" doing nothing to ease her fears. Zeke must have sensed that because he leaned forward and signaled to the pilot to give them a private channel. Instantly, the ground control communication ended, but she and Zeke could still talk to each other.

She wasn't sure if that was better or not, but at least the pilot wouldn't hear now how scared she was. She let her taut posture loosen slightly as Zeke repositioned his headset and mouthpiece to talk to her.

"I can distract you," he offered, taking both her hands in his and holding tight.

He could and he did. And that was almost more dangerous than the winds that buffeted them.

"Hey." He tugged her hands to turn her right to him. "Talk to me. It'll help."

"I can't talk." The headsets magnified the tension of her words.

"Sure you can. You want to know about people you'll meet tonight?"

She nodded, trying to turn back to the window, but he wouldn't let her. She tried to think of something that would genuinely get her mind off the turbulence. "Tell me about your softball team. What's the name of it?"

"The Niners."

"'Cause there are nine on a baseball team?"

"No, because there are..." He hesitated, shaking his head. "It's kind of a joke."

"What's the joke?" she asked, keeping her voice steady despite the next rough bounce.

The chopper dropped hard, whipping to the right as it did. She let out a groan of fresh fear. "Please tell me something to get my mind off the fact that we're about to die."

He laughed softly. "We're not going to die."

"Niners, like it's a play on the 49ers?" she asked. "The football team?"

"No." He definitely seemed uncomfortable with the topic, and just as she was about to let it drop, he leaned closer and said, "It's a reference to zeroes."

Zeroes? They're all a bunch of zeroes? She shook her head, not understanding.

"In our net worth," he added.

A slight frown pulled as she visualized that many zeroes and then...holy shit. "Nine?" she asked, all the fear gone and replaced by astonishment.

That made him...a...she imagined a number with nine zeroes. "As in..." Her mouth formed a "b," but no sound came out.

Another shrug. "I told you, I've had some success."

"*Some* success?" She practically choked, the helicopter momentarily forgotten. "Wow. Really? Nine?"

He laughed, studying her. "You really didn't know that? It's pretty easy to find out with one Google search. The first story that comes up is from *Forbes*, calling me one of the top twenty most elig..." His voice trailed off, and the helicopter hit a welcome but rare smooth section of air.

Most eligible billionaires was what he was going to say, she assumed. "No," she replied. "I didn't Google you." Then her heart stopped. "Did you Google me?"

The helicopter jolted again, knocking them hard and turning her words into a soft shriek.

The pilot was too busy getting them down to even throw back an apology, so Zeke pulled her closer, but it didn't work. "Of course not."

But his words were lost as the whole chopper vibrated and rumbled, bouncing in the wind like a kid's toy on water.

"Oh, my God." She barely mouthed the words. "I'm sorry to be so scared. I hate this."

"Don't be sorry. But I promise, I travel like this all the time. This is really rare."

She nodded, biting her lip and holding his gaze. "I don't want to die before I start my business," she whispered.

"You're not going to die."

She closed her eyes without answering.

"Mandy." He pulled her into him, fighting the pressure of his seat belt to get closer and wrap her in his arms. "Don't be scared," he said. "Don't be..."

It wasn't working; she was shuddering. With one quick look to the pilot, he snapped his mouthpiece down and did the same to hers.

Just as they plunged another few feet, he kissed her. She moaned into his mouth but didn't move away because this…this felt so good. If she was going to die, it would be kissing this beautiful billionaire.

She grabbed his head and pulled him harder against her mouth. Taking the cue, he deepened the kiss, opening his lips, letting their tongues clash and collide.

He tasted like peppermint and safety, closing his hands over her face to hold her right where he wanted, each second of contact making the wind seem to die down. Or maybe she forgot to be afraid because this felt so good.

She took a breath, let out a soft sigh, and deepened the kiss. They stayed that way until they jolted one last time, hitting the concrete of Fisher Island Heliport.

"Uh, we made it, folks."

The pilot's voice, back in their ears, jolted them apart.

"Sorry for the rough ride."

She closed her eyes. "That wasn't rough," she whispered. "That was perfect."

Chapter Seven

Finally on solid ground, Amanda really tried to put that little tidbit of information on the back burner as Zeke ushered her to a private car, which took them around the island to the mind-boggling waterfront mansion owned by debonair Garrett Flynn and his vivacious and quite pregnant wife, Meredith. Still affected by the turbulence—and that kiss—Amanda managed not to swipe a damp palm over the couture dress before shaking their hands.

Instead, she took steadying breaths and tried not to ogle the surroundings as she was handed a crystal goblet of champagne, greeted by some of the other twenty or so guests, and introduced proudly by Zeke as his girlfriend, Mandy Mitchell.

His *imaginary* girlfriend.

Well, that made sense, because everything definitely had a fantasy-like feel to it. From the wall-to-wall aquarium stocked with sharks—real ones—in the living room to the multi-layered pool with at least fifteen canopied bed-like lounges around it, nothing seemed *real*. So it was fine to pretend to belong to the attentive man at her side as twilight descended over paradise and the first few sips of champagne took away Amanda's nerves.

But every once in a while, in the middle of light, breezy conversations with people who all looked like they'd stepped out of a Ralph Lauren ad, she'd glance up at Zeke, and he'd give her a smile that was very real.

After one conversation ended and that couple stepped away, Zeke and Amanda were alone, side by side, facing the deepening-blue ocean that grew darker as some evening clouds gathered.

"So, what do you think?" he asked softly, the question innocuous, but the tone was intimate.

"About?"

He didn't answer right away, but smiled. "The house? The party? Your boyfriend?"

The word did a really unholy thing to her insides. "The house is breathtaking. The party is exquisite. And the boyfriend..." Is breathtaking *and* exquisite. "Has really honed his social skills since Mimosa High."

He laughed. "You know you could totally wreck my reputation with that secret knowledge about what a loser I was in high school."

"Loser?" She scoffed at the word. "If so, you shook that label quite nicely."

"You're being kind," he said. "As far as the social skills, some networking comes with the job."

The job of being a billionaire. "Speaking of jobs, this isn't quite what I pictured when you said you had a business dinner you wanted me to attend." Amanda gestured toward the infinity pool and the yacht just beyond it, taking in the small crowd, harpist, and white-jacketed waiters. "I thought I'd be surrounded by stodgy old men in a dark restaurant where I'd be sitting next to you like an accessory while you planned to take over Wall Street."

"No stodgy old men or dark restaurants in business anymore," he explained. "And Wall Street takeovers are so last millennium. But you know what's most wrong with your picture?" He leaned closer, his hand secure and seductive on her shoulder, his mouth kissably close. "You could never be an accessory to any man."

The words sent a splash of white hot emotion into her stomach. Yes, she could. And she shouldn't let champagne, chiffon, or sharks let her forget it. "Not again," she said softly.

A frown pulled his brows together. "One of these days you'll have to tell me about this jerk you married."

Her whole body tightened. "One of these days, I will." She tried to inch away. "But not tonight. This is too beautiful and too much fun for ancient history. This is really..." So not the time and place for that particular confession. "Are all *your* houses like this one?"

"I'm more understated than Garrett. I have a nice place in the city, though, overlooking Central Park. And a really pretty Victorian in San Francisco with plenty of room if you want to come and visit California."

She let the invitation pass. *Pretend would end,* and she couldn't forget that.

"Flynn likes to flash his money," he said quickly, as though he'd read the look of discomfort on her face. "But he's much more settled down now that he's married and has a baby on the way. Much happier."

She couldn't help detecting a wistful note in his voice. "Is that what you want?"

He didn't answer right away. "Isn't that the American dream?" he finally asked.

She gave a disdainful, but soft, snort. "You're *living* the American dream, Zeke."

"Not entirely." The subtext in his voice couldn't be ignored this time. "Not like Garrett," he added.

"Garrett seems happy," she agreed. "But, trust me..." She looked hard at Zeke, wondering how honest she should be. Under the circumstances, not too open. "Marriage can be a nightmare."

He didn't flinch, his eyes reflecting the water beyond them as he gave her a questioning look. "Did he hurt you that bad, Mandy?"

Why sugarcoat it? "Yes."

"I'm sorry." He turned her so that they were facing each other, the breeze lifting her hair and the way he looked at her lifting her heart. "I'm sorry he broke you so badly."

Denial rose up, swift and certain. "I'm not broken. And, thanks to you, I am well on my way to complete independence, which is all I crave, ever." She lifted her glass in a toast, even though the champagne was nearly gone. "So thank you, Ezekiel Nicholas, for doing deals great and small, even with me."

He tapped his glass to hers. "Mandy." Never had anyone made her name sound so pretty. "I'm having a hard time."

Having a hard time breathing? Because that simple task was next to impossible for her right at this second, under the onslaught of this man's insane attention. "How so?"

He let his gaze fall to her mouth, his expression telling her he was remembering the kiss on the helicopter. Done to distract and calm her, it had had the opposite effect, making her focused on him and completely unnerved.

"I'm having a hard time keeping this imaginary."

A ribbon of heat twirled through her, but her body betrayed her with chills. "Ah, yes, the man who hates to lie." She tried to keep it light, but her voice was tight. "You're doing a good job of pretending, though. I'm sure every person at this gathering believes I'm your girlfriend. Not that I understand why they need to."

"So I'm not lying. Remember? The contract." With his free hand, he held her chin, lifting it slightly as if he were getting ready to kiss her again. And, God help her, she would kiss him right back. "I'm a man who honors a contract, no matter what it's written on. Ask any of my business associates in this room."

"Whoa, Nicholas. Please tell me this is your long-lost sister you've brought to meet me."

Zeke closed his eyes and broke into a wry smile. "Except this one," he said under his breath. "Don't ask this one *anything*." He turned, shaking his head, still smiling as he extended his hand. "I didn't know you were here, Becker."

"When Garrett Flynn sends his private jet, I board and fly where it takes me, because it's usually somewhere cool. Or hot. And speaking of hot..." He shook Zeke's hand but kept his dark, penetrating gaze on Amanda. "Hel*lo*." He positively drawled the word. Nearly as tall as Zeke and every bit as well-built, this man had a face that looked more rugged, less clean shaven, and raw.

"Mandy, this is Elliott Becker, who is best kept at arm's length. Becker, let me present Mandy Mitchell, who is *not* my sister and quite immune to your fake Texas twang and oversized, uh, ego."

Elliott's easy smile crinkled tanned skin and made his midnight-black eyes dance with humor. "The twang isn't fake, darlin', and the ego isn't the only sizable thing on me. God, you're gorgeous. Ditch this human computer and marry me."

She laughed, instantly charmed. But Zeke speared him with a look. "She's too smart for you."

"Who isn't?" he joked, winking at Amanda. "I'm still amazed they let me on the team. I'm the dumbest third baseman ever."

Dumb as a fox, she suspected, if he was one of the Niners. "I doubt that."

Elliott reached for her glass. "Smart enough to know when a lady needs a drink." He put the glass under Zeke's nose. "Get with the program, Genius. Your girl's parched."

Zeke took the glass, giving him an amused glare. "Do your best, Becker. It won't work. She's mine."

"You can't blame a man for trying."

Zeke laughed. "No, I can't. Excuse me, Mandy."

He stepped away, and instantly the other man got a little closer, a scent of sandalwood adding to his allure. "Where did he find you?"

"High school," she said.

"No shit. Sweethearts?"

"Not exactly. We had longing eye contact across the cafeteria."

"Really? I pictured Zeke more of the lost-in-the-library type back then."

"You can't imagine." She gave him a slow smile, wanting to protect—and even improve—Zeke's reputation. "Every girl in school wanted him in the worst way." Wanted his GPA, so that wasn't a lie.

Both his eyebrows shot up. "Including you?"

"At the front of his line."

He made a little snort of surprise, which gave her a weird jolt of pleasure. "So where you been all these years?" he asked.

Married and held prisoner. She lifted a shoulder and kept the banter going. "Just waiting for him to sow his wild oats."

"Zeke? The brainiac? He's never been the biggest ladies' man on the team."

"How many of, uh, you guys are on this team?" There couldn't be too many Niners running around.

"Well, they have been dropping like flies lately. Flynn was one of the founders, but he's obviously off the team, and I'm a little worried about Lord Leo, who is rumored to have fallen flat on his face in love with a librarian, no less, up in someplace called Sanctuary Island."

There were lords on the team? "So if you move away, you're off the team?"

"Not exactly. If you—"

Another man sidled up next to Elliott, nudging him to the side. "You're out, Elliott. Zeke sent me over to pinch hit while he gets a drink."

What was this? Another god fallen down from Mount Niner? Amanda looked up at this newest arrival, meeting smoky gray eyes that looked...familiar. Recognizable. Even a little famous.

"I'm Nathaniel," he said with a picture-perfect smile.

"Nathaniel...Ivory." She managed to keep the stunned shock out of her voice, as a member of a family that some would call "American royalty" stood right in front of her—and not on the cover of some magazine. "Hello. I'm Amanda Lockhart, er, Mandy. Just call me Mandy."

Damn, her composure had slipped a little. But whose wouldn't? Naughty Nate, as the tabloids liked to call him, had hair a thousand shades of chestnut, a jaw like it was chiseled from marble, and that smile that every member of the Ivory family seemed to be blessed with. Along with…a reputation for trouble with a capital T.

"Mandy," he nodded, openly admiring her. "Well, now I understand why our poor Zeke is a puddle of nerves tonight."

"He is?" She glanced over her shoulder, seeing Zeke leaning against a bar, chatting with a woman. "He doesn't look nervous."

"Watch," Nathaniel said. "Give him three, two, one…there." As if on cue, Zeke turned from the woman and looked at Mandy, a little surprised to be caught by all of them.

The other two men lifted glasses to him in mock toasts, and Zeke shook his head, fighting a smile, before saying something to the woman.

"Mandy knew Zeke in high school," Elliott said, lifting one brow. "Apparently, Einstein was quite the catch back in his day."

Nathaniel let out a loud laugh. "Not a chance. He's a card-carrying nerd who, thanks to some very good friends, discovered that even rich men need to hit the gym."

"Oh, really?" She feigned surprise. "And here I recall they named a set of bleachers after him since he did the deed under them so many times after football games."

"He was on the football team?" Nathaniel choked.

"And not a virgin?" Elliott added.

She gave a broad smile, careful not to lie. "Trust me, a cheerleader never forgets."

She could feel Zeke coming up behind her. Maybe she could smell his cologne or sense the other two men shifting toward him, but his hand on her shoulder was no surprise. In fact, it was welcome.

"What are you telling these clowns?"

"I'm sharing what you were like in high school." She felt his hand tighten on her shoulder, a flash of disappointment darkening his eyes.

"Who knew you were Most Likely to Get Laid?" Elliott drawled, giving Zeke a playful punch.

Surprise flickered on his expression, then it slipped back to cool and calm as he pulled Amanda a little closer. "I don't like to brag."

"Your girlfriend is doing it for you," Nathaniel said.

"Are you, now?" He rubbed her arm affectionately. "And here I thought she never even noticed me back then."

She looked up at him, lost for a moment in the warmth and invitation in his eyes. "If that was the case, I was blind and stupid."

His eyes shuttered as if she'd kissed him, the compliment obviously going straight to his heart. He didn't reply, but they shared an achingly long look.

"Well, she sure as heck is noticing you now." Elliott put his glass up for a toast. "Let's make a bet on how soon we'll need a right fielder."

"Why would you need one?" Amanda asked.

The other two men fought a laugh, but Zeke looked serious. "Careful what you say, gentlemen. I don't want to scare her off."

"Why would I be scared?"

Elliott leaned closer. "We have a strict 'bachelors only' rule on the Niners. Once you lose that status, you're off the team."

Oh, dear. Pretend really *did* have to end. She managed to keep her face expressionless.

Zeke, on the other hand, seemed completely relaxed at the implication, his hand slowly moving up and down her arm possessively. She wanted to hate the sensation, but, damn it, she didn't hate it at all. Still, she didn't look up at him, too terrified to see what she might read in his eyes.

There was no way they'd need a new right fielder because of her. She simply couldn't get in any deeper than she already was.

After dinner, the party moved inside as the breeze picked up and rain threatened. While Zeke and Mandy chatted with Meredith about the latest addition to the shark tank, Garrett joined them and wrapped a loving arm around his wife to whisper in her ear.

Zeke watched the exchange, aware of the tug of envy for what they shared. His friend had been lost and lonely a few years ago, bouncing from woman to woman and bed to bed. Then Meredith had appeared, and wham, Zeke had witnessed Garrett transform from playboy to peaceful.

Zeke had never been much of a player, though the women were

available at every turn. That wasn't what he wanted. Under his possessive arm, he stroked Mandy's bare shoulder, the contact getting far too familiar, too good. Could she fill the hole in his heart? Did he dare give another woman a chance, after—

"Gotta steal Zeke for some business," Garrett said to the group.

Meredith reached for Mandy's hand. "I'll entertain your beautiful girlfriend, Zeke. Go talk shop with my husband."

"I'm fine," Mandy said, though he had to say there'd been a subtle shift in her demeanor since Nate and Elliott had made their stupid jokes about losing a right fielder. Nothing he could exactly pinpoint, but he didn't relish the idea of leaving her.

Still, he knew Garrett's invitation to the dinner party hadn't been strictly social, so he owed this time to his host. "I won't be long," he whispered, adding a kiss to her soft hair.

She glanced up and smiled, that wariness that had shown up earlier still taking her eyes from grass-green to the dark shade of a raw Colombian emerald.

"We'll be in the study with Nate and Elliott," Garrett told his wife. Then he gestured toward the window. "Looks like Mother Nature refused to cooperate with your plans for an after-dinner cruise."

Meredith waved her hand. "Can't control the weather. We're fine inside, but..." She gave another look at the sky. "I think some of you will not be getting in a helicopter tonight."

Zeke had already thought of that but hadn't suggested turning the evening into an overnight—not with Mandy so skittish. He let Garrett lead him away to the study before they could start that discussion.

In Garrett's oversized and over-masculine two-story library, Elliott and Nate lounged, talking.

"We were just making friendly wagers," Nate said, as Zeke joined them in another leather chair.

"On what Garrett's latest insane scheme is?" Zeke asked, grinning at their host, who had a reputation for outrageous ideas. Obviously, they paid off, but it took balls of steel to do a deal with the guy. Zeke had done many, of course, all profitable.

"No, we're betting on how long until you're off the team."

He didn't answer, but Garrett brought over a bottle of port and gestured toward crystal glasses, eyeing Zeke. "She's a lovely young woman."

"She is that," he agreed.

"You sure she's legit?" Nate asked.

"Legit?" He scoffed at the word, using it to avoid confirmation or denial. "Coming from you, I suppose you're asking if she's got blue blood that can be traced to Plymouth Rock."

Nate angled his head in consent. "I never heard of Lockharts."

Had she introduced herself that way? Why did she insist on using that name? "That's a married name. She's divorced."

Elliott leaned forward. "I like her, Zeke, but you have to be careful."

In other words, watch out for money-grabbing gold-diggers. As if he didn't know that. "I am."

Garrett had his phone out, tapping the screen, almost as if he weren't listening. "I'd like to be sure she isn't going to break our boy's heart."

The other two men laughed softly, but Zeke put his hand on Garrett's phone, pushing it down. "No need to run a search on her. We're safe in that department." Except, he knew for damn sure his heart wasn't safe at all. It might already be a lost cause. "And if not?" he added, digging for a certain kind of casual he didn't exactly feel. "I don't like to play things safe, as you all know."

"Good," Garrett said, settling into the fourth chair. "Because I have one hell of a dangerous proposal, and you are the three to make it happen."

Happy that the conversation was off Mandy, Zeke shifted his attention to business. "Let's hear it."

Garrett folded his arms and looked from one to the other. "I've heard each of you on different occasions proclaim that you'd like to own a professional baseball team."

He had all of them instantly. They didn't bother to share a look; they'd talked about this over post-game beers many times. Elliott, Nate, and Zeke shared a love of the sport and deep desire to be team owners.

"Oh, baby." Nate leaned forward and put his elbows on his knees. "You got that right. The only problem is there isn't one in the entire country interested in selling right now. Trust me, we've looked."

"What about starting one?" Garrett asked.

"Too much legwork," Elliott said.

"And years before you have a competitive team," Nate added. Of course, that would matter to Nate, who didn't know the definition of defeat.

"Not to mention that buying a Major League team would take more money than the three of us would part with that easily," Zeke said, already doing the math in his head and coming up with...astronomical.

But Garrett ignored the arguments. "I didn't say Major League." They all started to speak, but Garrett waved them off. "Hear me out. I'm talking about a privately owned minor league baseball team."

"None of those for sale right now, either," Nate said.

"You can buy equity stakes, though," Zeke told them. "I've looked into a couple of teams. Quite profitable. But..." He gave a shrug. "Not the game we're interested in, right?"

The other two men agreed.

"I'm not talking about an equity deal," Garrett said. "I'm talking about starting a minor league team from the ground up. Including building a stadium that can be used for MLB spring training, which would pretty much pay for itself in a few years."

All three men looked at each other, Elliott's eyes the widest. "Build a stadium?" The real estate mogul in him looked fascinated. "I like that idea."

"It needs to be in Florida," Garrett said. "Because I'm here now more than I'm anywhere else, but it can't be the east coast of the state because of spring-training travel logistics. The big teams have almost all moved to the Gulf Coast. We need to find a location, do a land deal, get the stadium built, and start recruiting players. I've got more friends involved, but I want you to be the core team. I know your hearts are into this."

Zeke knew where he stood. The closest thing he'd ever gotten to playing ball as a kid was running algorithms on statistics. He played softball now, and each game made him want to be more involved with baseball. And not as a spectator; that wasn't good enough for him. He'd always known that someday he'd buy a team.

"I love this idea," he said, unable to hide his enthusiasm. "I'm all in."

Garrett beamed as Nate lifted his port glass. "I'm interested if I can have a hands-on role. I don't want to be an angel investor."

"Same here," Elliott said. "What's our next step?"

Garrett beamed, obviously expecting this response. "Lawyers, of course," he said. "And we have to scout a location. We can hire someone to do that because I don't have time to drive up and down the state, but I do have a few locations I think could sustain a medium-to-small stadium."

"I'm over on the west coast all week," Zeke said, already loving the realization that the project would have him back in Florida—with Mandy—on a regular basis. "Give me your list, and I can check out some sites. Then we'll turn it over to professionals—"

"Like me," Elliott said. "I think I've proved I can close the deal on a good piece of land."

Considering that Becker had made his fortune at twenty-five by buying an innocuous property in New England that happened to have two billion dollars' worth of solid Goshen stone on it, he certainly had the qualifications there.

"You can have that job, Becker," Zeke agreed. "And when we get close to building—"

"I'll handle that," Nate offered. His family money meant he never had to work, but Nate had proved himself to have excellent project management skills.

"Gentlemen." Garrett stood and raised his glass, and they all followed suit. "Let's play ball."

They toasted just as a thunderclap shook the house and rain splattered on the window. "Didn't you come by helo?" Nate asked.

Zeke lifted his glass. "But not going back that way," he said.

"Not tonight," Garrett agreed. "You and Mandy can stay here, of course. I'll get a guest suite prepared." He took a moment to lift his brows. "One room or two?"

Zeke didn't hesitate a second. "One." Yes, they had a contract...but he could definitely find some loopholes tonight.

Chapter Eight

There never was a moment to say no. The party ended, the weather escalated, the overnight guests were ushered to their rooms. Or room, as the case may be. Of course, Amanda and Zeke weren't flying back to Florida's west coast in a storm, and it seemed crazy to go to a hotel when they were in a house this size, but...

Amanda swallowed against a dry throat as she entered the softly lit guest suite on the second floor and heard Zeke behind her, saying good night to their hosts, giving her a minute to get situated.

She looked around, admiring a floor-to-ceiling fireplace in the middle of a cozy sitting area. French doors lined one wall, looking out to a wide veranda, only partially covered by an awning, the rest designed for private sunbathing. Tonight, however, rain blurred what must have been a million-dollar view beyond that. Large double doors opened to a bathroom the size of a small country, and another set led to a walk-in closet. In the middle of the room...the elephant—an ultra-king-size bed covered in silk pillows and draped in sheer curtains.

One great big mistake just waiting to be made.

"Your dress is going to be a mess."

She wheeled around at Zeke's voice, catching him as he closed the door and locked it behind him. "Excuse me?"

"From sleeping in it." He took a few steps closer, fighting a smile. "I mean, if you're going by the letter of our law."

The contract that said no clothes would ever come off. She'd thought that would be enough to keep them out of bed. Of course, she hadn't planned to be trapped in a suite overnight with him.

"Then you're going to be uncomfortable, too." She gestured toward his dress shirt and trousers. "Maybe you should have thought of that when you told Garrett we only needed one room."

She gave him a minute to deny that, but he lifted a shoulder. "I didn't want to leave you."

Points for honesty. And the ability to turn her lower half into a pool of lust with so few words and one hot look.

"Anyway, if you read that contract closely, it doesn't specify *whose* clothes," he said. "I can take mine off."

Oh, please don't do that. She'd never manage to keep her hands off him.

"Or you can take yours off."

She narrowed her eyes and crossed her arms. "You know damn well what I meant when I put that line in our deal. All clothes stay on. All hands kept to ourselves. All...stuff...is off-limits."

"Stuff? Is that what the kids are calling it these days?" In three long strides, he closed the space between them, his eyes bright.

"Whatever you call it, I was trying to keep us from a situation like..." She angled her head toward the bed. "This."

"Yeah, that." Eyeing the bed, he sidestepped her and lifted one of the sheer drapes off a hook to slip it a few inches across the canopy. "Nice bed. You could sleep in here without clothes on, and I wouldn't even see you." He fingered the fabric. "Although, this is pretty sheer. But if we turn the lights off, you're safe."

"I know I'm safe," she admitted. He'd never lay a hand on her if she didn't want him to. The problem was...look at him. *That* was the problem. His hair was a little messy from the wind outside, his collar open, his sleeves rolled up to expose strong forearms.

He sat on the bed, the flouncy comforter puffing up around his legs. "I'll sleep on the floor."

"Don't be silly."

"I bet the tub's huge."

She smiled. "Safe bet, but no."

He fell back and spread his arms across the bed. "I'll fit on that settee."

"I doubt that."

He patted a pillow as if inviting her. "There's a chaise on the balcony. I don't mind rain."

"Saying one thing, doing another." Laughing softly, she took a few tentative steps closer, unable to resist the sheer pleasure of looking at him spread out on the bed. His hair dark against the shades of cream and ivory, his arms open as if she could…climb on. His eyes closed, and she ventured closer, quietly inhaling the clean scent of him.

"Is that a yes?" he asked when she didn't answer.

But she crept one step closer, careful not to touch him. His eyes stayed firmly shut, and his chest rose and fell with slow, even breaths. If she hadn't known better, she'd have thought he was asleep, and that gave her the confidence to get so close she could see his eyelashes brush against his cheek and the shadow of his whiskers. She let her gaze drift lower, counting a few stray hairs that peeked from the top button of the shirt pulled over well-developed pecs.

He still didn't move, so she kept looking, at his narrow waist and hips, and the rise…oh.

He snagged her hand so fast she gasped as he yanked her onto the bed next to him with a slow, easy laugh, curling his whole body around her. "You're staring at me, Mandy Mitchell."

She tried to deny it, but that came out as a soft catch of her throat at the pressure of his body next to hers. The sweet, sweet pressure.

"I guess you owe me some staring." His voice was gruff. "I stared at you enough."

"In high school?"

"Tonight." He eased her even closer, lining up their bodies on the bed. It felt so natural and right. But it wasn't, and she couldn't forget that. "Didn't you feel it?"

"Mmmm." She closed her eyes and nodded, ignoring the warning bells to enjoy the solid man next to her. "I did."

"And you know what I was thinking?" With one finger, he traced her profile, brushing lightly over and over across her lower lip.

"About that contract you signed?" She tipped her head to the side to catch his smile. He was so close, she could see the different shades of blue in his eyes, the silver rims, the dark pupils. Eyes that held hers, then searched her face as if he were looking for the perfect place to…

"Yep," he whispered. "And all the ways I can get around the terms of our deal."

She didn't breathe, slowly realizing that her hands were locked on to his upper arms, the rock-hard muscle pressing into her palms. His leg rested over her thighs, and that rise she'd noticed?

Rising against her hip.

Everything in her—every single female cell in her body—ached for him. She wanted to turn, to press, to feel his hard maleness right where she wanted it. "You can't…" Her voice was barely a breath.

He pressed his lips against her temple. "I can." And he…was.

"But you can't…"

He feathered kisses down her cheek, making his way to her mouth. "There's nothing in that contract about…" He grazed his tongue over her lower lip, making everything tight and hot and painfully aware of every inch of his body hardening against her. "Kissing."

"But I can't…"

"You don't have to do a thing, Mandy." His fingertips brushed along her jaw and chin, the touch so gentle it could have been air. Unable to stop herself, she felt her back bow, her face lift, her throat exposed to his touch. He ran his thumb over the skin, circling the dip between her collarbones, trailing a hot line lower and lower.

"I have to breathe. And think. And stay sane." She turned her face to him. "All of which I am right now forgetting how to do."

His hand flattened over her breastbone, a strong, huge, masculine hand with enough pressure to make her want to beg for him to…keep going. He leaned over her, his mouth barely an inch from hers.

"You're breathing." He kissed her gently. "What did you think of that?"

"Nice."

"See? You're thinking. What was the last thing you said you forgot? Oh, sanity." He lowered his head and nestled under her throat, sucking softly at her skin. His hand dragged down over the silk of her dress as his erection grew mighty against her. "Sanity is overrated."

She wanted to laugh, but nothing was funny. Nothing was real. Just the touch of his hand and the heat of his body and the taste of his lips. "Zeke…"

He lifted his head and looked at her, his eyes dark with arousal. "You want to break the contract?" he asked hopefully.

She shook her head, biting her mouth closed to keep the "yes" from popping out.

He slowly moved his hand, her breast under his palm now, shooting sparks between her legs and making her want to scream. Instead, she squeezed his biceps with all the strength she had, and he slowly eased himself further on top of her. "Zeke."

"What do you want, Mandy?" He pressed harder, making everything hot and dizzy and so, so needy.

This. She wanted this. And, oh, that. And...oh, that gentle kiss. His mouth was like warm water, his hands sure but kind, his legs wrapping around her...he rocked into her, the unforgiving might of his erection shocking her.

"It's been so...long." She rose and fell against him, completely unable to stop the waves. "But I'm..." How could she even say the word?

He rose an inch. "Please don't be scared of me, Mandy."

She wasn't, but she was scared of this. Of how close this was getting to something she'd absolutely sworn she'd never do. His serious tone made her open her eyes and look right into his. She should tell him the truth. She should tell him what she'd had to fight and how ugly this beautiful act had become for her.

But that would ruin everything.

"I'm not scared of you," she said softly. "Just men like you."

Very slowly, he lifted his hand from her breast and took all the pressure of his body to the side, releasing her. Instantly, she was cold and lonely and achy in a completely different way.

"I'm not like anyone you've ever met," he said simply. "And if keeping that contract will prove it to you, well, then..." He inched her bodice higher, getting her strapless dress right back in place. "I can wait."

She didn't answer, searching his face, knowing he had to feel her heart thump the way she felt his. A billionaire with a good heart? Was this even possible? Could she trust him?

"You can wait?" she asked.

"What's another few days after twelve years?" He kissed her cheek and inched her toward the pillow. "Sleep with me. Just sleep."

She could do that. The realization that she most certainly could do that, and it wouldn't be wrong or stupid or anything but amazing washed over her as cool as the rain pounding on the balcony.

"Yes," she sighed, rolling into his arms. "I can sleep with you."

Hours later, Amanda woke up sweating and tangled. Without thinking, she turned to the man she'd fallen asleep next to, ready to make a joke about how her dress—her three-thousand-dollar designer dress—was wrapped around her legs.

But the pillow next to her was empty. Sitting up, Amanda blinked into the darkness. Cool air ruffled the drapes shrouding the bed, the sound of steady rain loud enough for her to know the French doors were opened. Thunder rumbled in the distance.

They'd fallen asleep on top of the covers, but at some point, Zeke had pulled the comforter down and covered her with a sheet.

She threw that off and pushed back the sheer drape, peering into the darkness toward the balcony. It was hard to see, but it looked like he stood leaning against the railing, face up to the sky, rain pouring on him.

He needed to be alone. Needed to do his…waiting.

Her heart folded as she remembered the words he'd whispered to her. *I can wait.*

But could he wait forever? She let out a long, slow breath of sadness and frustration. She should tell him now. She should tell him what he was getting into and how…unavailable she was emotionally and physically and every other way a man might want her.

How would he take it? She barely knew him, but she had a sense that he was a man of honor. He was also a man who got what he wanted. A man who could tear a paper-towel contract in two with one sexy, talented hand. He could lick a contract apart, kiss it to pieces, make a mockery of…*legalities*.

And he seemed to want more than sex, or was that her dreaming and fantasizing that he truly was the perfect man?

Another long, low rumble of thunder rolled over the Atlantic Ocean, echoing in the room. Her entire being longed to bring him back to bed. But she couldn't—she *shouldn't*—do that.

She slipped her feet to the floor, the sheer dress damp from sweat and discomfort. The bodice squeezed her top, the material stuck to her legs. Her fingers brushed something cool and crisp, and she lifted Zeke's shirt, which he'd left on the bed.

Without a second's hesitation, she slipped out of the dress, wearing nothing but a tiny silk thong. The room lit with distant lightning, enough for Amanda to see Zeke's silhouette standing on the wide balcony, the marbled section protruding out further than the overhang, rain drenching him.

She stuck her arms in his shirt, buttoning a few buttons and standing so that it fell to her bare thighs. Taking a breath, she calmed herself and walked slowly toward the storm outside, which

could only be a little more dangerous than the one raging inside her.
She had to do something. She had to.

Water sluiced down Zeke's bare chest, dousing his hair, soaking his
skin, and plastering the pants that still hung unbuttoned to his body.
Mother Nature's cold shower was doing its job, and he didn't have to go
into the bathroom and run water to keep his erection at bay.

Around three, he'd awakened, a curvy, sexy, soft, sweet woman in his
arms, her breath against his cheek, her sleepy sighs as intoxicating as the
port he'd had in Garrett's library. With each moment, he'd grown hotter,
harder, and more desperate to touch her.

He'd stroked her arm, let their feet brush, and listened to the music of
a moan she'd never know she'd let out. If he'd touched Mandy, she
would have responded. Their bodies were meant for each other, ready for
the inevitable.

But the pain in her eyes after their kiss had told him the ice-cold
reality that some heartless bastard had slashed her heart. No, he couldn't
do anything that would—

He shuddered as arms wrapped around his waist, stunning him with
warmth and invitation.

"What are you doing out here, Ezekiel?"

Her voice was musical, gentle against the distant backdrop of thunder.

"Solving a quadratic equation."

He felt her laugh. "What a geek."

"It's that or break the contract."

She scraped her fingers over his chest. "You already did. This is not
your shirt."

He put his hand on her arm, recognizing the feel of familiar fabric,
already wet from the downpour. "No, but this is."

"I borrowed. Is that okay under our contract?"

Mandy was in his shirt. The thought shot fire into his groin, taking
him back to the state he'd tried for the last twenty minutes to drown.
"No," he said, the roughness in his voice surprising him. "Not okay."

In one easy move, he pulled her around his body, getting her right in
front of him against the railing. She was rain-soaked already, the water

battering her hair and pouring down her face. But she looked up at him, undaunted by a little smeared makeup and a storm.

"The rules didn't say whose clothes we had to wear," she whispered. "And it was the closest thing to you in that empty bed."

Her words slayed him, punctuated by a flash of lightning in the distance. The light was just enough to highlight his wet dress shirt flattened against her body, molded to her form, the shape of her breasts visible, the points of her nipples like gumdrops he needed to taste.

Instinctively, he leaned her back so more rain poured over her. She dropped her head and let the water cover her face and slide down her neck and into the shirt.

How had this happened? What lottery had he won? What good deed had he done? What karmic retribution put her in his arms? "Mandy Mitchell."

She smiled, her back still arched, pressing her against him. "I really never thought I'd be called that again in this life," she said.

Still holding her with one steady arm, he lost the battle not to touch her hardened nipples. He flattened his hand over the shirt, right over her heart, and slowly, easily, gradually dragged his palm until he cupped her breast.

She gasped softly, straightening, her eyes wide. He braced himself for the word "no" or that look that said sex terrified her. But her expression was soft, her jaw slack, her eyes dark with arousal.

A loud shot of thunder made her startle and suck in a breath, coming closer.

"All those nights, Mandy," he whispered into her dripping wet hair.

"All what nights?"

He thumbed her nipple, gratified by the hard, relentless point under his fingertip. "All those nights I'd sit in my room and solve equations and make graphs and torture my brain with mathematics..." He unbuttoned the top button, easily able to reach into the shirt and caress her breast.

For a minute, he couldn't talk, his whole brain flatlined by the perfection of her skin and the slope of her woman's body.

"But then I would think about you." His cock underscored the sentiment, growing harder against her belly.

She smiled, either because of the words or what she felt. "What did you think about, Ezekiel?"

"These." He squeezed her breast. "This." Soft, sweet, tender woman filled every sense as he brushed her lips with his. "And…" He slid his hand down to the bottom of the shirt, sliding easily between her legs, finding sweet, soft, soaked silk, the sexiness of it jolting him. "Of course, this."

She moaned as he stroked her panties and found a sweet spot.

"And what did you do?" she asked.

He wanted to laugh at the question, but he wasn't capable of anything but feeling her buckle a little under his touch. "Not calculus."

"Did you…" She wiped her hands down his chest, over his abs, lower to his already open pants, a question in her eyes.

He closed his eyes and hissed when her fingertip made contact with him, the slight touch injecting more blood to an already engorged hard-on. The rain was useless now, doing nothing but making this even sexier. "I did," he admitted. He buried his face in her hair, nestling into her neck, fighting the urge to howl and slam himself into her fist.

She moaned, clearly turned on by the thought. Pulling her in, he kissed her, tasting rain and the remnants of lip gloss, tasting sex and desire. "I want you, Mandy," he murmured as he broke the kiss. "Here, there, anywhere you'll have me. I want to be inside you. I want to make love to you."

The lightning answered for him, the shock of light catching unmitigated fear in her eyes.

There was no doubt about it. "Sex scares you," he said flatly.

She didn't answer, looking down, the distant rumble like an echo of her pain. "It does more than scare me," she said softly. "I…can't. I may never…again. I just can't."

Then he knew. All the comments about powerful men, her hesitation about sex, her assumption that everything between a man and a woman caused…pain.

She didn't say a word, the rain rolling over her cheeks like tears he knew with certainty she'd shed a million times. "He hurt you."

Her eyes shuttered. "I told you he did."

"No, he physically hurt you."

She didn't answer, biting her lip, looking down in shame.

"Tell me."

She shook her head.

"Please, Mandy. Did he…" God, he couldn't say the word. It made him recoil, a testosterone-induced rage bubbling through him. "If he hurt you, wherever he is, whoever he is, I'll kill him."

He could see her eyes fill despite the rain. "No, you can't. And that's not…please, Zeke. I can't talk about it."

"You should talk about it," he urged. "Let someone share your anger."

She shook her head again. "I'm past anger and, honestly, I didn't come out here to talk about that." Her fingers brushed his abs again, but the fire was gone.

Until she got over this—until she talked and healed—he wasn't going to have her. Not the way he wanted.

Far-off thunder rolled, and rain splattered around them, chilly now and not nearly as seductive as it had been a minute ago. No, until this pain was gone from her heart, every time they kissed and touched, some asshole came into the room with them.

He might want Mandy in every way a man could want a woman, but before they could share that, he had to at least try to help her forget the guy who'd wrecked her. Sighing, he put his arm around her. "Come in with me."

"I can't go to bed," she said, and he understood what she meant.

"I have a better idea."

Chapter Nine

Zeke brought Amanda towels and wrapped her in them, then sent her into the bathroom where she found a thick velour robe. She stayed in there a few minutes, corralling her composure, toweling off her hair, then staring in the mirror to see herself through Zeke's eyes.

But all she saw was…Doug Lockhart's wife. A shadow of the woman she could have been, and certainly not the woman Zeke thought she was.

She closed her eyes and released a pained sigh. She couldn't go the rest of her life alone, could she? But anything else meant…

A shudder passed through her whole body. She wanted him. Really, truly felt the desire that she'd long ago thought Doug had killed. But there it was, alive and sparking in every nerve ending in her body.

Oh, it had been so long since she'd made love to a man who cared about her feelings. In the early days of their marriage, Doug had, but then…things had escalated.

If he hurt you, wherever he is, whoever he is, I'll kill him.

Well, good luck finding him.

It would never get to that point. She couldn't let it, even if she did give in to her body's urges. In a week, Zeke would be gone. Pretend would end. She'd start her business, and he'd go back to his life in New York, and this would be nothing but a lovely interlude that made her feel beautiful again.

Holding that thought, she opened the door to find a fire raging in the fireplace and Zeke on one knee, adjusting the glass enclosure around the flames.

He was still bare-chested but must have found a pair of sleep pants. In the firelight, the muscles and cuts of his bare chest looked like an artist had painted them.

"Wow." Amanda ventured closer. "I'm impressed."

"Don't be. All I did was find the switch and turn on a gas fireplace." He stood, his body on full display, the drawstring around his waist loose enough so the pants fell over narrow hips, revealing more of his masculine form. "And I found some basic necessities in the armoire there. I should have known our hosts would provide sleepwear."

She pulled the robe a little tighter, more for protection than reluctance to give up its warmth for some flimsy nightgown. "They thought of everything."

"C'mere," he said, reaching for her hand. "Unless you want to go back to sleep."

She shook her head and walked closer, where he'd laid their comforter on the floor between a small sofa and the fire. The French doors were ajar, so she could still hear the sound of rain and thunder.

"The wet bar's stocked," he said. "You want anything?"

She considered that but then shook her head. "Too early for coffee and too late for wine."

"That magic hour of four AM." He took her hand. "Let's enjoy the fire, and maybe you'll fall back to sleep."

Doubtful, but the offer was too good to fight, so she let him guide her to the floor, fluffing the down around them, making a soft bed. He leaned against the sofa, facing the fire, and she naturally—so, so naturally—curled against his chest and let him wrap an arm around her.

Silent for a moment, he stroked her hair.

"I don't trust many people," he said, the low baritone of his voice as soothing as the thunder outside.

Grateful he was initiating the shared revelations, she snuggled closer.

"I would imagine," she said, staring into the dancing flames, "that when you are as successful and wealthy as you are, lots of people are out to use you."

He made a small grunt of agreement in his throat, his fingers threading her hair slowly, circling one damp strand.

"I'm always stunned by how many fakes there are in the world," he finally said.

The words hit low and hard, making her close her eyes while he continued.

"I guess because most of my life, I've really lived in and around numbers. Before those numbers translated to money, I knew who and what I could count on. But as the years went by, and I made more and more, I discovered that it is almost impossible to sift genuine people from phonies."

"You have to trust your judgment," she said.

"Funny thing about judgment. Mine seems to be in excellent working order when it comes to finance and business. I can smell a good investment, and my gut instinct is rarely wrong when sitting across the conference room table from a potential business partner."

She waited, knowing there had to be a "but" to this confession.

"But with women?" He gave a wry chuckle. "Man, I suck in that department."

"I find that hard to believe, Zeke. You're gorgeous, you're charming, you're genuine, and you're…"

"Loaded," he finished for her.

"I wasn't going to be that crass."

He shrugged, moving one sizable shoulder under her head. "I am. It's great, don't get me wrong. Money buys freedom and houses and four-million-dollar baseball jerseys and a hell of a lot of security. I suppose, if I so choose, it could buy me companionship."

Something dark in his tone made her look up. "They say it doesn't buy happiness."

He cupped her cheek, holding her face in his hand with such a gentle touch it made her eyes sting. "They're right."

"Aren't you happy, Zeke?"

He didn't answer, and her heart slipped a little. He stroked her cheek and met her gaze with one full of hurt and promise.

"Maybe you need…someone…" But not her. This was pretend…and pretend would end. It *had* to.

"Now you sound like my mother."

"Maybe she's right. Maybe you should…" She swallowed and rooted around for the right way to say this. "Maybe you should give some of those girls she's bringing to the party a chance."

He looked at her like she'd lost her mind, and then resumed his hair twirling and cheek caressing, their legs stretched out in front of them, his body stone still.

"I don't want one of those girls."

An icy cold fear tiptoed up her spine. Because she couldn't be what he was looking for. She couldn't.

"Have you ever given anyone a real chance?" she asked. "Surely you've met someone who you trusted."

He didn't respond, and she started to move to see his reaction, but he tensed his arm and kept her where she was, gathering up a handful of hair and bringing it to his nose to sniff. "You smell like rain."

"Mmm." She nestled closer, drawn to his warmth and body. "Good subject change."

"I'm not...okay. Yeah. I got hurt." He snorted softly, as if to say that was an understatement.

"I'm sorry to hear that." She gave him a second to continue, but he didn't. "How long ago?"

"Couple of years." Another sarcastic snort. "Three years and three months, seventeen days."

"Wow." She sat up this time. "Must have been serious if you remember the date."

"Well, I'm a math guy," he said quickly, and then he gave a shake of his head, as if he were trying to erase that. "Everyone remembers their wedding date, Mandy."

She opened her mouth, then closed it, letting the heartbreak in his voice settle over her. "Oh, no. Really?"

"Technically, rehearsal dinner."

She inched back. "She broke up with you at your rehearsal dinner? Was she crazy?"

He laughed. "I'm going to take that as a compliment."

"As you should. What kind of lunatic would leave a man like you?"

His eyes tapered into icy blue slits, zeroing in on her with enough intensity to send chills over her whole body. "Someday, Mandy Mitchell, I'm going to hold you to that."

Only he wasn't being playful. And if she wasn't careful, she would have herself in way, way too deep. But, honestly, the man was attractive, rich, and had a heart of gold. "What was wrong with this woman?" she asked.

"Apparently, everything, but I was too blind to see." He shook his head, pulling her back into him and drawing the comforter over their legs. "You want to hear the whole story?"

"Every gory detail. I've got all night."

"It's not that long. Or gory. We were at the rehearsal dinner, a banquet for family and friends at the Waldorf, and she got a call." He paused for a minute, as though traveling through time to remember.

"I could tell it was urgent and upsetting because she left the table in a rush and was gone...a long time." His fingers stilled on her hair. "I was worried about her, of course, so I went to check on her and finally found her..."

"Oh, no. She wasn't..." Images of finding his fiancée in the middle of a tryst flashed in her mind.

"No, she was sobbing. Absolutely bawling her eyes out in an empty meeting room at the end of the hall."

Amanda sat up. "What happened? Cold feet?"

"She was still in love with her *other boyfriend*." His voice grew tight. "And he had broken up with her."

"What the *what*?"

"No kidding. She'd been seeing someone for months, a married guy." His voice went flat—absolutely dead from an old pain. "She thought they'd stay together while we got married, and eventually they'd both get divorced, and she'd walked away with money because chump, moron, trusting guy that I am, we had no prenup."

"Oh, God." And Amanda's heart folded in half, stabbing her chest. No prenup. He'd trusted someone that much. "That had to hurt."

"I made it out safely, but, bottom line, I blame myself."

"Why?"

"Because I didn't see through her. I let lust and love and what I wanted more than anything—a partner in life—put blinders on me. She never loved me. She told me that night, all weepy and sobbing. She never loved me and..." He trailed off. "Man, I must sound like a loser."

"No, not at all." Her voice sounded thick in her throat, making it hard to talk. "You gave your heart and trusted and..." Heat crawled up through her as his words replayed. *What I wanted more than anything—a partner in life.*

What she wouldn't give to be that woman.

The thought stunned her, making her instinctively pull away.

"Hey," he said instantly, drawing her right back. "It's your turn."

No, her turn had come and gone, sadly. And now...knowing without a doubt what he wanted? Now she really should tell him everything.

"I did the same thing, Zeke. Only I married him, and it took about seven years to realize that he never loved me, either. And there was a prenup, not at all in my favor. You're lucky you didn't have to go through that kind of pain."

He turned his face to press his mouth against her palm. "I don't think it has to be painful. Not love and not...any part of being together."

She knew exactly what he was referring to. She could tell him that much, right? "You've already figured out the gist of it."

"Sort of." He took her hand and pulled them both down to lie next to each other. "But since I told you my story, you have to tell me yours."

She let him line up their bodies with him on his back and her head on his shoulder, their legs entwined. They sank into the fluffy down, and he wrapped them tighter together. The rain had slowed to a drizzle, and the thunder had quieted, and the only sound was the soft hiss of the gas fireplace and the steady thump of her pulse against her throat.

Waiting for that to slow to a normal rate, she didn't talk, but let their breathing even out and match, her fingers on his chest, unable to resist touching him.

"He was a control freak," she finally said. "In every aspect of life."

"What does he do?"

Now? Who knew? "Commercial real estate." She flattened her hand and enjoyed the steady beat of Zeke's surprisingly dear and trusting heart. "He was very good at it, too. Well, when the market was strong, I mean. But I met him my senior year in college, and he was older by almost ten years and so...impressive. He seemed like the perfect husband. I really didn't have any great career dreams, to be honest. I wanted to be a great wife, do volunteer work, have some kids, be happy. I could lie and say I was ambitious, but I wasn't. Ironically, I'm more ambitious now."

"And were you happy?"

"For a while. Before we got around to kids, though, I had a sense that things weren't...perfect. Work was stressful, and the market was bad, and that made him..." Mean. "Rough."

He puffed out a disgusted breath. "He hit you?"

"No, he never hit me. He didn't beat me or ever make me scared for my safety. I wouldn't have stayed with him, I swear. When I say he was rough, I mean..." She swallowed, then took a deep breath. "Sex. He liked things...not tender." She almost laughed at the understatement. "Let's just say he had a domineering streak that really got, um, exaggerated in the bedroom."

Under her fingers, she felt his muscles tense and heart rate increase. "I take it that didn't, um, do it for you."

"Nope, not my style," she said softly, slowly. "I didn't want to do what he wanted to do." She closed her eyes, washed with the degrading memories. The truth rose up, ready to come out. She should tell him…everything. But something stopped her. Fear, remorse, shame, the knowledge that this had to end one way or another so why make admissions that would only haunt her and hurt him?

"Everything needs to be mutual," he said. "Whatever people do together, it has to be mutual."

"Well, it wasn't. So, eventually, we did nothing and he did whatever he did somewhere else. Of course, I filed for divorce."

"You're smart. You got out. Mandy, I admire your guts."

A chain of guilt snagged her heart, squeezing her chest. "It didn't take that much guts. But…" She swallowed the rest, absolutely unable to say the words.

"But what?"

"Well, I guess I feel kind of dumb, too. I signed the world's most horrific prenup, and now I'm…" She looked up at him and smiled. "Now I'm a maid."

"Not for long," he reminded her. "You'll be a business owner."

She patted his chest and nodded. "Thank you, Zeke."

"Hey, I'm happy to help you out."

"I mean, thank you for this. For holding me and talking to me. For not trying to… I mean, I was…" Ready to fall into bed with him. "Not sure how this would go."

He pulled her up closer, brushing a kiss on her temple, wiping away more damage with one kiss than he could ever realize. "I'd never hurt you, Mandy."

"I know."

"No, you don't," he whispered. "But I'll prove it to you. And once you're sure, once you're absolutely one hundred percent sure, we'll make love."

She closed her eyes and lifted her face, accepting the sweetest, softest, most beautiful kiss she'd ever had. "I'll never be—"

"Yes, you will." He feathered another kiss on her cheek, and her temple, and her ear. "You will be sure and ready and free. And the only tears you'll shed will be from pleasure and joy."

For a long time, Mandy just stared at the fire, both of them perfectly still until Zeke fell asleep in exactly that position. She watched him slumber, drank in the sunrise, and somehow managed to fight the tears as his last words played over in her head.

She might be sure. She might be ready. But she'd never be free. Not the way he wanted her to be. And that was the saddest thing she ever knew because sometime in the last few hours, this had ceased to be "pretend." But it still had to end.

Chapter Ten

Amanda couldn't breathe. Her heart pounded so hard she could hear each beat in her ears, and both of her palms sweat so much she had to turn them over to get some air on her skin. And she was shaking.

But Lacey Walker didn't seem to notice any of that as she turned the last page of the proposal.

"I'm impressed, Amanda," she said, finally looking up. "Simple, smart, incredibly efficient. I know I didn't give you much time."

Next to none, in fact. Amanda had called Lacey the day before to ask for a meeting, certain she'd be pushed back a week or more. But Lacey herself had called back almost immediately and invited Amanda to come in bright and early the next morning with her proposal.

Which wasn't ready. But thanks to Zeke, who'd stayed at Amanda's house until three that morning helping her put a plan together, she'd arrived here at nine, ready for Mimosa Maids to be considered for the outsourcing. They'd laughed, they'd argued, they'd finished, and somehow, they'd kept true to the letter of their contract. Clothes stayed on, even during a heated goodnight kiss.

A kiss that was going to lead to—

"But you wouldn't do that, would you, Amanda?"

She might. For three days, she'd been getting closer. She blinked at Lacey, digging for a suitably vague answer to cover her wandering mind. There wasn't one. "I'm sorry, Lacey, I'm nervous this morning and had about two hours' sleep."

Lacey broke into an easy smile. "I love that this means so much to you. I know the feeling."

She was counting on that. "My plans are a lot smaller than building a resort."

"Trust me, my plans were small, too." Lacey tossed back some curls with a laugh. "Then I met the architect, and his ideas were much bigger than mine." She held up her left hand to show a gold wedding band. "Much bigger."

Amanda's already pounding heart kicked up a notch just thinking about that, taking her back to the mantra that had put her to sleep the last few nights. *Pretend has to end. Pretend has to end.*

After his father's surprise party, Zeke would head back to New York, and his visits to Mimosa Key would be so infrequent, he'd surely forget her. Would she forget him?

She'd have to.

"My question is about the staffing. A big part of J&T's plan is to hire existing staff we have now and dedicate them to Casa Blanca. Are you prepared to do that?"

"There are several staff members I'd like to interview and consider, and I may hire new as well. I'm not afraid of working here every day until we have a fully trained housekeeping staff."

She nodded, considering that. "I like that. I know Jared is planning to move Tori into the office, and she won't be training staff." She sighed, shaking her head. "I need to give this some thought, Amanda, but I'm very intrigued by your ideas. Especially this Mega-Green cleaning line, which you've managed to make cost effective. Others promise similar things, but the fees for environmentally friendly products are sky-high."

Because Zeke owned a stake in the chemical development firm looking for beta testers of the new product line, she'd been able to get an amazing price on "green cleaners."

"I'm excited about that, too," Amanda said.

Lacey fluttered through the pages again, slowing on a spreadsheet and graph Zeke had created, nodding slowly. "Yes, this is quite an impressive piece of work." She closed the binder with a snap. "I'll be making a decision shortly."

"If there's anything else I can do, Lacey, just let—"

"Yes, there is."

Amanda leaned forward, ready for whatever she suggested. A test run, another interview, more numbers. "Anything."

"Accept my apology," Lacey said softly.

Didn't see that coming. "It's fine, Lacey. You're running a business."

"Mr. Nicholas came and personally spoke on your behalf."

She nodded, knowing he'd done that from the first night he showed up at her house with five thousand dollars in his pocket.

"I shouldn't have assumed the worst and fired you."

"I'm not a business owner, yet," she added with a quick smile. "But I imagine you have to daily weigh what's best for your company versus what's best for your employees. I don't blame you for making that decision. In fact, I'm glad you did. It motivated me."

"To find the money, yes. How did you do that, by the way?"

"Creative financing," she said, confident that was no lie.

Lacey's smile was rueful enough that Amanda suggested she knew more than she was letting on. "Give me a few days, and I'll get back to you."

Outside of Lacey's office, Amanda took a minute to lean against the wall and close her eyes with a sigh of relief. This was all so close now. She started to head to the back door, then checked herself. She wasn't in uniform; in fact, she'd decided to wear a simple, but crazy expensive, polka dot dress the personal shopper had left when she'd delivered clothes for the surprise party. Right now, there was no reason to avoid the lobby, which was a much faster way out.

Opening the door that took her behind the front desk, she froze at the sight of Tori Drake clicking away on one of the computers. That wasn't unusual; the head housekeeper of the day often used the front computers to monitor checkouts to get the rooms cleaned while they were unoccupied.

But Amanda really didn't want a run-in with her now. She moved quickly, hoping Tori wouldn't notice her.

"What are you doing here?" The icy demand made Amanda freeze and swallow a curse.

She turned and smiled. "Seeing old friends."

The other woman's gaze dropped over the dress, her lip curling slightly. "You've been banned from the property."

Not true. "Sorry, but you don't own the place."

"But I'm about to own housekeeping, and if you think you can come slinking around for your old job, you can—"

"Mandy!"

They both turned to see Zeke strolling across the lobby, his light, loose, linen shirt accentuating his body, his blue eyes locked on Amanda like she was his personal target. He had one hand behind his back and a very sexy smile on his face.

"Well, well, well," Tori ground out under her breath. "It's your favorite guest."

Amanda slipped out from behind the desk to get away from Tori and closer to Zeke.

"How did it go?" he asked, still not noticing Tori.

She nodded. "Good. It was—"

He brought his arm around and presented her with a single long-stemmed red rose. "I'd have brought champagne, but I figure after last night we both need coffee and rest before the party tonight."

She took the rose, pulling it to her nose to sniff but gave him a warning look, whispering, "Be careful what you say."

He looked past her, and she could have sworn she saw his lightning-fast brain compute the whole situation. "Excuse me for a second," he said softly, stepping away to the desk. "Ma'am?"

Tori gave him a sultry smile. "Yes?"

"My villa is ready for cleaning. My girlfriend and I will be out for the day. We'd like fresh sheets and champagne chilled by four. Will that be a problem?"

Her smile drooped like whipped cream thrown against the wall. "Of course not."

"Thank you." Then he turned to Amanda and put his arm around her. "Let's go, Gorgeous."

As he hugged her close to his side, Amanda looked up. "Why did you do that?"

"Never liked that girl in high school. She made fun of me."

On the way out, Amanda couldn't resist one look over her shoulder, expecting to see daggers in Tori's eyes. But that very second, Lacey stepped out of the management suite and asked Tori to come into her office.

It was almost midnight when the last of the non-family guests finally left the country club. The band was packing up, the waiters were cleaning, and Mom and Dad were hugging some old friends at the door. It was time; Zeke was ready to make his announcement, but he had to be extremely careful who heard what he had to tell them.

Nothing would be public for a while, but he was ready to tell his family the news. And Mandy, of course. He hoped she'd be as happy as he was.

"I guess she's lost her touch after all." Jerry sidled up next to Zeke at the bar, gesturing toward their mother with his glass. "The liedar is broken."

Zeke threw a look at his brother. "What makes you say that?" Had Mom figured out their ruse? He sure as hell hoped Violet hadn't cornered her older son to complain that the younger one wasn't really dating the girl he'd brought.

"You couldn't tell?" Jerry choked a laugh. "Dad wasn't surprised in the least when they walked in."

"I thought he was," Zeke said. "And Mom thought he was, which was all that mattered."

Jerry still shook his head. "He's known for weeks and that whole jaw-dropping, stuttering, and tears? He's been practicing that for days."

"And Mom couldn't tell? Impossible."

"I'm telling you. Her liedar must have been tied to hormones, and those are gone now." Jerry grinned, flashing his easy white smile and crinkling eyes as blue as the set that stared at Zeke in the mirror every morning. "Unless she's just so happy to see you in love that all internal systems went on the blink."

In love? Was his infatuation with Mandy that obvious? He glanced at the dinner table where Jerry's wife and Mandy were laughing, the connection between the two women easy and natural from the beginning. Everyone liked her, of course. Even Mom. Mandy had absolutely charmed Mom, of course, reminding him with a whisper during one particularly nice slow dance that she was only doing her job as his imaginary girlfriend.

Except, not one second of this evening had felt "imaginary" to him. And when he made his announcement, all that pretend business would be over. Anticipation and something that felt as close to a happiness more raw than he could ever remember rolled through him.

"So tell me more about Mandy," Jerry said, interrupting Zeke's thoughts. "You met her at the resort, you said. I'd love to hear about that."

"No, I would." From behind Zeke, their mother stepped between her sons. "I've been dying to get you alone, Ezekiel." She slipped her arm through his. "You see, I have so many mothers and daughters angry at me right now, I'll be needing you to write a lot of checks to charities to make up for the empty promises I made."

He smiled down at her. "I told you not to go to that trouble, Mom."

"Are you *really* dating her?" she asked. "Because I know she's divorced and works as a housekeeper, but—"

"Those details don't make her who she is," he said defensively.

"I know that," Mom insisted. "I'm trying to tell you I like her. She's charming and pretty and..." Mom sneaked a look at the table. "Maybe she won't insist on going to work so much that she can't have a baby."

On the other side, Jerry gave a soft grunt. "Mom, Laura's the—"

"I know, I know." She waved a dismissive hand. "I'm putting my hopes on Ezekiel now. Please tell me this is not some short-term fling of the week."

He easily met her eyes, unafraid of liedar, whether or not it had disappeared with menopause. Because this wasn't a lie. "It's not a short-term fling."

She scrutinized his face with the same distrusting expression she'd wear when he'd tell her he'd gone to bed at eleven but really stayed up until four on his computer. "How can I be sure?"

Just that moment, Mandy looked over her shoulder and caught his eye, sending that same happiness zinging through him. And only a little trepidation. She should be happy about his news.

It was time to find out.

He set his glass on the bar and put an arm around his brother and mother. "I'll prove it right now. Let's get Dad and go sit down. I have something I want to share with you."

His mother's eyes widened. "Really? Oh, my God, really?"

He didn't answer as he walked her to the table and Jerry went to retrieve Dad. In a moment, they gathered together, Jerry and Laura, his wife of six years, Mom and Dad, and Zeke and Mandy. It felt so natural, like she belonged in his family.

"I have some news," he said without preamble.

Jerry and Laura shared a look, and Dad launched a snow-white brow to the north, and Mom beamed like a Christmas tree.

"I love news," she said.

Next to him, Mandy gave him an uncertain look. "Good news?" she asked.

"Fantastic news." He gestured them all a little closer, despite the fact that only the wait staff was in hearing distance. But wait staff could talk. "This is family confidential. You cannot breathe a word."

"Why not?" his father demanded. "If it's good news, we share it."

"No," Zeke said. "We have to handle the announcement very carefully, because this could be a delicate situation."

Mom's gaze zeroed in on Mandy's stomach. "How delicate?"

"No, no." Zeke waved her off with a laugh, putting an easy hand on Mandy's back and feeling her stiffen at the implication. "Different kind of good news."

Mom pressed her hands together under her chin, nearly jumping out of her skin. "Oh, this is so exciting."

"Yes, it is," Zeke agreed. "This is something I've wanted for a long time." All five of them looked at him expectantly, and he breathed the words quietly, "My own baseball team."

"*What*?" Mom's and Dad's simultaneous questions shot like a bullet across the table.

"Really?" Jerry leaned forward. "You're buying a team?"

He could have sworn he felt Mandy sigh with relief.

"Starting one from scratch," he said, reaching under the table to find her hand, hoping she liked the important part of his news. "My buddy Garrett Flynn proposed the idea to a few of our friends, and I've spent some time this week doing some site selection for a location to build a facility for a minor league team and to possibly use for Major League spring training."

"Is that what you've been doing?" Mandy asked.

"I wanted you to come, but you were so busy with your own business, I couldn't take you."

Mom's face had slowly faded to abject disappointment. "That's it? That's your news?"

"No. That's not the best part." He squeezed Mandy's hand. "I've found a location after spending a lot of this week searching up and down the west coast of the state." He turned to Mandy and met her gaze, hoping to see joy in those bright green eyes. "I found about a hundred and fifty acres of undeveloped land right on Mimosa Key in the northeast corner of Barefoot Bay. Which will get me back down here…all the time."

He felt her gasp more than heard it, nothing but shock and…well, not joy in her eyes.

"Northeast Barefoot?" Dad leaned forward before Zeke could interpret Mandy's reaction. "There's nothing up there but an old goat farm."

"That man died, I heard," his mother said. "Cardinale. His granddaughter's been living there since he passed. Is she selling?"

"She's going to," he said confidently, turning to Mandy. "Once we put Elliott Becker on the job."

But she didn't laugh or even reply, her face pale, her eyes still registering disbelief. Inside, all the excitement numbed as he realized...she wasn't happy.

Jerry and Laura were throwing questions at him, Dad was adding to the melee, and Mom looked torn between disappointed and hopeful. But all that didn't really matter because he'd expected Mandy to look thrilled, but she was anything but.

In fact, she barely smiled.

Chapter Eleven

The low-grade panic that had started when Zeke shared his news bubbled up in Amanda's chest, squeezing everything until she couldn't breathe. Her heart walloped her ribs, and every once in a while, she got a little dizzy. Somehow, she managed to chatter with everyone else and hold Zeke's hand as they all left the country club to wait for their cars.

This shouldn't have happened. She had no right and no desire to fall for someone again. That wasn't the plan! That wasn't independence, plus she—

"Here's our car," Zeke said as the limo pulled up to the country club entrance. He guided her into the back seat, gave one last wave to family members then slid in next to her. The car smelled rich, like clean leather, the lights barely on, the windows black.

"My girl is upset." Zeke eased them both to the wide back seat, folding her in his arms. "Isn't she?"

She let out the breath she'd been holding for a long, long time. "This would be a hell of a lot easier if you'd please be an asshole rich guy I'd like to punch."

He grinned.

"And it would help if your family weren't so nice."

He laughed.

"And if you wouldn't do things that make me want to…"

"Want to what?"

Break every rule for you. "Kiss you."

"What did I do that made you want to kiss me?"

"Pretty much just standing, sitting, being, and breathing."

He let out a soft moan and pulled her into his lap. "The party's over, sweetheart."

It sure was.

"Now we are free to…" He dragged her dress up to her thighs, and then eased one of her legs over him, so she was straddling and facing him. "Break the contract."

"I'm not fr—"

He stopped her with a kiss, pulling her with both hands on her shoulders, situating her right over a mighty erection that pressed hard against her bottom, her pearly pink dress balled up between them.

As he broke the mouth-to-mouth contact, he slid his hands down, over the neckline and onto her breasts, making it impossible to talk or think. She had to *feel*. His hands erased everything.

He rocked once, making her gasp. She dropped her head back, the blood rushing through her doing exactly what she wanted it to do—clearing her head of any thoughts. Of any rationalizations. Of any truths or fears or problems this was going to lead to.

Instead, she felt the burn of his lips on her skin, the heat of his fingers as they wandered up her thighs, cupping her bottom, and caressing the most tender spot between her legs.

"Zeke…" She couldn't breathe, her body coiled tight with how much she wanted his fingers on every bit of her skin, his mouth everywhere else, and his whole manhood deep, deep inside her. Just thinking of that made her roll against his hard-on, earning a grunt of pain and pleasure and an intensified sucking against her neck.

The rumble of the causeway under the tires told her they were almost home, and when they got there…

"I want to make love to you," he rasped into their kiss. "I want every inch of you, Mandy Mitchell." He slipped a finger into her wet panties, deep enough to know without a doubt that she wanted the same thing. "I will be so gentle," he promised.

The words tore her heart out. "I know you will, but…"

"Don't be scared, honey. I will go so slowly." He stroked her with his thumb. "So soft and sweet and easy." Sparks ignited between her legs, fueled by the seductive words.

She could barely nod, her breath so twisted in her lungs, fighting the orgasm that already threatened. One more second, one more caress, one more promise, and she'd be gone.

"This is…wrong."

"It's going to be all right," he assured her. "We're going to tear that contract to shreds. Along with this dress."

"No, I mean—"

The limo came to a stop in the driveway of his villa. She eased off him, straightening her dress and hair, trying to get her breath. He could tear that paper-towel contract and this dress, and it wouldn't change anything. She was…who she was.

And she could never be his.

Except…maybe this one night, before he left. One night, one time, one sweet, sweet night…she could be his. Doug couldn't steal everything from her. He couldn't take away this one night.

Zeke had Mandy in his arms before the lights of the limo disappeared, scooping her right off the ground and carrying her up to the door, her laughter like music as she dropped her head back.

"What are you doing?"

"Sweeping you off your feet. And, shit, the key's in my pocket."

She reached her hand between them, going for his pocket but landing on his throbbing hard-on instead. He hissed. "Don't make me drop you, Mandy."

She laughed again, giving him a squeeze, then finding her way into the pocket to produce the card key. "Voilà!" She held it up, and he positioned her so she could unlock the door, and he pushed them in.

"Are you going to put me down?"

"On the bed." He took her straight down the hall to the bedroom, where the efficient staff had followed his secret instructions and left about two dozen hurricane-style candles burning around the whole room.

"Zeke!" she exclaimed as he set her on the bed, kneeling over her. "This is so romantic."

"I wanted our first time to be perfect for you, Mandy." He slowly lowered himself to the bed. "As perfect as you are."

Her eyes fluttered in acknowledgment of that, each breath she took slow and strained.

"I never want to hurt you." He traced a line along her cheek and jaw, sliding up to her parted lips.

She whispered something he didn't catch. Pretend end? "What was that?"

Her eyes darkened under a frown. "Zeke, this was only supposed to be for a week."

He kissed her softly, tracing his lips to her ears. "What is this 'supposed to' you speak of?"

She shuddered a little, and he kissed her with every ounce of tenderness a man with a raging boner could manage, letting her warm to the intimacy and relax in his arms. But she seemed more tense.

"Deep breaths, Mandy. I'm not going to hurt you."

A fine sheen of sweat glistened on her shoulders, so he kissed it, tasting salt and perfume and sweet, sweet Mandy. He lifted her body enough to unzip her dress in the back.

"Zeke, I really shouldn't…"

"Shhh." He feathered kisses over her breastbone, tugging the strapless dress lower and lower until her breasts were revealed. He dipped his head to kiss one and caress the other, making her gasp and arch her back.

"Oh, my…"

He ran his tongue over her nipple, loving the hard bud and sweet taste, sucking hard enough to make a noise. Blood rushed in his head, amazing him that there was any left there, considering how much had flowed to his lower half.

Still, he fought to hold back, easing that dress down, watching her chest rise and fall and seem to fight a losing battle.

Her head moved back and forth, almost as if she was saying…no. He paused for a moment, so hyperaware of her fears, stilling his hands.

"Zeke, we…can't."

"We can," he whispered, inching his way up to kiss her mouth and talk to her. "We really can."

"But…there's this paper…"

He laughed softly. "You're going to hold me to that contract?"

For a minute, her whole body stilled, and then she looked at him. "What good is a contract if you ignore it?"

Was she serious? "How about I burn it?"

"Zeke, I have to… there's something—"

A soft tap on the outside door cut her off and made him frown. "Did you hear that?"

"Housekeeping!"

Her eyes widened. "It's Tori!"

"Shit." He pushed off the bed. "Don't move. I'll take care of her."

"Zeke, wait." She grabbed his arm. "I have to tell you something. It's important. I have to—"

"Housekeeping!" She was *inside*!

He let out a disgusted grunt. "Does she think this is how to keep guests happy? Hold your thought, I'll be right back."

Why would she come in, he wondered as he marched down the hall. The wall safe where he kept valuables was hidden in the dining area, but she'd know that. She wouldn't know the combination, though. He turned into the living room and found her putting something on the coffee table.

"What the hell do you want?"

She straightened, unafraid or even surprised to see him. "I've left something for you, sir."

At this hour? "What is it?"

"Oh, a special gift from housekeeping." She gave a tight smile. "Hope the sheets were clean enough for you and Mrs. Lockhart."

She pivoted and walked to the door, yanking it open and disappearing into the dark. What the hell? He grabbed the envelope but didn't bother to open it, too eager to get back to Mandy.

On his way out, he stepped into the dining room and opened the cabinet where the safe was, tapping in the digital combination he'd set. Deep in the safe, he found the paper towel they'd used to write their contract.

It was time to put those candle flames to good use.

In the bedroom door, he paused, blinking into the flickering light when he didn't see Mandy on the bed. Or anywhere. "Mandy?" He checked the bathroom, but the door was open and the lights were off.

Where did she go? The French doors to the patio were open, and he stepped closer, seeing her immediately, walking by the pool, her arms wrapped around herself as she whispered, like she was…

Talking to herself? Like she was…practicing what she wanted to say to him?

His heart nearly collapsed. She'd had so much pain, so many fears. But he didn't care. He'd conquer every one of them. He'd beat anything and anyone down to have her in his arms, afraid of nothing.

He started to go outside but decided to give her a minute. Let her gather her thoughts and make her speech.

Instead, he dropped into a chair in the sitting area and ripped open the envelope that had his name on it. He unfolded the paper inside, frowning at the legal document as he tipped it to read by candlelight.

"What is this?" He turned the paper closer to the flame and squinted at the tiny print, a seal at the top, and names…he recognized.

A slow, icy chill wormed through his body as the words almost made sense. All of the words. Even the maid's parting shot.

Hope the sheets were clean enough for you and Mrs. Lockhart.

"Zeke."

He looked up, surprised to find Mandy a foot away, her arms still crossed, her face streaked with tears. He blinked at her.

"I'm still married." The words were barely a breath of air.

He let the paper flutter to the floor. "I know."

Chapter Twelve

The thing that buckled Amanda's knees wasn't that he knew her secret…it was how stricken he looked. He stared at her with vacant eyes, the slightest frown of pain and disbelief pulling his brow, his whole body hunched in a self-protective posture.

She knelt in front of him. "I was trying to tell you."

"Now?" The word ground out like one syllable of agony. "How about, oh, a week ago?"

"I didn't think it mattered a week ago."

"You didn't—"

"This wasn't real, Zeke!"

He straightened at the force of her words, leaning back, looking at her…as if for the first time. With all that awe and joy and interest and attraction she'd been basking in for the past week wiped away, replaced by raw hurt.

That was the worst part. "The fact is, I'm legally bound—"

"To your husband." Anger darkened his words.

"To a nondisclosure agreement that is part of the world's most horrific prenup. I really cannot talk about my husband or where he is, but that's easy enough because I don't know where he is."

He stared at her, the only thing moving on his body were the tips of his fingers, which slowly dug into the armrests of the chair with the same pressure she imagined they'd like to dig into her chest and rip out her heart right now.

And that was the only reason she had to break the agreement and risk the truth.

"He's a criminal," she said softly.

He still didn't speak, searching her face and waiting for more.

"He took millions of dollars for a fake real estate investment and to develop this big park and residential area in Tampa. He swindled five investors out of about ten million dollars and claimed to have a bank guarantee from somewhere in Switzerland and a commitment from some fund in New York. It was all lies. He thought he could float money, finish one project and start another..." She closed her eyes, almost relieved to be saying this to someone other than a federal investigator.

"We were divorced, for all intents and purposes. I'd moved out, had a plan, even had a little bit of money. All the paperwork was done, I was walking away with nothing, but he had one more paper to sign." Her voice cracked. "He refused and disappeared that night."

His fingers pressed harder. "Why wasn't he arrested?"

"They can't find him, and he won't come back into this country. Because we weren't divorced, I had to turn over whatever money I could to the federal government. My name is on many of his documents, and I'm trying, dollar by dollar, to pay people back, and the investigators insist I use my married name so anyone he owes money to can find me."

"They don't know where he is?" He sounded incredulous.

"I've heard he's in Croatia, and Australia, and Singapore, and the latest sighting was Hong Kong. There's some extradition glitch with criminals there, so he might think he's safe. I used every dime I had left to pay for a private investigator. All I want him to do is sign the piece of paper and let me be free of this marriage and this debt and the weight of... my past. I want to be free."

She dropped down to sit on the floor, the pressure of the story almost too much for her. Zeke made no effort to reach out to her or even soften the look on his face.

"In my prenuptial agreement, there is a line that says I can't reveal anything I know about his business, so I'm in a really bad position."

"That's void if he's a criminal."

"One would think, and I certainly told the investigators everything I knew, but...I'm afraid if I break that agreement, I'll never get him to sign that decree. I keep hoping he will meet a woman and *want* to sign it, but..."

She'd never imagined *she'd* meet someone. Someone so good and right and real that he made everything she thought she knew about powerful men seem wrong.

Quiet for a long time, he finally swallowed and nodded. "If you really wanted to, you could find him."

The allegation stung. "Trust me, I want to." Now, more than ever.

"Do you? Or are you protecting yourself, Mandy? Do you want to be certain you don't have to take another risk so you stay…married?"

"No," she answered without hesitation.

"Really? Because you crave independence, but you don't go after it."

She let out a soft, shuddering sigh. "I don't know how," she admitted.

Finally, he nodded. "I understand."

"You do?" She barely understood, so how could he?

"I wish you'd told me, but—"

"I thought this was strictly business, Zeke."

He closed his eyes, like the words were a direct hit to his heart. "That's where I made my first mistake." He pushed up, stepping around her. "But I won't make a second."

The words sounded cold and harsh and…deserved. She inched back as he walked away.

"Would you like me to drive you home?" he asked.

For some reason, that question did her in. The dismissal of it. The finality. And, no, she didn't want him to drive her home. She couldn't bear to be alone tonight.

"I'll sleep upstairs, if you don't mind."

"I don't mind."

Tears burned behind her lids. Pushing up, she stood and watched him walk across the room, not sure what to do. Then he stood very still, as if he was having an internal debate.

Turn around, Zeke. Turn around and forgive me. Turn around and take me in your arms and tell me that we'll figure this out.

He didn't move.

"Zeke…"

"I have to make a phone call," he said, the tone still utterly…icy.

She deserved that. Without a word, she walked out and padded up the stairs, closing the door in the guest room but not locking it. Because she still hoped he'd come up to her.

An hour passed, and she was still alone. Still in a frothy pink dress he'd bought for her, alone in a guest room she'd cleaned for him not a week ago.

She rolled up on the bed, pulled the comforter over her and finally, fitfully fell asleep. When she opened her eyes, the very first whisper of dawn touched the morning sky beyond the plantation shutters she hadn't bothered to close.

And she was still alone.

Pushing up from the bed, she wiped sleep away and waited for the realization that she'd had a very bad dream. But it was no dream. She opened the door and peered into the dark, and then tiptoed down the stairs, sensing something different about the villa. Emptiness.

"Oh, no, please." The words slipped out from behind her fingers, as if she could contain the pain she knew she was about to endure.

She went straight down the hall to the master bedroom and into the open door. The room was empty, the rose petals and candles out of sight, the Egyptian cotton sheets stripped off the bed.

Any sign that Zeke Nicholas had been a guest was gone.

Amanda wasted no time doing what she had to do. At eight-thirty that morning, she was waiting outside Lacey's office, hoping to be the first meeting of the day for the Casa Blanca owner.

As Lacey came around the corner, she slowed her step and gave a warm smile in greeting. "Amanda, I love your ambition," she said with a laugh. "You aren't going to wait for me to make this decision, are you?"

Amanda swallowed hard, smoothing her hands over her dress. "Actually, I've come to withdraw my proposal, Lacey."

Amber-brown eyes widened in surprise and disappointment. "Why?"

She'd never say. "And I also am here to ask if you'd consider letting me have my old job back."

Lacey let out a low sigh, clearly not thrilled with either request. "Come on in, let's talk."

But there would be no talking—not openly. Just some begging. She had to repay Zeke somehow. She'd spent two thousand of his loan starting her business, and she wanted to pay back every dime, as quickly as possible. This was the most expeditious way she could think of.

In the office, Amanda perched on the edge of the guest chair, while Lacey followed her in, hooked her bag on the back of the door and closed it with a sharp snap. "What happened?" she asked before she even sat down.

"My...my..." She hadn't expected Lacey to ask. "My financing fell through," she finally said. And that was kind of the truth.

"Yes, I saw his name on the morning checkout list."

Amanda closed her eyes, unable to meet Lacey's gaze. "Don't judge," she whispered.

Lacey surprised her with a sharp laugh. "Judge? You are talking to the wrong woman. Honey, I have been there and done that and have the baby to prove it doesn't always go south when a man helps you out. So, what happened?" she repeated.

"I...he...we..." She laughed at her pathetic stuttering, taking a deep breath to find some composure. "It's a long story."

"I like long stories, but give me the abbreviated version. He wanted more than you're willing to give?"

A warm blush rose up. "Am I that transparent?"

"No, he was. When he came to our house, the guy was already half gone. But I know you're a private woman, so I haven't been able to read your take." She leaned forward, dropping her chin on her knuckles. "He's a catch. Great-looking, wealthy, caring. What's his fatal flaw?"

"He doesn't have one," Amanda admitted glumly. "I do."

"And it is?"

She nodded. "You're right about me. Private. And so's my answer to that question."

Lacey grew quiet, considering a reply. "You know what meeting my husband made me realize?" She lifted her hand as if to say, *Don't bother, it's a rhetorical question*. Then she leaned closer, narrowing her eyes. "When it's real, anything is possible."

Her chest squeezed. "This wasn't real." It was, in fact, imaginary.

"Then better you learn that now before you make any lifelong mistakes, right?"

Right. "I guess."

"I was going to give you the business."

Damn, damn, *damn*. "I can't do it, Lacey. I have to pay back his loan. Otherwise..." *I'm no better than my husband, the swindler.* "I shouldn't have taken it in the first place."

"Well, that's a shame, because I loved your proposal. And I have some serious issues with Tori and Jared. For the time being, I'll continue to manage housekeeping through the resort and revisit the outsourcing at a later date. Maybe by then you can re-bid for the job."

"Maybe." But she sounded about as confident as she felt. Like, maybe pigs could fly. "But right now, I need an income. Can I work for you again?"

Before she answered, her phone rang. "Hang on," she said, lifting the receiver on her desk. "Lacey Walker."

As Lacey listened to her caller, Amanda waited, her heart still hammering from making the request.

"She did *what?*" Lacey's voice rose as she stood, sounding astonished by whatever news had just been delivered. "Take her passkey and send her to my office."

Lacey clicked off the call and remained standing, looking down at Amanda. "When he checked out, Mr. Nicholas reported that Tori broke into his villa at one in the morning. Do you know if that's true?"

"She used her passkey, I was there."

Lacey puffed out a breath and fell back into her chair. "I'm letting her go."

Ding, dong, the witch is dead. Small consolation now.

"But then I have some scheduling problems."

"I'll help you," Amanda said, leaning forward. "I'll work anytime, any job, anything."

Lacey's smile was slow and kind of sad as she shook her head. "You really need to have your own business. I'll take you up on that offer and give you triple time if you work the reunion I'm having in a week. I'm really short that night, and it will definitely count as overtime, since working the reunion means you'll miss enjoying it."

Amanda frowned. "What reunion?"

"Oh, you weren't here for the last all-staff meeting. I had a great idea for some local marketing. I'm holding a Mimosa High reunion for everyone who ever went to the high school that we can find. It's going to be all day on the beach. We've located lots of former Mimosa Scorpions through the Internet and Facebook."

"Wow." A Mimosa High reunion. Could there be *anything* less appealing?

"And we're giving everyone a name tag with their senior adjective. Isn't a reunion an awesome way to spread the word about the resort and get people of all ages together?"

Amanda swallowed her response, because Lacey wouldn't understand that she'd been Mandy the Magnificent but would now be Mandy the Maid. "Awesome," she agreed.

"I'm sorry you have to work, but I'm desperate that day."

And the last thing she'd do was turn down triple time when she'd just groveled to get her job back. The only thing that mattered was accruing the money and sending it to Zeke Nicholas. "It's fine, as long as you don't make me wear *my* senior adjective."

"What was it?" Lacey asked.

Amanda shook her head. "I forget." Even though they both knew that no one forgot their senior adjective.

"I'm sorry Zeke isn't still here to attend," she said quickly. "Because meeting him really did give me the idea." She eyed Amanda. "Any chance he'll be back?"

She remembered the baseball team—had thought about it a lot, as a matter of fact. But he'd find a new location for his minor-league plans. He hadn't disappeared in the middle of the night only to return to build a baseball stadium. She'd already practiced squashing all hopes of that.

"I really don't know," Amanda answered honestly. "He left before I could ask him." *Or tell him how I really felt.*

Lacey nodded, pushing back from her desk to end the meeting. Amanda stood right away. "Thank you so much, Lacey."

The other woman came around her desk and reached both arms out. "If it's any consolation," she said, giving Amanda an easy and warm embrace, "Clay and I broke up once, too. But he came back."

It was, in fact, no consolation at all.

Chapter Thirteen

The giant orange ball dipped over the cobalt waters of the Gulf, moments from melting into an aww-inducing puddle of gold. Barefoot Bay had never looked more glorious for the reunion that spanned class members from almost sixty years. They didn't have senior adjectives before the 1970s, so the oldest party guests were over sixty and making up the nicknames now, based on memories.

And those tables were definitely having the most fun, Amanda thought as she bussed another set of martini glasses and carried them to the open-air bar. Although, to be fair, Lacey's idea was a huge success, with two hundred people falling in love with Casa Blanca, many sharing pictures on social media sites that would surely increase the resort's visibility and bookings.

Everyone was having fun...except Amanda. She was doing what she'd done for the past week. Cleaning up other people's messes and wallowing in her own. She missed Zeke more every day and here? At the reunion, where he'd be a superstar and she'd be...

No, she wouldn't be. If she'd ever had a chance with him, she'd blown it by lying and hurting him. Sighing for the sixtieth time that hour, she glanced around, hating the tiny little tickle of hope that played with her heart, imagining he might...

Stop it, you moron! He's not coming back.

There weren't that many representatives from the class of 2002 in the crowd, though Amanda had run into a few people she remembered. No one commented on her lowly maid status—at least not to her face. Overall, the atmosphere was too festive, the music too upbeat, and the booze was flowing too freely for anyone to be mean.

"Until now," Amanda muttered under her breath, squinting across the beach to confirm that, yes, the bitch was back.

Alone and dressed in her usual too-short, too-tight, and too-much, Tori kicked off her shoes and sashayed onto the sand.

"What's Tori the Tiger doing here?" The question came from behind the bar, making Amanda turn to meet the gaze of another housekeeper, who was also doing double duty working the big event.

"Class of 2002," Amanda said. "I guess she has as much right as any former Mimosa High student to be here."

Still, Amanda glanced around for Lacey to see if there was any reaction to the arrival of the former employee. Lacey stood in a large group, her baby—dressed in Mimosa High red-and-white overalls—on her hip. With her husband, Clay, at her side, Lacey was surrounded by friends and guests, reveling in the success of her party and her ever-growing business. She had no need to be concerned about Tori.

So Amanda wouldn't worry, either. Instead, she finished bussing the glasses and scooped up her empty tray, ready to go look for more to clean up. As she turned, she almost smacked into Tori.

Oh, man. Really? "Excuse me," she said, trying to sidestep Tori.

"Oh, hello, Mrs. Lockhart." Her smile was tight as she slid her gaze over Amanda's uniform. "Interesting outfit for the reunion. No designer polka dots anymore? Oh, that's right. Turns out your sugar daddy wasn't so sweet after all."

Irritation skittered over her skin, tightening every nerve. Amanda forced a fake smile, refusing to make a scene at this event. "I'm working," she said through gritted teeth.

Tori glared at her, her gray eyes turning into angry slits. "Not if I have anything to say about it."

"You have nothing to say about it," Amanda replied. "You did your work, you wrecked enough things for me, now get out of my way."

One eyebrow tipped up. "Wrecked things for *you*? We lost the outsourcing, and Jared dumped me."

Smart man. "Sorry to hear that."

"Are you? No doubt you'll be after him next."

"Actually…" Amanda had to bite back a laugh. "There's plenty of doubt. I'm not interested."

Tori leaned in close enough that Amanda caught a whiff of beer on her breath. "Does Lacey know? Does anyone else at Casa Blanca know? It wasn't hard to find out you're still married to Mr. Wanted By The Law."

"Mandy Mitchell!" They both turned at the exclamation, Tori inching back and Amanda almost dancing for the reprieve. A beautiful young woman with long black hair stepped forward, her dark eyes focused on Amanda. "You don't remember me, do you?"

"I'm afraid...wait." Amanda took in every detail of the woman's striking, unforgettable and exotic looks, but couldn't remember her name.

"Frankie." The woman put her hand out. "Frankie Cardinale. I was a freshman when you were a senior, so you probably don't remember me."

The name was familiar, but she really couldn't place a memory. "I'm sorry, I don't."

"Well, I remember you," she said, nodding.

For a moment, Amanda froze, waiting to hear of some horrible mistreatment she'd done back in her glory days.

"Don't tell me, she kicked you off the cheerleading squad for being too pretty."

The woman looked at Tori like she had an extra head. "Not by a long shot. My locker was by yours, Mandy. Because of some mistake, I was the only freshman in that hall." She gave Amanda a slow smile. "You were the only senior who gave me the time of day during what was a really challenging year for me."

Tori let out a little snort of disbelief.

"Oh! I do remember you," Amanda said, returning the smile, seeing a scared, dark-haired little girl in her memory. She reached out a hand to Frankie. "And I'm glad you're here."

"Mandy's glad because it gives her more work to do," Tori said. "She's on staff at the resort. A *maid*."

Frankie nodded, her interest piqued. "Cool. I'm trying to meet people who work here because..." She let her voice fade as a low thumping filled the air and all around, people started looking up to the sky, a crowd-wide cheer of excitement rising.

Amanda turned to the sunset, which often elicited applause, but this was different. The sound walloped through the air, drawing her gaze to the helicopter that hovered directly overhead.

For one long moment, Amanda stared slack-jawed and suddenly filled with so much hope she could taste it. Was it possible that—

"Well, someone wants to make a grand entrance," Tori said wryly.

Yes, someone did. Amanda's traitorous heart leapt into her throat as she closed her eyes and let the thudding blades match her pulse. He was coming back for her!

She fought the urge to run out and wave him down, watching the chopper dip left and right, zooming over the crowed and getting a huge hoot of pleasure from everyone around. Lots of glasses were raised, and people clapped and hollered, the sound deadened by the blood rushing in Amanda's head.

Once again, the bird tipped to either side, turned and flew over the crowd as if...he was looking for someone. Looking for...*her*?

Stop it. Stop it, she ordered herself. She hated the slow heat that crawled over her, hated the expectation and thrill that clutched her heart and wouldn't let go.

Suddenly, the helicopter popped higher into the air and flew to the north.

"Is he leaving?" someone called out.

No, Zeke! Don't leave! Amanda squeezed the tray so tightly it could have cracked in her hands. It had to be him. Who else? He was—

"Looking for a place to land!" another voice announced.

"Who is it?" a couple others called out.

Amanda squinted into the setting sun to see Lacey and her group, but they all seemed as surprised as anyone. Lacey even covered the ears of her crying baby.

Even this far away, Amanda could feel the pulse of the wind as the chopper dropped down on a deserted section of the beach. As though drawn magnetically, the crowd turned, and many started walking toward the new arrival.

"Let's go see," Frankie said, putting her hand on Amanda's arm. "Don't you want to know who from Mimosa High can afford to take a helicopter to the party?"

She ignored Tori's gaze locked on her. Only one man could...

No. She refused to let this hope steal her very breath. But how could she not? How could she not wish and dream that he rode in for her?

Still carrying her tray, Amanda let Frankie lead her with the crowd, closer to the thumping drum of helicopter blades, the rhythm matching the voice in her head.

He'd come back for her. He'd come back to help her. He'd come back...

It was crazy, it was wrong, it was stupid. And it was impossible not to fantasize.

"Hey, you're shaking," Frankie said.

"Hey, you're dreaming," Tori added, on her other side.

Amanda refused to look at either one of them. The crowd gathered closer to the helicopter, fifteen rows thick, with Amanda at the back as the noise finally abated.

And then the door popped open, and Amanda lifted the tray, pressing it to her heart as if she could stop the insane pulse that shook her. It had to be him. It had to be—

A man in a cowboy hat.

She had to bite her lip to keep from letting the cry of disappointment escape her. *Stupid, stupid girl.*

"Would you look at that?" Frankie whispered under her breath. "Take me to your rodeo, cowboy."

Tori elbowed her. "Not who you were expecting, was it, Cinderella?"

She fought the overwhelming urge to smack the tray right over Tori's head.

"'Scuse me?" The cowboy stepped closer to the crowd, his long, lanky body moving with purpose. He took the hat off and shook out some dark hair, peering into the crowd.

Holy cow, she knew that guy. It was Elliott Becker, one of the Niners she'd met in Miami.

"Anyone here know a man named Frank Cardinale?"

Next to her, Frankie gasped. "What the *eff?*"

And suddenly, it was all clear. The name Cardinale was familiar because she'd heard it at the party—the owner of the land they wanted to purchase for the baseball team. No Prince Charming had blown in on his chopper to sweep her away. He'd stayed away from a woman who'd lied and hurt him so bad…and sent someone else to do his work.

That didn't stop her from peering around the crowd and the tall cowboy to see into the helicopter on the off chance…

No. Elliott had come alone.

The only thing worse than the disappointment that crushed her chest was the fact that Tori was right there, witnessing Amanda's defeat.

"I'm looking for Frank Cardinale," Elliott called out.

Still staring at him, still wishing to God he was someone else, Amanda whispered to the woman next to her. "I think he wants to buy your land."

When she didn't answer, Amanda glanced to her left, but Frankie was gone. She turned, looking at the crowd behind her, but the other woman was darting away, headed in the other direction down the beach.

"Excuse me, miss." A man tapped Amanda's shoulder, and she whipped around, thinking...

Oh, she had to stop this right now. She smiled at the older man. "Yes?"

"Could you clean up our table over here? We had a martini spill."

Amanda had to remember why she was here, and it wasn't to entertain fairy tales that did not come true. "Of course."

One more time, Tori jabbed her. "Give 'em hell, Mrs. Lockhart. I got some drinking to do."

On an exhale that caught in her too-tight throat, Amanda turned from the scene and headed back to her tables. The senior citizens were definitely getting rowdy, and someone had clocked two glasses and spilled gin over the table.

She reached for her rag, but she'd left it at the bar...where Tori now stood. Damn it, she didn't want to go back there. She glanced around again, tapping her pocket and wishing a dishrag would magically appear.

"Here, hon," that same older man said, holding his hand out. "Use this."

She gave him a grateful smile and took the paper towel, opening it to—

See words. Words written on the paper towel. She blinked at them, not able to read anything but seeing dark ink that had bled into the soft paper. A slow, agonizing trickle of awareness tiptoed up her spine, stealing her breath and making her head light.

Using two fingers, she spread the paper.

...do agree to pay...

She dropped the tray on the sand with a thud.

...imaginary girlfriend...

She squeezed her eyes shut. Was this a trick of the fading light? Tori's idea of a joke?

...activities that require the removal of...

"Where did you get this?" she whispered, tearing her gaze from the paper towel to the man next to her.

Silently, he pointed over her shoulder. Very slowly, as if in a dream, she turned around, and there he was. His hands in his pockets, his linen shirt loose in the breeze, his smile as sweet and warm and stunning as the sunset behind him.

For the time it took her heart to stop then speed into overtime, they stared at each other.

Zeke took a few steps closer, his blue eyes intent...and on her. Everything around them fell away, the laughter, the music, the world. When he was right in front of her, he dipped down on one knee, and then she heard the collective gasp from people around them.

What was he doing? "Zeke..." His name came out in a croak.

Looking down, he reached for the tray she'd dropped and lifted it to her. Oh, God, what a fool she was. She'd thought—

And he placed a folded piece of paper on top of it.

Still on one knee, he hoisted the tray higher, the paper on it fluttering in the breeze.

"All this needs is your signature."

The look on Mandy's face was all Zeke needed to be absolutely certain he'd done the right thing.

Not contacting her for a week had been one of the hardest things he'd ever done. But those achy nights—and all the effort to get back here— were worth the pure happiness he could see in her eyes.

She reached for him, closing her fingers around his forearm and tugging him up to her with enough strength in her touch for him to know she wanted him right where he wanted to be...closer.

"Is that what I think it is?" she whispered.

He nodded, keeping his vow not to say a word until her signature was on the divorce decree he'd paid a lot of money to some of the lowest people on Hong Kong's food chain to get signed by her ex. It hadn't been that hard, based on what he was able to find out about Doug Lockhart. Not hard for a man like Zeke, who had connections all over the world.

Information and location and access were all easily bought with a few million dollars.

The job had been expensive, yes. But he'd have paid six times that much if he'd had to. Ten. A hundred. Whatever it took for this moment and Mandy to be his.

As he stood, she held his gaze, a gorgeous glisten in her green eyes, the tears the kind he'd hoped she'd shed.

"How?" she asked.

He angled his head as if to say, *Do you really need to ask?* Next to him, Paul Jameson, one of Zeke's longtime top managers, produced a pen.

"I will witness and notarize the second signature," Paul said.

"The second..." Mandy looked from one to the other, letting out a soft laugh. "You *are* relentless."

Zeke didn't answer, but Paul nodded to the document. "Go ahead, ma'am," Jameson said. "It is one hundred percent official."

Her hands trembled as she opened the paper and then let out an audible sigh as she read the words Zeke had memorized already.

Final decree of dissolution of marriage.

Paul had only included the last page, the important one that required her signature. Right next to Douglas B. Lockhart's. B for bastard.

The bastard who was already in the hands of federal authorities. But not, Zeke had made sure, until he'd signed his divorce decree.

Once again, Mandy looked up at him. "Thank you."

He mouthed one word. "Sign."

Without hesitation, she put the pen to the paper and scribbled her name. Still looking down, she set the pen on the tray and took a slow, deep breath.

"That doesn't make anything legal." Tori muscled her way closer, her face pink with anger and jealousy. "She's still married!"

Taking the signed paper, Zeke turned and shoved the tray into Tori's hands. "Would you mind? And while you're at it..." He sneaked a wink at Mandy before adding, "Get some class, Tori, because you obviously have none."

Her jaw unhinged, but Paul nudged the woman away, so Zeke could return his attention to Mandy, who still looked bewildered...and beautiful. She reached her hands up to his face, putting her warm fingers on his cheeks.

"I can only guess how, but...why?"

She didn't know why? "Because I..." *Love you.* "I want you to be happy." Which were one and the same, weren't they? He would make her happy...forever.

"I am," she admitted. "Happier than you can imagine. I saw the helicopter, and I thought..." She blinked a tear. "I hoped you'd be on it."

"As if I'd be that much of a cliché. I leave the grand gestures to Becker. Paul and I drove in a few minutes ago."

She stifled a half-laugh, half-cry. "I really wanted you to come back to me." Her voice cracked, and that did such stupid things to his heart.

"You doubted that I would?" How could she?

"Of course. I lied to you. I hurt you. You disappeared in the middle of the night."

"I had work to do, Mandy. Work to make it completely right for us to be together." He wrapped his arms around her and pulled her into him to whisper in her ear. "I never considered for one second that I wouldn't come back to you. But I wasn't going to say another word until you were—*are*—a free woman."

"I am free." A soft shudder ran through her. "That's all I've wanted. Not independence, freedom...to love. There's a difference, isn't there?"

"Huge," he agreed, stroking her hair as he held her close. "As long as you love me, you can have all the freedom you want and need."

She inched back, her eyes darkening. He couldn't breathe as he watched emotions play over her face and realization settle on her heart. "I could," she sighed. "I could love you."

"What's this 'could' business?" Without a second's hesitation, he reached down and scooped her into his arms, getting a small shriek of surprise as he cradled her. A crowd had circled them, cheering and clapping.

"Zeke!" she exclaimed, wrapping her arms around his neck. He hoisted her higher and started across the sand. "What are you doing?"

"What I should have done in high school," he said loudly. The crowd parted as he powered through, the sound of her laughter and cries of joy almost drowned out by the cheering and the thump of the chopper blades as they started up. "Watch out, world. Ezekiel the Geekiel got the best girl of all!"

A few familiar faces came into his view, blurred like they were in high school, except for the one that had never been anything but crystal clear. The face of the woman he loved, holding on for her life.

Mandy laughed as he lifted her into the helicopter, and they both turned and waved at the crowd.

"I can't believe you did that!" she said, breathless. "Oh, look!" She lifted her left hand, holding a balled paper towel. "I still have our contract."

He snagged the paper, holding a corner so the document that brought them together fluttered like a dragonfly in the wind. "We don't need any contracts except the one that says forever and ever." He leaned over to kiss her. "And clothing optional."

The paper sailed off over the Gulf of Mexico, floating on their love and laughter.

He yanked the door closed and pulled her into him. "Buckle up for the ride of a lifetime, Mandy Mitchell."

"Is that my name again?"

"Not for long."

Seduction on the Sand

Dedication

Dedicated to Cathy Woodcock Henderson,
a loyal reader, supportive fan, and tireless member of the team!

Chapter One

Elliott Becker climbed out of the helicopter and strode across the beach without bothering to apologize for his dramatic arrival that unexpectedly halted a high school reunion. A lot of faces in the crowd stared back at him, all easy to read. Men narrowed their eyes in distrust because he was wearing a Stetson and arrived by chopper. Women ogled openly because, well, he was wearing a Stetson and arrived by chopper.

He cleared his throat, tipped his hat back, and applauded himself for choosing this reunion to start his search. His goal had nothing to do with Mimosa High, but this was an easy way to reach a lot of island residents at one time. And *easy* was the only way he rolled.

"I'm looking for a man named Frank Cardinale," he announced to the crowd that had gathered when his helicopter had landed on the sand.

From under the rim of his hat, he scanned the crowd, catching a quick movement in the back. Long dark hair fluttered as a woman darted away, moving with just enough purpose that her retreat couldn't have been coincidental.

No one answered his question right away, so he zeroed in on the lady who'd left. With some luck, she'd lead him right to Mr. Cardinale. And if there was one thing Elliott Becker had a ton of, it was luck. And money. And charm. And some damn fine looks. He was about to put all of them to good use.

He followed his instinct and the sway of wavy waist-length hair the color of coffee beans. In a sheer cotton skirt that clung to her hips and danced around her ankles, she made an easy, and lovely, mark.

She power-walked down the beach, away from the resort and the party, heading straight to the frothy white shore where the Gulf of

Mexico swirled in low tide. Just as her bare feet reached the water line, she glanced over her shoulder, too quickly for him to get a look at her face. But he could easily see her narrow shoulders tighten and her long legs pick up speed.

Interesting. Maybe someone didn't *want* him to find the owner of the twenty acres in Barefoot Bay that he and his partners needed to close this deal. The plans to build a small baseball stadium and start a minor-league team on Mimosa Key were supposed to be secret, but he and his partners had already nailed down verbals on three plots in the northeast corner of the island. Word could have gotten out that they wanted that last twenty acres, even though the other landowners had signed nondisclosures. On an island less than ten miles long and three miles wide? Even scads of money didn't buy silence.

He matched her quickened steps. No, she wasn't out for a sunset stroll; she was running. Not literally. Not yet, anyway. But definitely moving away from Elliott for a reason. A reason he had every intention of finding out.

It didn't take more than a few long strides to catch up, but he stayed about a foot behind her.

"I bet you know where I can find Frank Cardinale," he said, keeping his voice low and unthreatening.

She didn't turn, pretending not to hear him.

"Otherwise, why would you take off like a twister in a trailer park?"

That slowed her step. In fact, it stopped her completely. Elliott felt his mouth turn up in a satisfied grin. The Texas drawl always got 'em. Of all the moves his military family had made, he'd lived in the Lone Star State for only a year, but it was enough to pick up a few expressions and work on the twang. And, hell, he looked excellent in a cowboy hat. Now if she'd only turn—

"I live in a trailer." Her words were nearly lost with the splash of a wave at her feet.

Shoot. Way to blow the first impression. "It's just a turn of phrase, ma'am."

"More like an expression of condescension and mockery."

"No, a way to say you're moving too fast, not an insult to your home." He took two more steps, close enough to notice how the late afternoon light made her skin glow and pick up a whiff of something flowery and pretty. "After all, home is where the heart is," he said. Not that he'd know, but he'd certainly heard that enough in his life.

"It's not for sale." She spun around, making her hair swing like a curtain opening to a stage play. "So get back on your fancy helo, cowboy, and leave me alone."

He blinked at her, still not fully processing the demand because, man, oh, man, she was pretty. No, she rounded pretty and slid right into gorgeous, despite the fire in whiskey-gold eyes and the daring set of a delicate jaw.

"What are you staring at?" she demanded. "Are you deaf or just dumb as dirt?"

"Blind. By your beauty."

"Oh, *puh*lease." She looked skyward and sighed. "Spare me the lines."

"That's not a line."

Her eyes turned into golden slits of sheer disbelief.

"Okay, it's a line," he conceded. "But in this case, it's also true."

"Did you hear me? It's not for sale."

Yeah, he'd heard her, and the statement was starting to make sense, considering he'd come to the barrier island for one purpose, and it wasn't to flirt with sexy brunettes on the beach. Not that he'd fight the inevitable, but his goal was to buy land, and these words were not what he wanted to hear, no matter how scrumptious the mouth that spoke them.

"Do you know Frank Cardinale?" he asked.

She crossed her arms, which was patently unfair considering what that did to her cleavage. "I *am* Frank Cardinale."

He snorted softly and didn't fight the need to examine her breasts further. 'Cause, hell, now he had an excuse. "Considering ol' Frank is in his eighties and a man, I'd say you have one hell of a plastic surgeon, Mr. C."

"Miss," she corrected. "Miss Francesca Cardinale." She squeezed her upper arms as if nature and good manners were telling her to reach out and offer a handshake but she had to ignore the order. "Frank was my grandfather. He's dead."

The lady wasn't married, and the landowner was dead. Meaning this little excursion to the remote island would be fast, easy and possibly quite fun. He refused to smile at the thought, but took off his hat with one hand and extended the other. "I'm very sorry for your loss. I'm Elliott Becker."

She didn't take his hand, but met his gaze. "I know why you're here. You're not the first person to come sniffing around the land. Although you're the first to drop down like you owned the place."

"Which I don't." But he intended to.

The thump of helicopter blades pulled his attention. There went Zeke, whisking away the woman he'd recently gone stupid in love over. Zeke had taken the chopper for the day, leaving Elliott with the task of finding Frank—er, *Francesca*—Cardinale to close the land deal.

"But you're not getting my land, Mr. Becker, so you better find another ride out of Barefoot Bay." She gave him a tight smile, which only made him want to see that pretty face lit up with real happiness.

"Maybe you could give me one."

"A ride? Maybe not." She took off, not even bothering to end the conversation.

"I can walk with you, then."

"No."

He fell in step with her anyway. "Can I call you Francesca?"

"Make that a hell no." She refused to look at him.

He kept stride. "So, what's your price?"

That got him a quick look and almost—*almost*—a smile of admiration. Of course. Women loved relentless men. In cowboy hats. With Texas twangs.

"My price is too high for you."

And money. Women *loved* money, and he had even more of that than charm and sex appeal. "Not to be, you know, immodest or anything, but cash really isn't an issue."

She stopped and closed her eyes, so close to a smile he could almost taste it. And, damn, he wanted to. "Good for you, but let me make this clear: I don't want to talk to you, walk with you, or sell you one blade of grass that I own." With that, she powered on, shoulders square, head high, bare feet kicking up little wakes of sand and sea.

Damn, those were pretty feet. Would be even prettier if they weren't moving so fast in the wrong direction.

"Course there is the fact that you don't, uh, actually *own* that land." He cleared his throat. "Unless you really are Frank Cardinale."

Her speed wavered, her shoulders slumped, and she let her head drop in resignation. "What do I have to do to make you go away?"

"Smile."

She slowly turned to him. "Excuse me?"

"Smile for me."

She did, like a kid being forced to say cheese.

"A real smile." He gave her a slow, easy one of his own, lopsided and genuine enough to melt hearts and weaken knees and remove any clothing that needed to go. "Like this."

For a second, he might have had her. He saw the flicker of female response, the ever so slight darkening of her eyes, the thump of a pulse at the base of her throat. "The property is not for sale, and please don't bother taking this conversation one step further because the answer will be an unmistakable, unequivocal, indisputable no."

"A hundred thousand?"

She practically choked. "What part of that didn't you understand?"

"The long, unspellable words might throw me, but I got the 'no' loud and clear." He winked. "A million?"

Very slowly, she shook her head.

Oh, for cryin' out loud, let's get this done. "Five million? Ten? Fifteen? Everyone has a price, Francesca."

Then her face relaxed and her lips curled up and her eyes lit with something that reached right down into his gut and sucker punched him. "Not for a billion. Which I doubt you have."

She started to walk away again, and he lost the fight not to touch her. Reaching out, he closed his hand over her elbow and stopped her, pulling her very gently toward him so he could turn over his trump card, low and sweet and right in her ear.

"I have two billion. And a half, to be precise. I'm willing to part with enough to buy your land, make you a rich woman, and celebrate over dinner together. Do we have a deal?"

A glimmer of amusement lit her eyes, as gold as the sunset behind her now. "Is everything this easy for you?"

He laughed softly, mostly at the truth of that statement. "Just about."

"Was it easy to become a billionaire?"

Disgustingly so. He went for a self-effacing shrug. "Mostly a mix of good timing, dumb luck, and my irresistible boyish charm."

"Really?" One beautifully arched eyebrow lifted toward the sky. "Well, guess what, Elliott Becker?" She cooed his name, already softening. The *B* in billion usually did that when his world-class flirting missed the mark. "Your luck ran out, your timing sucks, and I don't find you charming, boyish, or the least bit irresistible."

Undaunted, he took a step closer and lifted his hand, grazing her chin. "Bet I can change your mind."

"Bet you can't." She pivoted and took off so fast, she kicked a clump of sand on his jeans.

Brushing it, he just grinned. "How much are you willing to bet?" he called out. "I put fifteen million on the table!"

She stuck up her middle finger and kept running.

Sweet.

The only thing Becker liked more than a sexy woman with attitude was a sexy woman with attitude *and* a piece of real estate he wanted. This could be a good time. Maybe not quite as easy as he'd thought, but sometimes *hard* could be fun, too.

Chapter Two

D on't look back. Don't look back. Don't give him the satisfaction.
Of course, Frankie looked. What red-blooded human female wouldn't? And the cowboy was already ambling down the beach in the other direction, as fine from the rear as the front.

Under the cowboy hat, long, dark hair brushed the collar of his T-shirt. Faded jeans rested casually on a stare-worthy ass, drawing every woman's eyes to narrow hips and long, lean thighs that took huge strides as he loped away.

But she was a sucker for shoulders and, son of a bitch, he had those for days. Broad, strong, muscular. Along with a killer smile and bedroom eyes and...a billion freaking dollars. No, no. Two and a half billion freaking dollars.

Hello, deal breaker.

Had he actually said *fifteen million* dollars?

That blew every other offer out of the water, and from by far the best-looking bloodhound to come sniffing after her prime property. But, like the others, he'd soon learn she was serious about not selling. The land belonged in the Cardinale family, and it would stay in the Cardinale family as long as there was blood in her veins and breath in her lungs. No man—not even one who no doubt got whatever he wanted from 99.9 percent of the female population—could ever make her break that promise to her grandfather.

He'd learn soon enough that Frankie was the exception to whatever rules got him through his charmed life.

With a quick glance behind her, she abandoned the event and any chance of playing more verbal volleyball with the cowboy billionaire. She'd been there long enough to introduce herself to the Casa Blanca spa manager and arrange a meeting, which had been her only goal at the reunion.

Happy she'd left her sandals in her truck, she headed home before the sun disappeared in the water. Well, not home. *Kind of* home. Temporary home. Home for the moment, which was supposed to be a week or two and had extended to three months now.

It *felt* like home a lot more than that high-gloss, high-tech high-rise in DC. How had this tropical island stuck in the middle of nowhere become her home? For the second time in her life, too.

Sure, the place was a lush, undiscovered gem glittering in the Gulf of Mexico. A few years ago, the hills and lakes of central Barefoot Bay had been lost among the more desirable real estate along the coasts. But ever since Casa Blanca Resort & Spa had been built along the shore, money had been dripping into this island. Or dropping in by helicopter, she thought with a mirthless smile.

It was like they'd gotten a newsflash when her grandfather had died without a will. Well, too bad, suckers. Florida's probate and intestate laws were crystal clear, as was her extremely sparse family tree. She'd inherited the twenty-some acres of glorious tall pines and gently sloping hills…and all that was on it.

Coming around the last corner, she slowed down to brace for the sight of exactly what that entailed: seven goats, two dogs, a milking shelter, and a less-than-luxurious single-wide that Nonno had rolled onto the land after his house was wiped out by a hurricane a few years ago. Yep, oddly, inexplicably, this wretched little goat farm had become her home.

Not *so* inexplicable, she thought as she rolled up the dirt road. This was the very place where she'd taken refuge thirteen years ago when her world came tumbling down. On those bleak days in the fall of 2001, when the world mourned people they didn't know and she mourned the parents she'd lost, she'd loved the security and simplicity of the goat farm. It was sunny and easy, with sweet goats and precious Nonno to make her forget the ache of being an orphan. She'd loved it then, and she loved it now.

Only now, without Nonno, it was lonely.

As she rounded the last bend, her gaze froze on a black SUV parked in front of the trailer. Holy hell, would these bloodhounds never give up? *It's not for sale, people!*

Sighing, she did a mental count of the days until this could end. Nine.

Nine days until the full ninety-day probate period would be over, and she could officially wave a property title in her name in the faces of these relentless developers. All of them. Even the ones with bedroom eyes and ride-'em-cowboy shoulders. Shoot, was this *him*?

The thought rocked her as she slammed on the brakes next to the SUV. Had Wile E. Coyote somehow *beaten* her here?

She shoved her bare feet into sandals, trying to stomp away the tendril of heat and anticipation. Surely she wasn't going to be *that* girl...the one who went all breathless and giddy at the sight of a sexy rich guy. Not a chance in hell.

She threw open the door to hear Ozzie and Harriet from inside the mobile home, their high-pitched barks welcoming her home. Not the warning snarl of a Rottweiler that she *should* have to keep these idiots away.

Stepping out, she scanned the pen first to be sure all the girls were safe. Four of her goat does were visible, all offering their own distinct bleats to alert her that something was wrong. Still, no one was in sight. Was he around the side in the buck's pen? Maybe Billionaire Becker was stupid enough to let a horny male goat out of his gate? That might actually be amusing.

"Hey, where are you?" she called out.

"Don't take another step."

She froze, inching back at the low voice, searching side to side but unable to see who'd issued the warning. Someone with a serious amount of balls.

"I mean it." A man stepped out of the milking shelter that ran along the back of the pen. A man who was definitely not Elliott Becker.

Not nearly as tall, and wiry thin, the man wore a beige polo shirt and sported thin hair flopped over to cover a bald spot. Before she could get out a word, he held up a phone as if he were taking a picture of her. A wannabe landowner, of course. These nine days could not pass quickly enough.

"What the hell are you doing?" she demanded.

"I'm afraid you can't come any further, ma'am."

"Excuse me?" Was this a joke?

"You're on private property."

"I sure as hell am. *My* private property." She plowed toward the pen, ignoring the happy greetings from her goats. "Who are you and what are you doing on my farm?"

Inside the pen, he approached the gate, reaching it at almost the same time she did. His eyes were pale blue behind wire-rimmed spectacles, giving her no smile as he shot out his hand to deliver a business card.

"I'm Michael Burns, attorney-at-law and the personal representative with full power of attorney on behalf of the owner of this land."

She almost choked, closing one hand over the metal gate, the other automatically taking his card. "I don't have a personal representative."

"You're not the owner."

A little white spark of anger blinded her for a second, stealing her breath with its power. "I am—"

"Not the owner," he interjected, reaching to his back pocket to remove a piece of paper folded in threes, as though it had been in an envelope. "My client, Island Management, LLC, owns this property and has sent me to clear it off so it can be sold. I'm afraid you'll have to take your animals and find another place to squat, ma'am."

There were so many ways to respond to that, she couldn't even grab hold of one because nothing made sense. Island Management? Clear it? "*Squat*?"

"Technically, that's what you're doing." He gave the paper an officious snap to open it. "I have here the Last Will and Testament of Francesco Antonio Cardinale."

She blinked, digging for anything that could be an explanation as she opened the pen gate and stepped inside, her grandfather's voice a soft echo in her head.

I no have a will, piccolina. I came to the world with no birth certificate and go out with no will.

The next breath got stuck in her throat, leaving her speechless. "No, that's not..." *Possible.*

Or was it? All she could do was shake her head and steady her hands as she reached for the paper. Words swam as she tried to make sense of them, a slow pulse pounding in her ears.

"That's his signature, a legal witness, and the seal of the great state of Florida." He pointed to the embossing at the top of the page, but Frankie's gaze stayed riveted on the signature.

Don't need to sign a will, piccolina. What's mine is yours.

And he'd been right...except not if there *was* a will. Was that possible, or was this particular shyster just incredibly creative?

"Who is Island Management, LLC?" she asked, absently closing the gate behind her because Clementine was already pressing her little white nose closer.

"I can't say."

"You can't..." She looked up, those white flashes of fury blinding again as everything suddenly fell into place.

The billionaire cowboy, of course. Forget beating her to the property—he'd beaten her to the punch. Somehow.

Oh, she knew how. Money can buy anything. "Don't tell me. Island Management is owned by an egotistical, smart-ass hotshot in a helicopter named Elliott Becker."

"I'm not at liberty, nor am I required by law, to reveal my client's identity."

Disgust and anger roiled up, matched by the sound of Ozzie's endless bark and Harriet's desperate whines for Frankie to come and greet them. Next to the man, Clementine and Ruffles bleated softly, staring up at him like they were actually following the insane conversation.

Then all those sounds disappeared at the purr of a motor and the crackle of tires spitting dirt in the distance.

Turning, Frankie wasn't even surprised to see a sleek silver sedan worth more than all twenty of the acres she was clinging to barreling onto her land. Coming in to hammer a nail in the coffin, Billionaire Becker? Oh, man, it was going to be fun to take this bastard down a few pegs.

Except, what if Nonno *had* signed a will? No. No, she refused to let herself even entertain that possibility.

"Oh, look, here's your client now." Still holding the paper, she whipped open the gate to go back out to the yard. Then she sucked in a slow, deep breath to be sure she had enough air in her lungs to give him holy hell. A strong hand clamped on her elbow.

"No one sent me," the lawyer said. "Hold it."

She yanked her arm free. "I know what this is about. Good guy, bad guy. You're going to play hardball with some fake"—she flicked at the paper—"piece-of-crap forgery, and he's going to throw insane amounts of money around. But trust me on this, neither one of you will get a thing."

The sedan door opened and, sure enough, Elliott Becker emerged, this time without his stupid ten-gallon hat. Which, God help her, only made him more attractive. He stared at them, his head angled as if he were sizing up the situation. Wondering if she'd caved yet, no doubt.

"It won't work, Becker!" she called.

Behind her, the other man grabbed her again. "Who is that?" he demanded.

He didn't know? She threw him a surprised look and attempted to wrench her arm out of his grasp, but he held tight. "Let me go, asshole!"

"Hey!" Elliott's voice boomed across the farm as he strode forward. "Let her go."

Oh, yeah, good cop, bad cop. She wasn't falling for it.

"You're trespassing," the man behind her barked.

True enough, but...they really didn't know each other? Frankie looked from one to the other, then tried again to free her arm. "Let go of me!"

When he didn't, Elliott charged closer, hoisting himself over the fence in one smooth move. "Get the hell off her," he ordered through gritted teeth.

Clementine snorted while Agnes and Lucretia, the wee pygmy goats, trotted closer like kids on a playground attracted to a fight.

"You know this guy?" Elliott asked without looking at her.

"Don't you?"

He threw her an incredulous look. "I landed on this rock less than an hour ago. Is he hurting you?"

The anger and protectiveness in his voice touched her, but she squelched the female reaction. "He just showed up here with"—*phony papers and lies*—"threats."

Elliott's eyes tapered even more as he practically breathed fire at the smaller man. "Get out of here."

"I have business with Miss Cardinale."

"Business to maul her?" he fired back, looming over the man. "Do you want him to leave?"

"Yes." She wanted them *both* to leave.

"Get out." He got his chest—a big, mighty, impressive as hell chest—right in the smaller man's face.

"I have a legal docu—"

Elliott reached out and closed a sizable fist over the guy's collar, jerking him toward the gate. "Get the hell out."

The other man's eyes widened as he fought to keep his composure. "Fine. Let me go."

Elliott didn't move, his nostrils flaring.

"Let me go," the lawyer said again. "And I'll leave."

Very slowly, Elliott opened his fingers, and the lawyer tried to shake off the contact, brushing his polo shirt.

Elliott leaned in to make his point. "If you ever lay a hand on this woman again, you will regret it for the rest of your life."

The threat hung in the air, until Arlene let out a long nay and nuzzled her flat nose into Elliott's thigh. She might as well have sighed, "My hero!"

"You can keep that paper, miss," the lawyer said as he opened the gate to leave the way normal men did. "The old man signed two copies, and I have the other one. You have exactly nine days to get yourself and your stinky animals off my client's land."

He walked away before she could react, but Elliott whipped around and looked at her. "What did he say?"

"You really don't know him? You really didn't send him?"

He gave her a shake of his head.

She stuffed the business card into the twisted wire of the gate like a little white flag of surrender. "Then you just became the lesser of two evils."

Chapter Three

When the SUV disappeared around the bend, Elliott finally took a moment to drink in exactly where he was. In a cage full of strange-looking animals. Two no bigger than a medium-sized dog, and the bright orange one stuck its nose in his belly and started to bleat like a...

"Are these...nanny goats?"

"These are does," she replied. "The buck is in another pen around there."

"And that's, like, a billy goat?"

"Only if you are a graceless clod. No one with any real class would call them nannies or billies unless you are referring to meat goats. Mine make milk and soap." She closed her eyes as if an adrenaline dump hit her system. "I guess I should say thank you for getting rid of him. He was peskier than most."

She raised goats? And scoffed at a legit offer of a million? More? He inched back, taking another look at her frilly skirt and sandals, the wild-from-the-wind long hair, and the natural cream of her skin, sizing her up in a second.

A hippie chick earth mother who might be hot as Hades but surely could be bought. Maybe a million didn't make her go all gooey and send her on a beeline for the mall like most women, but a sweet little donation to her cause *du jour* and enough cash to take her critters to another farm? Easy peasy.

All righty then. Game on, goat girl.

He slipped his hands into the pockets of his jeans and tipped his head to look a little modest and respectful. "So, what was that all about, if you don't mind me asking, ma'am?" He held out his hand in a quick correction. "Not that you look like a *ma'am*. Can I use your first name? Francesca?"

"Frankie," she corrected absently, focused on the paper she held. "This can't be real."

"May I?" He reached for the document, their fingers brushing in the exchange, allowing him to feel the tension in her knuckles. "Relax," he said softly. "He's gone."

"For now."

"I won't let him hurt you."

"I hate to break it to you, big guy, but I probably could have handled one wormy lawyer with a bad comb-over. But that paper?" She curled her lip at the document. "That's a little scary, because my grandfather didn't have a will."

"This would say differently." He scanned the words, simple enough to follow: Frank Cardinale had left his property and everything on it to Island Management, LLC. "Do you know what that company is?"

"Don't have a clue. Do you?" There was enough accusation in her voice that he knew she suspected he did.

He shook his head, rereading the document. If this was real—and it sure looked legit—the person he should be negotiating with was that lawyer he'd just tried to punch, not the lady and her Billy Goats Gruff. "Didn't you say you had other interest and offers on the land?"

"Plenty of interest, and I just ignore the offers. I have no plans to sell." Next to her, a brown and white goat with massive ears nuzzled into her waist, and she stroked its head, the only noise the incessant barking of dogs inside.

He gestured toward the trailer. "You want to get them?"

"They'll settle down," she said. The goat next to her nayed again, pushing Frankie harder while another—a miniature with a twin—did the same on her other side.

"I know, I know, ladies," she cooed, rubbing their bodies. "I'll take care of you in a minute."

Elliott handed back the paper. "What are you going to do about this?"

"I don't know." She crouched down, face-to-face with the orange goat, reaching under its belly before looking up at him with a disarmingly pretty smile. "But first I'm going to milk my goats. You can leave anytime or...watch."

Holy hell, that sounded...unappealing. "By all means, milk."

She stood and nudged the animal toward the back of the pen, to a long, enclosed wooden structure with no doors and square holes for windows and a corrugated tin roof. "I have to do this every twelve hours whether I want to or not. That's my life now." A mix of irony and humor tinged her voice, piquing his interest.

He followed her, another goat at his side and two more behind her, fuzzy, noisy, curious little things that had no sense of personal space.

"So you're, like, a goatherder?" he asked.

As she stepped into the building, he heard her laugh softly. "Just like one."

He followed her in, his eyes adjusting to the dim light, his nose swamped with the musty, earthy smell of hay. Bales of the stuff were piled to the rafters of the wooden structure, filling up half of it. The other half was much cleaner, with a tile floor and a small kitchen-like area with a sink, cabinets, and an industrial-size fridge.

"You can sit by the milking station." She indicated a bench under a window that let in the last of the fading light and some fresh air. The bench faced a contraption that looked like a long wooden chair with a hole in the seat. One of the goats walked up to it, then turned to stare down Elliott.

"Hi." Elliott bent over and looked into two massive brown eyes and big teeth bared in a… "Is he smiling at me?"

She let out a sharp laugh as she wove her fingers into her hair and started sliding one strand over the other. "*He*? I'm about to milk *her*."

"Oh, yeah." Elliott settled on the bench not far from the goat, much more interested in the other female in the place. She faced him, her hands still busy with her hair—braiding it, he realized—with deft, swift hands. The position showcased a narrow waist and nicely round breasts that he had to force himself not to examine too obviously. "I don't know much about goats," he admitted.

"You don't say." She turned to the sink to wash her hands, and then opened a drawer, pulling out a box of latex gloves and an array of stainless steel equipment that she placed on a tray with easy grace.

With her back to him, he was free to take in every curve of her feminine form. The long braid settled down the middle of her back, pointing to a sweetly shaped backside. She tied an apron around her waist and turned, catching him staring at her.

"You don't look like a goatherder," he observed.

As she carried the tray to the contraption where the goat waited patiently, she fought a smile. "Just goatherd. You don't say shepherd-er, do you?"

He didn't say either one very often. "I didn't even know people still owned goats. I thought they were at petting zoos and in kids' books."

She laughed again, a sweet, musical sound that made him only want to hear more, as she got her pretty face close to the flat-nosed, floppy-eared goat. "You are so misunderstood, aren't you, Ruffles?"

Straddling a small bench so her skirt fell to either side, she placed a bucket and patted the platform next to her. "C'mere, girl, and let's do this."

The goat let out a long staccato nay and then ambled into place, jumping up a foot or so to get her hind legs over the hole where the bucket was.

"I'm going to guess you've never seen anyone milk a goat before," Frankie said as she snapped on a pair of gloves.

"Or a cow."

She looked up, surprise in her eyes. "With that hat and accent? I figured you just walked off the range."

Busted. "City Texan," he admitted. "Big difference." The year they'd lived in San Antonio hardly qualified him as a real Lone Star Stater, but he'd gotten his use out of it.

The goat bayed again as Frankie's hands started to squeeze and stroke, followed by the sound of liquid splashing into the stainless steel bucket.

"There we go," she whispered into the goat's ear, adding a soft kiss. "That's the dirty part, Ruffles."

She pushed back and dragged the bucket out of the way, then replaced it with a fresh one. Her feet hooked under the bench as she leaned forward, serious now, the muscles of her legs visible through the thin skirt. With spare, confident movements, she stroked the goat's...udders? Teats? He had no idea what a goat rack was called and wasn't about to amuse her any further by asking.

"Nonno was a little confused before he died."

The statement threw him, coming from nowhere and yanking him back to the real business at hand—who really owned the land he wanted.

"Your grandfather?" he guessed.

She nodded.

"Confused enough to sign a will you didn't know about?"

She sighed, her fingers squeezing and moving like a well-practiced professional. He sat stone still and watched the choreography, mesmerized and suddenly, surprisingly uncomfortable. Damn, who would have thought a woman milking a goat would be sexy?

"Do you think the will might be legitimate?" he asked.

She didn't answer for a long time, concentrating on her goat. "I guess anything is possible, but unlikely." She looked up, a single strand of dark hair that had escaped her braid slipping over one eye. "For example, you showing up at exactly the same time as this lawyer with a fake will. Why did that happen in the same hour if you aren't teaming up on me?"

"We're not," he said honestly.

"Then that's one hell of a weird coincidence. Which, by the way, I don't believe in."

"I do."

She snorted softly. "Well, I don't."

"Coincidence, karma, good fortune or lady luck, whatever you call it, I happen to be a living, breathing believer in it all," he said, leaning back and crossing his legs. "And my guess is the universe is trying to tell you it's time to sell this land. To me."

The fire in her eyes damn near fried him. "The universe is not telling me a damn thing except to stay away from smarm-fests like that lawyer and…and…"

He grinned. "I can't wait to hear how you describe me."

A slow, deep blush gave away how right he was. "How do you know what I'm going to say?"

"Your eyes. They're eating me up trying to come up with something insulting, which, of course, you can't."

She choked a hearty laugh. "And egotistical, arrogant, entitled billionaires. How's that?"

He answered with a shrug. "I've heard worse. On the beach an hour ago, as a matter of fact. From you."

"What you didn't hear, obviously, is this: My property isn't for sale."

"It might not even be yours."

Her hands froze, and tension tightened her shoulders. "It's mine."

But was it? "Are you sure your grandfather didn't make some kind of backdoor deal you didn't know about? I have to admit, it wasn't easy to find any record of him alive or dead when we were tracking this property."

She made a face but didn't reply, her hands moving a little faster to wring milk out of poor Ruffles. After a few minutes, she backed off, and he could have sworn the goat sighed with relief.

"All done, Ruff." She swatted the goat's backside and scooted her off the platform, twisting to pick up the bucket and carry it to another tray. "Clem, you're up!" she called, and another one, a little smaller and almost all brown but for a spot on her forehead, ambled over for her turn at the station.

"How long have you been doing this?" he asked.

"Eighty-one days."

Eighty-one days, twice a day, with half a dozen goats? "No wonder you're such a natural."

She worked on the next goat in line, repeating the same series of actions she had with the first animal.

"It's not that difficult." She swiped that stray hair with the back of her gloved hand and then blew out a long, slow breath. "And as far as my grandfather, he was never big on paperwork. He used to say he was born without formalities and he'd die without them, too."

"No one is born without some sort of paperwork," he said.

"Nonno was. He was born in a farmhouse in Italy, and they didn't bother with a birth certificate."

"Not a town record?"

"He did have a baptism, and that was logged in a local church, but they weren't sure how old he was then. Best we can tell, he was eighty-eight, maybe eighty-nine when he died."

"How long ago did he die?" he asked.

She stopped milking for a moment, closing her eyes. "Eighty-one days." The pain in her voice was undeniable.

"Oh, wow. Really sorry." And this time, he meant it. But he couldn't help assessing the situation with this new information. She'd been here only since he'd died, which could mean she had no idea if that will was real or not. "Were you close to him?"

"Not close enough," she murmured, inching closer to her goat.

"But you are his next of kin? Or would that be one of your parents?"

"My parents are both dead," she said quietly. "And I was Nonno's only relative, so the land belongs to me." She finished this goat and turned to Elliott. "It's a very clear-cut law in Florida when a person doesn't leave a will. I've already looked into it and talked to the County Clerk when I moved back here. That guy, that lawyer? He's a fraud."

But if Island Management really *did* own this piece of property, that's who Elliott needed to be doing business with, not the gorgeous goat girl. Sad, but true.

"You know," he said softly, trying to lessen the blow of the truth. "Your, uh, Nonno wouldn't be the first elderly citizen to get scammed when they were sick, dying, and had no will."

She closed her eyes with just enough misery for him to know he'd hit the mark. "That lawyer's just more imaginative than the other people who want this land. My property is desirable, as you obviously know." She stripped the gloves off slowly. "What are your plans for it? Hotel? Condos? Planned retirement community?"

Worse. He knew without a shadow of a doubt that she'd hate what he and his partners were planning. A minor-league baseball complex? No, that would never fly. And if the lawyer was a fraud, Elliott would still have to buy the property from this lady who would no doubt recoil when she found out her little goat farm would be turned into an access road and parking lot.

"Don't tell me," she said with a laugh when he didn't reply. "You're an eccentric, unhappy, lost, and lonely billionaire who has decided to reconnect with Mother Earth and wants to live on a working farm."

Bingo. Answer supplied. "How'd you know?" He managed to keep all humor out of his voice, earning a surprised look from her.

"Seriously?"

"Well, all except for the lonely part. I can usually scare up a date."

She rolled her eyes. "I bet you get plenty lucky."

"I told you, I am—"

"Lucky, yeah, I got that a few times. But I'm not—"

"Selling, yeah, I got that a few times, too." He pushed off the bench, impatience growing. Maybe she was just hardballing for the best offer. It's what he'd do. "I want the place," he said, leaving no room for argument. "I'll double your best offer."

"No, thank you." She stood, shoulders square, eyes narrowed, feet apart. Damn, she looked good mad. "I am not interested in money."

"Then how about I put that entire amount, and another few million, into..." What would be her soft spot? Something with animals. "Your favorite...goat charity."

"A *goat* charity?"

"Don't tell me, that's the wrong word. Shoot, I'm trying to make this painless for you, Frankie."

"Painless? *Painless?*" She took a step forward, as if she were about to induce some pain of her own. "You don't know what you're talking

140

about, cowboy. The pain happened when the only family I had left died in my arms. You're just an...an..." She swatted the air like a fly had buzzed her. "An annoyance."

"I'm sorry about your grandfather, Frankie."

She glared at him. "Here's what you should be sorry about, Becker. I made my grandfather a promise. This land, these twenty measly acres of scrub and swamp, is going to stay in this family no matter what. And I will raise goats and make milk and soap and cheese for as long as I'm capable of it because that's what he wanted. Do you know what a deathbed promise is?"

One based entirely on emotion, which was just stupid when it came to land. "One you won't break."

"Finally, something you know." She blew out a breath like she'd been holding it for ten minutes, ignoring the next two goats bleating for their turn on the table. "Trust me when I say that no amount of money is going to take this land out of the family. No amount. So do us both a favor and leave." She pointed to the door and held the position for a good fifteen seconds.

He could change her mind. With sweet talk and a few promises of his own. He knew his power with women. But why bother? If the lawyer had a will, then, in nine days, the lawyer would have a deed. Becker's business wasn't with this woman, no matter how attractive she was. They needed her land to build *his* dreams.

"I'll show myself out," he said, stepping away and to the door.

Outside, the late daylight had faded, and twilight had descended over the goat pen. He kept an eye on the grass and dirt in case he might step in literal shit instead of the stuff he'd just walked away from.

He stole a look over his shoulder, a little disgusted at just how much he wanted her to be standing in the doorway, calling him back, asking for help. Which was moronic. She couldn't have made her aversion to him any clearer.

He reached for the gate latch, his gaze landing on something white wedged into the wire. *Michael S. Burns, Attorney at Law.*

Of course the business card would be there for the taking, because Becker's luck made his life easy. He snapped it up, climbed into his rented Audi, and had the guy on the phone before he'd reached the end of her dirt road.

Chapter Four

Sunday afternoons were usually Frankie's favorite time of the week on the farm. Instead of the impending press of Sundaynightis that used to plague her up in DC, she relished the end of the week because she didn't dread the beginning of it.

No paperwork, bureaucracy, rules and regs, or unbearable office politics loomed the next day at a desk job she'd once thought could make her happy. In the three months since she'd slipped into this unexpectedly blissful existence, she'd come to think of Sundays as a gift.

She groomed the goats most Sundays, spending the day cleaning and trimming hooves or brushing their fur. And she talked to them because, hell, there was no one else around.

But today, Frankie was restlessly moving about the farm, starting chores but not finishing, picking up the hoof clippers, then getting distracted by the oils she used for soaps, not accomplishing anything but watching the dirt road and listening for cars.

It was if she *wanted* Elliott Becker to come back, which was just so lame it hurt.

"Crazy," she whispered, snapping her fingers to get Ozzie and Harriet into the goat shed with her. The dogs trotted inside, more at home on this farm than they'd ever been pent up in that downtown apartment. Just like her.

Inside, the dogs sniffed and wagged and looked up at her with curiosity, as if they still wanted to know who'd invaded their home with a brand new smell the day before.

"A bad man," she told Ozzie, his big brown eyes staring up at her like he followed every word. Australian terriers might be a little stumpy and slow, but they had brains. At least Ozzie did. The little short-haired wiener named Harriet didn't have the smarts, but she was sleek and sweet and pretty as a picture. All beauty and no brains. Kind of like Cowboy Becker, who wasn't even a cowboy at all.

"A fake man," she muttered as she finished cleaning out the last stall. "A pretend cowboy who's probably not even a billionaire and no doubt is lying about...everything."

Ozzie barked his response.

"And dumb as a box of rocks!" she added, swiping her hands on her jeans. "A *goatherder*. What kind of big, dense, lug nut even says something like that?" He was big, all right, and gorgeous.

She shook her head, closing her eyes, more than a little disgusted with herself for being swayed by his good looks. Frankie had never been that kind of female. Swooning over his heroics with the lawyer, flirting with him while she milked the goats, sneaking peeks at his pecs? What was wrong with her?

She guided the last of the does out to the pen, except for Isabella. About six weeks ago, Frankie had realized the doe wasn't just fat—she was pregnant, though Nonno had left no record of how far along she was. Frankie guessed by feel that she was nearing her term, so she let Isabella sleep in her hay, no doubt dreaming of the love of her life.

"Let's go feed him now." Both dogs trotted after Frankie to take the walk to Dominic's private quarters, far from the girls in case someone who wasn't ready to breed went into heat. Being the Italian stud he was, Dominic would have fought his way over to the pen for some good times with the does. She'd seen his temper a few times, and without a doe in heat, he was getting downright nasty lately.

As they passed the back side of the trailer, Ozzie stopped, and both his little stick-up ears turned, like radar dishes seeking a signal. A fine chill waltzed up Frankie's spine as she stood still, listening for whatever had attracted Ozzie's attention. A squirrel? A rabbit? A...*man*?

Maybe not Becker. Maybe that lawyer?

That's why she was restless, she thought. Tomorrow she had to go to the County Clerk's office—oh, that would be a fun five hours in a place not unlike her old office—and figure out if a legitimate will had ever been filed. They'd never even checked for that when she was last there because Nonno had told her...

She swallowed hard. Had he *really* told her? Or was she fooling herself? Because she knew damn well a will *could* have been filed. It *could* be legit. She hadn't been with him for two years, both of them too stubborn to say they were sorry. And during those two years…

A slow, sickening heat turned in her belly as she watched Ozzie listen even more intently while Harriet rolled around on something delicious-smelling, her little paws in the air, her white teeth showing in a dog smile.

Ozzie finally gave up the audio hunt and continued to trot to Dominic's shed. The old buck bellowed as soon as they reached his long, narrow pen, this one surrounded by much sturdier fencing than what the girls had. His shed was much smaller, too, more for shade than anything else. Dom needed far less attention than the female goats. All he required was food, water, and regular sex, which basically made him like every man on earth.

"Hey, big guy." She reached over the thick railing to give Dom's dark head a pat and stroke his horns. His golden eyes settled on her with no small amount of longing. Longing that, if not satisfied, could turn to downright fury.

"Gotta wait awhile for Agnes to be ready, okay? A week or two, best I can guess." Of course, Nonno had left no records of any of the goats' cycles or births. It was like he'd lost all interest after the hurricane, after Frankie had moved to DC.

She swallowed guilt and refocused on Dominic, who blinked once, his pink gums sliding into what she'd swear was a smile. She tunneled her fingers into his wiry fur and scratched, thinking of how happy Nonno had been when he had Dominic shipped over from Italy. When his plans for "La Dolce Vita" were in full swing, before they'd had their fight, before she'd been a complete and total idiot who needed to "find herself."

She scooped up grain and feed, poured fresh water in the trough, and fluffed his hay. Finished, she whistled for the dogs and trudged across the field, eyeing the tiny one-bedroom trailer through the eyes of the cowboy who'd been here yesterday.

Why couldn't she stop thinking about him? Okay, it had been awhile since she'd had anything that resembled a date. In fact, let's be honest, the ladies in her pen got more action than she did and they had to share the same guy.

That was no excuse for her obsessing about him and wondering what he'd thought of the humble place where she currently lived. Without knowing why the trailer was there, he probably thought Nonno was dirt-poor and she was "trailer trash" who'd swoon over a multimillion-dollar offer for her land.

Man, he couldn't be further off base. He so completely didn't know what he was dealing with. He was—

Sitting on the first step of the trailer.

Ozzie exploded in an outburst of sharp, loud, frantic barks, launching toward the stranger.

"Whoa." Elliott didn't even stand, reaching out a hand, which Ozzie immediately sniffed. Harriet scampered around, trying to get a piece, so he reached his other hand to her, getting a total tongue bath for his trouble.

"Hey, pooches." He looked up and grinned, like his sneaky, unexpected arrival was completely normal and welcome. "And goatherd. Not goat*herder*."

Nothing was normal and welcome—especially the way her knees weakened and the rest of her tensed up at the sight of him. Well, of course, she was shocked. That had to be why her body went into this state. Nothing else.

"You scared the crap out of me."

"You're vulnerable out here." He tipped his cowboy hat back so she could see his eyes glint with humor and then travel up and down her body with open male appreciation. "Not really safe for a woman as beautiful as you."

"You going to play that card now, Becker?"

He took off the hat and set it next to him on the step, but Harriet launched onto it like the brim was dusted with bacon bits. "Which card?"

"Vulnerable? Beautiful? Heroic? Who knows with you?"

With an almost imperceptible flinch, he leaned forward to give Ozzie even more love, his fingers seeming to know exactly how to calm the high-energy dog.

"Of course, you have your vicious guard dogs to protect you." Ozzie was practically rolled on his back now, with Becker's big hand tunneling the dog's fur for a rare and prized belly rub. Ozzie was toast, his tongue already hanging out, his stub of a tail vibrating with joy. Harriet jumped off the step with the hat locked between her teeth as she trotted around the end of the trailer.

"You may never see that hat again," she warned.

He shrugged. "I've got plenty."

"What are you doing here?" she demanded, fighting the urge to press a palm to her pounding heart, but not willing to let him know he had any effect on her at all.

"What can I say? I'm drawn to"—one more sweep with his eyes and, damn it, she felt heat rise—"this place."

"I didn't even hear you drive up."

"My point exactly." He finally gave up on Ozzie and leaned back on locked arms, a move that made his biceps...huge. Ozzie threw both front paws on Elliott's lap, letting out a demanding bark for more attention. Which he got from those incredibly large and surprisingly tender hands.

Oh, Frankie, come on! They're just hands.

"I have an offer for you," he said, squinting up at her with an irrepressible grin.

She puffed out a breath, dropping her head back to let out a grunt of sheer exasperation. How could she make him believe she didn't want the money?

"One week." He stood slowly, taking a step closer. "Let me stay for one full week."

Her eyes widened, because she certainly couldn't have heard that right. "Excuse me?"

"I need to know if this is what I really want and need in my life."

"And you want to, what, try out the farm life to see if it's for you?"

"Exactly." His lips curled up, revealing stunning, perfect, white teeth and a hint of dimples hidden in the whisker scruff that was probably created using a special Hollywood clipper to get that perfect two-day-old-beard look.

"Nothing about you is real, is it?"

He recoiled a little at the question. "What makes you say that?"

"You really are a fake."

She had him; she could tell he didn't know how to answer that.

"You'll just be whoever you need to be to get a job done, am I right?"

"Um, I'm a little more complicated than that."

She lifted her shoulders. "I think you're simple. In every imaginable way." She started to walk past him, but he sidestepped and blocked her.

"Come on, Frankie. I really want to know more about this...goat life. I've been reading all about goats, all night. They're really quite a huge business and fantastic pets. I've been thinking about"—his gaze moved to the pen—"Ruffles. And..." He lifted his hand as if he were going to touch her, then dropped it, catching himself. "You."

Don't do it, hormones. Don't listen. Don't react. Don't go surging into high gear.

"Don't shake your head," he said. "You know the attraction is there."

"You're attracted to Ruffles?"

He laughed. "You can't deny it."

No, she couldn't. "All the more reason for you not to be here for a week." As if she actually needed a reason. But the idea...oh, Lord. Why did the idea appeal to her? Was she *that* lonely out here?

Yes.

"I won't bother you, Frankie, I swear."

"Too late for that."

"And I won't sleep...near you."

"Have you seen my lavish accommodations?" She gestured toward the trailer. "One bedroom and a lumpy sofa in the living room."

Undaunted, he looked around. "I'll sleep in the barn."

"It's not a..." She closed her eyes, hating the thoughts that played at the corners of her mind.

"You wouldn't have to be alone when creepy lawyers and other people who want this place come circling like vultures." His enthusiasm was infectious, she had to give him that.

And he was dead-on about the vultures. He'd surely get rid of them.

"And you wouldn't be lonely."

"I'm not..." She swallowed the lie. "I have plenty of company with seven goats and two dogs."

"And a lot to do. I'd be happy to help."

She had to laugh. "Why do I think goat's milk soap-making is not your forte?"

"Is that what you do here?"

"This week, I will be."

"I can help you make soap. I know a lot about soap. I use soap every day."

She didn't know whether to laugh, cry, or beg for mercy. What had she done to deserve this?

"You can't handle a farm, Becker. It takes...experience."

"Says the woman who's been here for eighty-one days."

"Eighty-two, and I lived here when I was a kid."

"You're still not safe out here alone, and you know it."

"Please." She waved him off, along with the sense that he was right. "I have a .22 rifle, and I am not afraid to use it."

He snorted. "That'll get the evil squirrels, Annie Oakley."

"It could stop someone."

"Didn't stop me."

Damn it, he was right about that. "Well, something has to." She managed to get by him, powering straight for the trailer door. She pulled it open, aware he'd followed.

"And you don't even lock your door," he chastised.

On the top step, she whipped around, a little taller than he was now. She used the advantage to glare down her nose. "I will from now on. Goodbye, Becker."

Ozzie barked, loud and sharp, making his displeasure at the word *goodbye* clear.

"She doesn't want me to leave."

"Yes, *he* does."

He exhaled and shook his head. "Clearly, I need lessons on farm management and…and animal husbandry."

"Science," she corrected. "It's known as animal science, and I have a degree in it."

"Which will make you an excellent teacher."

Ozzie kicked it up to a deafening yelp, no doubt loving this idea.

"Oh!" She blew out pure exasperation, at him, at Ozzie's relentless barking, at the situation. "Come on in," she said, holding the door open.

"Nice work, partner." He scooped up the little terrier and followed Frankie in so fast, she could feel the warmth of him at her back.

"It's an invitation to come in, not sleep here."

She closed her eyes and turned one way and then the other, the tiny trailer closing in. Or maybe that was him, six feet of unstoppable testosterone and determination who'd just filled it. She moved a few steps into the tiny kitchen, flipping on the faucet to quench an inexplicably dry throat.

"So what's your real game, Becker?" she asked as she reached for a glass. "You think you can distract me or change my mind somehow? You make a bet with someone that you could spend a week with me and get my land?" She turned and caught him looking at the dog in his arms, wide-eyed like they shared a secret.

Like she'd just hit the nail on the proverbial head. "Did you?" she demanded.

"No." He stroked Ozzie, shifting his attention from the dog to her. "I really am intrigued by...this. And you. And I think you shouldn't be alone until you...you figure out what you're going to do with this place."

She frowned at him. "I've got it all figured out. And no other buyer figures into it."

He nodded, still stroking Ozzie. She refused to look at his hands. Hands that could...oh, boy. She took a deep drink of water.

While she drank, he dipped his head closer and closer, like he was going to...put Ozzie on the floor. Her heart almost stopped. Oh, brother. He moved one inch and she'd thought he was going to kiss her.

Instead, he reached over her head for his own glass. "Why, thank you for offering, I'd love a glass of water."

She tried to duck away to let him get it, which was damn near impossible because he was so big and filled her kitchen with all his body and...hands.

Enough with the hands, Frankie!

"I still don't completely buy this you-want-to-live-on-a-farm business," she said.

"I don't either," he admitted. "That's why I'd like to try it."

"They have dude ranches for that kind of thing."

He filled his water glass, smiling.

"What?" she asked, seeing the smirk.

"You're not a dude, that's all."

"Oh, God." She leaned against the counter, half-laughing, half-sighing. "You really think you can flirt me out of my land? That you can woo me with cute jokes and a drop-dead smile and a sudden interest in goats?"

He turned. "Drop-dead? I like that."

"Then why don't you?"

He just laughed and looked down at Ozzie. "She totally likes me, don't you think?"

The little traitor barked twice and wagged his tail.

"He speaks English," she said.

"Obviously." Elliott crouched down. "Talk some sense into your mom, will ya, bud?"

He barked twice again.

"What's that mean?" Elliott asked.

"Go away."

He laughed again, an easy, playful, masculine laugh that sounded…good. There'd been no laughing in this little trailer for three months. No flirtatious banter, no combustible chemistry, no sexy side glances, no…man. No laughter, no music, no connection, no…romance.

And yet she'd thought she was content here. Nearly content, anyway. Almost content. Wasn't she?

He put the glass to his lips, giving her only his profile. He drained the whole glass, his Adam's apple bobbling, like he'd walked miles through the desert. Well, he had trudged up here from far enough away that she'd never heard the car.

As much as she wanted to, she couldn't take her eyes off him. Good God, the man was a specimen and a half of perfection. And protection. A thick bicep with the shadow of a vein running through, strong forearms dusted with dark hair. Then she was back to his hand, curled around the glass, all tanned, long, powerful.

But she didn't really know anything about him at all.

From behind the glass, she saw him smile.

"What?"

"You have a camera?" he asked, lowering the glass. "'Cause it would be easier to take a picture, Francesca."

She felt a warm rush to her cheeks at the use of her full name. And being caught staring. "You're standing in front of me gulping like a hog." She forced herself to turn, leaning on the sink and looking away. "How'd you get so"—*built*—"rich?"

He chuckled as if he knew exactly what her real thought had been. "Told you already. Dumb luck."

She gave a scoffing grunt, pushing off the sink to go back into the living room. He followed, with Ozzie practically crawling up his jeans, of course. "Not buying it. Nobody's that lucky."

"I am." He sat in Nonno's old recliner, the first man—the first human—to sit there in three months. Pushing back, he popped the footrest with a loud snap. "Haven't been in one of these for a long time."

"No La-Z-Boys in the mansion?"

He grinned, getting comfortable and, of course, making room for Ozzie on his lap. "I might have to change that."

Didn't deny he owned a mansion, she noticed.

"Anyway, to answer your question, I bought a very valuable piece of property." He crossed his feet and looked at her from under thick lashes. "I paid forty-six thousand dollars for about six acres of land in western Massachusetts."

"And selling that made you rich?"

"Nope. I never sold the land and never will."

She eyed him, curious, watching his smile grow and his dark eyes dance.

"But the first time I put a shovel in the ground, I hit some stone. Beautiful gold stone."

She gasped. "You struck gold in Massachusetts?"

"Close enough. Goshen stone. Rare and desirable, and the amount I had on my land—land that I bought as a favor to my cousin who really needed to sell, I might add—netted over two billion dollars."

"Wow." It was the best she could do because, wow. That *was* lucky.

"I know," he agreed. "So I might be arrogant about a lot of things, but not my money-making skills. I literally fell into wealth, so it doesn't really change who I am, just how I live. And, yes, I gave my cousin a cut."

He searched her face, probably looking for the usual drool women have to wipe when they learn his net worth. A flicker of discomfort registered on his expression when she imagined what he saw instead. "I mean, I live well," he said slowly. "I have a—"

"Yacht."

His eyebrows lifted. "Sure, I have a pleasure boat."

"And a private jet."

"It makes travel easier."

"Multiple expensive homes."

He lifted one shoulder. "I like to stay in my own place if I can."

"Butlers and staff and, of course, some ridiculous collection like art or horses or..."

"Rare cars," he supplied. "I'm not going to apologize for how I live. I told you I was in the right place at the right time."

But, still, she knew all she had to know about him. He worshipped at the money altar, and she despised people like that. She learned at a tender age that when you put money in front of everyone else, the ultimate price is too high. Her parents paid that price, and it still hurt her to think about it. You can't love people and money at the same time or with the same intensity. One wins out, everytime.

"Look." She took a steadying breath. "I really appreciate your concern for my safety and your interest in goats and whatever else you're going to dream up to persuade me to give you access to...me. But I don't think this is going to work out."

He didn't move, except for his infernal petting of her dog. "It's the money, isn't it?" he finally asked.

She scowled at the question, not believing she was quite that transparent.

"You have issues with money," he explained.

Well, yes, she *was* that transparent. "Who doesn't?"

"Most women—"

"Hey, newsflash, Becker." She snapped her fingers three times. "I am *not* most women."

Charcoal-black eyes raked her, from face to body and back up again, just as smoky and sexy as a man could look. "I noticed."

Damn it, she hated the heat that generated. Two words. One look. And a couple of billion dollars. "I don't believe money buys you happiness."

"So says everyone who doesn't have it."

She managed not to scoff at that. "Money buys nothing but misery. Trust me, I know firsthand. *Misery.*" If her parents hadn't been chasing the almighty dollar...they'd still be here.

He finally smiled. "This is good, Frankie. Really good."

"What is?"

"This arrangement." He gestured to her and then to him, as though they had actually made an *arrangement.* "You can teach me about goats and farms and animal science, and I can teach you that you are completely wrong about people who have money."

Could he? Maybe someone needed to do that, otherwise, she was never going to fully heal from the pain of losing the two people she'd loved and needed so desperately. Without giving herself a chance to think deeper than that, she nodded.

"Okay, then." She put her hands on her thighs and pushed up.

"Can I stay?"

Ozzie let out four furious barks, as though he could answer for her.

"I have six sets of very dirty hooves waiting to be cleaned and trimmed. That's a total of twenty-four goat hooves, which means forty-eight toes that need your attention."

He frowned, making her wonder if the simple math threw him. "I thought you had seven goats."

"One's a buck and, trust me, you cannot handle him."

He pushed up from Nonno's chair and smiled at her. "You have no idea how I live for a challenge. If I clean all twenty-four feet, can I stay?"

"Their called hooves, not feet. And, we'll see."

He scooped up the dog like he weighed nothing. "Let's go, Wizard of Ozzie. Farmwork to do."

As soon as she opened the door, Harriet came bounding over with his cowboy hat in her teeth. Well, what was left of it. The brim was shredded.

Frankie bit back a laugh, but Elliott just hooted as he put down one dog to give his attention to the other. "Would you look at that?"

"Sorry," Frankie said, fighting an outright giggle.

He gave her that slow, sexy, careless smile as he set the hat on his head and the ragged brim dipped over his forehead. "Let's get to the hooves, boss."

Damn it. *Damn* it. Did he have to be so stinking sexy?

Chapter Five

Elliott rolled over, a jolt from head to toe. Pain jabbed his back and something fuzzy scraped his ear. His forearms ached from compressing the damn shears, using every ounce of strength he had to snap off hard chunks of goat toenail. His thighs hurt from squeezing the beasts between his legs as he bent over goat butts and held their hind legs up to do the work.

Holy mother of misery.

Everything hurt and needed rest and a five-hundred-dollar massage and sauna at the club in Manhattan. Later. He'd make an appointment later. Now, he had to sleep, the need pressing his lids closed and numbing the pain. In his ear, a soft sigh pulled him a little further from a dream, and he reached out to...

He dug through sleep-fog for a name. Francis. No, Frankie. Fiery, feisty, funny, and...*furry*?

With a grunt, he threw himself backward, as far away from the little goat as possible.

Ruffles.

A musical laugh filled his ears. That pretty, girlie, bell-like laugh he hadn't heard nearly enough while he cleaned shit—actual, *real* manure—out of goat hooves. Shifting in the hay bed he'd made the night before, he squinted to see Frankie at her milking station, already wringing the crap out of Clementine's titties.

Holy hell, he knew their names. Plus, it couldn't be seven in the morning. Did it never end, this goat business?

Well, this was part of the deal he'd made with the lawyer, right? Burns had salivated at Elliott's offer and asked for one week to close the sale. During that time, Elliott had to make sure Frankie hit nothing but roadblocks until he and his partners owned the land. That required constant supervision and, evidently, sleeping in a goat barn.

"How'd you sleep?" Frankie asked, the splash of milk into a metal bucket not hiding the little note of concern in her voice. She might act like she didn't care that he had to sleep here, but she did.

"Like hell in a haystack." He leaned up on one elbow, scowling into early sunlight that streamed through the opening behind her, backlighting her so she looked...great. Really great. "You're up early."

"It's a farm, big boy. That's how we roll."

Too tired to argue, he rested his head and let his eyes focus on her. Jeans today, faded but tight enough to show every curve. And an oversized T-shirt so loose that when she leaned over to adjust the milk pail, he could see right down to a tank top. Her hair was pulled back in her Heidi braid. Small, taut muscles in her arms bunched as she squeezed out milk, her lower lip tucked under her teeth in concentration, a glisten of perspiration giving her a glow.

"You can use the facilities in the trailer," she said, not even looking at him.

"In a minute. I'm mesmerized by milking." And the milk maid.

She tried to hide her amusement by tucking her head under the goat's belly instead, but he caught the smile. "Good, you can finish for me. I think you learned how to do it last night."

Yes, he had. Squeezed the udders till those suckers were dry as bones. And never wanted to put his hand on another goat nipple as long as he lived. "Aren't you almost done?" he asked.

"Still have Ruffles and the little girls. And I need to leave in less than an hour."

He sat up completely. "Where are you going?"

"County Clerk to get to the bottom of this Burns guy and his bogus will."

Except, the will was not bogus. Elliott was certain of that. How Burns's client was able to coerce the old man to sign it might not have been the most ethical of means, but the will was legal. "I'm going with you."

That earned him a vile look. "No, you're staying here to milk the goats."

"I'll do both, but I'm going with you."

"I can handle it. I've already started, to be honest. Last night I Googled that lawyer and the name of his client."

Oh, that was not good. "What did you find?"

"He's a real lawyer, sadly. But Island Management doesn't have a Web site or anything trackable. But I have some contacts in the county government who helped me after Nonno died without a will or a deed to this land."

Brushing some hay out of his hair and off his jeans, he finally got up from the homemade bed, his real estate experience taking over his brain for a moment. "How can he not have a deed to the land?"

"He was a founder of the island, back in the 1940s. A group of people actually settled the island, and were able to claim ownership of land. That's how the lady who owns Casa Blanca got a lot of that land, from her grandparents who were part of the founding group. But there's a deed now, on file, and in eight, no, seven more days, it transfers to my name."

Not if it transferred to another name first. In six days, if all went according to plan. An unwanted pressure of guilt punched hard enough to push him to a stand. "Let me hit the head and I'll finish the goats, shower, and go with you."

Her jaw unhinged.

He ignored it. "C'mon. You know you want company."

Before she could argue, he was crossing the pen and headed for the trailer, blinking into the blinding sunrise, making plans for who to call first and exactly what strings to pull and palms to grease. He *had* to be at those government offices with her.

Her grandfather was a founder of the island.

He silenced the voice in his head with a litany of rationalization. This place was perfect for the stadium, great access, close to a good population base on the other side of the causeway, still small and out of the way enough to be a real tourist draw. Plus, they'd already secured the surrounding properties, and this little plot shouldn't hold them up. The whole plan wouldn't work without a good access road and parking. This was too *easy* to start over.

Fast, easy, simple, lucrative, and…a shitty thing to do to Frankie.

Swearing softly, he stepped inside the little mobile home to find the bathroom in the hall. He'd have to go get some things from the resort if he was going through with this plan, but Frankie had thoughtfully laid out an unopened toothbrush package with toothpaste, a washcloth, and something that looked like a bar of soap. It was brown and lumpy and smelled…amazing.

He sniffed again, getting a mix of sweet and peppery smells. When he turned on the water to lather up, the scents got stronger, and the soap slid around in his hands with a buttery, luscious texture.

If she washed in this stuff, then he wanted to...touch her.

Oh, hell, he wanted to anyway.

He stripped his T-shirt off and took a French bath, imagining how good a whole shower would be, except he didn't think he'd fit in that phone booth of a shower. Once he'd dried off and brushed his teeth, he checked outside and, not seeing her, pulled his phone out of his back pocket and called Zeke.

The hello was very sleepy and not real pleased. "What?"

"Did I interrupt the honeymoon?"

He got a low groan. "We're not married...yet."

Geez, the guy fell hard and fast. "We need to talk."

"You didn't close that Cardinale deal yet, Becker?" Zeke was awake now.

"Working on it."

"Call me when it's done. I'm sleeping." A female voice in the background, followed by a soft laugh, told Elliott that his friend wouldn't be going back to sleep anytime soon. Lucky bastard.

"Well, sorry to delay your morning exercise, but you have to hear me out. I put an offer on the land through a lawyer who appears to have a legitimate claim naming his client as the owner of the land."

"And?"

"Owner's granddaughter is going to fight it, so I have to delay, distract, and divert her for a week while we slip in under the radar and get the land. And, just in case this lawyer's a shyster and he's lying, then I have to work on buying the land directly from her. Either way, I'm going to win." He felt better just saying it out loud. He had a plan and needed to stick to it.

"Hmm. Okay. Sounds...okay."

"Oh, it's more than okay," he said, reassuring himself as much as Zeke.

"Why, is she hot?"

"A ten."

Zeke snorted. "You are the luckiest son of a bitch on earth."

"Says the man who is in the sack with a gorgeous female while I have a goat waiting to be milked."

"What?"

"It's a goat farm," he explained. "The late owner ran a goat farm, and she took over."

"So why doesn't she want to sell?"

"Sentimental value, best I can tell."

"You can outbid that, Becker."

"Yeah, but she doesn't know about my deal with the lawyer, and she doesn't know what we're planning to build." Another one of those little guilt pricks stabbed at his chest, so he paced the trailer. In three steps, he was in a bedroom he knew had to be Frankie's, decorated—if you could actually use that word—with a simple beige comforter and a few pillows, some pictures of the great outdoors on the walls, and a single dresser with a hairbrush, mirror, and two small, framed photographs.

It didn't look like any woman's bedroom where he'd spent time. He was used to counters that looked like the makeup department at Saks and overflowing closets with a zillion pictures of...themselves. This room was as simple as the farmer who lived in it. And all that did was intrigue him more.

"So, what's your plan?" Zeke asked with a yawn.

"I'm going to, um, stick around her farm." He cleared his throat. "And work."

"What?" Zeke barked out a laugh. "You? Work a farm?"

"Yeah." Leaning over the dresser, he squinted at one of the small pictures. But his focus was on the girl in the photo—definitely Frankie, though a good dozen or more years ago, with the gangly body and braces-heavy smile of a preteen. She stood between two people who were undoubtedly her parents, the mix of features easy to discern.

"Then she must be an eleven, not a ten."

"Grow up, Einstein." Hey, was that the Plaza in the background? A limo driver behind them, waiting with an open door, the small family dressed for a special event. Vacation in New York City? The other picture was of an older man, he'd guess the grandfather she called Nonno, leaning against the shelter Elliott had just slept in. A bull of a man, with a shock of white hair and some teeth missing in his broad grin. One hand was on a goat, the giant, gnarled fingers nearly covering the animal's whole head. Next to him, that same little girl, the braces still on.

"So, can you make it?" Zeke's question brought Elliott back to the conversation.

"Sorry, make what?"

"Brunch tomorrow at Casa Blanca. Nate's docked his yacht in the harbor, and he's meeting Mandy and me for brunch. Why don't you come over and join us? I mean, if you can get away from the goats." He chuckled, and in the background, his girlfriend was laughing, too.

But Elliott ignored them, looking from one picture to the other, both of which had to have been taken in the same year. With her grandfather, she had hunched shoulders and a shadow of pain around her young eyes.

"We're meeting around noon at the restaurant. Be there, because I have some great news to announce."

Elliott pictured that great news in bed next to Zeke—the woman he'd known from high school and found not so long ago cleaning his villa over at Casa Blanca. "I can only imagine."

"No, you can't," Zeke said, his voice rich with a contentment that Elliott had never heard in Einstein's tone before.

No surprise, really. Zeke had confessed his longing to settle down awhile back, when he and Elliott had become friends. They'd had Yankees season tickets near each other and had then joined the same recreational softball team. But the very idea of settling anywhere with anyone made Elliott's teeth itch.

Zeke covered the phone, muffling his words but not the woman's laugh. Okay, it didn't sound exactly like hell to be that happy, but the same woman forever? That was not easy enough for Elliott Becker. That was downright…difficult.

He signed off the call and picked up the two pictures again, looking at them side by side, imagining that little—

"Can I help you find something?"

He jerked around, stunned that he hadn't heard her come in. "Just looking at your pictures."

"Also known as invading my privacy." She strode closer and took the photos, placing them exactly where they'd been on the bureau.

"What happened to your parents?" he asked, letting his gaze shift to the other picture.

She swallowed, hard. "9/11." Her words were so gruff, so soft, he almost didn't understand. But then he did. And he felt his own shoulders sink with the truth.

"Both of them?" God, that wasn't fair. So, so not fair.

She blew out the slowest, saddest breath he'd ever heard, closing her eyes. "Both of them." Her voice cracked on the last word, and he couldn't stop himself from reaching to her and pulling her into his arms.

"Frankie, I'm sorry."

She was stiff at first, but then she molded into him with the next sad sigh. "Not as sorry as I am."

Something in his heart just twisted and cracked and fell right open. Easing her down on the bed purely so he could sit and hold her, he stroked her hair off her face and looked into her eyes.

He shouldn't do this. He shouldn't get personal or care. Zeke and Nate wanted this land, and when they wanted something, they got it. She'd just be the collateral damage of their unstoppable success. Well-paid collateral damage.

His job was to figure out how to get this land, not how to understand her heart. That's why they'd sent him.

Still, he couldn't help himself. "Tell me about them," he whispered.

He felt her lean further into him, one step closer to trust he knew in his gut he didn't deserve. Trust he'd be betraying soon. But he held her anyway because there was no way he couldn't. No way.

Chapter Six

Comfort. Sweet, strong, delicious comfort in the form of muscular arms wrapped around her and a bare chest beating with a heart she wanted to rest against. The consolation felt so good and necessary when she let herself slip to that sad place, so Frankie just let herself fall into Elliott's embrace.

"I really don't talk about it, about them." She swallowed against the rock in her throat, sniffing the lingering smell of lavender and sea salt. "You used my goat's milk soap."

"That creamy stuff?"

She nodded and sniffed again. She'd never smelled it on anyone but herself, and on him it was divine. "I made it."

"Nice." She could feel his face move in a smile against her head. "And nice attempt at a subject change. Talk to me, Frankie."

She exhaled, knowing this man well enough to realize he wouldn't let her stand up and go on until he got what he wanted. Inching back, she met his gaze, unashamed of her tears. "My parents are the reason you can't sway me with money. I really do believe it is the root of all and every evil, including the greed that stole their lives."

He narrowed his eyes. "Greed didn't drive jets into the World Trade Center, Frankie."

"No, but greed had my parents insisting on being workaholics, never missing a day, even an hour. Even that day, when…" She fought the lump again, the injustice, the bad timing, the big fat *what if* that had ruled her life for so long after September 11, 2001.

Every time she'd heard a miracle story about someone who hadn't gone to work at the Twin Towers that day, she choked on her own "what ifs."

"What if they'd skipped work that morning to come to the school open house instead, like they promised they would?" she asked, giving voice to a question she'd asked herself a million times. "What if they'd chosen to meet my new teacher like all the other parents? What if they had a story like that...and they'd been saved?"

He stroked her hair, not saying anything or passing judgment on her bitterness.

"They didn't have to be there that day," she whispered. "They were supposed to be at my school, but some big multimillion-dollar client was coming in that afternoon and at the last minute, they bailed on the school meeting." She closed her eyes, remembering that last breakfast, the punch of disappointment because, once again, money trumped everything else. Not even one of them would pick school over a client, so she'd lost them both.

"And they could be alive if they could have been somewhere else, and they would have been if their priorities had been in order."

"Everyone who died could have been somewhere else, Frankie." His voice was as calm and sweet as the fragrant soap he'd washed with, but the words did nothing to help her.

"But they *should* have been somewhere else," she insisted, clinging to the regret and anger that always bubbled under the surface. "I've forgiven them, but..."

"Not if there's a but you haven't."

Well, she'd tried. It had been thirteen years and she wasn't angry at the world anymore. "But I'll never be a fan of anyone who is motivated by the desire to have more. That's what drove my parents—the need for more. More money, more things, more status, more success, more multigazillion-dollar deals." She puffed out a disgusted breath. "They died to have more."

He didn't respond—how could he? He was a *billionaire* who no doubt worshiped at the altar of More Is Never Enough. But his gentle caress on her back felt like that of a kind, caring man, so she tried to forget that he was cut from the same cloth as her money-hungry parents and let him soothe away the old beast of bitter who reared his head more often since Nonno had died. So maybe it wasn't bitterness that had her blue, maybe it was just a far too familiar sense that she had no one.

She closed her eyes and rested on his powerful shoulder, practically purring at how good he felt.

"I came here after it happened," she finally said, not wanting to talk about her parents anymore. They weren't why she wanted to hold on to this land. It was because of her savior, Nonno. "To live with my grandfather."

"Was he your only relative?"

"No, my mother's sister in Long Island also wanted me, but according to my parents' will, I was supposed to live with Nonno. So I left a four-thousand-square-foot apartment on the Upper East Side and a private school, driver, and a life of pure luxury to move to a goat farm in the middle of a swamp island."

It was his turn to back away and look at her incredulously. "That must have been horrible."

She fought a smile. "I loved it."

"Really?"

"Well, not immediately, no. I mean, it was a bit of a culture shock and I was a typical teenage brat full of denial and anger, but Nonno? Boy, he just loved me like I was another one of his darling does. He was just the most amazing, sweet, terrific guy in the whole world. My grandmother had died a few years earlier, and the farm was fading, but only because he needed a second pair of hands and he was too stubborn to ask for help. His middle name was stubborn," she said, trying to make light of the character trait that had nearly cost her that last goodbye. "But once he started teaching me how to do things, I really, really loved the life."

"You lived in this trailer?" he asked.

"Oh, no. We had a little ranch house, but it was messed up badly in a hurricane that hit the island a few years ago. He put this up temporarily."

"I guess it was a great escape from the pain of what you'd gone through in New York," he said.

Everyone thought that, and it made sense. "It didn't seem like that to me at the time. I enjoyed the animals and loved Nonno and he loved me. Completely and wholly and unconditionally. Way more than my parents did, or at least than they acted like they did."

"Like, he went to your teacher conferences instead of working?"

She laughed softly. "Even better. After the first year at Mimosa High, he yanked me out and homeschooled me because the teachers were all 'from hunger,' he used to say."

"He educated you himself?"

She shrugged. "More or less. He certainly taught me how to milk goats and breed them, and how to make soap and cheese, and get a doe ready to give birth. But that's not exactly what qualifies as an education in the state of Florida."

Comfortable now, she tucked her legs under her and shimmied back to look at him. That was no hardship. His dark gaze was right on her, every word hitting his heart, she could tell.

"And that was a problem," she added. "Enough of a problem that my Aunt Jenny swooped down from New York, went to war with the courts, and got me to go live with her in Roslyn Heights, Long Island, also known as living hell for me."

Which was actually the understatement of all time. "My cousins were entitled, obnoxious, partying bitches, and my aunt and uncle were as money-obsessed as my parents. I don't know how I survived there, but I did."

"Then you came back here?" he guessed.

"I went to Florida State and got a degree in animal science and, of course, I stayed with Nonno on every break and in the summer. The more I learned, the more I had ideas for this place. It has so much potential to be a real money-making operation if he had only brought it into the twenty-first century. But Nonno didn't like...the twenty-first century. He had a rotary phone here until the day he died."

"So that's what you want to do now? Make it a twenty-first-century goat farm?"

"No." She pulled her legs up again, wrapping her arms around her jeans, not liking this part of her story any more than the part about her parents. "I made him a promise that I wouldn't and, honestly, I lost interest in high-tech farming."

"Why?"

"After college I...we..." She closed her eyes against the tears that welled. "We had a bad fight about modernizing this place. I'm telling you, there is no creature on earth as pigheaded and close-minded and obstinate as an old Italian man. I wanted to expand and install a whole milking and dairy system, and he just wanted to make soap and cheese and maybe have a little petting farm and retail storefront when he rebuilt the house. I was on fire with youth and ambition, and he was mellow with age and the simple joys in life. We fought pretty badly." She managed a wry smile. "I may have inherited that stubborn streak."

"Ya think?" Laughing softly, he brushed a strand of her hair off her face, the gesture so intimate it sent an unwanted rush through her, but also encouraging, so she kept talking.

"Anyway, after our big argument, I went to DC and got a really important job at the Department of Agriculture and Nonno…" Her voice hitched, and he reached for her hand, swallowing it in his much more sizable ones. "He had a stroke."

"And you weren't here."

She looked at him, touched for some reason that he would understand just how horrible that was. "No, I wasn't. And if I had been…"

"He still would have had a stroke."

She shook her head vehemently. "But I might have gotten him to the hospital sooner or maybe I would have seen an early symptom." Guilt wracked her voice and pinched her heart. "But I was in Washington…and…" She swallowed but forced herself to make the admission. "I was no better than my parents in being somewhere other than where I should have been, chasing success and big dreams and—"

"Big dreams? In the Department of Agriculture?" He couldn't hide the incredulity in his voice.

"I was on a fast track to a directorship," she countered. "But that's all over now, thankfully."

"Because you promised him you'd run the farm the way he wanted you to?"

"I promised him…" She wasn't really sure if he'd heard that promise, so what did it matter? Damn it, her voice truly cracked then.

"Tell me, Frankie." With a little pressure from his hand, it felt natural to let go of her grip on her legs and allow them to drop, removing the protective barrier she'd created as she told her story. Automatically, Elliott took up the space by getting closer.

She closed her eyes and reminded herself that the promise *did* matter. "He was in a coma when I arrived from DC," she whispered, letting herself be transported back to that night. "I sat with him in the ICU and apologized and promised and begged him to stay alive. But he just stayed completely still and asleep."

Elliott stroked her knuckles, as if to gently coax the story out of her.

"One night, after about two weeks, he woke up, and we talked for hours."

Hadn't they?

"What did you talk about?" Elliott asked, leaning forward, fully invested in the story.

"He wanted me to know he'd forgiven me for leaving and he loved me..." She swallowed so her voice didn't hitch, but the way Elliott caressed her hand nearly did her in. "He wanted this farm to be a perfect slice of heaven with a herd sired by the buck he'd brought over from his home country. So I promised him I'd do exactly that, and I also promised him that I would never, ever let this land be owned by anyone who wasn't in the Cardinale family. And I'm keeping those promises." She closed her eyes. "He died...that night. In fact..."

Her voice faded out, a sob threatening. "Shhh. That's all. You don't have to tell me any more."

But she did. He had to know why this mattered so much to her. "I promised him I'd keep the land and do exactly what he'd wanted to do with it. Then I moved in here for what was going to be a week or two while I figured things out and sifted through his belongings and figured out someone to take care of the farm before I went back to DC."

"How were you going to run the farm from DC?"

"I didn't know," she answered honestly. "But I stayed here a week, then two, then three..." She smiled. "Then I quit my job and decided to stay...for a while."

He lifted a brow. "You just quit this job that was on the fast track?"

She shrugged. "I have, you know, some money from my parents, and I never expected to like it so much here. To feel so...at home." Lonely, but at home.

Something flickered in his expression. A little hurt maybe? A little fear? Perhaps he'd just realized how crappy it would be to try to buy her home. He lifted their joined hands to his mouth, breathing a soft kiss on her knuckles. Goose bumps flowered up her arms, and chills trickled down her spine, but she managed to stay still.

A centimeter of space closed between them, but she wasn't sure who leaned closer to whom...it was like a magnetic force pulling them toward each other for a kiss.

His lips were warm, soft, sweet, and Frankie didn't even bother to fight, opening her mouth just enough to taste his tongue and hope that this wasn't fake and neither was this very sweet man.

"Let me go with you today," he said, his voice surprisingly gruff. "You don't want to be alone."

No, she didn't. Not today, and not...tonight. "Yeah, cowboy. You can come."

Morning sun bounced off the massive glass building that took up a city block when Frankie and Elliott reached the entrance to the County Clerk's offices on the mainland. Despite the brightness, Frankie knew a maze of lines and cubicles lay behind those shiny walls, populated by frustrated people and overworked clerks and wrapped in red tape.

If only she could find Liza, the amazing clerk who'd helped her last time.

"I can't believe I have to go in there again," she sighed. The last time, when she confirmed that the property was hers despite the lack of official paperwork, she'd lost nearly six hours in the place.

Elliott kept a light hand on her back and squinted up at the place, and glanced around the campus of Collier County government buildings. "Nice real estate, though."

"Not if you're stuck inside." At least today, she'd have him next to her, and for some reason she didn't want to examine too closely, she was happy about that. Maybe it was his steady presence or close attention, but she liked having him here.

And she'd liked kissing him back home. A lot.

Just as they stepped under the entrance awning, Elliott paused and reached into his pocket, glancing at his cell. "I have to take this call. Why don't you get started without me? Who are you meeting with, so I can find you?"

"Just call me. Take down my cell."

He looked at the phone with a face that said he had no time for that now.

"Okay, best bet would be in Official Land Records," Frankie said. "The lady who helped me last time was Liza..." She dug into her memory for the woman's last name. "Lemanski! Liza Lemanski."

"Got it." He gave her an impulsive kiss on the forehead and stepped away with the phone to his ear. "This is Becker."

Becker. Even the way he said his last name was sexy. He didn't even look back to say goodbye as he walked away, obviously seeking privacy. Trying not to be disappointed—hell, how had she gotten so used to him already?—she went inside to start the long process of waiting in lines, filling out forms, taking a number, and waiting some more.

About fifteen minutes later, Elliott came up behind her in line.

"I have an emergency," he said softly. "It could take an hour or two. You can handle this on your own?"

"Of course I can," she said quickly, fighting irritation that he would even imply she couldn't. Or maybe it was irritation because he kept disappearing. Or these bureaucrats kept giving her a runaround. Truth was, everything had her irritated right then. She closed her eyes. "This is just frustrating."

"I know." He stepped closer and put a gentle hand on her shoulder. "When we're done, we'll stop by my place at the resort and..." He let his voice fade and, damn it all, didn't her imagination and hormones go wild. "Maybe take a walk on the beach. Have a drink. Relax."

And fall into his bed.

She inched back, not sure where the thought came from, but it sure wasn't the first time she'd had it. With a quick and unexpected peck on her lips, he was gone.

She shifted to her other foot and checked her number again, furious at the way he'd left her so electrified. And disappointed to be alone. Why in God's name would his leaving affect her like that? He was a billionaire, for crying out loud, and it was Monday morning. Of course, he had more important things to worry about than her little property problem.

Just like her parents.

She shoved that thought out of her mind, scrunching her eyes shut to mentally erase the words. Over the course of the next two hours, she met with ineffective clerk after ineffective clerk. Keyboards were pounded, file drawers were opened, then she was sent to another department, then another.

It all reminded her so much of her old job that her stomach clenched. She'd never go back to that, never. She really did just want her farm and her goats and...

Becker's face flashed in her mind. And his body. And the whole cycle of thoughts started all over again.

Finally, she got to Land Records where she was greeted by a familiar face, and the first one smiling all day.

"Liza!" Frankie reached out to shake her hand, not surprised when the other woman added a friendly hug. They'd gotten pretty darn friendly the last time Frankie had been here, and Liza had been an absolute treasure helping her navigate a maze of red tape and brick walls.

"What are you doing back here?" Liza asked, her stunning turquoise-colored eyes dancing with warmth. "The ninety-day wait period hasn't passed yet."

"I know, but I've been informed that someone has tried to file an illegal will in my grandfather's name."

Liza frowned and gestured to the hall. "I've been digging around since I got the message that you were worming your way through the processing system from hell. C'mon, let's go in my office and talk."

In the windowless room, Frankie took the guest chair, remembering the homeness of the little office, despite its lack of windows and abundance of government-issued ugly furniture. Frankie had seen her share of these four walls, but Liza made hers welcoming, with a lamp on the table instead of fluorescent light and a few pictures of a darling little brown-eyed boy she assumed was Liza's son.

"It's very puzzling," Liza finally said as she slipped into her chair behind the desk. "I found that will a few hours ago when I first got the notification from documents pending that you were looking for it."

Frankie shot forward. "And it's fake, right?"

She blew out a breath. "I don't know. It's disappeared right out of the system not twenty minutes ago."

"What?"

"It's the strangest thing," she said, turning to tap on her computer keyboard as if she hoped it might magically appear again. "I wouldn't have even looked, but a notice came that you were in the process office and would eventually make your way here, and, of course, I remembered you and how there was no will and no deed for your No... What did you call him again?"

"Nonno," she supplied. "It's Italian for grandfather."

Liza smiled. "Yes, I liked that and your story about your farm. It sounds so dreamy, you know?"

"It is," Frankie said, understanding the longing to escape bureaucracy. "You should bring your son to my farm sometime. He'd love the goats."

Liza's smile faltered, and her gaze shifted to the framed picture next to her computer. "Oh, he's not my..." Liza gave a tight smile. "Sure. I'd love to bring him over, thank you." A box flashed on the screen, taking her attention back to the computer. "Ugh, still says 'file not found,' but..."

"But what?" Frankie leaned forward, trying to get a better look at the screen.

"Well, when I saw that notice that you were trying to track down a will and I found it, I had a chance to see the document scan." Her pretty mouth drew down. "I hate to tell you, it looked legit."

"It did?" Worry clamped her chest.

Liza's gaze softened and grew sympathetic, like a doctor about to deliver very bad news. "Frankie, we do see this kind of thing from time to time."

"What kind of thing?"

"Older folks do get scammed like that. These con artists and developers comb old-age homes and even some neighborhoods looking for elderly citizens who haven't written a will, then they persuade the person, who is oftentimes not completely, you know..." She tapped her temple and gave a sympathetic tilt to her head.

"Nonno was pretty alert," Frankie said. But then, she'd been gone awhile. How did she know how alert he was? She didn't know he was sick enough to have a stroke, either.

"I'm sure he was, but in some cases, these people don't know what they're signing because they don't have family to advise them."

And neither had Nonno, because she was in Washington, DC. Tamping down guilt, she leaned forward. "Can you fight that?"

"Oh, absolutely, with the right attorney. Unless, of course, the land gets sold before you get a hold of it. Then you're in trouble."

Frankie pinched the bridge of her nose, squeezing against the frustration headache that had started hours earlier. "So, what happened to the document?"

Liza whooshed out a breath that fluttered her bangs. "I do not know, and I tell you, I'm freaking Sherlock Holmes when it comes to investigating things like this. I've dug through every file I can find, but it's gone."

"Then, that's good, right?"

She shook her head. "It's just weird. It could mean that it was flagged by someone, somewhere, and pulled from the system, or it could mean that someone made an offer on the land and a Realtor has the will."

Frankie sucked in a breath. "No!"

"Don't panic yet. I'm going to make this a top priority, and I promise to call you when I find it. Is this still your cell number?" She read from the open file, and Frankie confirmed.

Liza walked out with her, still chatting as they went down the hall, but when she opened the door, she went stone silent. Then she turned to Frankie. "Brace yourself. Hottie in the office."

Frankie laughed, remembering how a handsome man could send a reaction fluttering through the otherwise dull halls of a government building. She inched around to take a peek, her whole body tightening at what she saw. Not a hottie...*her* hottie.

"There you are," Elliott said, coming toward her with outstretched hands. "I thought you got lost in the maze."

Instead, she was lost in an unexpected embrace.

She turned to say goodbye to Liza, who was staring hard at Elliott, a frown tugging as if she was trying to place him.

"Liza, this is Elliott Becker. Elliott, Liza Lemanski, the most helpful person in this building."

Elliott nodded hello. "Helpful, as in you straightened everything out?"

"Not exactly," Frankie said. "But thanks for trying, Liza."

She gave a wave, and another scrutinizing look at Elliott, which Frankie imagined he was used to, though Liza wasn't exactly salivating; she was more curious than anything. "Nice to meet, you Elliott Becker." She said his name slowly, as if trying to place it or remember it for later.

With a final nod, he gave Frankie a nudge forward. "Let's go celebrate."

She eyed him. "Celebrate what? The brick wall I just ran into?"

He shrugged quickly. "Well, my business situation went well."

"I guess one of us should be happy." The weird thing was, despite the frustrations of the last few hours, she felt oddly happy right here on his arm.

That was weird, wasn't it?

Chapter Seven

"I don't believe it." Frankie stood with her hands perched on her hips, turning once to survey the plush, high-end villa, called Rockrose. Tucked into a garden and looking out over the aquamarine waters and pure white sands of Barefoot Bay, this one-bedroom vacation home was private, expensive, and perfectly appointed.

"You don't believe what?" Elliott asked as he joined her.

"That you would willingly choose to sleep on hay in a goat shelter when you are paying God knows what for this place."

He laughed. "I told you I'm eccentric."

"Or nuts."

"A little of both. Wait here, I'm going to get some stuff." He headed to the back, presumably the bedroom, giving her a moment to inspect the luxurious furnishings and finishings. Light, tropical fabrics accented the dramatic Moroccan-style architecture of the whole resort, with rich wood floors leading to a pool and patio. But it was the front veranda and the water view that captivated Frankie, so she stepped back outside to lean against the rail and drink in nature's finest work.

At the sound of male laughter on the beach, she spotted two men, both tall and shirtless, talking as they walked up the beach, straight toward the villa. Speaking of nature's finest work. Both great-looking, both built to break hearts, they got closer and Frankie couldn't decide which one was easier on the eyes.

Might have been a tie.

She zeroed in on the man on the left, his chestnut hair and square jaw so familiar, she couldn't resist squinting to get a better look. He laughed and made a gesture, and even that seemed like something she'd seen before.

They glanced at the villa then, and both men slowed their steps as they noticed her.

"Holy shit," she whispered, recognizing the man on the left. "That's Nathaniel Ivory."

Behind her, Elliott stepped onto the veranda. "Holy shit is right. What the hell do they want?"

"You know him?" She wanted to turn to see Elliott's face, but didn't want to miss a minute of "Naughty Nate." Shirtless, no less.

"Yeah, I know him."

"Dang, I left my phone in the car. I want to get a picture."

He choked softly. "To sell to the tabloids for fifty grand? Thought you didn't care about money, Frankie."

"Who said anything about selling it?" she teased.

He was next to her in an instant, but both men lifted their hands in greeting.

"Nice of you to show up, Becker," Nate called.

"You really *do* know him." She couldn't keep the awe out of her voice, which earned her a dark look.

"He's not your type."

She bit back a smile and looked at Nate again. "Oh, honey, Naughty Nate is everyone's type."

He mumbled a curse and practically leapt off the veranda, heading them off as they came closer.

"I want to meet him," she called playfully.

Elliott purposely ignored that, and Frankie didn't know what gave her more of a secret thrill—that he was jealous or that she was about to meet the equivalent of American royalty. The Ivory name was synonymous with power, money, and juicy scandals. With hands in every business and half of Hollywood and a lot of Congress, there was an Ivory on the front page of the news regularly.

Out of earshot, the three of them talked for a minute, then Nate and the other man gave her friendly waves. Frankie took that as an invitation and joined them on the paved path that separated the house from the beach.

"These are some friends of mine, Frankie," Elliott said, gesturing to the men. "Zeke Nicholas and Nate Ivory."

She looked from one to the other while she shook hands, politely not ogling their chests, but still stealing a few peeks.

"So this is who has Becker's full attention this week," Nate said, giving her a world-famous once-over that had made millions of women swoon. Oddly, it had no effect, but that might have been because Becker held his own with these two men.

"It seems he has a strange desire to be around goats," she told them.

Both men could barely hide their amusement. "I think it has a lot more to do with the goatherd than the herd of goats," Zeke said, grinning at her.

The statement did crazy things to her insides, far more than Nate Ivory's flirtatious wink that said he agreed.

"So, what brings you here?" she asked.

"It's a...baseball thing," Nate said.

"Softball, actually," Elliott corrected him. "We're all on the same softball team."

"Really?" Well, it certainly made sense that they were athletes with those bodies. "That must be fun to watch." For any female with a pulse. "Are you planning to play while you're all here? I'd love to see a game."

"No," Elliott said quickly. "We're not, we're—"

"Bad," Zeke added. "Not pretty to watch."

She smiled up at him. "I doubt that."

"What are you two talking about?" Nate asked. "The Niners are fantastic to watch."

"The Niners? That's your team?" Frankie shifted her gaze to Becker, who looked more than a little uncomfortable. Was he jealous of these guys? That seemed a little preposterous, but something was bugging him.

"Yeah," Zeke answered. "The Niners."

"What does the name mean?" Frankie asked.

They all shared a look and a silent communication that she couldn't decipher.

"It means..." Nate dragged out the words.

"Nine on a team?" she guessed.

"Zeroes," Becker finally said. "Net worth."

It took a few seconds for that to register, then she understood those nine zeroes meant a billion. "All of you?"

"More or less," Elliott said. "So now I'm sure you don't want to see us play."

Because she'd made her feelings about billionaires clear enough to him. She gave an easy shrug. "Might still be fun."

Elliott put a hand on her shoulder and started to steer her away. "Great to see you guys. I'll try and catch lunch in the next couple of days, but I'm really busy."

"On the farm," Nate said, fighting amusement.

"With the goats," Zeke added, equally entertained by the thought.

"And the goatherd who is obviously a helluva lot better looking than you two clowns." He whisked her away, calling over his shoulder, "We'll be in my villa. Read the sign: Do not disturb."

He sure seemed anxious to get her away from them. Or at least…alone in the villa.

Elliott wasted little time throwing the rest of what he needed in his bag, making sure Zeke and Nate were gone. He'd warned them off any mention of the baseball stadium, but the chance of letting something slip worried him. Plus, witnessing Nate flirt with Frankie irked the crap out of him.

She was…his. At the moment, anyway.

"This place is really amazing," she said as he came out of the bedroom with his bag.

"As you said, it beats the double-wide." He gave her a wink. "Anytime you want to move over here, I'm game."

She angled her head and gave him a *get real* look. "I'd like to see more of the resort, though. Especially because I have a meeting with the spa manager this week. Can you give me a tour?"

He'd risk running into Nate and Zeke again, but it beat goat work. "Sure."

An hour later, Elliott snagged a picnic lunch from the restaurant and persuaded Frankie to walk to the nearby harbor, where they settled on a wide, whitewashed dock to enjoy the afternoon sunshine. It was warm enough that Frankie slipped off the sweater she wore over a strapless sundress, revealing shapely bare shoulders and a surprising sneak peek of cleavage.

He couldn't help admiring the lovely picture she made as she leaned back on her hands and lifted her face to the sun which, despite being February, was quite warm.

"Your friends are funny," she said. "And that Nate is as good in three dimensions as he looks on the covers of tabloids in two."

He faked a choke. "And here I thought you were different from most women."

"I am," she insisted, taking the cold shrimp he offered. "But I'm still human."

He looked skyward. "Change the subject."

"Deal. What do you want to talk about?"

Her land. Besides a deathbed promise, what else was he taking from her? The question had plagued him, and it felt like the right time to ask. "So what exactly are your plans for your grandfather's farm?"

"It's my farm now," she said quickly. "And my plan is to fulfill the vision he'd always had. La Dolce Vita."

"The Sweet Life." He'd heard the expression.

"That's what Nonno called it. He didn't want to turn it into some big high-tech farm, but he always wanted to see it be a little country store and destination for families. Before Casa Blanca was built, not enough people came to Barefoot Bay to make that a reality, which is part of the reason I fought him on it and wanted to go in a different direction. But now I see the wisdom of his ways, and that's exactly what I'm going to do."

Except, she wouldn't if La Dolce Vita was transformed into an access road and stadium parking. He swallowed, but the bite lodged in his throat, making him down half a bottle of water while she stared out at the horizon, deep in thought.

"Don't you feel you're making his dreams come true and not yours?" he asked.

She considered that, then shook her head. "I've wrestled with what to do, but the more I'm there, the more it feels right. I think I'll build a cute two-story house made of stone like the ones in Italy. I'll live upstairs, but downstairs would be the retail shop. Something small, you know? I would sell my soaps and milk and cute little goat-related products. I'd have a petting pen and a much nicer milking shed and production area."

Whoa, these plans were a little further along than he'd realized. "Sounds like you might need some cash to make all that happen." With cash from the sale of her land, could she build her farm somewhere else? Would that assuage his guilt?

She shrugged. "I told you, I have some money tucked away."

"But do you have millions?"

She turned from the water to stare hard at him. "You're still convinced you can buy me."

"Not you," he corrected. "But your land."

"I haven't dissuaded you from your eccentric farm dreams yet?"

"Absolutely not. And if you had a lot of money, you could make that dream bigger, better, even more beautiful"—he took a breath and leaned closer—"somewhere else."

"So could you," she replied. "Why my land?"

Because it was next to the other three plots they'd already secured. Because this location was perfect. Because it was easy, and Elliott liked things to be easy.

Except...he also liked them to be fair.

"Anyway," she said, unaware of the war of words raging in his head. "Until I settle that issue with the lawyer who claims someone else owns the land, I couldn't sell it if I wanted to. Second, I don't want to. And I don't care if you call me stubborn, since I told you I come by that trait honestly."

He shook his head, recognizing the impact of a brick wall when he hit it.

He reached for a stray hair and brushed it off her face, studying her strong profile, the little bump on her nose and the thick lashes that brushed her cheek when her eyes were closed. "You're pretty when you're stubborn."

She tilted her head to rest against his hand. "Now you're just trying to play me."

He threaded some hair through his fingers and added a little pressure so she would turn to face him. "I swear I'm not doing anything but sitting in the sunshine with a gorgeous woman, enjoying food and conversation, and thinking about how much I want to kiss her."

With a sigh, she scooted around to face him with her whole body, crossing her legs under her flouncy skirt and forcing him to make eye contact. "I never know when you're being real."

"I'm always..." But was he? "I'm being totally real about wanting to kiss you."

She shook her head, helping herself to a chocolate-covered strawberry, nibbling while she scrutinized him. "I think I know what bothers me most about you, Becker." She pointed the bitten end at him.

He had to laugh. "Now there's a loaded statement. Sounds like the whole 'bother' list is pretty damn long."

"Endless," she agreed with a wry smile. "But this is the big one: Sometimes you're Texan, sometimes you're not. Sometimes you're cocky, sometimes you're sweet. Sometimes you play a little slow on the uptake, sometimes your smarts are daunting. Sometimes you say you're on my side, sometimes you're clearly on the other team."

For a long time, he said nothing, debating all of the different possible responses to that, and not liking any of them.

"And sometimes..." A slow smile curved her lips and her eyes sparkled as she flipped the strawberry stem on a paper plate. "I really like you and, yeah, sometimes I want to kiss you, too."

"I don't want to hear about the other times," he said softly, meeting her almost halfway. "Let me know which Becker you like, and that's the one I'll be."

She popped back. "See? That's what I don't like. The ability to change and shift and transform to suit the moment. You do that, you know."

Why lie? "I know. I like things to be expedient. So I've learned to, I don't know..." He dug around for the least offensive way to describe himself. "I've learned to blend in with whoever I'm around," he finally said.

She curled her lip like her last bite had been bad. "Don't you want to fix that trait?"

"I'm not quite thirty yet," he said. "I will, in time."

"Then call me when you do, Becker." She reached out and trailed a featherlight touch on his cheek. "If it's the guy I like, I might be up for some of that kissing you mentioned. If it's the phony guy who says what he thinks he needs to say to get what he wants, I'm out."

He snagged her wrist before she could pull her hand away, wrapping his fingers around the narrow bones. "I want to be the Becker you like," he said gruffly.

"Just be the only Becker there is. I mean, how can you be anyone else?"

He rubbed his hand up and down her arm, then let their fingers entwine as he managed to get a little closer. "I moved a lot as a kid."

She regarded him, silent, waiting for whatever that had to do with his ever-changing personality. A lot, he knew.

"I developed an incredible ability to fit in, no matter where I was. Vermont, Texas, Carolinas, big city, small town, on the base or off, every year or so I was in a completely new environment, and I knew survival depended on fitting in."

"Lousy excuse for being a phony," she shot back, the utter lack of sympathy causing a ping inside but not really surprising him.

"I'm not phony," he insisted. "I prefer to think of myself as a chameleon."

She rolled her eyes. "Semantics. Fake is fake."

"I'm not fake. I don't see what's wrong with bending with the wind a little if it makes other people happy and moves things along smoothly. When I'm hanging with my softball team, I'm one of the masters of the universe with nine zeroes. When I'm doing a deal, I'm a commercial real estate mogul. When I'm home with my folks, I'm their ordinary son."

"Who are you right now?"

He smiled and opened his mouth, but she put her fingers over his lips. "The honest truth, Becker. No jokes, no saying what you think I want to hear. Right now, who are you?"

"A guy who really, *really* wants to kiss you." He leaned closer. "Honest, unwashed truth."

She shook her head. "And you're also that real estate mogul who wants to buy my property."

He gave a shrug, not denying that. "He wants to kiss you, too." He closed the rest of the space between them. "A lot."

He expected her to dodge him, but she stayed perfectly still, letting him place his lips on hers for a slow, tender kiss. A strawberry and chocolate kiss, as warm as the tropical sun and light as the bay breeze that lifted her hair and ruffled her skirt.

With a barely audible moan, she tilted her head and let him intensify the contact, their clasped hands separating so they could add light touches. He caressed her bare shoulder, and she tunneled her fingers into his hair.

"I like *this* Elliott," she whispered into the kiss. "But I don't know when you'll change."

As much as he didn't want to, he leaned back, far enough to allow their eyes to focus. "I don't change. I adapt to a situation. It's me, all the time, but I won't deny I know how to work people to get what I want. Is that so bad?"

She smiled, shaking her head. "Only to the people who are being manipulated by you—and I have a feeling I'm one of them right now."

"You call it *manipulated,* but I call it really nice and natural kissing." He underscored that with a longer, deeper kiss, teasing her lips and teeth with his tongue, enjoying a pure rush of pleasure through his body. His hand slid into her hair, easing her even closer. "God, you smell pretty and taste good."

She let out a little sigh as he dragged his lips across her cheek and along her jaw. "You smell like that soap I used in the bathroom," he murmured.

"I made that."

"Mmm. Nice work."

Her throat caught, making him want to explore that skin with his lips, too, but she backed away. "And speaking of soap, if I don't stop making out and start making soap, I won't have a batch ready for that meeting with Jocelyn Palmer. So…" She was trying to push away, but he did his best to hold her in place.

"Am I really going to lose to goat soap?" he asked.

"Goat's *milk* soap," she corrected. "And, yes, I need to get back to work."

He let her stand, easily rising with her. "I can help."

"But…" She hesitated as he got closer, looking up at him as he loomed taller. "There's nothing for you to do. It's a one-person job."

"Then I'll watch and inspire."

She made a face of pure disgust. "How on earth am I going to get rid of you? Don't you have something else to do? Sell buildings? Count your money? Play with your Niners?"

He shook his head, slipping his arm around her. "Nope. You're all I've got this week."

"Lucky me." She snorted with derision, but he could tell she didn't mean it, not the way she was looking at him. "I wish you *were* real, Elliott Becker. You're funny and great-looking and kiss like a dream."

"I *am* real. What do I have to do to prove that to you?"

She pressed a little more into him, her curves fitting nicely against him, her upturned face as beautiful as any view around him. "Kiss me again."

"With pleasure." Lowering his head, he tightened his embrace and kissed her mouth, lifting her up to her tiptoes and into his body. This time he didn't let go, opening his lips and letting their tongues curl and collide, dragging his hand down her spine to settle low on her back and press a little more.

She let out a tiny moan of pleasure, and her fingers tightened on his arms. Both of their hips rocked imperceptibly toward each other in a natural, ancient, raw movement that neither one could have stopped if they'd wanted to.

Blood thrummed from his head to his lower half, and her body shuddered at the first pressure of his.

Finally, before he grew so hard he couldn't hide it, he let her go.

"How'd that feel, goat girl?"

"Real."

He gave a smug smile and took her home.

Chapter Eight

On any other day, Frankie found the process of making soap from her goat's milk relaxing and pleasurable. Today, with Elliott right behind her, glued like a shadow, taking every chance to touch or bump or make body contact, she was anything but relaxed. Each touch was electrifying.

Ozzie circled Elliott's feet, staying as close as possible while the goats positioned themselves around the kitchen area of the milking shed, mostly content to watch. Not Elliott. He wanted to be right on her heels—or ass, to be more precise—nosing over her shoulder, asking clueless questions, making her...jittery.

He practically kissed her ear as he leaned over her to watch her stir the lye into the mixture.

"Back away or you'll get burned," she warned.

But of course he didn't. "Is that stuff making the soap hot?"

"Kind of." Like he was doing to her. Ugh. She had to give him something to do or she'd melt like the waxy soap ball. "What are you good at, Elliott?"

"Besides everything?"

She laughed. "In the soap-making department."

"Whatever you need me to do, I'm good at it."

She had to smile at his infectious confidence, inexplicably attracted to it. "You're probably pretty good at marketing. I need to come up with some catchy names for my fragrances. See that row of bottles?" She indicated the shelf stocked with tiny vials of essential oils she used in the soaps. Go smell them and tell me what they make you think of."

"Okay. Do you have a certain theme you're looking for?"

"Something that would capture the essence of this island, I think.

Something that has a local flair, so it would be tropical and beachy and sunwashed."

"Sunwashed?" He gave a soft laugh as he unscrewed one vial and sniffed. "Whoa. Too strong for sunwashing."

"Well, I dilute them, and be careful, some of them are super potent. It's best to put a tiny dab on a cotton ball and sniff that."

After a second, she heard him inhale deeply. "Oh, that's nice. Smells like a really sultry woman. Someone who likes to…"

She cringed, not knowing what to expect.

"Milk goats." He was close to her again, so close she startled, almost dropping the spatula. Without warning, he lifted her hair, exposing her neck. She'd changed into jeans and a tank top, covered with an apron and was currently up to her elbows in rubber gloves and lye… but he made her feel naked.

"What are you doing?"

"Testing the fragrance. I need to smell it on you."

Soft cotton tickled her skin, followed by a warm breath. "Mmm. Almond?"

"Yes." The scent was strong and distinctive, but her whole body was reacting to touch, not smell. Tingling, tightening, bracing for a man.

"It gave you goose bumps," he observed, kissing a few and making the chills worse.

"Now there's a fragrance name. Goose bumps."

He chuckled into another light kiss, disguised as a sniff.

"That won't sell." He kissed her skin again. "You know what gave me goose bumps?"

She wasn't sure she wanted to hear, but waited while he stroked her shoulder.

"The first time I saw you at the resort." He rubbed a slow, small circle. "Running away from me with your hair flying and your cute little bare feet in the sand."

She stood stone still, not caring that the soap might gel if she didn't stir fast enough. She had to hear the rest.

"When you turned around, with the sun setting like back lighting on you, it gave me chills." He kissed the spot he'd been rubbing, pressing his lips to her skin until it burned. "So let's call this one…Casa Blanca Sunset."

She couldn't help sucking in a surprised breath. "That's so pretty!"

"Exactly what I thought when I saw you."

Laughing, she tilted her face toward him. "You really are good. Gifted, in fact."

He let their foreheads touch. "One down. How many do I need to name again?"

"As many as you can, but I'd like four." If she could take it.

Another kiss, and he was gone, opening more bottles and sniffing. She busied herself by pouring out some of the mixture and finding her emulsifier to make the froth that would give the soap its creamy texture.

"This is nice." He inhaled loudly. "What's a mimosa flower?"

"It's why the island you're on is called Mimosa Key. They're incredibly bright pink, fuzzy flowers that bloom everywhere in the spring."

"Sounds like a drink to me. Do you have anything that smells like an orange?"

"Extract. There should be some over there." She touched the button of the electric emulsifier, the low hum drowning out other sounds and sending a slight vibration up her hand as she worked the liquid into a froth.

Suddenly, his hand was over hers, gripping the tool with her, his other hand under her nose with a cotton ball. "What's that smell like?"

Tangy oranges and sweet flowers. Maybe... "Brunch on the Beach?"

"Yeah, but let's go with something more poetic. Mimosa Mornings."

"Oh." She dropped her head back, letting it hit his solid shoulder. "You're a genius."

He dragged a finger over her lips, her chin, and her throat. "You inspire me."

She kept her eyes closed, flicking off the emulsifier to revel in a different buzz, the slight touch of his fingertip on her breastbone.

"Let me put it right here and see how it smells." Turning her to face him, he held her gaze for one second, then dipped his head, past her mouth, lower, lower to brush his mouth right along the top of her protective apron. His tongue flicked in her cleavage.

"Um, Becker. People aren't going to eat my soap."

He chuckled and slowly lifted his head. "When a woman smells this good, I want a taste."

The aroma wafted up, as sweet and light as the kiss on her lips. He kept it chaste and quick, leaving her wanting more when he stepped away. "We've got morning and sunset covered. Let me see what I can cook up for nighttime."

That she knew she couldn't take. "That's probably enough."

He inched back. "Don't you want four?"

"I want..." She let out a nervous laugh. "To stop giving you excuses to kiss me."

His eyes gleamed with satisfaction. "Be right back."

When he stepped away, she finished creaming the mixture and catching her breath, not daring to look over her shoulder at him. Maybe she should find a reason to go into the trailer, lock the door, and wait him out. Maybe she should—

"Night-Blooming Jasmine," he said. "I like the sound of that."

"It's—"

"Seductive."

She smiled and slipped off her latex gloves, stepping away from the soap mixture to get her molds. As she turned, he was right there, inches away.

"Close your eyes," he ordered.

"I don't need to."

"Close and enjoy this."

Enjoy what? Another trip down to her breasts? What did he have in mind now? "Elliott..."

He lifted a cotton ball to her nose, his expression disappointment. "I really like this one, but I want you to close your eyes so you can really appreciate this scent."

She inhaled, a zing going to every pleasure center in her body. "Oh, what is that?"

"Chamomile and lavender."

She took another whiff. "What do you call it?"

"I call it..." He hesitated a few beats, making her look at him.

"You have no idea, do you?"

"Barefoot at Twilight," he finally said.

She let out a soft gasp at the perfect name, and he caught the inhale in a kiss, wrapping his arms around her to pull her into him. "You like it?"

Really, what wasn't to like? "I think that Jocelyn will love these fragrances and this whole concept and then she will buy tons of my soap, ensuring that I have every reason to stay right here on my goat farm where I belong, which..." She inched back and winked at him. "Makes me wonder if you really know what you're doing."

He didn't smile but looked at her for a long time. "Makes me wonder, too," he said, his voice hoarse. Suddenly, he let her go. "So, we've got one more. We have morning, sunset, and twilight. What's left?"

"Midnight."

"I'm thinking something tropical, like that coconut—" He froze, eyes wide. "Did you hear someone scream?"

"Oh, that was Dominic." She was so used to the bays and bleats, she barely heard her buck calling. "He's..." She laughed. "He's kind of frustrated and...you know. Worked up."

"Must be something in the water around—"

The goat cry was louder now and followed by the metallic smack of his pen gate hitting the fence.

"I think he got out!" Frankie whipped around to run to the shelter door. Not good. This was not good.

Elliott was on her heels, and they both rushed outside at the same time, to find Dominic charging straight toward them, wailing in fury and excitement at his freedom.

"Holy shit, he's mad," Frankie said. "He could bust right into this pen."

"He won't." Elliott tore to the gate and leaped over it again, going straight for the buck, who hesitated and stumbled in surprise. "Whoa, slow down there, big boy."

He was a big boy, too. A Salerno goat the size of a small pony, with a shiny red and black coat and powerful twisted horns, Dominic was everything one expected from an Italian boy.

"Careful," she called. "He has a temper. And he's obstinate. And can be a little stupid when he's this horny."

Elliott grinned, slowly approaching the goat, holding out his hands. "Easy, boy. None of the girls in the goat pen are interested in hotheaded, stupid, stubborn guys."

But behind her, Agnes and Lucretia bayed and danced, as though they could contradict that statement. They were always ready for a party, and that just made Dominic throw his head back and howl.

"Damn, he's ready to rock and roll," Elliott said, taking a step closer.

Just then, Dominic whipped around, his full focus on Elliott. He lowered his head and charged, head-butting Elliott right onto his ass.

Frankie slammed her hand over her mouth, not sure if she should laugh or go try to save him, but Elliott rolled and got up so fast she didn't have a chance to do anything.

"I don't think so, goat boy," Elliott muttered, his muscles tense, his backside dusty. He took a few more slow steps, jumping to the side to miss another butt. "We're done here, Dominic."

"We have to get him back into his pen," Frankie said. "I don't know how to do that, either, because he's never escaped since I've been here."

"Let's go, Dominic." Elliott carefully approached him and got his hand on the goat's neck. "Let's go—"

Dominic whipped from side to side, butting hard again, but this time Elliott held his balance and managed to get his arms around the goat's neck.

All the does were out of the shelter now, screaming and scuffing their hooves, the acrid smell of the buck as exciting as the fight. Frankie held two of them back, walking closer to the fence, mesmerized as Elliott tried to lead Dominic back to his pen.

Dominic bucked again, snapping with open teeth at Elliott's arm.

"Shit, he bites!"

No kidding. Frankie nodded, half-laughing, half-holding back a moan. Dom bit, kicked, and head-butted when he was content, for crying out loud, and right now he was one pissed-off buck.

"Come on, boy, come on." Elliott braved another bite, swearing furiously as he worked to keep his balance and move the buck away. "You gotta go back home."

As if he understood, Dominic jerked out of Elliott's grip again and started to run in the direction of the road.

"Sonofabitch!" Elliott took off after him, a few feet behind, both running full force with dirt and stones flying.

Elliott grabbed hold of him, practically wrestling the goat to a stop, getting yet another buck and bite in the process. But Elliott held on tight, his legs wide, his powerful arms finally, finally subduing the goat.

"We're going home," Elliott said through gritted teeth, clearly in control now. "Move it!"

Like a chastised puppy, Dominic gave up the fight and plodded back around the trailer to his pen, each step more humble than the one before. Elliott, on the other hand, looked downright victorious.

And sexy as sin.

Frankie didn't even hesitate, leaving the does in their pen and rushing to join Elliott at Dominic's enclosure. Battling for breath, his face red, two bites swelling on his arms, Elliott led Dominic into his pen, standing over him just to let the poor buck know exactly who was in charge. Frankie stayed on the outside to right the latch, watching with a pounding heart and soaring affection.

Finally, Elliott patted the buck and led him to the water bowl. "That's enough of that shit, Dom." Wiping his face with a dirty arm, he ambled out of the pen and double-checked the lock.

"Elliott." Frankie was almost as breathless as he was. "That was—"

She threw her arms around him and kissed him so hard she knocked him right back on his ass.

High on the fight, humming with a surge of adrenaline, and inhaling a heady mix of pretty perfumes and disgusting goat, Elliott took Frankie's kiss and gave it right back to her. He rolled her over on the grass, getting right on top of her to savor his win and this woman. She clutched his head, then his shoulders, almost as if she wanted to stop what she'd started, then wrapped her arms around his whole body and gave in.

Pressing her into the grass, he kissed her mouth, their tongues instantly tangling, their bodies rocking against each other like they'd been waiting all day to do that.

He had, that was certain, and it sure felt like she had, too.

Elliott gave in to the urge to explore whatever inch of her body his hand could find. Face, neck, shoulders, then he slide lower to her breast, making her hiss in a breath when he brushed over her nipple.

"Looks like more than one gate broke around here, Frankie," he teased between kisses.

"I just wanted to…thank you." She was fighting for control, he could tell. And every time he touched or kissed her, she lost a little more of the fight.

They rolled again, and this time he pulled her on top, loving the pressure of her body on his, already responding with blood rushing to harden him. Her eyes widened as she felt that between her legs.

"You know," he whispered with a sly smile. "We can't let poor Dominic see this. He'll go nuts." Laughing, he pushed her up and brought them both to a stand, kissing her again and walking her away from the pens, around the trailer, to the shade of a massive oak tree.

Still joined at the mouth and hip and hands, he leaned her against the tree trunk and pushed his entire body against hers as they kissed. His fingers found the apron tie in the back, snapping the string so he could get one less layer of material between his body and hers.

But it was stuck around her neck. "Take this off," he ordered.

"Becker..."

"Not everything, just the apron. I have a no-apron make-out policy."

She put both hands on his shoulders and inched him back. "You have two buck bites on your arms, your face is bleeding, and my guess is this"—she gave a gentle squeeze to his ribs, making him grunt in pain—"hurts like a mother."

Still cringing, he nodded. "But, so does"—he rocked his lower half into her, biting his lip to hold back a groan of pain and pleasure—"this."

She searched his face, desire crashing with common sense in her golden-brown eyes. "I should take care of your other injuries...first."

"First." His smile tipped up. "That's encouraging."

"Becker, come on. I barely know you."

He slid his hand up her arm, lingering over her shoulder, tempted to take it south and torture her by touching her breasts again, but he dragged his palm in the opposite direction to cup her jaw. "What better way to get to know me?"

"Oh, I can think of several. Talking. Exchanging information. Watching you to see what kind of man you are."

"I'm a buck-saving, goat-toe-clipping, soap naming, hay-baling assistant goatherd."

She laughed. "Well, when you put it that way, what more could I want?"

"Exactly." He smothered her neck with kisses again, licking her lightly until he got to her mouth, where he gave it full force. She stiffened and melted and moaned, meeting each sweet press of his lips with one of her own.

"Becker..." She gave his bruised ribs another squeeze. Hard.

"Yeow!"

"Let's get you cleaned up and in a shower." She reached up and kissed his cheek, stinging the spot where he knew a goose egg was growing under his eye. "A cold one."

She should have said *freezing*, because fifteen minutes later, he was stuffed into a Hobbit-sized shower under biting cold spray. But after having Frankie's tender hands all over him with antiseptics and wet cloths, he needed a cold dousing.

Facing the stream of water, he closed his eyes and ignored the sting on his cheek where he'd come in direct contact with a goat horn.

He breathed carefully, since every deep inhale hurt his ribs. But the pain wasn't what shot fire through him. It was the memory of Frankie under him, the hunger in her kiss, the smell and taste and rawness of their connection, which was so real.

She might think he was a fake, but this attraction was genuine. He glanced down at his growing erection. Didn't that prove it?

He leaned against the plastic wall, slightly out of the stream of water, automatically fisting himself and thinking about the way her breast had felt in his hand. The first stroke just made his stomach drop, so he let go, blinking water out of his eyes to find some soap.

Not seeing any, he took a steadying breath and put his face under the water, unable to resist the burning need to touch himself again. To imagine her slender, feminine hands stroking him just...like...that.

"You need soap?"

His eyes popped open at the sound of Frankie's voice on the other side of a flimsy white shower curtain.

"Yeah." His response came out gruff as he flattened his hands on the wall to keep them off his dick as the water picked up temperature. "Bet you have plenty of that, huh?"

"And none of it has a name yet." Her hand reached in, holding one of her brown and yellow bars of goat's milk soap. "I call this one...Morning Shower."

Reaching for the soap, he captured her hand, too, giving it a slight tug. "Man, do you lack imagination."

She laughed and slipped out of his grip. "That's why I need you."

He took the soap and sniffed. "Spicy," he said.

"Yes! There's sage in there." She was so close, just one thin piece of plastic away. All he had to do was slide that curtain and...

Instead, he rolled the soap in his hand, foaming up. "Nice lather."

"That's not a very good name."

Laughing, he gently soaped his ribs. "Shit, that hurts."

"I'm afraid 'shit that hurts' won't sell, either." The curtain moved slightly, and he waited, not breathing, but she didn't draw it back. "I was thinking about something a little more, you know…sexy. Got anything?"

Right here, sweetheart. He stroked himself, once, quickly, closing his eyes as the suds intensified the pleasure against his insanely sensitive skin. "I might be able to come…up with something."

He heard her throat catch with a laugh. "You know what I mean. Does that scent make you think of anything…evocative?"

Like her mouth when she opened it to his or the sweet curve of her ass when she bent over to pick up a milk bucket? That was *evocative* as hell.

With his palms covered with lather, he tried to wash his body, but his hands just went right back to the place where he wanted her fingers to be. Sliding up and down, fondling his tingling balls, rounding the tip with her—

"Got anything?" she asked.

Other than a raging boner? "Um…let's see. I'm thinking about…" *Sliding. Into.* "You."

She chuckled. "Very sweet, but 'you' isn't going to sell soap. How about some words like…"

Like *that*. He squeezed himself, unable to fight the battle now.

He could have sworn she laughed. "Like…I don't know. I'm not very good at this. Luscious? Can you work with that?"

Her lips were luscious. If they would just close over him right…there… "Yeah, that's good, but…"

"I know, I know," she agreed. "Not good enough."

Not nearly, but he couldn't stop now. He pumped a little harder, fighting to hold back any sounds of his self-pleasuring, silently rocking his hips and wishing like hell he was rocking into her.

"Succulent?" she suggested.

Yes. Please suck it.

"Sweet?"

That would be so damn sweet.

"Oooh, how about tantalizing?" She dragged out the word, low and sexy and just enough to put him right over the edge. "Sultry? Sensual? Steamy and…Elliott? Elliott, don't you have any words for that fragrance?"

Yeah. Not anything that would go on a soap label. "Nothing terribly…soapy."

"Try harder."

"If you insist." Giving in completely, he leaned against the wall, biting his lip to keep from grunting, pumping furiously now. "It just isn't"—good enough—"real."

She laughed again. "Is anything that has your hands all over it?"

He looked up at the curtain, certain she was watching, but it held firm to the wall. Fire danced up his back and down his thighs, his whole body hot and hard and...finished. Biting his lip until he could taste blood, he shot an achy, unsatisfying, completely inauthentic load against the wall, momentarily satisfied, but hollow as hell.

Easy, yeah, but not good enough.

"Elliott? Are you okay?"

No, he wasn't okay. He was a shell of a man who wanted more than fake sex. Damn it! He wanted her, and he wanted it to be real. No matter how difficult it would be for a man who liked things easy.

"I said..." He cleared his throat and turned his hands under the stream, rinsing them. Finally, he inched the curtain back, but she wasn't there. "Frankie?"

"Right here."

He jerked around to see her at the other side of the shower, looking in. She raked him with a gaze that made him want to scream out in a wholly different kind of pain.

She gave him a hungry look, her gaze lingering on his partial erection. "Maybe we should call that one Party of One."

He snapped the curtain closed and swore under his breath. "That name sucks." And so did a self-inflicted handjob when he wanted the real thing.

He heard her laughing as she left the bathroom.

Chapter Nine

"**B**ecker, is that woman biting you?" Nate slipped his sunglasses down his nose, just to get a better look at Elliott, but not far enough that anyone at the outdoor pavilion restaurant would recognize him.

Elliott brushed the mark on his arm, faded in the few days since Dominic had inflicted it. "Had a run-in with a buck."

On the other side of the table, Zeke leaned in. "A buck? Like a bronco?"

"A buck is what you call a male goat, Einstein."

Zeke and Nate shared a look, cracking up.

Elliott looked up at the deep blue sky and blew out an exasperated breath. He knew this lunch wouldn't be easy. They weren't going to like what he had to say, they weren't going to let him off the hook, and he hadn't really wanted to come to lunch at all. The days on the farm had slipped into a nice routine, next to Frankie from dawn to dusk, sneaking a few kisses whenever he could, laughing a lot, getting to know her. And, hell, he'd finally gotten promoted to the sofa at night.

Surely a move into the bedroom couldn't be far away. It was inevitable, except...he couldn't do it until he got out from under the only dark cloud in his otherwise blissful week. And that's what he'd come to tell these guys, whether they liked it or not.

"What's so funny?" he demanded, taking a sip of a spicy Bloody Mary.

"It's just..." Zeke tried to keep a straight face but failed.

"It's you," Nate supplied. "Knowing about goats. If you don't think that's fucking hilarious, then you're dead inside."

But he wasn't dead inside. And that was the problem. For the first time in recent memory—and that went back years—Elliott felt completely alive. He wanted a woman in a way he'd never imagined possible. And he couldn't have her until his ill-conceived plan to screw her out of her land got killed.

"Goats happen to be very cool," he said. "And there's good money in goat's milk and the products. They're among the fastest-growing domestic animals in the world."

Zeke had to bite his lip, nodding, mirth dampening his eyes. "I'm sorry, Becker, but...*goats?*"

Ire and defensiveness zipped up his spine as he thought of all Frankie had been teaching him about goats this week. "They aren't just cute little weird animals, you know. People like to visit them. Kids love to pet them, and women buy the goat's milk products. And goat's milk—"

Zeke held up two hands in surrender. "Sorry, you're right." He couldn't wipe the smile off his face, though. "Really, that's good. You're right."

"Damn right I'm right," he said, reaching for his drink but choosing cold water instead. His throat was parched with the pressing need to say what he had to say, hear them piss and moan about the change in plans, and get back to Frankie.

Nate seemed less amused by the goats, though it was hard to tell with his shades firmly in place in his never-ending effort to hide in a crowd. He rarely appeared in public without sunglasses, knowing every iPhone in the joint would be taking pictures and videos, and the line for autographs would form at the right. Maybe not in a classy place like Junonia, the outdoor restaurant near the pool at Casa Blanca, but for the most part, fame and the Ivory family fortune haunted Nate.

"You know what I think?" Nate said, leaning down just enough so his hazel eyes peered over the rims of his Ray-Bans. "I think something doesn't smell right, and it's not just the goats."

Nate might have been bad to the bone, spoiled rotten, and competitive to the point of death, but he was also surprisingly intuitive.

"What makes you say that?" Elliott asked, although he knew the answer, and he was grateful for the door his friend had opened for him.

"I think you're getting a little too cozy with the goat girl, and you're dreading the moment she finds out you screwed her in more ways than one."

"Just one," Elliott admitted. "I've only screwed her on paper." So far.

Nate and Zeke shared a look that said they didn't buy it. Well, too bad. It was the truth. He hadn't slept with her, but…he wasn't going to be able to hold off much longer. She'd made enough overtures and responded to enough kisses to know the feeling was more than mutual. The only thing stopping them now was the look on her face when she found out he'd slipped Ol' Comb-Over a deal on the side and stolen her property.

A white hot splash of self-loathing rolled through his gut.

But these weren't men who responded well to letting emotions get in the way of profit. Especially Nate. There had to be another way, an easy solution. Elliott always found the easy way…no matter how hard it was to spot.

He blew out a slow breath and turned to look at the beach and horizon on his right. "When you did the first site reviews, Zeke, did you talk to the owner of the land exactly to the east of the top end of her farm?"

Zeke shook his head. "It's scrub, utterly useless land."

"But who owns it?"

"I never bothered to look it up because the land didn't pass the most fundamental feasibility study. You're in the real estate business. You know useless land when you see it. You're the expert."

Someone had once told him a particular piece of land in Massachusetts was worthless because it was too hard to dig a foundation, and so far, that land had made him a very rich man. Feasibility studies could be proved wrong.

"I want to talk to the owner," he said.

"Don't bother," Zeke said. "The cost to clear that kind of land and make it usable for our needs would be astronomical."

Good. If a problem could be solved with money, it wasn't a problem. "But if we used that plot, she could keep her farm."

"No, she couldn't." Nate was pissed enough to take his glasses off to make the point. "I was just in Miami with Flynn and saw a preliminary site drawing of the whole stadium complex. There is no physical way to follow any configuration that Flynn has had drawn up without putting parking somewhere on her land. And that's where it's going unless you're too whipped by a goat leash to put it there."

"Look, couldn't the parking somehow include her goat farm?" He'd been thinking about this, but hadn't yet put it into words. "It could attract tourists."

Nate hooted softly. "Yeah, 'cause people *always* want to stop at a goat farm when they go to a baseball game. Geez, Becker, I know we give you shit you about being a moron, but in this case, it might be true."

"But I—"

"He likes her," Zeke said, all the amusement gone from his eyes now, replaced by understanding and rationality. Thank God. "And he's trying to make her happy and give her what she wants."

Nate must have agreed, because he fell back in his chair and threw his hands up in resignation. "Well, there you go. Another one bites the dust."

"What dust?" Except Elliott knew exactly what dust he meant.

"Might as well start recruiting new team members for the Niners right now. Oh, hell, why don't we just change the name of the team to the Bucks? In honor of our goat-lover and former third baseman."

Elliott knew what Nate's comment meant. No one played on their softball team at home who wasn't rich and single. A walk down the aisle meant a walk off the team.

He shook his head. "I just met her," he said, and even that level of denial felt wrong. "I mean, she's special, but..."

"Trust me," Zeke said. "When it happens, it happens fast."

"Are you and Mandy, uh..." Elliott tapped his left ring finger, unable to even say the word.

Zeke finally smiled. "Shopping for the rock this afternoon, buddy."

Nate let his forehead thud onto upturned palms. "What the hell is *wrong* with you two?"

"What's wrong with finding someone to spend your life with?" Zeke demanded.

"What's *right* with it?" Nate fired back, then he turned his disgust on Elliott. "She's a *goatherd*, for God's sake."

"Hey, Mandy was a maid," Zeke said, clearly coming over to Elliott's side in the conversation. "Look, why don't we look into other options before the deal that Becker set up goes through? Maybe we can do something with that other land."

He could tell Nate wanted to explode as he shook his head and no words came out. "Wait, wait," he sputtered. "Did you tell him about Will Palmer?"

"Who's that?" Elliott asked.

"He's a local," Zeke answered. "He's really involved with this resort, and his wife runs the spa. They're friends of Mandy's."

"What about him?" Elliott asked.

"Will Palmer." Nate dragged out the name like Elliott was an idiot for not recognizing it. "Former minor-league player, well connected, coaches, recruits, and absolutely loves the idea of baseball on Mimosa Key. He's already got some major names lined up to come to the announcement when we go public. He's going to bring in players from Miami and Tampa for an exhibition game right here at this resort, against the Niners, maybe in the next few weeks."

The announcement? An exhibition game with pros? In the *next few weeks*?

He could practically feel Frankie slipping through his fingertips.

"Whoa, whoa." He made a slow-down gesture with both hands. "Nate, we don't have that land deal yet. We can't *announce* anything."

Nate thunked his elbows on the table and stared at Elliott. "You want me in on the announcement?"

"Of course." They all knew that Nate added the glitz factor and that his family's name meant huge coverage for them.

"Well, my time is limited."

Elliott almost choked. His time? Time was all this trust-fund billionaire bad boy had. "Might have to reschedule a trip on your party barge to Greece this spring?" Elliott shot back.

Nate's jaw tensed as he gritted his teeth. "You're a riot, Elliott. We sent you down here to do a job. Do it or we can find someone else to take your place."

For a long, crazy minute, he thought about the offer. Really thought about Frankie and her farm and the goats and—

Zeke reached in to referee the argument. "We don't want to do this without Becker," he said to Nate. Then he turned to Elliott. "But I also don't want you to hurt someone you care about."

Elliott looked from one to the other. "She doesn't want to sell," he finally said. "The land has sentimental value to her."

"Sentimental value?" Nate's voice rose in shock. "Surely you offered enough money to crush any sentiment."

"It's *family* land, Nate. You understand family."

"I understand that I'd like to shoot mine." He curled his lip. "Did I say that?"

"Yeah." Elliott tilted his head toward the next table and lowered his voice. "And you better shut up or that'll be online in about three minutes."

"Listen to me." Nate pointed at Zeke, his voice low and soft. "You're thinking with your heart. And you"—he shifted the finger to Elliott—"are thinking with your dick. I guess that leaves me to use a brain."

"I am not," Elliott denied. If he had been thinking with his dick, he'd have had her in bed already instead of waiting to clean up this mess that he made first.

"Your tongue *is* hanging out to the floor," Zeke agreed.

Nate just shook his head, disgusted, as an older woman slowly approached their table, tentatively holding out a pen and paper. "Excuse me, but are you Nathaniel Ivory?"

He pushed his sunglasses back on, as if that could hide the truth.

"Could you..." She offered the pen to him.

Nate scratched his signature, but gruffly refused a picture. When she walked away, he threw back the rest of his champagne and pushed up. "Now it'll be all over Twitter that I'm an asshole who won't let my picture be taken. I'm out of here. If you need me, I'll be on my forty-million-dollar yacht. Or, as some call it"—he gave a lazy grin, softening his famous Ivory family jawline—"the party barge."

He walked away, sunglasses in place, body language set to *bother me and you die.*

"What's the bug up his ass?" Elliott asked Zeke when they were alone.

Zeke shrugged. "He's been acting strange. Lying even lower than usual. Maybe another Ivory family scandal on the horizon?"

"What day *isn't* there an Ivory family scandal on the horizon?"

Zeke looked around, frowning as he zeroed in on someone on the other side of the restaurant. "Hey, isn't that your goat girl?"

Elliott turned to see two women chatting under an awning, his gaze drawn to the familiar one. The beautiful one. The one he wanted more than his next freaking breath. How had that even happened to him? "She said she had a meeting here with—"

"Jocelyn Palmer," Zeke supplied.

"How'd you know that?"

"She's the one we were just talking about. Will Palmer's wife." Zeke frowned and gave Elliott's arm a warning tap. "Will knows about the baseball stadium, so it's a safe bet his wife does, too. And Will knew where we were going to put it, so..."

"So, shit." Elliott pushed up. "I should find an excuse to get those two apart."

Zeke pulled out his phone. "Good, you're leaving. I'll call Mandy." His voice was totally without sarcasm, just...happiness.

"It's good, isn't it?" Elliott asked.

Zeke beamed. "Like nothing I've ever known."

That hollow feeling that had gotten so familiar in the last few days deepened in his chest. "Do me a favor and look into that other land. I'll cover the clearing costs, no matter how astronomical they are. I'm getting out of the first deal I made."

"I will. I'll work on it this afternoon, but you have to do me a favor," Zeke replied.

"Whatever you need, buddy."

"Don't fight it."

Elliott knew exactly what the other man meant. "I'm...working on it."

"No, I mean it." Zeke stood up to level Elliott with a straight gaze. "You always go for the effortless way out of things. If it's real, it's worth doing the tough stuff, even if it hurts."

"Tough? I've been living in a trailer and cleaning up goat shit for her."

"It can get much tougher than that, my friend. Especially if you want it to be real."

Elliott turned again to look at her, just at the very moment she spotted him. Her face brightened, and her smile blinded and, damn it, his every nerve cell threatened to fry. Felt real enough.

"It is real," he said softly, unable to take his eyes off her.

"Not as long as you're lying to her, it's not."

His heart dropped a little. "Look, I'm going to tell her everything, but not until after I call that lawyer and kill the deal. It can't be pending, she'll never believe me. I'll track him down this afternoon and pull the offer that I put in."

"And then what?"

"Then I'll tell her and..." He finally turned to Zeke. "Who knows, Einstein? Maybe the Niners will be looking for two replacements."

Zeke gave him a nudge. "Get 'er done, cowboy."

Elliott snorted. "I'm no more of a cowboy than you are."

"But you are a straight shooter. If you want to talk to Burns first, do it, but make it right with her as soon as you can."

"I will." And he meant it.

Frankie's soaring heart rate had to be her excitement over how well the meeting had gone with the spa manager who'd walked her outside to say goodbye. It simply couldn't be the sight of Elliott Becker on the pavilion having lunch with his friend, his dark gaze locked on her like she was his one and only target.

Except he'd been looking at her a lot like that lately. And, every time, a thousand butterflies in her stomach made a mockery of her attempts to be cool. But cool had become warm, and warm was fast reaching the boiling point.

She wanted him. The kisses, the touches, the secret looks and sexy words and his poor, pathetic attempt to hide her effect on him in the shower...it had taken every ounce of self-control she'd ever had not to climb in there and finish the job for him and every time he'd taken a shower since then.

She'd been relieved when they'd gone off in different directions this morning, happy to have some time where her head didn't feel light and her limbs heavy with need.

"I know, it's amazing." The comment yanked Frankie back to the moment, and she instantly returned her focus to Jocelyn Palmer, who was still holding and smelling some of the soap samples.

She closed her eyes and inhaled the mimosa and orange bar. "Mimosa Mornings," she said with a smile. "I just love how you've given these such incredible names and tied them all to the island. We could have so much fun with that!"

"I already have," Frankie said with a laugh.

"We are all about locally grown." Jocelyn's dark eyes gleamed with an inner peace and joy that Frankie already admired. "And romance," she said. "With so many destination weddings booked, I'd love to offer these perfectly named products in welcome gifts and baskets, if you're ready to ramp up production. Our brides might like them for wedding favors, too."

"I can be ready. I'm..." Frankie turned to follow Jocelyn's gaze, not the least bit surprised to see Elliott striding across the deck toward them, a black polo accentuating every muscle, even though it hung loose over casual cargo shorts.

He trotted down a few steps, extending a confident hand to Jocelyn. "You must be the spa manager Frankie was so excited to meet with today. I'm Elliott Becker."

The other woman's eyes widened a little, as if she knew the name. Well, he was technically a guest even if he hadn't spent one night in his villa.

"Hello, Mr. Becker, I'm Jocelyn Palmer."

"I see you're crazy about Frankie's amazing work."

"We were just talking about the great names they have," Frankie said, unable to resist leaning into him a little. "Here's the man to thank, Jocelyn. He's a genius when it comes to that kind of thing."

"You have quite a way with words," Jocelyn agreed, but she kept looking at him, frowning slightly, and then she glanced at Frankie, obviously unsure of the connection.

"He's been visiting my farm for the last few days," Frankie said, hoping that would cover it.

"But aren't you part of the baseball thing? My husband is so thrilled about this—"

"Shhh." Still smiling, he put his finger over his lips. "We're really trying to keep it on the down low."

The baseball thing? Did she mean that the Niners were here? Frankie waited for an explanation, but Jocelyn was already nodding knowingly.

"I understand," she said. "But it won't stay quiet for long, not on this little island."

"We're trying, though. Are you two finished?" He gave an impatient tug to Frankie's hand, along with a look that said clearly how much he wanted to be alone with her.

"We were just playing with some ideas for more soap lines," Jocelyn said, missing the look completely. "Later this year, we have three wedding planners opening up a new bridal consulting firm in the resort, called Barefoot Brides, so we need to really amp up the romantic themes around here."

Elliott slid a comfortable arm around Frankie. "We can work on some romance," he teased.

Frankie laughed but couldn't bring herself to pull away. "I'm sure we can come up with all different themes and lines, Jocelyn."

"As you know, our resort motto is 'kick off your shoes and fall in love.'"

"We'll work on it." Elliott took a step away, effectively ending the meeting for her, his impatience palpable.

"Wait a second," Frankie said under her breath, giving him a warning look. He knew how important this meeting was to her, and it wasn't quite finished. "What's our next step, Jocelyn?"

"*Our* next step is the beach," Elliott replied. "Let's kick off our shoes and see what happens."

Jocelyn laughed. "Just call me as soon as you have the whole line ready to go," she said. "Oh, and Elliott, best of luck with the baseball project. It's going to mean great things for all of us and, honestly, I haven't seen my husband so excited since...well..." She looked down and tapped her loose-flowing top. "Since we found out some very good news."

"Oh!" Frankie exclaimed. "Congratulations! You certainly don't look pregnant."

"It's early yet, but we're very happy, thank you." She gave Frankie a spontaneous hug and whispered in her ear. "He looks like a keeper."

Frankie didn't reply but just said goodbye, her whole body warm from the sun and the encouragement. And the man who couldn't get much closer.

"So, she loved your soaps, huh?" he asked when Jocelyn went back inside.

She looked up at him, not that unhappy that he helped end the meeting. She wanted to be with him. "She loved your brilliant marketing, too. What's this about the baseball thing?"

That glorious smile faltered for a second. "Hey, can we walk the beach or are you afraid the slogan's really a prediction?"

"I'm not afraid of anything except an expertly changed subject to avoid answering."

He laughed, his easy, breezy, I-can-make-anyone-do-what-I-want laugh that Frankie had already learned to discern from his real laugh. The difference, she'd figured out after many hours with him, was in his eyes. Right now, they might be on her, but something was flat in his gaze.

"No expert anything," he denied. "You know some of my softball teammates are here. And you know one of them is Nate Ivory."

"Yes?"

"Well, he hates publicity, as you can imagine."

"Gets enough of it, though."

He nudged her out from under the awning and gestured toward the beach. "Kick off your shoes, Frankie."

And fall in love.

She toed off her sandals, and he did the same to his Docksiders and took her hand as they stepped onto the warm, fine sand.

"So why would Jocelyn's husband be so excited about you guys being here?"

"He's a former pro ball player and..." Elliott looked out at the horizon, his voice fading as he seemed to get lost in thought.

"And?" she prompted.

He turned and looked down at her, his expression so serious she drew back. "And..." He swallowed, searching her face, his seriousness growing downright dark.

"What is it, Elliott?"

"And we..." He shook his head. "It's not important. It's just some dumb baseball stuff." Before she could respond, he pulled her into his chest, wrapping his arms around her and dropping a kiss on her hair. "Tell me about your meeting with Jocelyn. Tell me about your plans for the farm. That's what's important."

Closing her eyes, she let the moment wash over her. The sand in her toes, the man in her arms, the lightness in her heart.

"What's important, huh? You're awfully philosophical. Did you drink at lunch?"

He laughed. "Busted. One Bloody Mary. You want one?"

She let out a soft moan, her head dropping back at how awesome that sounded. "Yes. Let's go." She turned back to the patio restaurant, where her gaze landed on his friends, sitting at a side table, deep in conversation.

"I knew he'd come back," Elliott muttered, steering her in the opposite direction.

"Don't you want to join them? They're looking right at us."

"Let them. Come on, I have a better idea." He rounded the deck, scooped up their shoes and led her to the back of the resort to the shaded, paved road that ran from the hotel to each of the private villas.

At the main entrance, he snagged a golf cart, offered a hand to help her up, and drove away toward his villa, uncharacteristically silent.

He definitely didn't want her talking to his friends.

"Are you really worried that I might be attracted to Nathaniel Ivory?" she asked, not sure what to make of that character trait if it were true.

"No," he said simply, his jaw set in a way she wasn't sure she'd seen before.

Without asking what was wrong, she hung on as the cart rumbled past picturesque villas, each tucked into their own tropical gardens. Some had front verandas that faced the bay with completely private pools in the back. Others were situated so that their elevated pools offered bay views. All of them were gorgeous, including the last one, Rockrose.

He turned to her, not climbing out of the golf cart. "Come inside with me so we can talk."

Talk? They'd been talking for days. "Okay," she said, leaning closer. "If you want to talk." She kissed him lightly. "But I'm kinda talked out today."

He fought a smile, a battle waging in his eyes, but still she couldn't figure out why he seemed so conflicted. She was practically inviting herself into his bed.

"We can talk, too," he said.

She smiled and lifted a shoulder. "Whatever you want." She started to slide her leg out of the cart, but he gripped her arm, holding her there.

"Francesca."

Her heart slipped around, helpless, as it always did, when he used her full name.

"I really like you," he said.

"I really like you, too."

"No, I mean..." He exhaled, frustration oozing off him. "I want to talk and tell you..."

"Hey." She wrapped her arms around his neck and pulled him close, putting her lips right over his ear. "I got a bag full of sweet-smelling cotton balls that I need you to name."

He grinned. "If that's not the sexiest offer I've ever had, then I don't know what is."

"This." She covered his mouth with a kiss, as hard and hot and sincere as she could make it, and he melted almost immediately. At least, his strange arguments melted. Nothing else melted.

Only her heart when he scooped her up and carried her inside, refusing to put her down or end the kiss until she was lying on his bed, breathless and ready for him.

Chapter Ten

What the hell was wrong with him? Elliott's body was ready—so, so damn hard and ready—but something in his chest, probably in the vicinity of his heart or, *worse*, his soul, wouldn't make a move. Instead, Elliott slowly sat on the giant king-size bed.

"So, where are these fragrances?" he asked.

From under her thick lashes, she eyed him suspiciously. "In my bag, which I dropped in the entryway when you Rhett Butlered me into bed and then...changed your mind."

"I didn't..." Shit. "I want to help you with your fragrances."

With a soft sigh, she rolled off the bed and disappeared out the bedroom door. For a moment, he froze, wondering if she'd just given up on him completely. And part of him was hoping she had. He could call Burns, kill the deal, and then, and only then, could he get in this bed with Francesca and probably stay in it for a week.

Ah, hell, he hated when shit that should have been easy got all complicated and difficult.

"Damn it," he muttered, falling back on the bed and throwing an arm over his face. Who *was* he?

"Smell." Frankie's hand closed over his arm, keeping it firmly over his eyes as a heady and rich aroma hit his senses. She straddled him on the bed without taking the cotton ball from under his nose. "How's that?"

"Nice." He used his one free hand to push her a little lower and get right over his... "Really damn nice."

"What's it smell like to you?"

"My sense of smell just gave in to my sense of"—he rocked his hips against her bottom—"woman."

Just a little, a traitorous voice whispered in his head. Just a few kisses and touches and maybe he could tell her without...

No. He had to do this right.

"I'm serious, Elliott."

Sadly, so was he. He would not...how had Nate put it? Screw her in more ways than one. He wasn't going to be that guy.

But then she rolled a little harder over his erection. "What's this smell like?"

Heaven. Trouble. Fun. *Frankie.*

He caressed her backside and hip, letting his fingers wander to the front of her skirt, skimming skin under her thin cotton top. "It smells like...coconut."

"Yeah, but what does it make you think of?" Her stomach was taut and silky and tensed up at his light touch. "Remember the assignment. Romance."

Romance. And until he was honest and real, this wasn't romance. This was...the tip of his finger glided over the bottom of a lacy bra. This was sex.

Which used to be just fine, thank you very much.

"I don't know," he said gruffly, yanking his hand away.

She tsked. "Losing your touch, Becker?"

He wanted to smile, but nothing was funny, not even her stupid pun. "What is this stuff?" he asked, trying to play along and remember the labels he'd read on the vials. "Lemon verbs or something?"

She laughed, tightening her legs, her bare calves against his thighs, and little else except that slip of a frilly skirt she wore. What else did she not have on under that skirt?

His dick grew harder, right into her bottom, earning a sweet little moan from her when she felt it.

"It's clearly making you think of something romantic."

"It makes me think of..." Sex. Sweet, fast, easy, hard, *now.* "Lavender?" he guessed.

"Becker," she sighed in frustration and lifted her hand so he could look up at her. She rested her hands on either side of his head, her hair dangling down to his cheeks, her top draped enough that he could easily slide his hand right...up...there.

"I need you to work your magic," she said.

Magic. She was magic. He put both hands on her hips and rolled her over his erection. And that was magic. Hot, needy, achy magic.

"Come and kiss me, Francesca."

On a sigh that sounded like pure relief, she lowered herself and pressed against him, kissing soft and sweet before adding heat and passion.

One hand found its way under her top, caressing skin as he reached around to unhook her bra and fill his hand with her bare breast. The other was already bunching up the skirt, desperate for skin and a long-awaited caress of her backside.

She was just as hungry and desperate, whimpering with each kiss, nibbling his jaw, threading her fingers through his hair, his name on her lips between strangled breaths.

"We never got a name for midnight, remember?" she said in between kisses, giving him the cotton.

He laid her on her back, bracing himself on one elbow next to her, lifting her hair to find that delicate spot right under her ear. "Let me smell it on you. That inspires me." He dabbed the fragrance gently, leaning in to kiss her eyes and cheeks and mouth.

And then back to look at how incredibly beautiful she was.

She looked at him. "How does it smell?"

"I need to find another place." He reached down to her skirt, pulling it higher to reveal her long thigh and bare hip. As he stared at her gorgeous body, his own nearly exploded. She wore nothing but a tiny strip of white satin, a thong he could take off with his teeth. "A place right...here," he said gruffly, drinking in the sight of her, trailing the cotton to a sweet spot on her inner thigh.

He lowered his head, loving that she guided him and pulled his hair just enough to show how much she wanted this, letting him kiss her hip and that wisp of material.

"Let me test it here."

"O...kay." She could barely talk, so he stole a peek at her face, eyes closed, mouth slack, her expression rapture and anticipation.

He could do this, right? This wasn't *everything*. They would do everything after he...after this.

He inched the tiny triangle of white to the side, revealing her sex-slick womanhood. He lowered his head, then dabbed her with the oil-scented cotton ball.

She sucked in a breath and let go of his hair, clutching the comforter instead.

Closer, he inhaled a mix of woman and lavender, of sex and spice. Very carefully, he kissed her and then slid his tongue around and around.

"Becker." She rocked up to meet his mouth. "Oh, God, don't stop."

Dividing his gaze between her heavy-lidded eyes and the visual of beautiful woman, he licked warm skin, curling his tongue then stroking her with feathery brushes of cotton, teasing her closer to abandon.

She gripped his shoulder, called out his name, and bucked against his mouth with the first full shudder of release. He pulled it from her, sucking and licking and holding her hips until she exploded with an orgasm.

She whispered his name, the sound of satisfaction and delight while her whole body quivered. She tried to pull him up, but barely had the strength, so he kissed his way back to her mouth.

"Becker, what do you call *that* fragrance?"

He laughed. "Well, I call it…" He couldn't even think of a word good enough to giving Frankie that kind of pleasure. "Where I belong."

She finally opened her eyes enough to let him see her surprise. "Not a very…soapy name from my marketing guru."

"What would you call it?"

"Amazing. Perfection. A prelude to…something."

They both knew exactly what something that was a prelude to.

"How about a prelude to a promise?" he suggested. "Too corny?"

"Well, it's for weddings planners. They love corny."

They both laughed, and she reached her hand to stroke his cheek. "I like you, Becker. So much it scares the hell out of me."

"What are you scared of, Francesca?"

She sighed and closed her eyes. "Everyone I love leaves me."

The admission was so simple and true, it hit like a punch between the eyes. He didn't even know how to respond, so he just lay down next to her, ignoring his body's needs to take this moment to connect.

"What are *you* scared of, Elliott?"

He thought for a long time, holding her hand, letting their heart rates settle back to normal.

"You *are* going to tell me the truth and be real, aren't you?" she asked.

"Yes." But not yet. He couldn't tell her yet. He'd have to tell her another kind of truth. A different revelation. "I'm scared that no matter what I do or where I go or how much I spend or make or accumulate, I will never be…" *Where I belong.* "Home."

She sat up slowly, leaning on her elbow to look at him. "Tell me why."

And for the first time ever, he wanted to tell someone everything. All his pain, all his missing parts, all the reasons why he had a hard time being real.

Because with this woman, being real was easy. Too easy. He'd never even thought there was such a thing.

Yes, Frankie wanted to have sex with Elliott Becker. More sex. Real sex. But something was stopping him, and Frankie suspected he just wanted one last wall to come down between them. He wanted to tell her something. That had been clear for a while now. And she wanted to tell him something, too.

So sex could wait. She had a feeling there'd be plenty, and often. This sharing was far more important.

They were both still fully clothed, but he nestled her into him, sliding a powerful leg over hers. He gently eased her head into the space right over his heart, his chin against her hair.

For a long time, neither spoke. Their breaths slipped into an easy unison, the afternoon sunlight slipping through plantation shutters to stream warmth on them. Frankie felt everything tense and scary and unhappy lift from her heart for the first time in a long time.

"Home," he finally said. He nodded, as though that sounded right to him. "I'd like a home."

She pushed up on her elbows again, certain she'd misunderstood the whispered words. "Didn't you say you have a few already?"

"I've got an apartment in New York and I keep a place in Paris, just because, I don't know. It's pretty there. My parents retired to San Diego, so I have a place there, and I like to ski so I bought a house in Aspen. And, of course, my gold mine in Massachusetts, but I don't live there. My place in Boston is in Beacon Hill."

She laughed softly. "Okay. What's wrong with this picture? You just told me of, what, five, maybe six different places you own and none of them are home? You live there, right? And something tells me that 'apartment' in New York isn't a walk-up."

"It's nine thousand square feet, three stories, with five different balconies and a three-sixty-degree view of New York City."

"Holy crap," she muttered.

"And by the way," he said softly, not breaking the slow stroke of her hair. "I looked up the quote. Money isn't the root of all evil. It's the *love* of money that's the root of all evil."

"Who said that? Shakespeare?"

"God. It's in the Bible."

"Really." She hadn't known that. "Still doesn't change my feeling about it or the fact that you own all that real estate and still don't have a place to call home."

"Because calling a house a home doesn't make it one," he said. "Now don't get me wrong, I love my places. But you'll never hear me call them home. The apartment in New York is jaw-dropping, I know. I have great parties there, and I actually live in about one-fifth of it, which includes the kitchen, bedroom, and media center. But..." He shook his head. "Nope, not my idea of a home."

"What is?"

"I don't know." He was quiet for a few seconds, thinking. "I started to think this week that..." His voice trailed off, and she didn't dare look up to see his face to figure out what he was thinking. Because if he was thinking...

No. Crazy fantasies. *Stop it, Francesca.*

"...that it must be nice to have something that's been in your family and has history like that."

Not exactly where she'd thought he might be going, that he might admit *her* home felt like it could possibly be *his* home.

"I've never lived anywhere for more than eighteen months," he said. "And now, I don't live in one place for more than a month or two before I jet off to the next apartment or house. I never had 'a room of my own,' a structure full of memories, or, you know, that place where you fall, where you can be..." His voice faded, and then he laughed softly. "A place where I can be myself."

She smiled at him, getting it completely. "So that's why you're a chameleon. You need a home base." Deep in her chest, so deep it was like a little black hole she'd never expected to find, a low, slow burn heated up, even though it terrified her. What if...could she be...was there a chance to make a home with a man like this?

"So why not build a house in the burbs and live there?" she asked quickly, trying to plug up that sensation.

"I don't know if I want that, either."

She slid her arm all the way around him, holding on to his substantial body, warm and close and so, so comfortable. "I think, ladies and gentlemen, that we have found ourselves a man who can have everything but doesn't know what he wants."

"You know..." He looked at her, his whole expression soft. "You're so damn right. I want..." His voice faded and, suddenly, a guard went up. Imperceptible, but she knew it.

"You want what?"

He didn't answer, still slicing her with his dark gaze, something—a lot—going on in his head.

"You're lucky, you know that?" he asked.

"Because I don't have that pesky pied-à-terre in Paris or the nine-thousand-square-foot place to keep clean?"

"Because you found a place where you...belong. I want that. I don't care if it's fancy or impressive or what people think I *should* be living in. I just want it to be a place where..." He shook his head, laughing. "This is cheeseball, but I want it to be a place where my heart is."

Her own heart took a dip and a dive. "That's where the person you love is," she whispered.

"Like your Nonno was."

Not exactly what she was thinking, but he'd opened a door she needed to step through. "Speaking of Nonno..."

She felt his gaze on her as she stared ahead, not willing to look in his eyes.

"What?"

"That promise I made?"

He shifted a little closer. "Yeah?"

She turned flat on her back and stared up at the ceiling, aware that her heart thumped with the need to be honest. She'd asked for him to be real and now she had to be, too.

"Frankie?"

"That night that I talked to my grandfather..." Biting her lip, she let the words fade with her next breath.

"Yeah?" He took her hand and gently, softly rubbed her knuckles with his much-larger fingers. She lifted their joined hands to look at his.

"Have I told you how attractive I find your hands?" she asked.

He squeezed her fingers. "Illegal change of subject."

She nodded, building up more courage. She owed him this truth. "It was about four in the morning, and I was with him in the ICU. The halls were so quiet and still. I wouldn't leave his side even though he was deep in a coma. There were no nurses in the room, just Nonno and me."

She closed her eyes, her whole focus on the warm place where their hands touched, transported back to that dark hospital room, the only sounds the steady beep of the machines monitoring Nonno's heart. She'd held his hand, too, just like this. But instead of the strong, young, powerful hand of Elliott Becker, she'd grasped the frail, wrinkled, sunspotted fingers of her Nonno. "I remember bending over to put my head against his chest, just to close my eyes for a moment and hear his heart. I knew his time was...close."

For a moment, neither spoke as she remembered the slightly antiseptic smell of Nonno's hospital gown and the thin bones of his old chest against her cheek. "And then he said, 'Don't ever let our land go, *piccolina.*'"

"When he woke up?"

And there was the rub. She looked up at Elliott. "I...think so. Maybe. I'm not sure." She took a slow, long breath. "He never opened his eyes, but his voice was clear and so was our conversation. But...he died." She swallowed hard. "I think he died before we had that conversation."

Elliott just looked at her, clearly not quite getting where she was going.

"I fell asleep after we talked..." At least, she thought she had. "And I woke up when the nurses came running in, and they said...he was gone. They told me he'd never come out of the coma because they would have known it. They told me...I imagined the whole conversation, but I talked to him, I know I did. I heard him and he heard me and we...talked."

Hadn't they? Sometimes it was hard to be absolutely certain.

And if it had never happened, how much weight could she put on that promise?

"Then the nurses were wrong," he said, at least *acting* like he believed her.

She sighed. Deep in her heart, she knew that they couldn't have been, but... "Sometimes, I think that he was already...gone." She shook her head, the memory of that conversation so vivid it *couldn't* have been a dream.

"So..." He got up on his elbow, looking down at her. "What you're saying is you aren't sure if you really made that promise or not?"

She didn't answer for a long, long time, then finally, she nodded. "It might have been, you know, my imagination."

He stroked her cheek, silent, thinking. "No, it wasn't. And you're lucky, then." He leaned closer and kissed her. "You've talked to angels."

Her heart folded in half and then burst in her chest. "Yes," she said, fighting tears. "I have."

"I'm lucky, too."

"So you've said a million times."

He smiled at her. "You talk to them. I get to fall in..."

She waited. What would he say? In love? In bed? In—

On the floor, her cell phone rang inside the bag she'd brought in, shredding the moment. She huffed out a breath of frustration, but he gave her a nudge.

"You can get that."

"No, I—"

"Really, you can get it." He leaned over the bed and snagged her bag, flipping it up on the bed. "It's the middle of the day and...it could be Jocelyn."

Did he want this intimate conversation to come to a crashing halt? It sure seemed so.

"Plus, I have something important I have to do today." He pulled her phone out of the side pocket and handed it to her, pushing himself off the bed.

Had they gone too far? Revealed too much? Bewildered, she took the phone and barely glanced at the screen, half-registering that it was Liza Lemanski from the County Clerk's office.

Before she could sit up to answer, Elliott was halfway across the room, and then he disappeared into the bathroom, closing the door. Frowning and ignoring the punch of disappointment in her chest, she tapped the screen and answered the phone.

"Hi, Liza."

"If you tell anyone I made this call, I will deny it until they tie me up and hang me in red tape."

Any other time, she'd have laughed. But... Frankie stared at the closed door and reached behind herself to hook her bra, a flush of embarrassment rising even though Liza couldn't possibly know where she was. "Your secret's safe. What's up?"

"I found the will. And the property deed."

"That's go—"

"And the multimillion-dollar offer from a third party that is set to close in forty-eight hours."

"*What*?"

"I'm not kidding, Frankie, someone has made a cash offer, and it is going through fast, fast, fast. That Burns guy has a one hundred percent legitimate will that your grandfather must have signed in a moment of weakness. He works for some seedy company that preys on old people who don't have official wills."

"Is that legal?"

"It isn't illegal if no one contests the will or they unload the property before a family member gets involved. And that's what Burns is doing. He's sold it to the highest bidder for so much more than market value, it should be a crime."

"How much?"

"I don't even want to tell you because I can't stand to hear a grown woman cry."

Oh, God. No. "How much?"

"More than you can beat, unless you have a few million or ten stashed away. Who even has that kind of money?"

She stared at the door. Elliott did. A man who could be…unreal.

"Who's the buyer?" she asked, the metallic taste of dread and shame filling her mouth.

"I can't—"

"Liza, please. You have to tell me. I have a feeling I just…I almost had sex with him." And, worse, dreamed of a future.

"Oh, God, I hate men. Have I told you how much I hate men? Hate."

"Liza?"

"The name is Becker. Elliott A. Becker. I'm guessing the A is for Asshole."

Frankie closed her eyes as the blow hit her heart. "You'd be guessing right," she muttered, already scooping up her bag and turning to the door. "Let me ask you something, Liza." She kept her voice low as she tiptoed down the hall to the living room.

"Sure. I've broken every rule in the County Clerk's bylaws and employee handbook by calling you. What's one more?"

Very quietly, without making a sound, she turned the front doorknob. "Can you give me a phone number for that Burns guy?"

"I...can't."

"He gave me his card, but I..." Left it in a place for Elliott Becker to find. Damn him! "Liza, please."

Outside, she slid into the golf-cart seat and reached for the start button. "I have to do this," she whispered, hating the catch in her throat.

"Can you write it down?"

"I won't forget it. I won't forget anything." Like just how close she'd come to being screwed in every way possible.

The electric cart barely made a sound as she rolled toward the paved road, memorizing the number Liza gave her before they hung up. But just as she passed the next villa, she heard her name, loud and clear.

"Frankie! Damn it, Frankie, where are you going?"

Feet slammed on the pavement behind her, but she gunned the cart and swerved around some shocked resort guests.

"Francesca Cardinale, stop that cart and listen to me!"

Did he have no idea who he was dealing with? Was he so shortsighted that he didn't think she could beat him at his own game of pretend?

"Frankie, please! I'm sorry! I want you! I belong with you!"

You belong in hell, Becker.

She shoved her hand in the air, thrust her middle finger to the sky, and kept driving.

Chapter Eleven

Voice mail. Voice mail. Voice fucking mail. Then nothing. The damn thing didn't even ring anymore.

It was like Michael S. Burns, attorney-at-law, no longer existed. Elliott flung the business card on the bed, tossed the phone on top of it, and let himself follow both, stuffing his face into the blankets that an hour later still smelled like...

Where I belong.

Except he didn't belong anywhere, especially not in the arms of a genuine, amazing, one-of-a-kind angel who deserved so much more than a fake. Because that's all Elliott Becker was. A phony, manipulative bastard who thought he could hedge his bets and play both ends against the middle and every other gambling cliché that always worked for him because it was easy and he was lucky.

Not anymore.

Now he was the empty shell of a fool who'd made a mistake and couldn't cover it up.

He flipped over, staring at the ceiling. Who'd called her? Burns? Why would he do that? Someone had found out. Maybe Jocelyn Palmer had alerted her. Hell, maybe Nate had sabotaged this.

At the thought, he shot up, furious and ready to kill his friend.

That would be just like that spoiled prick who got everything he wanted. Probably thought if he wrecked the romance, then Elliott would go ahead with the—

Three hard raps at the front door of the villa pushed him to his feet. If that was Nate, he might punch the bastard. If it was Zeke, maybe he could help. Elliott had to do something. He had to track the guy down and withdraw the offer and then go grovel in the hay and beg for—

"Mr. Becker! It's Michael Burns!"

Burns. Elliott whipped open the door and stared at the weasel with a comb-over, relief nearly buckling his knees. Thank God, his luck still held in some regards.

"Get in here." Elliott grabbed the guy's arm and practically yanked him. "I've been calling you nonstop for an hour!"

"Sorry. I was in a bank vault, and that cuts off the signal to my phone."

"I need to—"

"Here's your check, Mr. Becker."

Elliott stared at it, then closed his eyes. This transcended lucky. This was downright miraculous. "So you got my message that I wanted to end the deal before you finalized any paperwork?"

"Oh, I finalized plenty of paperwork, sir. The deal went through an hour ago."

Shit! "Then why are you giving me this check back?"

"Not your deal. I sold the land to the highest bidder, and I must say, that bidder doubled your offer with hard, cold cash. I honestly didn't think it was worthwhile to try to get you to counter."

Her land was gone? "No, you didn't sell it! You can't sell it!" He practically dove on the guy. "Whatever the amount, whatever it is, I'll beat it." He'd buy it back and give it to her. She couldn't lose La Dolce Vita. It was where she belonged. And where he—

"My deal's done. You can work with the new buyer, but I doubt she'll budge an inch. That woman laid down more money than I ever dreamed I could get and, between you and me, way more than it's worth. I have other—"

"Who bought it?" Except, he kind of knew, didn't he? In fact, who else would buy it?

"That squatter with the goats." Burns shook his head. "You just never know who has money, do you? I peeked over the bank manager's shoulder and got a whiff of her net worth." He leaned forward, eyes wide. "I could have sworn there were nine goose eggs in that number. Can you imagine?"

Yes, he could imagine. He could very well imagine that a girl who'd come from extreme wealth and never touched the money, investing it wisely for over a decade, maybe hitting some gold of her own, would have "some money" stashed away, as she'd said. Rare, unlikely, but who knew better than him how the right investment could pay off?

"Listen, pal, I have more land all over Florida that I—"

Elliott yanked himself back to the weasel in front of him. "Is it all land you scammed out of old people with no wills?"

"Not all of it and...and I don't do the visits or anything, I just handle the legal stuff. There are guys tougher than me that visit these old folks and try to scam them."

Elliott leaned into his face, taking the guy's collar in his hands. "Don't you have a grandparent, pal? What the hell's wrong with you?"

He tried to shake Elliott off, his face paling. "I need a job, man. I have bills and...problems."

"You want money? I'll pay you to get me the name of your dirtbag clients and a list of the people they're scamming. Then I'll pay you to be the lawyer for those poor old people and you won't have any problems."

His eyes widened. "Really?"

Elliott exhaled, shaking his head. "Problems that can be solved with money aren't problems, pal."

But his couldn't be solved with any amount of money. He took a slow step backward, trying to process all of this. Frankie had her land, so that was good. And he had...nothing.

Without her, he was right back to where he really belonged...nowhere.

"I'm serious," he finally said to Burns. "You have my number. Call my office." When the man left, Elliott stood in the middle of the living room, staring at the check. Millions of dollars that didn't matter to anyone without...a home, a partner, love.

How could he ever make her see that he understood that now?

He didn't know how, but he knew one thing. It wasn't going to be easy.

After Frankie returned home from the bank, she forgot about Elliott Becker. It took absolutely no willpower, because something else had completely captured her attention. Isabella was in labor.

Fortunately, she'd been feeling the doe's right side every day and had noticed some tension and change in the shape. Remembering how Nonno had handled the kid births when she was young, Frankie had prepared a clean stall with a bed of short-cut hay so it was extra soft, and had all the does milked and dogs fed, making them stay outside while she watched Isabella.

She had gloves and K-Y Jelly in case of breech, and a spool of thread, as well as lots and lots of towels. Since a goat could give birth to a kid on a mountainside with no boiling water, sterilized tools, or human in sight, there was little to do but make sure all went well and that her kids—she had no idea how many were in there—were all born alive.

Sometimes, intervention was necessary, but Frankie was certain she could handle it. And grateful for something other than Elliott Becker to think about. She cooed at the bleating goat, looking for the signs that she'd be delivering soon. Ears out, flank distended, some seriously gross stuff coming out of her.

"I think we're ready, Izzie," she whispered. "How many are in there, girl? We need a lot for our amazing farm, don't we?"

The farm she'd have without…him.

Grunting at herself, she focused on the doe. Her best guess was that Isabella had been in labor all day, so it wouldn't be too long now. Poor thing. She'd been here alone, while Frankie…was being had.

She stomped on the ugly thought and refused to let herself wallow in pity or sadness. It was over. She was done with Elliott Becker, and if and when he showed up to toss around his empty lies and phony words, she would tell him that. Now, she had to watch Isabella, who was pacing the stall, stomping, whining, and occasionally looking up for relief that Frankie couldn't offer.

Leaning against the wall, she tried to soothe Isabella by petting her, but the goat bleated and dug at the hay, over and over again, until her hind legs folded under her.

"You ready to go, girl?"

Isabella cried out and rolled onto her side, laying out her leg to make room. Suddenly, she jerked sideways and yelped.

Intervention time.

Frankie yanked on gloves and squeezed the jelly all over her hands, the whole time whispering and calming a very unhappy and uncomfortable doe. Outside, the dogs kicked up their barks, as if they knew something was wrong, but she blocked it all out as she reached for the doe's leg, sucking in a breath when a stream of blood trickled out. "Oh my God."

Should she call the vet and leave her alone? Or go in there and—
"Frankie!"

She jerked up at the sound of her name.

"Where are you?"

Becker. Thank God. Right now, she'd take help from Satan himself. "In the back. The birthing stall. Isabella's in trouble!"

She heard his boots hit the shelter floor, hating herself for how much she'd gotten used to that sound, and learned to love it.

"What's wrong?" He was next to her in an instant, the strength and security of him almost bowling her over as he reached out instinctively for the doe.

"No, wash your hands. Get gloves. No, no. Call the vet."

And then he was gone, taking her orders as Isabella screamed bloody murder.

"Where's your cell?" Becker asked from behind her. "Is the vet's number on it?"

"Yes, yes. My pocket." She reached her back pocket, finally looking at him for the first time. Holy mother, he looked like hell.

"Here, give me the phone," he said. "What's the name?"

Isabella bayed again. "Wait, wait. I need to find out if she's breech. Can you hold her legs open?"

He was on his knees, gloved hands reaching out with a surprising amount of tenderness, his face next to Frankie's. "Like that?" he asked.

Why did her damn heart slip around like that? She hated him. He'd screwed her—or tried to. "Yes. Let me reach in there." She looked up at him, expecting a curled lip of disgust, but he looked at Isabella with sympathy, touching her gently.

After a moment, she found the back end of the kid. "She's breech. I have to turn the kid."

"You want me to call the vet?"

She shook her head. "We can do this." She'd meant *I* can do this, but there he was, next to her, a partner, a friend, a lover... "An asshole who tried to steal my land."

"Now, Frankie?"

She almost laughed, except Isabella was howling with pain. "Sorry. Later." She pushed and prodded, sweat trickling over her face as she made careful, slow moves that wouldn't tear the placenta.

The whole time, Elliott held Isabella's legs. He talked to her and stroked her sweetly and, damn, if he didn't calm the doe down between contractions and give Frankie a chance to turn the kid.

Suddenly, a yellow bubble appeared.

"What's that?" he asked in horror.

Now she did laugh. "That's the placenta. And inside there, look..." A tiny brown foot came out first, then the face of a very pretty goat. "There's our first kid."

Both of them were silent as Isabella pushed quietly, the wee baby sliding out with its gooey overcoat.

"And maybe not our last."

The way he said it...whoa. She didn't dare look at him, didn't dare give away how that got to her. "Most times there are two," she said. "But there could be three or four or five. You ready, cowboy?"

The rest of a little brown goat plopped onto the hay, making both of them suck in a simultaneous breath.

"Would you look at that?" Elliott whispered, awe and a crack in his voice. "Even a goat birth is a miracle."

She finally found the strength to look at him again, inches away, his expression all dark and tortured and pained. He returned the gaze, the two of them inches away but worlds apart.

"Frankie," he whispered. "Is there any possible way you'll accept a simple apology?"

She managed a smile. "No." Then she turned back to Isabella. "But it looks like we've got another. And this one's coming out just as it should."

Isabella seemed to calm after she had a chance to greet her new baby girl with mama licks, and then she relaxed for the next delivery.

Frankie gathered her towels and gently cleaned the kid and got her ready for the tiny warm bed she'd prepared. For now, though, she let the baby stay near her mama.

Elliott cleared his throat against the silence. "I guess you'll never believe me if I tell you I was going to withdraw my offer."

She patted the tiny kid's head. "You'd guess right, then."

He sighed. "Well, I was."

Without answering, she laid a hand on Isabella's leg, feeling it tense for the second delivery. She shouldn't ask questions. She shouldn't give an inch, because this was Elliott Becker, and he'd charm and flirt and tease and lie his way to forgiveness that she had no intention of giving.

"So why didn't you tell me?" she asked, apparently unable to hear the rational voice in her head.

"I was going to, once I'd...undone my mistake." He leaned closer, but she refused to look. "That's why I didn't...why we didn't..."

"We did enough," she finished for him. Enough for her to feel like they'd had sex and she'd offered him her body...and all the time, he'd known he was trying to steal her land. "Enough for me to be hurt."

"I'm sor—"

She held up her hand and looked at him. "No amount of groveling in the world will allow me to trust you again."

He closed his eyes as if the words had been a direct hit.

"I know this isn't going to change things, Frankie, but—"

"Then don't say it. Just..." She shook her head. "You really don't need to be here."

"I need to explain a few things to you."

She exhaled slowly, peering down to see the next kid just starting to make an appearance.

"My friends, Nate and Zeke, we're joining forces to build a baseball stadium and start a minor-league team here."

Very slowly, she turned her head, the words flowing over her like a bucket of ice. "You wanted to build a baseball stadium on Nonno's Dolce Vita?" Surely he heard the dismay in her voice.

"Actually, the stadium's going to be over there, farther west. This land was for the"—he swallowed hard—"parking lot and access road."

She actually laughed because, how the hell else should she react to that? "Why not the men's room, while you're so busy demeaning my precious legacy of land?"

"But we could change that," he said quickly. "I've been thinking about a way to change that."

"By finding some other piece of land on some other island that's owned by some other unsuspecting, lonely, stupid, easily manipulated female?"

He just stared at her. "You're lonely, Frankie?"

Damn it. "No, I'm not," she ground out. "And notice how you didn't correct 'stupid'?"

"Because I know you're not stupid, but if you are lonely..." He reached for her, and she jerked away as if his hand were made of fire. His beautiful, large, sexy hand that she wanted...

Oh, Lord, have the kid already, Isabella!

"What if we worked the farm into the stadium?"

She blinked at the tiny baby in front of her, barely able to process the question. "Like a seventh-inning stretch and goat parade? What the hell, Becker?"

"I'm serious." He got a little closer, his dark eyes flashing like they did when he had some brilliant, grandiose, ridiculous idea that always ended up being…perfect. "We could have your whole idea for a stone house and a little store, maybe a petting zoo for the kids."

She frowned at him. "You're nuts, you know that?"

"Not if the team were called the Barefoot Bay Bucks. Then the goats would be mascots. It's amazing, don't you think?"

"Certifiable." She shook her head and pointed to Isabella. "Shhh. Here comes another one."

Just as slowly, but with much less drama, a little brown and white face emerged, protected by a shiny bubble. Isabella bleated with relief as the shoulders came through, then the backside. The kid plopped onto the hay with a soft thud.

"Would you look at that?" Elliott whispered. "We had a boy."

She gave a sad smile. "I might be able to keep one."

"Keep this one," Elliott said, putting his arm around her. "Let him be the Barefoot Bay Buck mascot. We can call him—"

"Stop." She cut him off with a harsh look and a sharp bark. "Don't do this anymore!"

"Do what?"

"Make me fantasize and imagine and dream and *want*. You're not real, Elliott A. Becker. You're not genuine. You're a fake. You're working me and toying with me and making me fall for you and then, wham, you'll be gone when the next investment or opportunity or lucky money-making scheme comes your way."

He still stared at her, a world of hurt in his eyes. "No, I won't, Frankie."

She turned away. "You will. Like everyone else, you'll…disappear." Like her parents. Like Nonno. Like any hope of having someone stay forever.

"Only if you want me to."

"I do!" she cried, hating the crack in her voice. "I want you to disappear. *Now*."

Without a word, he pushed up, the only sound the soft whimper of

Isabella's relief and the rustle of hay under his feet. She didn't turn to watch him go, but listened to his footsteps through the shelter, the barks of her dogs, and goodbye nays from the girls.

She stayed very still, petting Isabella and the brand new babies, while the sound of his car engine started, then grew quiet as he left her.

Ozzie came prancing over, barking his displeasure.

"I know, Oz." She kept him away from the stall with one hand, but looked into his sad brown eyes. "I liked him, too." Too much.

Ozzie made a soft harrumph and flattened on the hay, every bit as broken and bereft as Frankie.

Chapter Twelve

Twenty-one.

There were now twenty-one little cotton balls lined up along Frankie's soap-making counter. Three weeks' worth of fragrant messages.

But nothing else.

Agnes and Lucretia flanked her, their pygmy bodies pressed up against Frankie's knees as she neatly sealed the last of the soap bars for the meeting with Jocelyn that would start in less than an hour. Behind her, the doeling and buckling romped, still a little wobbly and high-pitched, alternating between crazy and exhausted every minute of the day.

She'd named the girl Daisy because of the flower-like white splotch on her forehead. And the buck? She hadn't named him yet. Still unsure if she could keep two of them here because of the complicated logistics of two bucks on the same little farm, she refused to let herself fall for him by giving him a name.

She just thought of him as Becker's boy, and that made her think of Becker, and that made her...not completely sad but damn close.

She picked up the cotton ball that had arrived today, hand-delivered by special messenger, who brought one every day when Frankie finished the morning milking. Each one arrived in a plastic box with nothing but a tiny piece of paper bearing a few words.

So now she had twenty-one obscure, impossible messages from Elliott Becker. Was he trying to tell her something or just help her with the soap fragrances he knew she was creating for Casa Blanca?

Hard to say, but with every new arrival, her heart softened ever so slightly. She picked up the one that had arrived today and sniffed it.

The first few had come with names that recapped so much of their time together. The good parts, when they were falling hard and fast. *First Kiss. Intimate Moments. Moonlight Madness. Secret Whispers.*

The following week, his messages reflected the state of her heart with uncanny accuracy. *Tender Ache. Empty Arms. Lonely Days. Sleepless Nights.*

What was he trying to tell her with the complex fragrances and cryptic messages? Each one confused and intrigued and delighted her. No phone calls. No texts. No letters or flowers or emails or postcards.

Just glorious fragrances and mystifying messages.

And this week, the tone had changed again. Now, instead of angst, she got...*Sweet Anticipation. Hopeful Heart. Counting Hours*. And, then, today's, the most perplexing of them all.

Coming Home.

Home? Her heart raced, but she calmed herself with a slow, deep inhale of the sweetest fragrance he'd sent to date. A marvel of vanilla and oak blend, like nothing she'd ever made before.

Maybe he was sending messages, maybe he was trying to help out, maybe he was the world's most creative groveler. She didn't care. The fragrances and names were a gift she gladly accepted. She'd re-created every one up until today's, producing a total of twenty new fragrances and beautifully packaged sets of soap she'd wrapped and ribboned and turned into a celebration of romance. Jocelyn would love these, use these, and sell these like crazy.

She took a sniff of Coming Home. She'd make that, but maybe save it for herself.

Putting the last of the baskets in the back of her truck, she absently ran a hand over Lucretia's soft neck, rewarded with a loopy goat smile.

"Wish me luck, girls."

Before she left she checked on Daisy and...that guy really needed a name. Black and shiny as his father, the little buck had a gleam in his eyes and a constant need for affection. She shouldn't get attached, but she reached down and gave him a hug anyway, his baby fur tickling her cheek.

"You know I'm going to end up calling you Becker and will regret it every time I have to say the name."

He whined noisily and stomped his tiny hooves in response. A chorus of goats guided her to the pen gate, but before she left, Frankie stood and looked at her little homestead. Her home. It was, now. And it was time to build La Dolce Vita. The resort would help get people over here, and she'd already talked to the gardener and head chef about using her goat's milk and selling that, too. First step, today's sale. Then tonight, she'd be...

Coming Home.

Alone.

She climbed in the truck and drove to Casa Blanca, trying to focus her thoughts on the meeting ahead with Jocelyn, a woman she'd grown to like and trust in the past few weeks. Jocelyn had confided that her father was very sick, with advancing Alzheimer's, and her dream was for him to live long enough to see her baby. She'd also shared the story of how she'd forgiven her father for the sins of his past, making Frankie think long and hard about letting go of the misplaced anger she harbored against her parents.

They'd only been trying to do the right thing for her. She had to stop blaming them and their careers for dying and remember that they loved her fully and wholly.

The parking lot of the resort was packed, but that wasn't so much of a surprise. Business in the restaurant, Junonia, was booming, and this late in the day, the promise of a gorgeous sunset brought people all the way from the mainland for cocktails and beach walks. Still, she'd never seen it quite this packed. She had no choice but to use the valet service, otherwise she would have had to cart all those baskets across the lot.

"Here for the event, ma'am?" the valet asked as he opened her door.

"I'm meeting with Jocelyn Palmer, the manager of Eucalyptus."

"No problem, we'll park it for you."

"I need to get those baskets out of the back."

He helped her take them into the lobby, which was even more crowded than the parking lot, with dozens milling about, sipping champagne, and waiters carrying trays of more flutes and food.

"Is there a wedding today?" she asked the valet.

"No, a press conference. ESPN is here!" His eyes bugged with excitement. "There's some big baseball thing. You should see who's here, too. Couple of Yankees, people from the MLB, and..." He leaned closer and looked side to side before lowering his voice. "Nathaniel Ivory is here."

"Oh." She had to get out of here before she saw Becker. Still holding one of the baskets with two hands, she shouldered through the crowd to the double doors of the spa, struggling to figure out a way to get the door and not put down the basket.

Suddenly, someone came up behind her and grabbed the oversized brass handle for her.

The tightening in her chest squeezed until it crushed her heart as she stared at the hand in front of her. Long, strong, tanned, masculine, and far too familiar. A hand she'd held. A hand that had touched her. A hand that—

"Let me help you."

She gathered her wits, took a breath, and looked up to meet the very ebony eyes that haunted her every night.

"You already have," she said, hoisting her basket a little higher, as if it could protect her from the impact of his size and proximity. "Thanks for the poetic and creative ideas."

"I have one more." His voice was low and intimate, and just a little too close for comfort.

"I got today's, thank you."

"One more creative idea. Would you like to hear about it?" Without waiting for her response, he took the basket she carried and opened the door for her, using his whole body to usher her in.

"I would not," she said crisply, walking to the wide receptionist desk. "Hi, I have an appointment with Jocelyn Palmer."

Elliott was right next to her in an instant. "She can't meet with you now. But I can."

The receptionist let out a soft laugh. "Is this the woman you've been asking about?" she asked him.

"This is the one. The one and only."

A totally unwanted and undeniable thrill danced through Frankie as she managed a smile. "But I have an appointment with Jocelyn."

He turned to the other woman and lifted his brows expectantly, giving her a moment to reply.

"Um, I'm afraid she's canceled that, Ms. Cardinale."

"What?"

"Her husband has asked her to be part of the announcement, and they're doing a walk-through meeting in the private dining room right now." She frowned at Elliott. "Aren't you supposed to be in there?"

"I have my own meeting." He put a possessive hand on Frankie's shoulder and gestured toward the hallway that led to the backrooms of the spa. "This way."

She refused to move. "I'm not..." She gave a pleading look to the receptionist. "Can I at least talk to Jocelyn?"

"I'll try and reach her."

"You do that," Elliott said. "We'll be in her office."

He pressed on her back, and Frankie let out a sigh, going toward the doorway she knew led to the spa manager's office.

"Why are you doing this?" she asked.

"I have to show you something." He opened Jocelyn's office door and guided her to the round table in the corner.

For a second, all she could do was stare at what was on the table. It was like...nothing she'd ever seen. She stood there and drank in every precious detail of a three-dimensional model of...a goat farm? She fell into the closest chair, a fine chill exploding over her skin as she tried to process the absolute perfection of the work.

"It's part of today's announcement." He stood behind her and placed his hands on her shoulders.

Questions bubbled up, but before she could ask anything she had to just look at it. Someone brilliant had designed this, someone who'd managed to climb into her imagination—and Nonno's—and create something that was as beautiful as it was functional.

"It's a 3-D scale model, but—"

She held her hand up to silence him, not wanting any more information while she absorbed what was in front of her. Acres of land, with a two-story. stone farmhouse that looked like it had been plucked from the hills of Tuscany perched in one corner, looking out over the expanse of a complex that included a large round pen, a bright red shelter and workhouse, and a precious little storefront surrounded by wooden benches and shade trees. A closed-off petting area filled one side and behind it, a series of larger pens, with a hand-painted sign above them that read: *The Official Mascots of the Barefoot Bay Bucks!*

"That's what we're calling the team," he said, adding some pressure to her shoulders as if he could underscore the importance of that. "So we'd love to expand the whole stadium complex to include this visitors' attraction, which we think the families and kids will love."

"It's..." She reached out and touched the gentle curve of a window dormer on the house, something so precious and inviting, it twisted her heart. "Dreamy." In fact, it was right out of one of her dreams.

"Do you like it?"

She looked up, over her shoulder. "I assume that's a rhetorical question."

He laughed, coming down next to her, taking one knee so they were face-to-face. "You and your ten-dollar words, Francesca. Is this what you want to do with your land? Did I understand what you told me?"

She searched his face, only slightly more appealing to her eyes than the work of art next to her. "Is this supposed to go on my land?"

"That's up to you. This is an optional piece of a master plan that's being announced in"—he glanced at his watch—"fifteen minutes. We can leave this out and build everything to the west of your property, with absolutely no infringement on your land at all. Or..." He took her hands, and only then did she realize she was shaking. All over. "This can be part of the plan."

"Whose plan?"

"Our plan, Frankie." He lifted her hand and pressed her knuckles to his lips, closing his eyes like a wave of relief and joy rocked him. "God, I missed you."

She tried to swallow, but a lump the size of, well, a baseball, filled her throat.

"Frankie, I don't know any way..." He opened his eyes, which were as shockingly damp as hers felt. "I don't know how to tell you in any other way how sorry I am that I hurt you and how much I want"—he inhaled a steadying breath—"a chance to be with you. A chance to hold you and make promises to you and to be completely real with you."

She'd dreamed of this moment, hadn't she? In fact, it was very possible she was dreaming right now.

Just like with Nonno.

Ignoring the quivering of her hand, she lifted her fingers to his face and grazed the rough shadow of whiskers and the smooth curve of his full lower lip. "You seem pretty real," she whispered.

Under her fingertips, he smiled. "I am. And so's this idea. Real and right and..." He blinked and glanced toward the model. "It feels like home."

Her heart slipped around and fell to her stomach. "My home."

"Our—"

She pressed on his lips to stop him. "Don't."

"Why not?"

"Because it will hurt too much when it's over."

"It doesn't have to be over, ever."

"Stop," she pleaded. "You're so good with words, with saying exactly the right thing, with…pretend."

"Said the woman who pretended to be dirt-poor."

"I did not," she shot back. "I'm just me. You never asked for a bank statement, so I never told you. You know how I feel about money. It's the source of all my pain."

He leaned closer, his expression warm and sincere. "Then let me be the source of all your pleasure. And contentment. And whatever else you want in the world, Francesca. Please."

She managed a slow but shaky breath. "What are you asking from me? Permission to use my land?"

"We want you to be a partner in the project. And you'll be in charge of…" He reached under the board that held the model and pulled out a miniature banner that he stabbed into the soft, fake grass. "La Dolce Vita."

The Sweet Life. And wouldn't it be? Couldn't it be? With—"Did you say a partner?"

"I sure did."

She swallowed, her mouth surprisingly dry. "A business partner?"

He took her face in his hands and held her head perfectly still so she couldn't look anywhere but right into his eyes. "A life partner."

The door pushed open, and they both backed away to see Jocelyn, who was equally surprised to find her office full—with a man on one knee. "Oh…oh, did I…Frankie! Did you see what's going on in the lobby?"

Frankie stood, vaguely aware she still held Elliott's hand as he came up with her. "The press conference?"

"Your soaps! Someone opened the baskets you brought and thought they were party favors, and they've been passed around to everyone, and people are asking for more."

"Well, I guess that's—"

"Good marketing," Elliott supplied. "Sorry we stole your office, Joss."

"Not a problem, but your team is looking for you, Elliott. They're ready to start the announcement."

He turned to Frankie, anticipation brightening his eyes. "Are you coming? We can easily bring this and add it to the plan." He lifted the corner of the model to show how light and portable it was.

She opened her mouth to answer, but nothing came out. Should she risk everything on him again? "I don't know," she said, her voice rough. "I need...time. To think."

He pulled her closer, putting a light kiss on her forehead. "The offer is real. Everything is."

With that, he left, nodding to Jocelyn on his way out.

"Please tell me I didn't just interrupt The Big Moment," she said with an awkward laugh when he was gone.

"No, *a* big moment, not *the*." She gave herself a little hug, smiling at the other woman. "I don't know what to do," she admitted, surprising herself with her honesty.

"You want advice from a pregnant woman who's watched her three best friends fall in love like dominoes and did the same thing right after she stepped foot on this island?"

"Really?"

"Kick off your shoes and—"

Frankie held up a hand. "Got it. But..." She turned to the model. "He's so big on grand gestures, I never know if he's real or not."

"Oh, he's real. My husband has been in on a lot of the planning sessions, and he's told me how Elliott's fought for this. The Barefoot Bay Bucks was his idea, and he's paid gazillions to buy land around and adjacent to yours so no one had to touch your farm. And he's masterminded this charity program where a portion of every game ticket sold is going to a foundation he's starting called No Kidding that gives goats to families in Third World countries to help feed them with goat's milk."

She just blinked at her. "I've created a monster. In a good way."

Jocelyn laughed. "He's the butt of their every joke, but he loves it because he loves..." She caught herself. "He's a good guy," she added softly.

"I'm scared." The admission came right from the heart and didn't even surprise her. She was scared. Scared to love and lose again. Scared to trust and believe and hope.

Jocelyn stepped forward with outstretched hands. "You wouldn't be human if you weren't a little afraid. You can't protect yourself from never getting hurt, Frankie. If you try to do that, you'll never live. You'll never know." She gave Frankie a light hug. "I'm going out to the pavilion to watch the show. Want to come?"

"I'll stay here, if you don't mind."

"Think about it," Jocelyn said as she left Frankie alone.

After a moment, Frankie sat down again and stared at the model. It was like he'd climbed into her imagination and her heart and made her dreams come true.

"All *our* dreams, *piccolina*."

She whipped around at the sound, but the room was empty. The door was closed. And she was alone. "Nonno?" A shudder passed through her, and then a complete and thorough sense of peace and comfort.

But there was nothing, no one, not even a flutter in the air. Only the fine line between her imagination and what was *real*.

And then she knew what she had to do.

Chapter Thirteen

Elliott stood to the far side of the makeshift platform stage, next to Zeke and their fourth partner, Garrett Flynn, the three of them content to stay out of the limelight. The media weren't here for anyone but Nate Ivory, who, despite his proclaimed distaste for the spotlight, looked damned at home with a ton of it pouring over him.

The patio of Junonia was full with media and VIP guests, but Elliott's gaze stayed locked on the doors leading into the spa, his every breath strained as he waited for Frankie. All he wanted was a chance to show her what he was made of, what he could be.

But she stayed conspicuously out of sight.

He turned back to the reason they were here, the news of the Barefoot Bay Bucks. In answer to a question about management, Nate explained that he'd be living in Barefoot Bay and supervising the building of the stadium complex and managing the day-to-day logistics of starting a new minor-league team.

"I'm planning to be here a lot, too," Zeke said under his breath. "You?"

Elliott slid him a glance. "Not sure yet."

Zeke tracked his gaze to the spa door. "Did you actually beg?"

"Like a pathetic dog."

"One knee?"

"Till I had carpet burn."

"I can't believe she didn't go for the goat-farm idea."

Elliott blew out a noisy breath. "I messed up so bad, Zeke."

"You never know."

But he knew. He'd taken his usual, easy, effortless shortcut to get what he wanted, and it had cost him everything. He wasn't quite sure when he'd become so certain that Frankie Cardinale was everything, but it didn't matter. She was, so now he had nothing.

Finally, the questions turned away from Nate and back to the Bucks, and the stadium complex, and that brought Will Palmer front and center. Thanks to him, they were well connected with the resort, including the talented architect who'd built the place, Clay Walker. Together with Clay, they answered questions about logistics and environmental concerns, and how to handle the increased traffic this would bring to the island.

All the while, Elliott watched that door, his heart sinking like the sun behind him, lower and lower as each minute ticked by.

"I have to talk to her," he murmured to Zeke.

"Now?"

"I have to." Before Zeke could stop him, he shot to the side of the patio deck, trying to stay inconspicuous as he hustled behind the crowd and jogged down the stairs. He pulled the door and swore softly to find it locked. Without giving it another thought, he set off to find another way back into the resort, determined and certain now. It took a full five minutes to work through the crowd, back into the lobby, and to the front entrance of the spa.

Without even glancing at the receptionist, he marched right into the management offices, yanked the door open, and...stared at nothing.

She was gone and so was the model of La Dolce Vita.

For a second, he couldn't breathe, his pulse slamming against his temples, a band of disappointment clamping his chest. Shaking his head, he stood in the doorway and let the power-punch of regret and disappointment pound him.

He didn't want to live without her, but she clearly felt differently. Taking one step inside, he fought a sting in his eyes and a lump in his throat.

Next time he'd be real. No matter how hard it was, he'd never fake his way through anything again. If nothing else, that's what a week on the goat farm had taught him.

Swallowing the pain and his pride, he turned and retraced his footsteps, all the way through the lobby, into the restaurant, and back to the deck where he heard...

A woman's voice through the microphone?

Stepping into the fading sunshine, he peered over the heads of the guests, to see Nate, Garrett, and Zeke on the stage alongside…Frankie?

"I'm thrilled to partner with the project," she said into the microphone, her voice clear and strong and like music to his ears. "My grandfather was a founding father of this island, and I know he'd be over the moon to see a team named after his beloved animals and this wonderful visitors' center…"

Elliott shouldered his way forward, reaching the front just as Frankie pointed to the table they'd set up with the three-dimensional stadium complex model, this time with the addition of La Dolce Vita.

She met his gaze, smiling through eyes as misty as his felt right then and reached her hand out. "We've been waiting for you."

He stepped forward, taking her hand and joining his partners. All of them.

Nate leaned up to the microphone. "And now for what you've all really been waiting for—the exhibition game! You know we have players from five different Major League teams and our own softball team for a game of sandlot." He pointed to the beach where a large area had been cleared for a makeshift ball game. "And I do mean sand."

A cheer went up, mostly from the other guys on the Niners who'd come down for the event, but Elliott barely heard. Instead, he gripped Frankie's hand.

"Partner?" he asked.

"Not only that," she said with a smile, lifting her hand to slide on a baseball cap with a stylized N. "I qualify to play on your team."

He reached to hug her, but Nate gave his shoulder a slam. "No kissing. We gotta win this game."

"He hates to lose," Elliott told her. "So we'll kiss later."

"Damn right we will, Becker."

"Frankie! You did it!" A beautiful young woman sidled up to Frankie, her arms outstretched. "I'm so happy for you!"

Frankie hugged her, laughing. "Thanks for breaking the rules, Liza." She turned to Elliott. "You remember Liza Lemanski, the great unraveler of red tape."

In a flash, Nate was next to him, his focus on the beautiful blue-eyed brunette. "I like a woman who can unravel."

Liza didn't giggle or flush or toss her hair like most women when Nate Ivory zeroed in on them. Instead, she pinned him with a dead-serious look. "Good," she said. "Because I've come to do a little unraveling."

Elliott looked skyward and finally got his arm around Frankie, pulling her into him and taking her down to the beach. "What changed your mind?" he whispered when they were finally alone on the sand.

"Nonno."

"You think he would have liked the idea?"

"I know he does." She smiled up at him. "He told me."

"He did?" Elliott raised his brows. "What else did he say?"

She turned, the sunset behind her a golden glow, her dark hair falling over one eye under the ball cap, her smile lit up from deep in her heart. "You're the real deal."

He let out a sigh and pulled her into his chest. "I been trying to tell you that."

"I had to figure it out for myself." She kissed him long and hard, and rested her head on his shoulder. "You really want to be a goatherd, Becker?"

"You really want to spend your life with a billionaire, Francesca?"

She smiled up at him. "Yeah. Come on, let's play."

Arm in arm, they walked together toward home base.

Scandal on the Sand

Dedication

Dedicated to faithful reader, avid fan, and dear friend
Ramona "Mona" Kekstadt who deserves her own umbrella
on the sands of Barefoot Bay!

Chapter One

I was her eyes. As soon as Nate caught a glimpse of the arresting color, somehow both impossibly ocean blue and bottle green, he had to talk to the woman, listening carefully as she was introduced to one of his friends.

"You remember Liza Lemanski, the great unraveler of red tape."

He didn't waste a second moving closer, getting a whiff of a barely-there citrus scent. "I like a woman who can unravel," he said with a wink.

"Good." When she turned to him, her turquoise gaze held no hint of playfulness. "Because I've come to do a little unraveling."

His friend made some kind of parting jab, reminding Nate that he was up third in the exhibition softball game that was about to start, but Nate's attention was on the beauty in front of him. "So, who's getting unraveled, blue eyes?" he asked.

"You."

Nice. "And I like a woman who doesn't mess around."

"That's not what I hear." She still wasn't smiling, making him wonder if the comment was a flirt or not. "We need to talk, Mr. Ivory."

That would be...*not.* Did he know her and forget those gorgeous eyes? Anything was possible, of course. With him, everything was possible. Or used to be.

How long would his past mistakes haunt him? Was he about to get an earful of how he'd made promises he'd never kept or taken phone numbers he'd never used or...worse? It could always be worse. Instantly, he felt his protective privacy walls rise like titanium barriers as he automatically reached for the sunglasses in his pocket.

"Sure, sure, let's talk after the game." Slipping them on, he took all the humor out of his tone and a step in the other direction.

She came with him, shaking back some long dark hair to make sure he could see she meant business. "Let's talk now."

"It'll only be three innings and then we're having a cocktail party at sea. We can unravel anything you want." He lifted his hand in a halfhearted wave goodbye.

"I prefer *now*."

Damn. He glanced around the large beachfront deck where he had just finished the press conference announcing the plan to launch a minor-league baseball team in Barefoot Bay. But no one came to his rescue. His business partners were already headed toward the sand for the softball game they'd put together to cap off the media event.

"Sorry, I gotta run. I'm batting cleanup."

"Yes, you are. Right this minute. With me."

Pushy little thing, wasn't she? Protected by reflective lenses, he let his gaze drift over her, lingering on fine cheekbones and lush lips that hadn't yet given him a real smile. Farther down, things got even better, with generous cleavage peeking out of a V-neck T-shirt and a tiny waist and soft curves under her jeans. She couldn't be five-four and a hundred and ten soaking wet.

"What's this about?" he asked, getting a sense that it *wasn't* about seeing her soaking wet, either.

"I need your signature."

"Oh." Relief washed through him as he let out the breath he'd been holding since he heard the edge in her voice. "You want an autograph?"

"No, I want your *signature*."

He didn't like the sound of that. "Listen, sweetheart, I have to play a ball game. So, later's better." Later, he'd be surrounded by his rec softball team and some pro ballplayers, safe from any accusations, suggestions, or sob story she might fling at him.

"Over here." She gestured toward an empty table that the wait staff of the Casa Blanca Resort & Spa had already cleared. Everyone had disappeared to the beach to watch the game.

Which was where he suddenly wanted very much to be.

"Whatever it is, make it fast." He purposely took all tease from his tone. She was hot, no doubt about it, but for some reason he smelled big trouble in this little package.

She responded by scraping a chair over the wooden deck as she pulled it out...*for him*. He stayed where he was while she took the other chair and opened up a large handbag.

"Okay...Liza." He rolled the name on his tongue, taking time to appreciate the sassy and sexy sound of it and wishing she were a little more of both.

"I really think you're going to want to be sitting down for this," she said.

"What do you have?" Irritation prickled his spine at her icy tone. Irritation and worry. He'd sworn on his life that there wouldn't be any more scandals, no more headlines, no more sexts that made their way to Perez Hilton's blog. Oh, that had been a bad week. The Colonel had *not* been amused.

She snapped a large manila envelope on the table.

"Pictures?" he guessed with a mirthless snort. "How original." Every stinking blackmailing female in a nightclub had their secret cell phone shots. Which was why he'd sworn off the club scene along with the rest of his far-too-active social life.

When she didn't answer, he ventured closer. "Oh, don't tell me, TMZ has offered five figures." He could only imagine what she had. "Let me guess. You've got 'Naughty Nate' bare-ass naked in Vegas or Cabo. He's got a joint in one hand and a fifth of Tito's in the other. Some dot-com billionaire's wife is grabbing his johnson, and they're about to fall into a hot tub with four more blondes."

Sickening that he could describe that situation a little too clearly. Swallowing a wave of self-loathing, he watched her slide a packet of papers onto the table, along with a spiral notebook.

What the—

"Nate! You're on deck!"

He ignored the announcement, hollered from the sand, instead dropping into the chair next to her.

"So, how much?" he demanded, a sixth sense already telling him what was going down here. The question went against everything he'd been taught as a member of a family with the iconic—and ironic—last name of *Ivory*. A family that was anything but pure and had trained all members that the first check was just that...the *first*. A blackmailer never went away.

But he absolutely refused to get embroiled in one more public mess and, damn it, if he had to pay to get rid of her, he would. Whatever it took to prove that he was worthy of the family name and…the chance to see that dark disapproval erased from his grandfather's eyes.

"I don't want money," she finally said.

Then what? Access to the Hollywood studio his older brother ran? A meeting with his other brother, the senator? Maybe insider-trading information from his cousin on Wall Street?

"Everybody wants something, Liza," he said on a sigh. Especially from an Ivory.

For the first time, the closest thing to a sweet expression settled on her lovely features. Her lips finally relaxed into a hint of a smile. Dark brows unfurrowed, and a slight blush of pink deepened her creamy complexion.

"Yes, everybody does want something," she whispered. "And I want you to sign this document." She slid the paper toward him. "And then I will go away and you can play softball and drink in Cabo with other guys' wives and have cocktails *under* the sea, for all I care." She flattened him with a dead-eyed look. "Sign, and I promise you will never see or hear from me again."

He had to slide off his shades to read the paper, blinking at the legalese, his name typed neatly in the blanks. And…*Dylan Cassidy, age four.*

"Who's Dylan?"

"Your son."

The words slammed like a power-punch to his temple, and for a second he actually saw stars. A *kid*? He'd been so careful. His whole freaking adult life, he'd been so damn careful about this. Very slowly, he lifted his gaze from the page to her face, digging like a dog in dirt for a shred of a recollection of this woman, a date, a night, an encounter, a damn quickie in the back room of a party.

Nothing.

"I don't even remember you," he said, the words sounding as jagged as they felt. How wasted had he been to forget this girl?

"Of course you don't remember me," she said. "I've never met you."

"But…this…" He tried to focus on the paper again, but a slow fire of horror sparked in his gut and rolled up to burn his chest as the words stopped dancing in front of his eyes. *Voluntary Termination of Parental Rights.* "This isn't a paternity suit?"

"No, this is my guarantee that I can live in complete peace without an ax hanging over my head."

What the hell? "I'm confused. Do you mind explaining what you are talking about?"

"I want you to sign this so that I don't wake up some morning and find out the Ivory family is out to take Dylan away from me."

"You said he…we…" He let out a puff of pure frustration. "I don't get this at all. If I'm signing away rights to your child, how can I have never met you?"

"I'm not his mother." She nudged the paper closer. "Not that you care about her or have bothered to check, but his mother is dead, and I'm his legal guardian. And all you need to do is sign right there, and I'll handle the rest of the red tape. As you heard, I'm good at that."

Dead? Was she saying this boy was an *orphan*? Another cascade of unfamiliar emotions squeezed some air out of his lungs, but he forced himself to breathe and get to the facts, starting with the obvious. "Who is his mother?"

Her expression was total surprise, followed by a resigned shrug. "I suppose more than one woman has told you she's pregnant in your lifetime. Her name was Carrie Cassidy."

Slowly, he shook his head to say he'd never heard that name in his life. "What happened to her?" Maybe that would jog his memory.

"She was in a car accident a year ago and died almost instantly." She held out a pen. "Please. Make it easy on all of us."

Easy? Nothing about this conversation was easy.

She leaned forward and speared him with her jewel-toned gaze. "She left enough details about how you dumped her, penniless and pregnant, to fill a whole issue of the *National Enquirer*. Imagine the headline: *Nathaniel Ivory, Deadbeat Baby Daddy*."

It didn't take much of an imagination to visualize how well that issue would sell.

She was right about one thing—signing would be easy. Two scratches of a pen and he could go play softball and drink scotch and live his life. No scandal, no problems, no…

No way.

"I'm not signing anything."

Close. She was so close that every cell in Liza's body was quivering, but somehow she managed to keep her cool. Finally facing Nathaniel Ivory, after eleven months of planning for this moment, she wasn't about to let him know that her insides were mush and her heart was exploding against her ribs and she could throw up from the nerves. She couldn't let him know how much this mattered or that she was totally bluffing about the *Enquirer* because...she wouldn't dream of dragging Dylan through mud like that.

She was doing this *for* Dylan, who was everything to her.

"What's in that notebook?" Nate asked, attempting to reach for it, but she snatched it away.

"No, you don't."

"I knew you were lying." He spat out the accusation with disgust.

"I'm not lying!" She clutched the book, holding it to her chest. "You could take this and run. I'm not letting you have it."

"Run? Run where? To the beach? Who *is* this dead woman and what fiction did she write in that book? What proof do you have? Have you ever heard of DNA testing? Do you really think I'm going to sign something without answers? You think I can't smell the stink of your scam from a mile away?" The questions came at her like bullets from an automatic rifle, each one lodging in her throat and chest and gut. "Forget the pretend mother and bogus baby, what is *your* deal, Liza Lemanski?"

Oh, she'd been so close. She saw the moment he'd wavered and nearly signed the document. Almost but not quite there...like everything in her life. And now he thought she was a con artist. Great.

"My deal is that you sign this paper." *Stay on point, Liza. Don't let him sway you.*

"Why now?" he asked. "Didn't you say she died a year ago? And this alleged son is four? What took so long to collect your cash, huh?"

"I'm not..." She shook her head. "You told her you wouldn't help her, and I didn't know you were the father until she died and left me as his guardian. I'm not scared of you or your family like she was." A white lie, but she had to appear strong. "I want a clean slate as I start the formal adoption process, so, please"—she tapped the paper—"let me have that and that will be the end of this."

"And you come up to me at the end of a press conference and throw this at me?"

"I read in the local paper that you'd be here this morning and I..."

Called in sick, grabbed the papers she already had prepared—working in the County Clerk's office did have its advantages—and put her plan into action.

"Why not approach my lawyer? That's how things like this are done."

"I thought it would be—"

"Easier to extort money."

"I don't *want* money." She fisted her hand, punching the air. "And I know you don't want a child."

"How do you know anything about me?"

Holding the brightly colored spiral notebook, she picked at the half-peeled $3.99 Ross price tag on the back. "It's all in here, your name, your description, your words to her. But when you read all that, I have to be sure this book is protected. It's all I have to prove my case."

"Then maybe you don't have much of a case."

"Oh, I have a case. And I have a child who..." *Looks a hell of a lot like you.* "Who I want to keep, without living in fear that someone is going to try to claim him."

"So you've said." He inched forward. A lock of chestnut hair fell over his brow, close to the golden-brown eyes that looked so much like...like Dylan's. "What do you *really* want, honey, because I don't believe a word you're saying."

Tiny beads of perspiration stung at her neck and temples, her cool slipping with each second that she had to face him. "I want that child. I want him safe and protected with me."

Something flickered in his eyes, a flash that went by so fast she wasn't positive she'd seen it, but she knew she'd hit some kind of emotional hot button.

"And you don't," she added, because what if *that* was the hot button she'd hit? What if he wanted a child? "It says so right here." She tapped Carrie's journal, maybe a little harder than necessary. "It says a lot of things about you that I don't think you want out in public."

Hollow threat, of course, but still she threw that trump card down again, hoping it would work. Surely a man with his lifestyle, money, and famously documented inability to commit didn't want a child he'd fathered almost five years ago.

Did he?

"Hey, Nate!"

Startled at the man's voice, Liza turned to see Zeke Nicholas, one of the other men who'd been involved in the announcement today, jogging across the patio deck, impatience darkening his expression. "You missed your at bat, man. Come on!"

Nate held up his hand and shook his head.

"'Scuse me," Zeke said to Liza as he reached the table. "But I have to steal this heartthrob for just a—"

"Shut it, Zeke!" Fury sparked in Nate's eyes, but he didn't take them off Liza, making her certain his anger was not directed at his friend.

Zeke froze midstep. "Everything okay here?"

"We're fine," Liza said, seizing the opportunity. "I'm getting Mr. Ivory's autograph." Not that she had any real hope left that he'd sign, but maybe with his friend here, he'd buckle. It was worth a shot. "Right here, sir. And then you'll make the second inning."

His nostrils flared as he took a slow breath and shook his head. "You have to play without me, Zeke." Suddenly, he stood, gathering up the papers and the envelope in one swooping motion. "Liza and I are going somewhere more private."

She didn't move but glanced at Zeke, who seemed as surprised as Liza was. "So we should meet you on board the yacht later, for cocktails?"

Nate shook his head. "Sorry, the party's canceled. Come on, Liza." He reached for her hand, and when she didn't take his, he closed his fingers over her wrist to gently pull her up. "I can't wait one more minute to get you alone."

Zeke looked skyward. "So much for 'the new Nate.'"

"Go play softball," he said through clenched teeth. "I've got something more important to deal with."

With a stiff nod, Zeke left, but Liza held her ground. "I'm not going anywhere with you."

"We're not talking about this here, out in the open with staff running around. Any one of them could be recording this conversation on a cell phone."

She glanced at the busboy who openly stared at Nate as he slowed purposely by their table. He was right, of course. Everyone was interested in his business.

"Look." He leaned closer, the low tenor of his voice practically vibrating the air between them. "I don't know you or this kid or this Carrie character from Adam. But if you think I'm putting my name on anything without details and dates, along with legal, scientific, and medical proof, you're out of your mind. Let's go."

She pressed the notebook to her heart, a flimsy four-dollar shield against his billion-dollar onslaught. "I have all that. And there's no doubt of paternity."

He tried to usher her away from the table. "Oh, there's plenty of doubt. I'm not stupid, and I don't make mistakes when I mess around with strangers."

"You're calling her a stranger? Your lover for almost two months until you found out she was pregnant and dumped her?"

His eyes widened, then he shook his head with a soft, sarcastic laugh. "I've heard some pretty creative scams, honey, really, I have. But I gotta hand it to you. This is good. Innovative, complex, and ballsy." He had the nerve to give her a salacious grin and openly check her out from head to toe, sending a completely unwanted awareness through her. "And all wrapped up in a hot little package with sex-kitten eyes and my kind of rack. It's good, kid. It's good."

Sex kitten? Kid? His kind of *rack*?

What had Carrie been thinking when she fell for this tool? "Nothing about this is innovative or ballsy and, honestly, the story isn't that complex. Let me spell it out for you."

"Not here."

"Right here, and right now."

Another waiter walked by, slowing his steps, and glancing in their direction.

"Okay, okay," she finally gave in, walking with him off the deck to the beach, to the opposite side of where the game was being played. When they were completely out of earshot of anyone else, she took a breath of salt-infused air, mustering up momentum for her power-plea. But her sandals sank into soft sand, giving him even more of a height advantage.

She refused to cower.

"Listen to me," she said. "You can deny this all you want or pretend you never heard of her or claim you're too smart to make a mistake. But the facts are simple: Carrie had your child after you made it perfectly clear you wanted no part of a baby, and she spent three years in fear that you'd find her and claim him. She lived with me since she arrived in Florida, pregnant and unemployed, and became my best friend. She was killed by a drunk driver on I-75 a year ago and left me guardianship of her child, whom I plan to legally adopt and raise. I can't do that until I know for sure and certain you will never try to take him away from me. What's *ballsy* about that?"

"Where does the money come in?" he asked with no hesitation.

"I don't *want* money," she repeated on an exasperated sigh. Was that so hard for him to understand? "I want freedom and peace of mind and my...this...Dylan." She swallowed as she said his name. "I want Dylan." Safe, close, happy. That's what she wanted. "Honestly, that's all I've ever wanted since the day a cop showed up at my door and told me Carrie was dead."

He had the decency to at least feign sympathy. "Sorry, but..." He reached for the notebook, tugging it from her fingers. "Let me see that. Let me—"

Something slipped out of the pages, fluttering to the sand. He stooped down and snagged it as she did the same, their heads tapping lightly. He got the picture before she did, but Liza had a second to see it was the photo of Dylan she'd slipped into the back of the journal.

She reached for it, instantly protective, even of his photo. "That's—"

"Me," he finished, staring at it, still crouched down.

"No, I took that..." Her voice faded as she realized what he was saying. "Yeah, he looks like you. So much for an innovative and complex scam for money, huh?"

Staring at the photo, he let his backside drop onto the sand to sit. "He's an Ivory," he whispered, awe and disbelief and recognition making his voice thick.

She plopped down next to him. "What do you think I've been trying to tell you?"

"That changes everything."

Her heart plummeted. "How?"

"I have to..." He struggled with the words, and her brain raced to fill in the blank. Meet him? Take him? Claim him? What did he have to do now that he didn't want to do years ago when Carrie told him she was pregnant?

He exhaled. "I have to see that journal. Somewhere completely private."

"We can walk on the beach."

He shook his head and pointed his thumb at the baseball game behind him. "They'll come after me. Where do you live?"

"Too far and..." She didn't want him there. "No, let's go inside and sit at a table or in the lobby."

He gave her a funny look, slowly shaking his head as he stood, still looking at the picture. "You don't understand. I can't do that. People know me. They take pictures. They approach me. Let's just..." He gestured for her to follow him. "I have an idea."

But she didn't move, looking up at him, feeling so small and helpless and frustrated and scared. "Are you going to take him from me?" she managed to ask.

He reached down and took her hand, his silence almost worse than if he'd said yes.

Chapter Two

Blackmail would have been better, Nate thought as he maneuvered his Aston Martin through the narrow streets of Mimosa Key, headed for the harbor where he had a shot at relative privacy. She'd agreed to come along, clinging to her precious notebook.

Blackmail he could handle. The family was used to that sort of thing. But a four-year-old child whose mother—with a name he'd never heard in his life—was dead and left nothing but a journal? This was big. This was problematic. This was life-changing, and not in the way he wanted his life to change.

But...

He's an Ivory.

The family sure had some powerful, unstoppable genes, and Nate had spent enough time with cousins to know an Ivory when he saw an Ivory. And mistakes happen, obviously, so nothing was impossible.

But no one told him! He never left anyone *penniless* and *pregnant*.

A sensation he couldn't name, didn't understand, and already hated welled up in him. A bunch of them, to be fair. Anger, fear, frustration, and disbelief coiled around his gut. What if he had *inadvertently* done something like that? What if this claim was real?

Next to him, Liza had situated herself as close to the opposite side of the sports car as she could be without actually riding outside. Silent, she stared straight ahead, gnawing her lower lip and clutching that cheap notebook like it was the crown jewels.

Well, in some ways, it was. Maybe it held information that could get her a lot of money. That had to be her game, with the strategy of acting like it wasn't. Hell, at this point, he *hoped* that was her game, despite her vehement denials.

He'd far prefer a little friendly extortion to *fatherhood*.

Who was this woman claiming to have had a relationship with him? He broke the silence after about five minutes. "Carrie…Cassidy, did you say?"

"Her real name was Careen. Does that help?"

Not a bit. "I have absolutely no recollection of meeting a woman named Carrie or Careen or Cassidy, let alone sleeping with her. Let alone spending *months* with her. I don't spend months with my best friends, let alone…women."

"So I've heard. And read."

He slid her another look, trying to see past the intriguing eyes and waves of thick, dark hair to the villainess underneath. But all he saw was a great-looking woman chewing a hole in her lower lip, her arms wrapped around her chest protectively, popping some luscious cleavage out of her T-shirt.

He returned his attention to the road. He would not be diving into that particular weakness of his anytime soon. "So tell me everything about this so-called Carrie."

She let go of that lower lip, whipping around, eyes flashing like the Sri Lankan green sapphires that decorated the backsplash of his master bath.

"So-called?" She flung the words back at him. "Carrie Cassidy was a living, breathing, lovely young woman who died far too young. And she's the mother of your child, so show some respect, for God's sake."

"All right, all right." Once again, he rooted around his memory banks, many of those vaults pickled by substances he'd recently sworn off. "Where'd I meet her? When and how?"

"In Key West, about five years ago."

Five years ago he'd been twenty-five, living off a generous trust fund, ridiculously wild, a bona fide jet-setter who went from party to party on any continent, with any socialite, without a moment's concern about tomorrow. He did not, however, stick his dick *anywhere* without a condom. He might be reckless, but he wasn't dumb, and he'd heard enough lectures from brothers and cousins.

So, had he been in Key West that year? That was possible, even probable. He went there on a regular basis. Had he had sex with a girl there? Likely enough. But hadn't she said something about being with her for months?

"So, she claims we dated for two months?" he asked as he turned into the harbor parking lot.

"You were lovers," she corrected. "And there's no 'claiming' involved."

Definitely a lie. "I can guarantee you if I was hanging out with someone that long term, I'd remember."

She made a grunt of disgust.

"What? I'm being honest."

"Listen to yourself. Two months is a long-term relationship, and calling what you did with Carrie 'hanging out' sounds so…" She closed her eyes and shook her head, unable to come up with something awful enough to describe him.

So he helped. "Cavalier? Uncommitted? Casual? Apathetic? Detached? I've heard them all, my dear, and every single one is true."

"Have you heard 'asshole,' too?"

He bit back a chuckle. "What do you think?"

"I think…" She turned away and looked out the window as he slid the car into a parking spot. "I hope none of those things are hereditary."

The sadness in her voice did something to his insides that he didn't like at all. He chose to ignore it. "Don't count on it," he said. "Those traits are stamped into the Ivory DNA."

"Or you're raised that way."

"Hard to say," he agreed.

"Which is exactly why I don't want Dylan raised like that. I don't want him part of that greedy, egomaniacal, power-hungry clan."

Her words shot a jolt of defensiveness up his spine. He turned off the car, flipped his belt, and reached for the door handle. Before he opened it, he flattened her with a look to underscore the warning he was about to give.

"Here's the rule, Liza. I can insult my family, but no one else can." Without waiting for her response, he opened the door and stepped into the February sunshine, which was plenty warm this far south. Instantly, she popped up on the other side.

"Well, here's *my* rule: I don't want Dylan to be, what was it you called yourself? Apathetic and cavalier and isolated?"

"I said *detached*. I'm not isolated."

She glanced around. "Then why are we here?"

"My boat is private." And isolated. He started walking toward the last

254

slip, where he'd docked. Liza had to hurry to catch up, shouldering her bag. He reached the twenty-eight-foot cabin cruiser, and when he turned to offer her a hand, he found her eyeing the boat suspiciously.

"I'd hardly call this a yacht."

"Neither would I," he agreed, purposely saying no more as he helped her on board and then unlocked the doors to the lounge inside.

"Can't we sit out here?" she asked, pointing to the leather sofas and captain's chairs on the deck.

He shrugged, though it was more comfortable inside with the living room and bar. But he felt relatively alone and safe, since very few people knew he'd rented this slip, so he sat across from her and reached out his hand.

"Give me that journal, please."

She looked back at him. "Are you going to throw it overboard?"

"No."

"Promise?"

"I swear, and my word is good."

Even in the sunlight, he could see the color wash from her face, and very slowly, she took out the maroon and pink notebook. He opened the cover, and the first thing he saw was another picture, this one of a woman holding a baby. Blond, blue-eyed, with pixie-like features and a sunny smile.

"That's Carrie, right after Dylan was born." She stood near him—maybe planning to dive in if he tossed the book—looking at the same picture.

He studied the woman's features, angling the photo so he could get every detail. And then something clicked. Something cleared. Something snapped into place like a puzzle piece.

Carrie? "No, not Carrie," he said, peering at her face, digging through a faded memory. "Her name is..." He closed his eyes, pulling the moment from the past. Yes, it was Key West. It was crazy. It was... "Bailey."

Liza lowered herself to the bench to sit next to him. "No, her name is not Bailey."

"Bailey Banks. I remember because she said she was named after a jewelry store, and I looked it up after...after..." After they had sex in the back of a limo. Fast, furious, forgettable sex. "I wanted to find her again, but I..." He shook his head, remembering the real frustration at the time. "No one knew her. I tried to find her. I asked around, but no one had ever seen her before. She must have crashed the party, and the number she gave me was bogus. I never heard from her again, and I wanted to."

And not because she was a good time. Not at all. Bailey Banks had been camera-happy, and that had scared the shit out of Nate, even back then before Instagram and Twitter. Right before she slipped out of the limo, she laughingly waved her camera and told him she'd had a video running the whole time.

So I never forget this night with Naughty Nate! Her parting shot was crystal clear in his vodka-soaked memory.

The next day, sober enough to be scared spitless, he went searching for the woman and her camera, but came up empty-handed on both. Eventually, he'd forgotten she existed, and no videos ever surfaced.

"That's not her version of the events at all." Liza gestured to the notebook. "You better read that."

"Are there more, um, pictures of her?" Or *him*?

"I have a few at home. Pictures I took."

"But no others? No pictures or…anything?"

She shook her head, and he took another look at the photo, everything from that night coming back to him, decadent moment by decadent moment. Bailey Banks. She'd been easy, sexy, and more than a little starstruck. And, of course, he'd taken advantage of that.

Self-loathing rose like bile, but he tamped it down. He was better now, different, and on the right road.

Wasn't he?

"I remember some of her story," he said. "She told me she ran away from home at fifteen."

Liza looked at him like he had two heads. "She didn't run away at fifteen. She was raised in Arizona, an only child, and close to her parents, who, as you know, because you *went to their funeral,* died in a fire. "

What the *hell*? "Someone is on crack," he said. "You or her. But I never went to anyone's funeral in Arizona."

"Read the notebook," she finally said, pushing up from the bench.

He didn't answer, but something was not right. Something was so not right with this picture. Nate leaned back and turned the page, to the picture of a boy who could have been him twenty-five years ago. "Let's see what we've got here."

Other than a big, fat mess.

Liza knew every word in that book. Every turn of phrase, every scrawled sentence, every gut-wrenching emotion that spilled out like Carrie's tears, every time she mentioned Nathaniel Ivory's name. The account of a naïve and innocent girl's relationship with a rich, famous, heartless bastard wasn't very long, maybe fifteen handwritten pages, but it made for good reading.

If you like fantasies with unhappy endings.

While he read, Liza walked around the deck of the boat, trying not to watch him, and failing a few times. She heard the pages flip, quickly, so she occasionally turned to catch a glimpse of him, bent over the notebook.

Any other time, any other circumstance, and she'd react like, well, like any other woman. He was easily six-one or six-two, with strong, square shoulders and the kind of chest a woman wanted to…rest against. Or explore with two hands. His face was classically handsome, with thick brows and a Roman nose, and a hint of shadow where his whiskers grew.

Easy wit, a sexy smile, and dark topaz eyes all attracted her more than she wanted to admit. But attraction wasn't an option…she needed that signature and then, just as she said, she never wanted to see him again.

He flipped the next page harder than the time before.

Did the truth make him angry? Unless…Carrie had lied.

No. Impossible. Carrie was sweet, simple, kind, loving, and guileless. The day she'd walked into Liza's cubicle at the County Clerk's office to apply for a job, the young woman nearly collapsed, whispering her secret that she was broke and expecting. And Liza had instantly liked her and soon loved her like the sister she never had.

In the following three and a half years, Carrie had never once revealed who Dylan's father was, except to say his family was powerful enough to scare her. But after she died, Liza found the notebook and finally understood just how powerful that family was. Her friend's secrecy and fears made complete sense.

According to what she wrote, Carrie worried that Nate would find her and change his mind about the baby. The journal filled in some holes and confirmed the hints that Carrie had dropped all along.

Right? Or had Carrie made the whole thing up?

"I don't know what to believe anymore," Liza whispered to herself as she stepped into the lounge area of the boat. Which was as visually stunning as the golden-eyed god who owned it.

Every piece of furniture and decor was a different shade of cream, covered in leather, suede, or marble, with masculine touches of gleaming teak. No surprise, money oozed from every corner, a testament to the famous Ivory family fortune.

He seemed to think money was all she wanted. Well, it would be nice if he wanted to throw a thousand into a college fund for Dylan, sure. But what she wanted—freedom from worry—was priceless.

"I read it."

She turned to find him standing in the glass sliders that separated the deck from the lounge, an unreadable emotion etched on his strong cheekbones and square jaw. Unless *ice cold* was an emotion, then she could read it just fine.

"This is complete and utter fiction. You know that, don't you? Pure fabrication."

Right now, she didn't know anything. "You said you recognized her when you saw her picture. You met in Key West. You...you had...you slept with her, didn't you?"

He huffed a soft breath and dropped onto one of the creamy sofas, tossing the notebook next to him. Liza stayed standing.

"Here's what's true," he said. "And I'm happy to swear on a stack of Bibles or in a court of law or whatever you want me to do that will make this legit."

What she wanted to "make this legit" was for him to sign and disappear forever. Both possibilities were becoming more remote with each passing minute. "Just be honest," she said. "And tell me your side of the story."

He nodded a few times, gathering his thoughts. "If your Carrie and this girl I recognize as Bailey are really the same person?" With his left hand, he flipped the cover of the book, opening to her picture. "I think they are. So, then about three paragraphs of this is true. I met her at a party, exactly as it says here, in the driveway of a beach house a friend of mine owns. She thought I was the valet, and I let her think that for a few minutes. It was funny, we flirted, exactly like she said. A few minutes later, she saw me inside and we had a good laugh, exactly like she said.

We had a few drinks and talked, exactly like she said."

"She called it love at first sight."

He closed his eyes. "I would categorize it as mutual attraction that led to lust. Nothing remotely like love took place."

Assuming a man like him even knew what love was. "And you took her home and were with her when she got the call about her parents that night, right?"

Very slowly, he shook his head. "That's not what happened."

She waited, crossing her arms and leaning against the bar.

"I did take her home. At least, I had my limo drop her off after we..." He swallowed, hard, then met Liza's gaze. "We, uh, got intimate in the back of the limo."

She lifted a brow. "Intimate?"

"We had sex," he said bluntly. "Wholly consensual, lightning-fast, and utterly meaningless sex."

Each word was like a hammer striking a nail into her heart. Was that how Dylan was conceived? That certainly wasn't Carrie's story.

"I dropped her off at an apartment building, but she wouldn't even let me walk her to the door," he continued. "She gave me her number and disappeared." A new kind of pain etched across his handsome features. "I swear to God I tried to find her, and it was like she was vapor. Bogus number, didn't live in that apartment, didn't know anyone at the party. She was gone." He cleared his throat and continued. "So that part she wrote about the phone call from the fire department in Tucson? Fiction. At least, it wasn't *me* with her that night, holding her, arranging for a private plane to get her home. Never happened."

Of all the possible responses she'd played out in her mind, Liza never expected this. Never expected the journal to be a half-truth.

"The trip to France?" she asked. "The vacation with your family? The two weeks at your place in Hawaii? The hot-air balloon ride when you said you loved her?"

With each question, his head slowly moved from side to side. "Never happened."

Her legs couldn't hold her anymore, so Liza finally eased into the closest chair, sinking into the buttery leather with a barely audible sigh. "Are you saying that whole whirlwind affair was a...lie?"

"That account of our relationship in that notebook is a story, a fabrication, a complete work of fiction," he said carefully. "Yes, I think I know this woman and, yes, we had sex. With a condom," he added. "What did she tell you?"

"She never..." She cleared her throat, having a feeling this wasn't going to get her the signature she needed and wanted. "She never actually told me your name."

It was his turn to stare in disbelief. "So you're basing this entire thing on some teenager's attempt at a bad romance novel? A woman who has, as far as we know, at least two names."

"She wasn't a teenager." But she wasn't much more than that. "I saw her legal document, and I know her name was Careen Cassidy. And Dylan looks like you."

He lifted a shoulder and nodded. "I'll give you that. But it could be a coincidence."

"And you did have sex with her."

"I had sex with a girl who had a different name and looks a little like that one in the picture." He leaned forward. "How well do you know this Carrie person?"

Ire shot through her. *This Carrie person* had been dear to her. "Well. Very well. We lived together, and I was in the hospital room when Dylan was born, and I've helped raise him."

"How did you meet her?"

"She applied for a job at the County Clerk's office when I worked in personnel, and we hit it off in the interview." Carrie's sob story had ripped Liza's heart out, and she'd invited the poor girl to stay with her until she found an apartment...and she'd never left. "We became really good friends and, well, she needed help and—"

"But not such good friends that she'd tell you who fathered the baby?"

The truth jabbed at her. "She told me you—he—had made it clear you didn't want anything to do with the baby, and she'd rather forget about you."

His eyes flashed. "I never told anyone anything like that, because we never had another conversation after I dropped her off at an apartment complex that night," he insisted, his voice rising with impatience. "She made it all up."

Was that possible? Inside, way down low in her belly, Liza grew cold and afraid. Had she been such a pushover that Carrie lied from day one? She'd always had a soft spot for strays, and she had the four cats to prove it. But everyone who met Carrie loved her, even Liza's mother, who didn't usually love anyone if they didn't have access to the right country club.

"What about the notebook?" he asked. "Where did it come from?"

"I found it hidden in her belongings after she died. When I read it, I realized just how rich and powerful a family she'd meant when I saw the name Ivory."

"And it didn't occur to you that this whole story was a product of her imagination?"

She shook her head, feeling incredibly vulnerable and foolish. "What occurred to me was that, if I could find you, I could get you to sign a TPR, er, a Termination of Parental Rights waiver, which is what I had urged her to do all along. I work with legal documents every day. I know they carry tremendous weight in court, and if you don't have them in order, it could come back to haunt you."

He didn't answer for a moment, his gaze on the picture that faced up. "Was she drunk?"

Liza blinked at him, the question throwing her. "Excuse me?"

"When she died. You said it was an accident on the highway. Was she drunk?"

She almost laughed. "I never saw Carrie drink anything stronger than iced tea. She was insanely healthy and, for your information, she never even went on a date in the time we were roommates. I tried to fix her up with a friend once, and she refused. She said Dylan was her only man."

That indiscernible flicker of emotion passed over his face again. He looked down, bracing his elbows on his knees to rest his chin on tight fists. "And what about Dylan?"

Her heart rate rose at the question. The tenderness in the tone scared her. "What about him?"

"How is he? His mom is dead and, well, he's an orphan."

"Not technically, since I—"

"No, I guess if he has a father, he's not an orphan."

She tried to swallow, but her mouth was dry and tasted metallic. Fear. She was tasting real, live terror that she could lose Dylan. Why in the hell hadn't she left well enough alone? This was exactly what Carrie feared. He'd have never come after Dylan, and now...

"How is he?" he asked again.

"What do you mean? He's..." Perfect. Adorable. Sweet as candy and as good as gold. But something in her kept her from sharing. What if

Nate fell in love with Dylan, too? And how could he not? Everyone fell in love with Dylan at first sight. "He's fine."

"Is he well-adjusted? Healthy? Normal? Smart? Going to school? Reading yet?"

She would have laughed at how much like a dad he sounded except…nothing about that was funny. He *was* Dylan's dad and, as such, had some rights. Not legal guardianship. She did have that. But, still, he had a right to know about his son.

She nodded. "Very healthy, very well-adjusted, crazy smart, and slightly temperamental. He's only four, so he doesn't read very many words yet, but he can spell." She laughed softly. "Oh, boy, he likes to spell." She smiled, thinking of the light in his eyes when she handed him a new pack of Matchbox cars last night. "He loves cars. Anything with wheels, actually."

"I was that way, too."

"Well, he's nothing like you." The words popped out, unfiltered, earning her a dark look. "I mean, well—"

"You don't know me."

Shrugging, she chose her words carefully. "In trying to find you and decide what to do about this situation, I read a lot about you, so—"

"Like I said, you don't *know* me."

"I know what your lifestyle is. I know you live on boats and have a dozen houses and go to parties in Monte Carlo and don't have a real job."

"I wouldn't call sitting on four *Fortune* 500 corporate boards, managing two charitable foundations, and handling a few billion dollars' worth of investments 'unemployed.'"

"I wouldn't call your lifestyle stable."

He made a guttural sound of disgust, pushing himself to a stand so he loomed over her. "A lifestyle is not a person. A lifestyle is a word the media made up. A lifestyle—" He turned and paced across the room, stopping to put his hands on the bar as if he actually needed support. "I am so sick of this conversation."

She drew back in surprise. "Excuse me?"

"Not with you. But, I've had it with…others." Keeping his back to her and his face down, he let his shoulders rise and fall with a silent sigh. "When can I meet him?"

"Why…*what*?" Her heart faltered. "Meet Dylan? You can't *meet* him."

Very slowly, he turned, and she nearly startled from the ragged emotion on his face. She couldn't quite decipher what he was feeling, but it was powerful and personal. "I have every right to meet this child you claim is my son."

"For what reason?"

He gave her a look of disbelief. "To determine if he's really mine."

"No, no, that's not necessary."

He narrowed his eyes and moved imperceptibly closer. "Just what are you hiding, Liza Lemanski?"

"Nothing! I'm not hiding anything. Look." Fighting a little wave of panic, she grabbed the bag she'd dropped on the table, flipping it open. "You don't have to meet him." If he met Dylan, he'd love Dylan. It was impossible not to. And then...he'd want to take Dylan. Just as Carrie feared.

"I have this. This is..." Her fingers closed around the small plastic box that she'd received from the lab. "This swab is a sample of his DNA. And these papers verify it's his, from my doctor. You can have it tested and compared to yours."

She put the box and a white envelope on the table.

"Why would I do that?"

"So you know I'm not lying."

"And then can I meet him?"

She looked up at him, swallowing hard, her whole body feeling like she was trying to turn a tide, and she'd never even expected this particular tsunami. "I really never thought you'd have any interest in meeting him," she said.

"Well, I do. Right now, as a matter of fact."

No, no, she would not let that happen. She gestured toward the DNA. "Just do the test and then..." *Sign the papers.* "Look, Nate, you don't want a child and you know it. How could you raise him? How would you guide him in life? When would you spend time with him? He needs parenting and I'm...I'm not his mother, but I love him dearly and deeply and the...the 'lifestyle' I'm giving him is normal, safe, and sane. I know I don't have a lot of money, but I give him love and attention and..." Damn it, her voice cracked. "Please don't use your family power to take my little boy." She stood up, driven by the need to plead and beg. Whatever it took to keep Dylan. "Please?"

For what seemed like an eternity, he didn't answer. But his gaze slipped to the box and swab she'd left on the table. "I'll think about it."

Right now, that was all she could ask.

Chapter Three

After a sleepless night, Nate texted Elliott Becker and they made plans to meet at the resort for an early run on the beach. When Nate jogged onto the hard-packed sand, he found Becker stretching, along with Zeke Nicholas, and neither one of them looked too happy with him.

"What the hell happened to you yesterday?" Zeke demanded.

"You wouldn't believe it if I told you," he said, though he'd already decided to confide in his friends. They were trustworthy and smart, plus they knew his family situation well enough to appreciate the magnitude of the problem.

"Some hot chick shows up and you disappear," Zeke said.

"Like you two haven't been MIA since you met Mandy and Frankie," Nate shot back, easing into a slow stretch to prepare for their run.

"We didn't ditch the game to get laid." Becker shook out his legs and started a slow jog.

If only he had, Nate thought. That would be so much easier to explain and so much more in character. Except, he wasn't that guy anymore.

"So who is this girl, Nate?" Zeke asked. "I saw her talking to Frankie at the end of the press conference, but no one else knew her."

Becker elbowed him. "Bet Nate knows her now. What bed did you leave her in this morning?"

"She's at home with"—*my son*—"a little boy."

Zeke threw him a surprised look. "She has a kid?"

"Long story." And Nate wasn't ready to delve into it all yet. Instead, he let his sneakers hit the sand near the water and picked up the pace. With his eye on the horizon, he let the morning sun warm his muscles.

"Better watch your step, Mr. Ivory," Becker said, slowing down to get next to Nate. "Zeke and I were just saying there's something dangerous to bachelors in the air down here."

Yeah, *fatherhood*. That was dangerous to bachelors. "Looks like it, the way you two fell like a couple of horny high schoolers," Nate shot back.

Unaffected, Becker and Zeke shared a grin, then looked at Nate like he was the one who'd done something stupid. In a moment, the three of them fell silent long enough to pick up the pace, run to the north end of the bay, turn around and get serious.

"Loser buys breakfast," Zeke said.

"Screw that," Becker said. "Loser buys the restaurant."

Zeke and Nate cracked up, but Becker didn't wait to hear them laugh at his joke, kicking sand as he sprinted away. Zeke swore under his breath and did the same thing, leaving Nate twenty feet behind them both in less than a few seconds.

Automatically, he took off, the wind whistling in his ears. But he didn't have it today, watching both of them get way ahead.

Thoughts of his fitful night before rose up and wrecked his speed like they'd wrecked his sleep. Damn, he had to solve this problem or it would wreck his work, too. And he had too much riding on this new stadium project his friends had entrusted him to run to risk having something like this steal his attention.

Still, did he have a son? What did that mean to his life? Could he walk away from that boy? Should he?

And, of course, the eternal question: What would the Colonel do?

As if there could be a question. Nothing, absolutely nothing, mattered more to the Colonel than family. They were, as the old veteran liked to say, his secret weapon in the war of life. Nate knew how his grandfather would act at the possibility of the Ivory DNA floating in anyone's bloodstream: *Claim that child. He's one of ours.*

But how could he? Nate had just begun to get his act together, and, now...this. Nate had jumped on the chance to own and manage a minor-league team, and not just because no one else in the Ivory dynasty had their hands in professional baseball yet. He had to prove himself to his grandfather, and this was his best, and last, chance.

And now, another potential scandal that would be eaten up by the media could devour his shot at the respectability he knew the Colonel wanted to see. Unless Nate walked away quietly...but would that move make the Colonel proud? A man who put family above everything else?

Lost in thought, he barely heard Zeke call to him. When Nate caught up with his friends, Becker was bent over, hands on his knees, a little winded but victorious. He looked up and caught his breath with a grin.

"Must have been quite a night for you, Ivory. I've never seen you lose a race."

"Or anything," Zeke added, eyeing him carefully. "What's wrong?"

"What's *right* is a better question. Let's eat, and I'll tell you."

A half hour later, at their favorite veranda table overlooking the beach, the three of them were still virtually alone in the beach deck of the resort restaurant. Comfortable that they had privacy, Nate told them everything and answered the questions he could.

"I hate to say this, especially because Frankie knows this woman, but I think it's a scam," Becker said, leaning back on the chair's back legs and crossing his arms. "She smells cash."

"But the kid looks like you?" Zeke asked. "Are you sure?"

"Freakishly," Nate confirmed. "And I definitely remember meeting the girl whose picture Liza showed me. And I happened to check the ship log last night, and sure enough, we were docked in Key West in April five years ago."

Zeke leaned forward. "If you got her pregnant in April, she'd have had a baby in January."

"Of course Einstein knows that," Becker joked.

Zeke ignored it, focused on Nate, always ready to use logic and math to solve a problem. "When's this kid's birthday?"

"I don't know, but he's four."

"He would have had to have turned four last month if you have any possibility of being the father. Find out his birthday, and if the math works, get a test and…"

"And then start writing big checks," Becker said.

"I told you she doesn't want money."

Becker snorted.

"Hey, Frankie didn't want your multimillion-dollar offer for her land," Nate shot back, not sure why he felt the need to defend Liza, but he did.

"Because she's a Niner in her own right," Becker replied, referring not only to the name of their rec softball team in New York, but also the qualification to be on it: nine zeroes in each player's net worth. "Your little friend is a secretary in the County Clerk's office living with a kid whose alleged 'mother' is dead." He air-quoted to make his point, leaning closer as he gathered steam. "And she has some notebook with a fake story in it—"

"The beginning was true enough."

Becker waved that off. "Maybe she *was* friends with some chick you nailed five years ago, and that girl died and Liza dreamed up this whole thing. She has access to all this legal shit. She's probably figured out a con. Hey, it happens. It happened to Frankie's grandfather."

Nate had to nod. His family name was a golden ticket to some people who tried to swindle money.

"So, what's your plan?" Zeke asked. "How did you leave it?"

"She gave me the kid's DNA for testing."

Becker looked skyward. "It's probably *your* DNA, and it will 'mysteriously' match."

"How the hell would she get my DNA?"

"With you? It's probably on sale on the Internet."

Nate fried him with a look. "You're an idiot, you know that?"

"Sorry, but this time, I'm thinking you're the idiot, Ivory. Sic some lawyers on her and make her go away."

Nate shook his head. "If my family—especially my grandfather—got wind of a paternity issue? Shit. Nothing would give him more pleasure than to add to his troops, as he likes to refer to us."

Zeke shrugged. "So a kid might be just the ticket to showing Grandpa just how legit you can be, right?"

"I thought of that," Nate admitted. "But how shitty a move would that be, on every level?"

Becker's shoulders moved in a silent chuckle.

"What's so funny?" Nate demanded.

"You with a kid. If you don't think that's funny, then—"

"Shut the hell up."

Zeke held up a peacemaking hand. "Listen, you need a plan of attack," he said. "A strategy to get through this."

"And a lawyer," Becker added.

"You're right," he agreed, more with Zeke than Becker. "First up, I have to find out more about this Carrie chick. I did try to find her after that night but only because she…" He shook his head, hating the admission. "Had a video camera."

Becker moaned, dropping his head into his hand in disgust. "A *sex tape,*

Ivory? That'll really help us get more investors for this project."

"It's five years old and quite possibly—hopefully—destroyed by now. But at the time, I wanted to get it back, but I couldn't find her or anyone who knew her. Now I have more information."

"So cruise down to Key West and have a look around," Becker said. "And take your new friend with you. Keep your enemies close, I always say."

Nate nodded. The suggestion—even though it was Becker's—made a lot of sense.

"And put her on the spot, test her a little," Zeke suggested. "Find out what she's made of and if she'd pull a stunt like this. She says she doesn't want money, so what does she want?"

"I'll tell you what you should do," Becker said, leaning forward as if an idea had grabbed hold of him. "Offer her a job."

"What?" the other two men asked in unison.

"No, I'm serious. That woman is plugged into the whole county system, and she can find her way around permits and waivers like no one else—she proved that with Frankie's land."

Frankie *had* introduced Liza as "the great unraveler of red tape." "We do need someone on staff who can handle that," he agreed, considering the idea. "But why would she want a job with me? She wants me to sign some form and disappear."

"Just offer the job," Becker said. "Make her an offer no normal County Clerk worker could refuse. Then you'll see if she's really serious about 'making a good life' for this kid."

"Damn, Becker, you took smart pills," Nate joked.

The other man gave a typically smart-ass Elliott Becker grin. "It's Frankie. She brings out a whole new me."

"Mandy does the same thing with me," Zeke admitted.

Nate looked skyward. "You guys are making me sick."

They just laughed, but then Zeke grew serious. "What about the DNA test?" he asked. "You going to do it?"

"I don't know." Truth was…the truth scared him. Absolute confirmation that he had a kid? "I have to figure it all out."

"Not at the expense of our stadium and team, I hope," Becker said. "Make sure your focus is where it should be: on the Barefoot Bay Bucks. We have a lot riding on this project, and we really need to rally some more investors."

"I know. I'll figure it all out."

"You will," Zeke said as they all stood to end breakfast. "Don't forget to—"

Something bright green whizzed by and slammed into Zeke's chest, shutting them all up as a Frisbee clattered to the table. They reacted with surprised laughs and turned at the sound of loud, fast footsteps. Two sets, in fact, both quite small. Two children approached, a tiny blond girl with her hand over her mouth and a matching tow-headed boy.

"Sorry," he said. "My sister..." He shook his head. "She didn't mean it. We're going to the beach, and she got excited."

He had to have been just about the same age as Dylan, Nate thought. "No problem, kiddo." Nate picked up the Frisbee and easily lobbed it to the boy, getting a grin when he clapped his hands over it and caught it.

"Emma! Edward!" A tall man in a white chef's coat came marching into the sunshine, a scowl on his face. "Don't bother the customers, you two. So sorry, gentlemen."

"No worries," Nate said. "We were just headed out." He took a step closer, sizing up the two of them. "Twins?" he asked.

"I'm older by a minute," Edward said, making them all laugh.

The chef extended his hand to Nate. "I'm Chef Ian Browning, by the way. I know Mr. Nicholas and Mr. Becker, but don't believe we've met."

"Nathaniel Ivory." He wasn't used to introducing himself, since most people recognized him, but this man was obviously British and probably didn't read the tabloids much. "Cute kids," he added.

"Thanks." He reached the kids and put protective and proud hands on their shoulders. For a flash of an instant, Nate imagined what that would feel like. "The children's program doesn't start until nine, and my wife had to go over to the mainland," the chef said. "So, you're with the new baseball business, too? Everyone in my kitchen is talking about—Edward!"

The boy went zooming out of his father's grasp, followed by his sister.

"We're going to the beach!" she called out, her shyness gone as the two tore down the stairs to the sand.

"Wait!" The chef darted after them, throwing the men an exasperated smile as he chased his kids.

"Got your hands full, huh?" Nate asked as the man zipped by.

"And another on the way, mate." He disappeared onto the sand, leaving the three of them sharing a look.

"You ready for that?" Zeke asked wryly.

"Hell no."

"So be careful what you wish for...*mate*." Becker added the chef's English accent and grinned at Nate. "You just might find it."

Chapter Four

"**C**ar, Aunt Liza? Now? N-O-W C-A-R!"

Liza tucked the dishtowel on the oven handle and smiled down at Dylan, her heart doing a little flip when she looked into his eyes—the very shade of tawny oak that had been haunting her every thought since the day before. Nate and Dylan did look so much alike. That fact was even more undeniable now that she'd seen Nate Ivory in person. Twenty-five years apart in age, but something in the eyes, the jaw, even the expression...had to be hereditary and not coincidence.

"Please?" Dylan dragged the word out, then frowned, no doubt wondering whether he could spell that one. "Now?"

"Yes. N-O-W." She nudged him to the kitchen door with one hand on his back, pausing at the dining room to call out, "Mom, I'm going to be in the driveway with Dylan!"

The announcement was a courtesy, but it didn't take away the fact that Liza still reported to her mom—thanks to the circumstances of her life—and she didn't like it.

After they unplugged the charger and maneuvered the bright red Power Wheels car into the driveway, Liza situated herself on the lawn where she could have an unobstructed view of the driveway, the street, and Dylan in his new toy.

"Do not go close to the street, Dylan," she warned as he climbed behind the wheel, his face bright in anticipation.

Mom had gotten him the Lightning McQueen electric car this past Christmas, and he lived for the chance to drive it, back and forth, in the semicircle driveway. That chance was usually the weekends, when Liza wasn't working. Mom watched him a few days, when she didn't have club meetings, lunches, tennis, or golf. Mostly, he was in day care, so Liza tried to spend every minute with him on the weekends.

"Here I go!" He gave it a little gas and started his circuit, waving each time he passed her.

She waved back, then leaned on her hands to look around the pristine neighborhood. Trimmed hibiscus, manicured emerald lawns, and rows of Queen palms lined the grid of streets that made up a painfully planned community full of pink and beige houses, all topped with the same barrel tile roof.

The sound of a car engine—a real one—made her open her eyes to check how close Dylan was to the street. Very.

"Careful," she called, though he was usually good about minding.

He stopped his little car suddenly, at the curb, and stood slowly. "C-A-R!"

"Yes, it's a car." She squinted into the sunshine, seeing a silver vehicle slowing as it approached her house. That was unusual in Blue Landing. Most of the retirees and snowbirds who populated the expensive development didn't even remember what it was like to have kids playing in the street. Living here was a great financial solution, and having her mother as a back-up for Dylan was convenient, but it sure wasn't the kid-friendly neighborhood she wanted.

Still, this driver was far more aware than most, slowing at her driveway.

"Wow!" Dylan slowly climbed out of his car, staring at the vehicle like it was a UFO. It was…different.

No, it was the sleek, space-age car she'd ridden in yesterday to the harbor. There couldn't be two cars that looked as if they'd been dipped in platinum and cost a million bucks.

Damn it all. *He'd found her.* Worse, he'd found Dylan, who walked toward the car parked in front of her mailbox.

Nate emerged like a god stepping out of his chariot, his hair streaked bronze in the sunlight, a loose white linen shirt accentuating his size and breadth.

Liza stood as dumbstruck as Dylan, her heart lodged firmly in her throat, denying her any chance to talk or breathe or demand to know what the hell he was doing here. But why bother asking that? She knew.

In two steps, she was behind Dylan, reaching a protective hand for his shoulder, but he shot away, running to the car.

"Car! Car! C-A-R."

A slow smile spread across Nate's face as he slipped off his sunglasses to get a better look. "You like it?" he asked Dylan.

"So pretty!"

Nate laughed, a low rumble of amusement that reached Liza's ears like a screaming alarm. He was already in love with Dylan, who, oblivious to any drama about to unfold, ran to the car and slapped his two hands on the curved spoiler in the back with a loud thwack. "Wow!"

Finally, Nate looked over to Liza, who had managed to swallow, find a shred of composure, and get to the end of the driveway.

"Hey," he said, the single word so simple and sexy and intrusive and intimate, she almost reeled.

Hey. *Hey*? Like it was no big deal that he'd hunted her down and come to her home and invaded her world *uninvited*?

"What are you doing here?"

"Aunt Liza!" Dylan answered for him. "Look!"

"I am looking," she said, her gaze flat on the car's owner and not the object of Dylan's fascination. "How did you find me?"

"Your address was on the paperwork you left." He turned his attention to Dylan, while Liza mentally kicked herself for the oversight. "You like cars, son?" he asked.

Son? Already? She must have choked a little, because Dylan turned to look at her, his eyes bright and his smile loopy.

"I love cars," he said.

So not fair. She'd told him that already. So, of course, he shows up in his one-of-a-kind classic something that someone with a Y chromosome could smell as special from a mile away.

"Well, maybe you can drive this one," Nate said to him.

This time, she choked loud and hard and purposefully. "Excuse me," she said, lifting her chin and refusing to be the least bit distracted or deterred by his size and looks and overall hunkiness. "He's four and he can't drive."

"I see that." He angled his head. "But he likes cars."

Didn't he see that kind of ridiculous logic was why she was trying to keep Dylan from him? What else would he let a child do? "If you suggest my little boy drive a...whatever that is—"

"Aston Martin. I usually have one shipped to me when I'm staying somewhere more than a few weeks."

She closed her eyes, just letting that simple statement sum up everything about Nate Ivory. He had an Aston Martin shipped to him when he stayed somewhere.

"How is that even normal?"

He laughed at the question and jutted his chin to Dylan, who was prancing around the car, leaving smear prints on every window as he tried to see in. "He thinks it's normal. Will you, uh, introduce us?"

She considered refusing the request. She could. She was Dylan's legal guardian and, as such, she could determine who even talked to him, but... No, she wasn't that scared of Nate Ivory. And not that cruel. Plus, Dylan would have a full-out meltdown if that car suddenly disappeared.

"Dylan, honey, come here."

He slowly lifted his little face from the driver's window, where he'd been pressing so hard he probably had licked the glass by now.

"Come and meet Mr. Ivory."

Nate shot her a look. "You can call me Nate," he corrected as Dylan came forward. Nate crouched down to his size. "If you give me knuckles."

He held out his fist, and Dylan knew exactly what to do. The fist-bump came with that sweet smile and childish giggle. "Who are you?"

And that pure and honest curiosity.

"I'm..." He struggled with the word, and every cell in Liza's body seized up in fear of what he'd say next. She couldn't talk or jump in or even move as time stood still and she waited for...*your father*. "I'm a friend of your Aunt Liza's."

She let out an audible breath, and he stood slowly, his expression saying what his mouth wasn't. *Don't worry.*

But she was worried. How could she not? "So you just, what, decided to cruise into Blue Landing for fun today?"

He looked around. "I could tell you're conservative, Liza, but I wouldn't have put you quite in the middle of Disney World."

"We're living with my mother right now," she said. "We've been staying here for a year." Did she have to explain her personal situation to him? Well, he was Dylan's father. "My mom lived alone in this big house and so, well, you know what they say."

"There's no place like home with your mother?" he suggested with a teasing smile.

"It takes a village to raise a kid."

He glanced around. "Pretty sedate village."

Irritation skittered as a need to defend the little development rose, but he was right. "It's also safe, secure, and comes with a backup babysitter who loves Dylan almost as much as I do."

"Car! Car! C-A-R!" Dylan had returned to his inspection, bored by the adults talking.

"I told you he's kind of obsessed with spelling." Liza tried to shift her attention to the little boy, but it was hard to stop looking at Nate. He looked different today, somehow. Calmer and more in control—but then, he'd ambushed her this time instead of the other way around.

"That's cute," he said, stepping closer to the car.

"Dwive!" Dylan insisted.

So Dylan had heard Nate suggest that. "Why would you plant that idea in his head?" she asked.

"Because it's what I'd want to do."

Dylan kept banging on the window and jumping up and down, until Nate opened the door. Little legs and arms scrambled right in, just as Mom came out of the front door.

"Liza?"

"Brace yourself," she whispered to Nate. "My mother is going to gush over you."

"Does she know about…Carrie and me?"

The question threw her a little. She hadn't expected him to care about things like that, or worry about how this affected her life in any way. A little knot of appreciation tightened in her chest.

"Nothing. You're going to be a total surprise. And I have to warn you, my mother has two weaknesses—she can't keep a secret, and she's a serial social climber. She'll tell everyone at the country club, on Facebook, and possibly stop by the local news stations to tell them that you were here. So, if she knows why…" She shook her head. "I'm not responsible for the ensuing scandal."

He put a light hand on her shoulder. "I got this." Instantly, a smile broke across his face as he turned to her mother. "Mrs. Lemanski?"

He's *got* this? He got her name wrong, for one thing. She hadn't been Mrs. Lemanski for…three husbands.

But the wrong name didn't make Mom stumble on her Manolos. The face she was staring at did. "Are you…" She put her hand on her chest, red nails gleaming. "Oh my God, are you…"

"Nathaniel Ivory."

Color rose from her heavy gold chain necklace right up to her perfectly styled frosted hair, her eyes popping. "As I live and breathe." She tapped her chest as though she couldn't do either one at the moment. "What on earth...oh, you are even better looking in real life! Gorgeous! Isn't he, Liza?"

"Stunning," she agreed dryly, getting a quick look from Nate.

"It's a pleasure to meet you." He held out his hand, and Mom practically lunged at it with both of hers, pumping mightily.

"Don't tell me you're moving into Blue Landing!"

Liza snorted. That'd be the day. He probably had servants' quarters nicer than this.

"I'm just here to see your daughter," he said. "I guess she didn't tell you we met at the press conference in Barefoot Bay yesterday."

"Oh, I read about that baseball team and..." Her mother finally took her eyes off Nate long enough to finally focus on Liza. "I thought you were at work. What were you doing there?"

Tracking down Dylan's biological father. "Uh, I—"

"Job hunting," Nate supplied. "And I'm here to deliver the good news. You're hired."

She just stared at him, utterly speechless.

"For what?" her mother asked.

"Yeah, for what?" Liza repeated.

He looked at her like she knew exactly what for. "My administrative assistant. We were so impressed with how you helped Frankie Cardinale navigate all that county red tape, we decided unanimously to offer you a job."

She tried—she really did—to say something, but not a word would come out. *I got this* meant offering her a job? "Are you out of your mind?" she asked under her breath.

But her mother heard. "Are *you*?" she demanded of Liza. "This is the best news in...well, forever! You say every day how miserable you are at the County Clerk's office and, Liza..." Her eyes darted to Nate, stealing a glance at his body and lingering over...all of it. "I mean, *Liza*. Why would you not accept?"

"Because..." It was insanity. Working for him? Was this his way of staying around Dylan? "I don't know the pay or benefits or—"

"Name your price," Nate said. "We'll triple your current salary, cover health care and—"

Dylan honked the horn lightly, making Nate smile.

"And there's a children's program at the resort where I'm setting up the office until we get further along on the site. Dylan can be in it at our expense."

"Liza!" Her mom practically squealed. "It's an answer to your prayers!"

"I wasn't praying for another job." Except that she kind of was. What she wasn't praying for was any reason to be near Nate Ivory. In fact, the opposite was far, far preferable.

"What do you say?" he asked.

Before she answered, Dylan laid on the horn with all he had, the deafening blare echoing over the quiet neighborhood.

Liza leaped at the excuse, rushing to the driver's door to stop the noise. "Dylan!" In the seat, his eyes were wild as he pressed the steering wheel with all his might.

"Stop!" she cried, lifting his hand for blessed silence. "Sorry, Nate." She tried to extricate Dylan from the seat, but his little hands clamped on the steering wheel, and he started kicking wildly, his sneakers slamming into the bottom of the dashboard, leaving tiny black scuffs on the cream-colored leather. "Dylan, stop that!"

"I want to dwive!" Smack, smack, scuff, scuff.

"Dylan, please."

"*Dwiiiiiive!*" He wailed, his voice rising exponentially from upset to temper tantrum. Full-blown meltdown was about fifteen seconds away. Actually, it might have already arrived.

She bit her lip, not sure whether to laugh or reprimand. *Welcome to fatherhood, Nate Ivory. How would this sound in Beverly Hills?*

Nate was next to her before she realized what was happening, large, strong hands reaching into the car to easily calm the kicking. "Take it easy, bud."

Dylan kicked harder.

"You can drive it."

And then he stopped. Liza whipped around to look at him, her breath taken away by how close he was, their shoulders touching. "Don't encourage him. He'll just be more disappointed. He's only four, Nate."

"I know, and such a big guy." He gave Dylan's legs a squeeze. "When's your birthday, bud?"

"Januawy twenty-fuhst!" He started kicking again, like it was his birthday all over again.

Nate seemed to pale for a split second—no doubt, the car had never been treated like this—but then he took control of the wild legs again, a catch in his voice. "Not if you kick."

Dylan stopped instantly. Because kids were traitors like that.

"And only if Aunt Liza says yes," Nate added.

"Aunt Liza, pleeeeease!"

"I don't...no. You can't take him in this car."

"I want to dwive!" Dylan screamed again.

Nate covered the boy's legs again. "In a minute—"

"No." Liza reached in and firmly took hold of Dylan, shouldering Nate out of the way. "Just no." He wasn't going to blow in here and do this. "You can't give a child everything he wants, and you can't make promises you can't keep." With a tight grip, she got Dylan out of the seat. "You can't let him drive." Her voice rose as she wrestled with a writhing, squirming, unhappy forty-two pounds of wild child. "And you can't..." *Take him away from me.* Which was really at the bottom of the low-grade panic rising in her chest.

Dylan kicked her thigh so hard she almost buckled.

"Liza." The reprimand and surprise in her mother's voice were loud and clear. Instantly, she was there, trying to wrest Dylan from her arms. "What's gotten into you?"

"Me? What about—"

"I want to *dwiiiiiive*!"

Sweat prickled under her arms, and all Liza's muscles bunched as she tried to still Dylan, looking over his shoulder to meet Nate's amused gaze. "You think this is funny?" she asked him.

"I think you're overreacting. Put him down, and let's all take a ride."

"There are two seats, Nate."

"Go, go." Her mother practically pushed her from behind. "I'll stay here, and you three go for a little zip around the neighborhood. You can talk about your new job. What are the hours?" she asked.

Oh, *Lord*.

"She can set her own." He slipped behind the wheel, touching something that made the seat shift way back, at least ten inches from the steering wheel. He reached out for Dylan. "Let's take a drive, tiger."

Dylan practically flew out of Liza's arms. "I dwive! I dwive!"

278

"Yep, you can drive." With an easy movement, Nate took Dylan from her arms and slid him behind the wheel. "You coming, Liza?"

"Aunt Liza!" Dylan cried, kicking again as excitement overtook his whole body. "Let's go!"

"You heard the boy, let's go." Nate had the nerve to grin at her as he pulled the seat belt across Dylan's little body, nestling the child into place on his lap.

On a sigh, she started around the back of the car, her mom instantly on her heels. "Liza! This is a miracle, isn't it?"

Not exactly.

"This job sounds wonderful." She squeezed Liza's hands. "And do you know he's one of the most eligible billionaires in the country? Billionaires *with a b*, Liza."

"Don't get your hopes up, Mom. This isn't about...us."

"Health benefits! Child care! Set your own hours!" Mom's voice rose with every empty promise. Because, really, what else could they be? "And look at him! You wouldn't be the first boss-and-secretary romance."

She looked to the sky, a full-headed eye roll necessary to calm her mother on a marriage roll.

"Let's go," Nate called. "I can't hold him still much longer."

"And he's so good with kids!" Mom slapped her hands on her cheeks in sheer wonder.

How good would he seem in a custody battle?

The words had a chilling effect on her heart, making her step toward the car to protect what was hers. Dylan was hers.

She couldn't forget that.

Except...he was also Nate's.

Chapter Five

As soon as the car was moving, Dylan relaxed into Nate, his tiny hands gripping the leather steering wheel, his little body finally still.

His guardian, on the other hand, was anything but relaxed. He threw her a reassuring look, but she had that lip trapped between her teeth again, her arms wrapped around herself as tight as the seat belt.

"There we go, now, we're going to make a right." Of course, Nate controlled the car completely, still holding the wheel with his own two hands and keeping them at a nice ten miles an hour on completely empty streets. "You got it, kid."

He felt Liza's stern look and met it with another smile. "S'okay, Aunt Liza," he said softly. "We got this."

"Like you had it back there at my house?" she asked under her breath. "With some bogus job offer?"

"We got this!" Dylan repeated in his high-pitched voice. A voice that reached into Nate's heart and twisted things around a little.

"Not bogus at all," he replied. "The offer is legit."

"Why?" she asked.

"Because you're exactly what we need and…" Dylan squirmed and giggled and stole a glance of pure joy over his shoulder. Because maybe he wanted to be near this kid? "It makes sense."

No, it didn't actually make sense, but he couldn't deny the sensation that had rocked him at the sight of Dylan Cassidy.

God uses the same flawless mold for every piece of Ivory glass!

He could hear the Colonel's proud voice, his announcement made at each birth and baptism in the Ivory family, celebrating the growth of the name built on the glass industry.

"It's just crazy," Liza said.

Yes, it was. But...it was true. And Dylan looked like he'd walked right out of that mold.

"Whoa, here comes a truck." Nate inched the wheel to the right and hugged the curb while a pickup rolled by.

"T-R-U-C-K! Truck."

"And what a great speller!" Nate gave the boy's shiny hair a ruffle, remembering his own hair being that honey color when he was small.

"Many words," Liza agreed. "But he shouldn't win when he has a temper tantrum."

"Does he have them often?"

She blew out a breath. "All the time. Daily. Hourly. Way more than you want to deal with, trust me."

He wanted to laugh, but he got her message. She didn't want him to like this child.

"He'll kick the heck out of your car," she added. "And he never sleeps through the night. Plus, he gets a lot of colds and..." Her gaze shifted to Dylan's face, and her eyes deepened in color, more blue with concern. "And he's..." She nibbled her lip. "He's a good kid," she finished.

"I'm sure, but—let's wait here for the mailman to pass, bud."

"M-A-I-L! Mail!" Dylan shimmied on Nate's lap, so delighted with himself. "Aunt Liza, I can dwive!"

The childish pronunciation and babyish enthusiasm were so damn sweet, Nate couldn't help but smile. But Liza's misery was apparent with every passing minute. "Just one more street, then we go back to your..." He had no idea what this child called Liza's mother.

"Just Paulette," she supplied. "And be prepared for half of the Gulf Shore Country Club to be waiting on the front lawn with cameras when we get back."

And how long until one of those amateur paparazzi calls the professionals in and someone takes a look at the kid and Nate only to put two and two together and come up with a new Ivory scandal?

One look at Liza, and he knew she was thinking the same thing. "I should probably lie low," he said.

"Ya think?"

"S-T-O-P! Stop!"

"Yep," Nate agreed, tapping the brakes at the intersection and waiting for a second before they continued on. He should probably stop, too. Stop soaking up this child and already imagining…a relationship.

He put a hand on the tiny shoulder in front of him, a dark, hollow sensation in his gut, a lone question burning since this news first broke. Was it possible he really had a son?

He pulled back into the driveway and turned off the car, relieved not to see a bevy of local socialites waiting for him. "Here you go, Dylan," he said, unlatching the seat belt and opening the door.

"Pauwette!" Dylan hollered, then ran toward the house, leaving them alone in the car.

After watching the boy disappear and leave behind a singularly confusing hole in Nate's heart, he had to pose the question that had been haunting him.

"Why wouldn't she find me and tell me?" he asked softly, knowing his voice was rich with pain and really not caring. The realization hurt.

"She did."

"She did not," he fired back. "I swear on anything and everything that journal she wrote is a lie. I never saw her again, and she…" A low anger seethed and bubbled in his veins. "What kind of person decides she has a right to keep that secret?"

He expected a defense of her dearly departed friend, but Liza lifted her shoulders and shook her head. "A person who wants to keep her child. She was afraid you and your family would want him."

"That's what she said in the notebook, which is riddled with lies."

"No, she told me that from the beginning," Liza said. "I always thought the father should have signed something, but she wouldn't do that. She was convinced you'd take the baby or your family would."

And she'd be right. Mimsy and the Colonel would pay whoever needed to be paid and sign whatever needed to be signed and weather whatever shitstorm the media threw at them, because Ivorys stuck together, no matter what.

"And would that have been a legitimate fear?" Liza asked when he didn't answer.

Nate looked at her for a long time, debating exactly what to say. In the end, he chose a simple course of action—his other reason for coming here today.

"I want to find out more about her," he said.

"I can tell you what you need to know."

He shook his head. "I don't think that girl I met and the one you knew were the same."

"What?"

"I mean, they might be the same person, but she was obviously a chameleon or split personality or something."

"Maybe she was," she admitted. "But that doesn't change this mess of a situation."

"Liza, I didn't go looking for this."

She closed her eyes and nodded. "I shouldn't have—"

"Oh, yes, you should have," he corrected. "A man has a right to know if he's had a child, and your friend was the one who made a huge mistake, not you."

"I agree," she said. "Except, she always said she'd told the father of her baby that she was pregnant and he told her to get lost."

"That conversation never happened with me," he said, a little tired of making this assertion. "Maybe Dylan's not mine."

"But her journal! She uses your name, describes your meeting exactly as you said it happened."

"Liza, she wouldn't be the first woman to fantasize about..." He realized how arrogant the statement sounded, and let his voice trail off. "I have some, I don't know what you'd call them, admirers? Fans? Desperate women who like my last name and want it."

She snorted softly. "Trust me, Carrie wasn't that woman."

"Like I said, I need to find out just who and what she was," he said.

"I know who she was, Nate. She lived with me for three and a half years. We were close friends, we talked about everything, we raised her child together, we...what?" She'd finally seen his look.

"She didn't tell you my name, though, right? She left it in some notebook that you found when she died? Did you ever meet her family?"

"Her parents were dead, and she was an only child."

"You really know nothing about her except what she fabricated since she moved here."

She closed her eyes, unable to deny that. "She never seemed anything but one hundred percent genuine."

"Are you a good judge of character?"

She didn't answer at first, then lifted a shoulder in admission. "I'm a better judge of things on paper, I'll admit. I can spot a phony legal

283

document a mile away, but..." She sighed. "I do things impulsively, and maybe I trust too easily."

He put his hand over hers, a sympathy he didn't quite understand but couldn't deny taking hold. "Let's do a little investigating, then. Maybe my friend who lives in Key West can help, too. We both deserve to know the truth."

"Remember, I work in the County Clerk's office, and that gives me access to a lot of official documents, from every county in the country. I can dig into that name, Bailey Banks, and of course, more about her parents and childhood in Arizona."

"If she was even from there. Sorry, Liza, but everything about her is suspect. Is she even really dead?"

Liza closed her eyes. "I identified her body after the accident."

"I'm sorry." He added some pressure to her hand, wanting her to know he meant that. "How did Dylan handle that?"

"Not well," she said. "He misses her, although I think he's forgetting about her as each month passes. He's always had me, and my mother, who adores him. I've been like a mother to him from the day he was born." She slipped her hand out from underneath Nate's, taking a second to nibble on her lip as she chose her next words carefully. "I need you to know something."

He nodded, waiting.

"I won't give him up easily, no matter what we find out about Carrie or what a DNA test says or what you want to do. I will fight for him because I love him with every cell in my body. His mother named me legal guardian, and that will carry a lot of weight in court."

Court? "The last thing I want to do is drag this to court."

"Then sign the paper and let me have him to raise and love," she said. "You can..." She closed her eyes as if the words pained her. "You can see him."

Two responses played in his head. *Maybe I will* was one. The other was the truth, so he said it. "He's an Ivory."

"What does that mean?" she demanded.

"It means he's...family."

"Define family," she shot back. "I've been with him since he took his first breath, first step, first bath and first birthday. I rock him to sleep every night. I take him to the park and supervise playdates and make sure he eats right. Except for a few strands of DNA, I *am* his mother."

"And because of a few strands of DNA, I could be his father."

For a long time, they just stared at each other, neither one willing or able to say a word. He studied her mysterious eyes, dark with distrust and fear and more alluring and beautiful than anything he could remember seeing in a long time.

"Why are you smiling?" she asked.

Was he? "I don't know. I guess because you're so pretty."

She inched back. "Now? You're going to hit on me now in the middle of the biggest crisis of either one of our lives?"

"I'm not hitting on you, Liza. Though I do wish we'd met under different circumstances."

"Like what? A party on your yacht? What did you say? Bare ass naked with some guy's wife's hand on your—"

"Shhh." He put his finger over her lip to stop the words from spewing out. For reasons he'd never, ever understand, a low burn of embarrassment started in his gut. He didn't want this lovely, caring, maternal young woman, who clearly gave with all her heart and soul, to even think about his...*lifestyle.*

"Listen, Key West is a couple of hours away on my boat. Let's go together and see what we can find out about her."

For a second, he was sure she was about to say no to the invitation, but then she stunned him with a direct look and a simple answer. "Yes, I'll go."

After they exchanged numbers and made plans for him to pick her up the next day, she climbed out of the car, pointedly not issuing an invitation for him to come inside. Instead, she walked slowly away from his car.

Then her front door flew open, and Nate glanced back to see Dylan running toward the street, arms outstretched. "N-A-T-E! I spell your name! N-A-T-E!"

The letters were screamed so loud, he heard them through the closed windows. Liza scooped the child up in her arms to carry him in without even looking back at Nate's car.

She was his mother, for all intents and purposes. But if he was his father...he simply had to know. And then?

He had no idea.

Chapter Six

He sent a limo for her. And a remote-control-operated toy sports car for Dylan. Liza didn't know whether to be thrilled or disappointed, but she was a little of both when the driver closed the door with a solid thud. With Mom waving goodbye from the driveway and Dylan dancing with excitement for his new toy, Liza dropped her head back on the cool leather and closed her eyes.

Everything smelled…rich. Was this just like the limo where he and Carrie…

Don't, Liza. Don't think about that.

This would be a fact-finding mission, a day trip to the Keys and back, a chance to smooth out the wrinkles in this messy situation. This trip was so impersonal that he sent a car and driver rather than picking her up himself. She had to remember that and put her mother's musings and any of her own really stupid secret fantasies to sleep while she focused on finding out what they could about Carrie Cassidy.

She held on to that thought until the limo driver pulled into the harbor on Mimosa Key and the first thing she saw was Nathaniel Ivory waiting on the dock next to the cabin cruiser she'd been on yesterday.

Bathed in sunshine, the breeze whipping his hair into a tousled mess, he stood with his hands on narrow hips, wearing khakis and a faded blue button-down shirt that fit his broad shoulders like it was custom-made for him—well, duh. Everything was custom-made for him.

His sleeves were rolled up to show corded forearms, the top button undone to reveal a peek of that impressive chest. His thick hair brushed the collar of his shirt with a hint of wave, the sun picking up the strands of burnished gold among the much darker shades.

He looked unreal, like a Photoshopped model who'd just stepped off the pages of a Nautica ad.

Who wouldn't buy what he was selling?

He approached the limo and opened the door before the driver even got out, dipping over to give her a dazzling smile. "Hope you don't mind the ride."

She laughed. "Yeah, all this leather and luxury. Really sucks."

"I wanted to get you, but I had some things I had to take care of on board." He reached for her hand to help her out, glancing up to the driver as he got out of the front. "Is her bag in the back?"

"My bag?" Liza stepped into the sunshine, warmed by it and the thought that he expected her to bring a bag. "Won't we be back tonight?"

"It's about a four-hour cruise down there, and I don't know how long it will take us to poke around Key West, and there might be some weather tonight."

Was he proposing they get a hotel or sleep on his boat? It was sizable, but she'd seen only one cabin. She leaned around his shoulder to check out the vessel again. "It looks pretty seaworthy to me."

"Good Lord, Liza, I wouldn't take you to the Keys on that." With a strong hand on her shoulder, he turned her to look beyond the harbor to the open water. "We're taking my *other* boat."

She couldn't do anything but stare. "I thought that was..." A freaking cruise ship. "Someone else's."

"*N'Vidrio*? I've been practically living on her for years."

It was a floating castle of a super-mega-over-the-top yacht, complete with colorful flags and a helicopter pad. "What does the name mean? Other than 'biggest boat in the damn ocean'?"

He laughed. "It's not. N for Nate. *Vidrio* is Spanish for glass, which is the basis of my family's fortune, and it's also close to the word for envy."

"Which everyone feels when they see that yacht." She turned back to the thirty-foot cabin cruiser. "And this is what? Your ferry boat?"

"Precisely. There's a utility garage on the lower deck of the yacht to house this."

His *utility boat* was nicer than some vessels the millionaires in Naples had. "Well, I didn't bring a bag," she finally said, still trying to get her head around the fact that she was going to the Keys on *that yacht*.

"No worries. We have everything you need on board. My sister, Beth, travels with me a lot, so her stateroom is full of anything a woman needs, and you're about the same size. If not, we can have some clothes delivered. There are personal shoppers in Key West."

Of course there were. She gave a smile and let it slide into a soft laugh. "Your life," she said, shaking her head, "is not like anything I've ever imagined."

"Then relax and enjoy it," he said, guiding her toward the boat. "Let's try to think of this as an adventure rather than a mission."

By the time they pulled out of the harbor, Liza started to relax. The breeze picked up, just chilly enough to make her glad she wore a sweater, and the briny smells of the sea made her enjoy a deep inhale and the rumble of high-octane inboard motors behind her.

An adventure rather than a mission.

Could she get that mind-set for this excursion? She peeked out from under her lashes to watch Nate steer them toward his yacht, enjoying the view of him as much as the glorious day on the water. It certainly was…adventurous.

How did a person actually *live* like this?

Every minute made her more convinced that she couldn't let Dylan be sucked into this life. There was nothing normal about it. Everything about Nate was too big, too much, too rich, too wild.

Nate angled the wheel and brought the boat around to aim right at the massive white vessel. Four stories and well over a hundred feet long, gleaming white with glossy black windows, *N'Vidrio* was nothing short of breathtaking.

"Wow."

He turned from the helm as they motored up to the back end of the yacht and two men in matching navy shirts came out to greet them. "It does have a wow factor," he conceded. "But most of the time, it's just home for me."

She stood and joined him, shouldering her handbag and bracing her legs for the docking. "Do you really live here?"

"When I am traveling near water, yeah. But the harbor in Mimosa Key is too small, so I keep it out here. I'm opening an office in the resort, as you know, so I'll split my time between here and there."

Because living at a resort was more normal than on a megayacht. One of the crewmen helped her on board, and Nate joined her, giving her a guided tour through the first deck, then the second, and by the time they reached the main living level, she'd seen so much leather and brass and marble and crystal, her head was spinning.

He took her to the bridge and introduced her to Captain Vicary, whose warmth and experience immediately put Liza at ease. After that, they moved to a private outdoor lounge with a Jacuzzi, a dining table, and a bar—staffed, of course, by another navy-shirted crew member.

"I ordered some lunch," he said as they settled across from each other on white leather lounge chairs. "Would you like a drink?"

When in Rome, right? "I'll have what you're having."

He stepped away and spoke to the bartender, leaving Liza alone for a moment. She soaked up the view, caressed the butter-soft lounge chair, and then opened her bag to see if she had any texts from Mom.

She did, a picture of Dylan and his new car.

When Nate came back with two Bloody Marys, she turned the phone for him to see. "Thank you, by the way. He was in heaven."

"C-A-R?" he asked, smiling at the picture.

"Spelled so many times, I couldn't wait to get in the L-I-M-O."

He handed her the drink and sat across from her, holding his for a toast. "Here's to Dylan, then. He's a great kid."

She didn't drink right away, gauging exactly what the wistfulness in his voice could mean. "You're still thinking about it, aren't you?"

He sipped, lifting a brow. "About him being mine and what that means? Of course. That's why we're here, right? To find out the truth about...her."

"You can't even say her name."

"I don't know what it was, evidently," he shot back. "She wasn't really my type."

She let out a soft grunt. "But that didn't stop you from—"

He held up his hand, palm out, silencing her. "I don't think my bad choices are a big surprise to anyone, including you. For what it's worth, I'm trying—and succeeding—to change my wicked ways."

"No more casual limo hookups?" she asked. "Why?"

He picked up the glass and studied the red liquid, toying with the leaves of the crisp celery stick garnish. "Those days are over." He slipped into a rueful smile. "They have to be."

She sat a little straighter, not sure what he was saying. Was it because of Dylan? "Why?"

"Because of..." He shook his head. "Look, Liza, I've had a good time. A professional partier. A wild lifestyle. But I've made a promise to settle down, and I plan on keeping it."

"A promise to who?"

"The Colonel." He shrugged, as if she might not know who that was. "Also known as 'Grandfather,' but he really hates to be called that. Thinks it sounds too soft."

She knew the famous patriarch of the Ivory clan, married to "Mimsy," as they called his eighty-year-old wife, both as famous as the king and queen of a country. "So you promised your grandparents, not your parents?" she asked.

"My parents?" He let out a dry laugh, then took a deep drink. "My mother lives in Belgium, a virtual recluse. My father is on his…fourth wife? I lost track and can't stand any of them. But suffice it to say he's in no position to pass judgment on how I live my personal life. No, the only opinion that matters in our family is that of one old ex-Marine who has some very impressive purse strings."

She couldn't help curling her lip. "That's kind of sad, don't you think?"

"What's sad is the Colonel thinking I'm a waste of the Ivory name." A wholly different kind of wistfulness colored his tone, surprising her.

"So you're cleaning up your act?" she asked. When he nodded, she added, "What's driving that? The purse strings or what your grandfather might think?"

"Not the purse strings. I have my trust fund, and no one can take it from me. No, it's his opinion that matters to me," he admitted.

Liza shifted on the lounge chair, taking a minute to have another spicy sip, letting the sunshine and alcohol and surprising confessions warm her. "For as much cyberstalking, as you call it, that I've done, I don't know much about your grandfather. He doesn't get as much media coverage as the rest of you."

"That's because he's the behind-the-scenes manipulator."

"Is that how he got so rich?"

He lifted his Bloody Mary and tapped the side. "This made him rich."

Ivory Glass was one of the most well-known brands in the world, as common as Kleenex and Coca-Cola. "Did he invent it?" she asked.

"Actually, his father did. The first James Ivory was a glassblower in Upstate New York at the turn of the twentieth century. He created the compound that made the glass nearly unbreakable but didn't do much with it.

When my grandfather was still in the Marines, working his way up the ranks after the war, he already knew his dad was sitting on a pile of gold. By the time he left the military as a colonel, he didn't let the wound that gave him a lifelong limp stop him. The post-World War II building boom happened, he mined that gold, making sure Ivory glass windows went into every new skyscraper in America. The rest is family history."

A history she knew in rough detail. The Colonel and his wife had six overachiever kids and they had kids. Everyone in the family either stayed in the business as it sat on top of the *Fortune* 500 list or went on to politics, entertainment, finance, real estate, or business.

"Ivory always turns to gold," she said, quoting a common expression about the family.

"Or a party." He set the glass down with a thud. "But, like I said, I'm out to change that."

"Is that why you've taken this role as the manager of the Barefoot Bay Bucks?"

"One of the reasons. Starting a minor-league team, building a stadium, yeah, the project has really given me a focus, and I'm stoked for the job and working with such good friends. But there are more steps in my non-evil plan." He made a sweeping grand gesture toward the yacht. "You might notice the distinct lack of dancing girls and drinking boys, also known as the regulars on *N'Vidrio*."

"Dancing girls?"

"A euphemism for..."

"The blondes in the hot tub you referred to the other day."

He didn't answer right away, but his golden-brown gaze turned warm as he regarded her. "I don't even like blondes."

Heat curled through her, unexpected and unwanted and way, way too strong. She should look away. She should make a quip or stand up or remind him that Carrie was a blonde. She should do a lot of things other than stare right back for five, six, seven straight heartbeats.

Holy hell, she realized with a start. *I could like this man.*

In fact, she already did.

When they were close to Key West, the captain tracked south around

Tank Island to work the ship to one of the few docks near town large enough to accommodate her. Nate was taking Liza to the bridge to enjoy the process of watching Vicary in action, when his chief steward signaled him for a private conversation.

"Excuse me, sir," Alex said in a soft voice. "Colonel Ivory is calling your stateroom."

A call from his grandfather was rare, but not entirely unexpected. Sometimes, the old man had to "spend time in the trenches," as he liked to say. "Have him hold, Alex. I'll be right there."

"Do you have to go?" Liza asked when the steward walked away.

"For a few minutes. Go up to the bridge, and I'll meet you there. Captain Vicary will make you feel at home."

"I doubt I'd ever feel at home here," she said. "But take your time, and I'll enjoy the scenery."

He followed another corridor to the oversized master stateroom that took up nearly half of the second deck. Taking a deep breath, he sat in a plush office chair and picked up the satellite phone.

"Hello, Colonel."

"Key West, young man? That's never a good place for you. Bad as Vegas, in my opinion. Why don't you go somewhere less colorful?"

Nate smiled to himself, not at all surprised at the greeting. "I'm entertaining a young woman—"

"Of course you are."

"—who we are hiring to work as an admin for the baseball team."

He harrumphed. "Don't get your milk where you get your bread, son. It's bad form."

It was impossible not to laugh at him. "I'll take your counsel, sir. Is that why you're calling?"

"I'm calling because we haven't seen you in over a month. Mimsy gets anxious, you know, and wants as full a table as possible for our family meal. Sunday dinner is critical time for the family."

Critical for bonding or for the Colonel to stick his nose into the business of every one of them? Both, Nate knew. Every Ivory who could make it was expected to show up at the "Ivory Tower" in "full uniform"—suit and tie for the men, formal dress for the women. It was tedious as hell, but they all knew better than to ignore too many Sundays and risk a surprise visit from the Colonel. "Maybe in a few weeks, sir. I'm really tied up with this new venture."

"If I know you, you're tied up, all right. To the bedpost with this female friend."

"Actually, you're wrong. She's not..." Well, she *was* hot. And he had been thinking about kissing her for the entire trip, but...they had too many complications. "She's got a kid."

"Really? Nothing wrong with that, long as you make your own."

Evidently, he had. He didn't answer, his gaze moving to the open view of Key West out his sliding glass door.

"Listen to me, Nathaniel." Nate knew what the softening of his voice meant. The Colonel often used a different tone when he really wanted to make sure his point got across. "I'm watching for that progress you promised. You know I'm not getting any younger."

He was eighty-three, going on fifty. "I know, sir."

"And no matter what situation you get yourself into, you can depend on your family—especially me—to help you."

"Thank you, sir." He thought about Dylan for a moment, longing to tell the Colonel more about the boy and the situation. It would be so easy to bring Dylan into the Ivory clan. He'd be accepted and loved and, regardless of what Liza thought, he'd be brought up right.

Shit, what a mess. "I'll be in touch with you, sir," he added vaguely.

They finished the conversation after a moment, and Nate headed back to the bridge, but before he turned the corner, he heard the pretty, musical notes of Liza laughing.

The impact brought him to a halt, making him realize how rare a sound that was. And how much he wanted to hear more of it. She had laughed over lunch, but she'd been cautious, asking a lot of questions about his family, keeping the subject on him and not her. Now he realized, with a little regret, he'd found out very little about her. And everything in him wanted to change that.

He came around the corner, and she was still laughing with the captain, but her face flushed slightly. "Everything okay?" she asked, her laughter fading.

No, he thought with a start. This wasn't okay. Every minute with her, things just got more complicated. "Yeah, yeah, I'm fine. Just...work things. You want to walk to the bow and watch the docking? It's a lot of fun from up there."

"It's fun from here, too," Captain Vicary said with a flirtatious wink at Liza. "But you can take her."

Without thinking—well, maybe he thought a little—Nate reached for her hand. "Careful, he'll have you working here if you show any interest in yachting at all."

She settled her pretty gaze on the captain. "We were just talking about that."

"She's working for me," he said, pulling her hand into his chest. "And it's time we finalize that arrangement right now."

She let him guide her around to the bow, their feet tapping the teak deck in unison. "He's a lady killer, you know that," Nate said.

"Captain Vicary?" Once again, the infectious laugh. "He let me steer for a while. It was great. I got us around that island all by myself."

He laughed. "With the help of a crew and a few engines, not to mention radar navigation. But I agree, it's a kick to drive this thing." And so was putting his hands on her waist and getting behind her, guiding her up the last narrow set of stairs to the tip of the bow.

There, he stayed right behind her, close enough that her body molded into his and the wind blew her hair against his cheeks.

"I swear I won't make a 'king of the world' joke," he teased.

She tilted her head back just enough to catch his gaze. "But you are king of the world, Nate Ivory. And this thing is damn near as big as the *Titanic*."

"But more seaworthy, I hope." The wind lifted more of her hair, and he reached out and got a handful, sliding it to the side to revel in the shape of her bare neck. And a sudden bloom of chills on her skin. "Are you cold, Liza?"

Her body, just close enough to his so that he could feel her from shoulders to thighs, relaxed a little. "Anything but."

"Good." He studied those chill bumps and the tiny dark hairs on the nape of her neck, fighting a very strong desire to lean forward a few inches and plant one little kiss on that smooth, smooth skin.

"You know what you are, Liza?" He dragged one finger over the skin, making her shudder.

"I bet I seem terribly pedestrian to you."

"Pedestrian? That is not at all the word I was thinking right now." *Delicious. Inviting. Feminine.* "Why would you say that?"

She glanced over her shoulder at him. "I'm not made for this, you know. This…life. I'm really kind of simple and ordinary, and my idea of an exciting Saturday afternoon is a trip to the Germ Factory with Dylan."

"The Germ Factory?" He laughed. "What the hell is that?"

"A play place with bins of plastic balls for jumping. That's what I do, Nate. And during the week I straighten out documentation messes for the county. I don't...drink cocktails on yacht decks with billionaires."

"Well, you do today." He looked at her for a long moment, then gently touched her chin, directing her face forward. "Now watch how fantastic your buddy Vicary is at docking. He's going to take this thirty-foot-wide monster and slide it right there, between those two piers."

He felt her sigh, doing as he suggested, and letting herself slip a little closer to him. She fit perfectly there, so he rested his hands on her shoulders, and neither of them spoke, letting the sounds of the crew dropping the dock cushions on either side of the yacht and the low rumble of the engines fill the silence. A few birds squawked in greeting, somehow intensifying the tangy, briny smell of the sea.

An unexpected lurch made Liza fall into him before she grabbed the railing for stability.

"And speaking of straightening out documentation messes for the county..."

"Yes?"

"Are you taking the job as chief unraveler of red tape for my organization?"

Slowly, she turned, trapped by his body and the railing, the look on her face saying she either didn't believe him or...maybe she liked the idea. He couldn't tell.

"You know you want to, Liza." As much as he wanted to kiss her right that moment, to seal the deal.

"I'm not going to lie, Nate. I'm intrigued and interested. But..."

"No buts, say yes."

"Not yet," she replied.

He added a little more pressure, pulling her forward as if he could just impress upon her how fantastic this idea was. "Look, I'm lost in this job. I've never had a freaking job in my life. I don't want to fail, and you're...you're like a secret weapon. You've worked your whole life."

"You say that like it's some kind of true accomplishment instead of a jail sentence. Plus, Nate, I hate to break it to you, but out here in the real world, *everyone* works their whole life. That doesn't make me some kind of Wonder Woman."

"You are a Wonder Woman when it comes to land documents and

official records. I'm going to work right at the Casa Blanca Resort until we get offices built on-site at the stadium, and it's beautiful there…"

He didn't have her, he could tell. She was definitely waffling between "you're out of your mind" and "no."

"And," he added with a smile he hoped charmed her, "they have that amazing kids program."

"I don't know."

"What don't you know?" he prodded. "It's perfect."

"I can't do anything until I know what's going to happen with Dylan. And how could you work with him around and…" She shook her head. "No. No. My goal with meeting you was to get rid of you, not get closer. I can't."

Without thinking, he pulled her into him, the very opposite of what she said she wanted.

She put her hands on his chest and looked up at him, those incredible sapphire and emerald eyes wide and serious. "You want to know something about me, Nate?"

"I actually want to know everything about you," he confessed.

She gave a vague smile. "Let's start with this, the thing I dislike the most about my…situation in life. The almost-not-quiteness of it."

"Excuse me?"

"It somehow always seems to haunt me. I almost-but-not-quite have an amazing son, but he's not, you know, mine. And I can't be sure he ever will be. I almost-but-not-quite have a beautiful, safe home in a nice development, except my mother owns it, and that makes her think she owns me. I almost-but-not-quite was in love once, too, but he…" She gave a dismissive wave. "Didn't work out. And now I almost-but-not-quite have the perfect job offer land in my lap, except it's…"

"It's what? It's not almost-quite anything. This is a bona fide offer."

"I can't spend that much time around you…with Dylan and…no."

Without thinking, he pulled her a little closer, just to erase the raw misery in those beautiful eyes.

"I *am* common and simple and pedestrian," she said softly, not lifting her arms to return the embrace but not pushing him away, either. "And I have very strong feelings about that child. I love him beyond description."

Her lower lip quivered just enough to show she was a little afraid of what he might say next. Or do. Because he couldn't stop looking at those lips and thinking about…

The ship lurched again, bumping the pier and slamming them together, his lips hitting right on hers in a completely unexpected kiss. For one flash of a second, neither moved, then they both slowly backed away.

He refused to apologize, and she just let a hint of a smile lift her lips. "You know what you just did, don't you?"

"Changed the dynamic between us?"

"You almost-but-not-quite kissed me." The smile grew. "The story of my life."

The boat stopped with a loud horn announcing their arrival and covering up his next sentence. "Might have to change that story, Liza."

Chapter Seven

The minute they stepped off the yacht to the pier, Nate pulled on a nondescript baseball cap. "Sorry," he muttered as he added his reflective shades. "Gotta suit up."

"I keep forgetting I'm with a celebrity."

He snorted derisively. "You're not. You're with someone people love to say they saw in person and prove it by taking pictures."

"That's a celebrity," she said.

"No, that's this stupid country that makes people idols and famous even though they've accomplished exactly nothing in their life."

She glanced up at him, wishing the sunglasses didn't deny her the chance to gauge how sincere that bit of self-deprecation really was.

"Oh, and this helps," he said, sliding an arm around her and tucking her tight to his flank. "Stay very close."

"A human shield?"

"No, but I won't get bothered nearly as often when I'm with someone and deep in conversation. When I'm alone, I'm like a walking target."

"Ugh," she said, and not at all because she fit perfectly under his arm like she belonged there. His body was warm and hard and so, so masculine, and there was absolutely no other way to stay there without sliding her arm around his waist. "That must be a craptastic way to live."

"You can't imagine."

A woman walked by and did a double take at him—not the usual check-out-a-cute-guy double take, either. The woman's step slowed, her eyes narrowed, her mouth dropped to a little O as she reached for her husband to whisper something.

Isn't that Nate Ivory?

Liza could practically read her lips. Nate steered them away with purpose, moving faster, keeping his head low.

"Just keep moving and get into a crowd."

"Holy cow," she murmured as they did. "You really can't go anywhere."

"I can, but I'm selective."

"Like you can't just go to the store and shop like a normal person."

"In some cities, I can. New York, LA are usually safe zones. In some places I lie low, in some I have the stores come to me, and in others, I hire bodyguards."

"Armed?"

He laughed. "Of course."

"Whoa." What would it be like to have to have a bodyguard? What a limiting life that would be and another really good reason for him not to have Dylan.

He guided her to a secluded sitting area between some stores, finding a bench under a tree and choosing the empty side that faced a wall rather than all the people.

"This life would totally suck," she announced as they sat down.

"What sucks is having to be rude to people when I don't want to. I don't want to come off as some kind of cocky asshole, because that does nothing to help my family's image, and really, it's just fodder for tabloids looking for the worst. I don't mind someone knowing who I am, but I hate when I have to be a prick in order to have privacy."

"Well, if anyone bothers you, I'll be a prick for you."

He eyed her up and down. "Sorry. You couldn't if you tried."

"I could be a bitch."

"Doubtful. Now, listen, we need a plan," he said. "I don't want to just wander around here like tourists. I thought we could start by going to my friend's house where I'd been to the party that night, but he's not answering his phone. I left a message, and he knew I was coming."

"Why don't we go to the restaurant where she worked?"

"You know what it is?"

She opened her purse and pulled out her cell phone, where she'd jotted down notes the night before. "I went into the office yesterday afternoon and did some digging around. I know where she worked, the apartment complex where she lived, and the number she gave 'in case of emergency' when she first applied for a job with the County Clerk."

He threw up his hands with a soft laugh. "See what I mean?"

"What? What's wrong with that?"

"Nothing, and that's the point. You're so…efficient. You're all prepared. You've gone through papers. You have names and addresses."

"That doesn't make me a rocket scientist." She laughed but had to admit the compliment warmed her.

"Maybe not, but it would make you a hell of a right-hand…woman."

"I thought I was going to be the chief unraveler of red tape?"

"You can call yourself CEO if you want." He took the phone and read the notes. "She worked at a place called Red Suns and Hot Buns?"

"We're in Key West, my friend. There are lots of suns and buns."

He just smiled. "Let's go."

Both the restaurant and apartment complex were well within walking distance, so a few minutes later, they were navigating the crowds again, with Nate holding her very close and keeping a running commentary in her ear.

That move easily hid his face from people.

It also sent a million chill bumps over Liza's skin and made her force herself not to turn to him and accidently almost-but-not-quite kiss him again. One woman watched him carefully as they approached, and instantly Nate pulled Liza even closer, pressing his lips against her ear.

"This one's going to be trouble."

"How do you know?"

"Experience. Do *not* make eye contact. That's like an invitation."

Liza sneaked a look at her, taking in the dark hair and bangs, khaki shorts and bright yellow T-shirt. "Nothing about her says trouble," she whispered, but just as they passed her, the woman turned, staring openly.

"Excuse me? Excuse me? Aren't you—"

Nate held up a hand. "Not now."

"But, please, you're Nate—"

"Not now," he said more forcefully, rushing them forward.

"I have to get your picture, oh my God." She spun around, looking behind her. "Karen! Karen, get over here." Her voice rose over the crowd, getting the attention of the closest people.

"Please," Nate ground out. "I'm on vacation."

"So am I!" she replied as if he were making small talk. "Oh my sweet fancy Moses, it *is* you!"

A few more people turned, and Liza could actually feel her own blood start to boil.

"Karen, I need a picture! I have Naughty—"

Liza jumped in front of Nate, right in the woman's face. "Stop it."

The lady drew back, her lip curling. "Who are you?"

"His bodyguard. Back off."

"Liza, you don't have to—"

She shook off Nate's touch and powered closer to the lady, nose to nose with her. "And I'm armed to the hilt and so are ten other people around him that you don't even see right now."

The woman's eyes widened, and she glanced to the side.

"Get the hell away from him, and if you take your phone out for a picture, I will give the signal to shoot."

The other woman sputtered, clearly not sure what to make of a five-foot-four woman making death threats. "I just wanted to..."

Nate put his hand on Liza's shoulder, easing her back. "We're okay now."

The lady looked from one to the other, and Liza stood on her tiptoes and gave the closest thing to a snarl she had in her.

Another woman came running up, breathless, a cup of ice cream in her hand. "What are you screaming about, Joanne? I had to pay for my froyo!"

"That's—"

Liza inched forward. "Don't even think about it."

Joanne held up both her hands, then looked at Nate, her face softening. "Sorry to bother you."

He took Liza's hand and tried to tug her away, but she stayed rooted in the spot, using what she knew was a soul-flattening look to slice the woman down. Finally, the two ladies took off, the others around them lost interest, and Liza slipped back under Nate's arm, both of them rushing through the crowded sidewalk.

He was chuckling, though, tucking her tighter against him. "I was right about you."

"I'm nuts?" She grinned, the rush of adrenaline still pumping through her.

"You're Wonder Woman." He looked down at her, his face so close, but all she could see was her own reflection in his sunglasses. Her eyes were shining, her color high, and her lips parted as if she...

Oh, Lord. Now she wanted to kiss him.

"That was sweet and not necessary and maybe a little dangerous. Don't do it again."

"But I saved you *and* your reputation."

He grazed her cheek with his finger. "You did something else you shouldn't have," he said, his voice low and gruff.

"Lied about being armed? Is that illegal or something?"

He laughed softly. "No."

"Then what did I do?"

For a long moment, he didn't answer, then he shook his head, refusing to say.

"What?" she urged. "I don't want to do it again if I did something wrong."

"You didn't do anything wrong." He smiled at her, then dipped his head to plant a soft kiss on her forehead, making the spot burn. "You made me like you even more."

Her whole body betrayed her with a splash of heat and hope she really did not want to feel.

She'd turned him on, damn it. That's what her little spitfire, protective, fearless bodyguard act did. And the next kiss wasn't going to be by accident.

Why the hell did he have to meet this woman under such stupid, complicated circumstances?

"There's the restaurant," she said, pointing to a bright orange sign that promised Red Suns and Hot Buns.

He led them across the street between a break in traffic, slowing down as a horse and carriage full of tourists trotted past. A woman in the back caught a glimpse of Nate. She pointed, then poked her partner, who turned, but the buggy moved too fast, and they darted behind it, into the restaurant.

It was late for lunch and early for dinner, but the outdoor bar was in high gear, with all the stools full and the jukebox wailing some Stevie Nicks. Nate led them to a table near the door, where he pulled out a chair for Liza and took the seat that had him facing inside.

In a few moments, a waitress appeared. A very minimally dressed waitress. She wore cutoff white shorts that revealed a third of her backside and a tight bright red crop top with a sunset emblazoned across her double D's—fake, in his expert opinion. The words Red Suns rolled over her chest, the tops of the letters covered by the ends of her platinum blond hair.

"Whatchya guys havin'?" she asked, shuffling her pad without really looking at them.

"How long have you worked here?" Liza asked.

That got her attention, right on Liza, which is exactly where he suspected she wanted it. If this one got all gooey-eyed over him, they might not learn anything.

"You lookin' for a job?" the girl asked, nodding as if she already knew the answer.

"No, I'm trying to find out about a friend of mine who used to work here, but it was more than five years ago."

"Before my time," she said. "But, hey..." She turned—revealing a matching Hot Buns written across her lukewarm ones—and waved over another server, a dark-haired young woman who looked like she was in her late twenties. "Tracy, c'mere for a sec."

The other woman pivoted on her sneakers and bounced over, a huge, friendly smile in place. "What up, buttercup?"

"You've been here forever, right?"

She rolled brown eyes. "Feels like it. I started in '05." She gave a throaty grunt and dropped her head back. "Why, God? Why can't I get my life together and not be a waitress?" She grinned at her joke. "Who wants to know?"

"This lady is looking for someone named..."

"Carrie Cassidy," Liza said. "Did you know her when she worked here?"

The woman shook her head, frowning as she considered the question. "No, no. I didn't know anybody by that name. When did you say she worked here?"

"About five years ago. I have a picture. Maybe you'd remember her." Liza got her phone, tapped the screen, and showed it to the waitress. "This is her."

The woman leaned closer, and their first server poked her head in to look, too.

"No, I don't..." She squinted and took the phone, staring at it. "Wait, I do know her. She worked here for almost a year. Um..." She snapped her fingers, digging for more. "Bonnie? Brandy? What the hell was her name?"

"Bailey?" Nate suggested.

She looked up, face brightening. "Bailey Banks! Yes. I do remember her." She looked at the picture again, thinking, then shaking her head. "Where is she now?"

"Well," Liza said, "I'm sorry to say she died in a car accident."

The woman's mouth dropped open. "No way! Oh my God, I never heard that. She just disappeared after...is that her little boy?" Still holding the phone, she dropped into an empty chair at the table, as if the knowledge that someone she knew had died pressed her down.

"Yes, it is," Liza said.

"That fucking bastard, excuse my French."

Nate leaned forward. "What do you mean?"

She glanced at him, then Liza. "Oh, her dickwad, deadbeat baby daddy."

He saw Liza suck in a breath, clearly unable to speak. So he did it for her. "Who?" he demanded. "You know him?"

"Oh, hell, everyone knows Jeff Munson around this town. He's been up every skirt in Key West."

"Jeff Munson, the old line cook?" the first waitress asked. "I know him. Whoa, yeah, total manwhore."

Tracy jutted her chin to the picture. "She loved the hell out of him, though. She even moved in with him for a while." Shaking her head, she sighed again. "God, I can't believe she's dead. I wonder if he knows."

So did Nate...what if Liza was all wrong? What if he wasn't anything but a fall guy?

"Do you know where we could find him?" Liza asked.

The other girl stepped closer. "I know where he lives." A soft flush bloomed under her makeup. "I've been there for, you know, after-work parties. It's over in Conch Harbor in those apartment buildings off Twelfth Street."

"Oh, God, no," Tracy said, leaning back and narrowing her eyes at Liza. "Please tell me you are *not* some HRS person who's going to give that kid to Jeff Munson, are you? Because I'm here to tell you, he is *so* not father material. Parties constantly, has a stream of 'ho bags in and out of his place, and hasn't had a legit job in his life. Trust me, he doesn't want a kid to hamper his style."

Nate swallowed, staying very still. She'd just described him.

"No, no, we're not from HRS," Liza assured her. "But it does seem fair to tell him what happened to her."

The waitress shrugged. "He won't care unless it involves money. That dude lives for the next get-rich scheme." She pushed up to get back to work. "Sorry to hear about Bailey. Sweet kid, but maybe not the brightest bulb in the bunch. She was always trying to make him jealous and making up shit about meeting celebrities at work. As if we get Leo DiCaprio in here on a regular basis."

She started to walk away, but Liza reached out her hand and stopped her. "Did she tell you she met Leo DiCaprio?" she asked.

Tracy snorted. "And Ryan Gosling and Adam Levine and, oh my God, that…that billionaire guy, the naughty hottie one from the messy family."

Nate froze—inside and out. To her credit, Liza didn't even blink.

"That girl had a *fertile* imagination and really tried to get Jeff's pants in a bunch over her 'celebrity' encounters, but…" She shrugged. "I just hope she died happy."

"She did," Liza said, her throat tightening. "She was really happy."

"Good, good. 'Cause, man, life is short." She gave a remorseful smile. "I better quit this gig and start living it."

When she walked away, Liza turned to the other waitress. "We're not going to have anything, sorry."

"No biggie. Good luck finding Jeff, and sorry about your friend."

Nate had no idea if she glanced at him, because he looked down at the menu they didn't need and made sure the bill of his cap covered everything but his chin. After a moment, they were alone, and he looked up at Liza, stunned to see her eyes swimming with tears.

"What's wrong?" he asked.

"She probably made you up," she whispered.

"Why would that make you cry?"

She bit her lip, hard, then blinked away the moisture in her eyes. "Maybe she made everything up. Her name, her life, her…everything. What if all those years of friendship were just a lie?"

He reached out a hand, no clue how to console her.

"Come on, Nate," she said, blinking away her emotions. "Let's go find this Munson guy. That place where he lives matches the address for Carrie's last address in Key West. I have a really good idea."

He was starting to know her well enough to know she probably did have an idea, and it probably was good. But something in him, something he really didn't understand, made him hope that this loser guy wasn't Dylan's father. He wasn't sure why he felt that way.

Out of pity for Dylan if that was the case?

Or maybe he was starting to like the idea of Dylan being his?

Chapter Eight

By the time they reached the complex, Liza had fully composed herself, forcing herself to pay attention to the surroundings, avoiding crowds as they walked briskly across town. She could not afford to get emotional about this yet. Not ever.

"All right, we need a plan of action," Nate said as they neared the destination.

"I told you, I have a plan for dealing with him."

"Not alone. Not with some guy who's been described as a douche-bag."

"I can handle a douche-bag. My goal hasn't changed, Nate. I want a signed Termination of Parental Rights so that no one has a claim to Dylan." But that wasn't all, and she had to admit that. "I also want the truth about who he is. Someday, I'm going to have to tell Dylan."

As he nodded, his expression grew darker, maybe realizing just how difficult a conversation that would be, no matter what was said. "That's why you got so worked up in the restaurant."

"This whole situation has me worked up," she confessed. "The sooner I have answers, the better."

"Then let's go." He led her through the open gate to the Conch Harbor apartment complex, both of them pausing to take in the half-dozen white stucco buildings with beaten barrel tile rooftops.

"This is it," Nate said. "I've been here before."

He was that sure? "Wasn't it dark that night?"

"Pitch, but I came back the next day, remember? I called the limo driver and had him bring me back, but I couldn't find her anywhere, and I even looked through all the mailboxes. No Bailey Banks. And before you ask, no, I didn't go to the apartment manager. I was trying to stay on the down low, but I really did look for her."

Having walked through town with him, she understood. "She was living with this Munson guy," Liza said. "Maybe her name wasn't on the mailboxes."

"Maybe. I know I tried to find her."

"Why did you, anyway? You said she wasn't your type."

He steered her toward the main building, where there was a bank of outdoor mailboxes for every building. "She took pictures," he said after a long beat. "Actually, a video."

Liza almost tripped, stopping cold on the sidewalk to stare at him. "Like of you guys…" She couldn't help making a face. "You mean a *sex tape?*"

He looked away. "I wanted to get it from her before she did anything stupid with it, like send it to the media."

Liza felt her eyes widen. "Did she?"

"The tape never surfaced, and I forgot about it until I saw her picture in that journal. It's not possible you have it, is it?"

"I doubt it. I got rid of all her stuff, and I don't remember any cameras in her belongings. She used her phone to take pictures."

"Let's hope that camera and what was on it is long destroyed," he said when they reached the mailboxes.

As they started to peruse the residents' names, Liza gathered up the courage to make a simple request. "Listen, if we find him, I have to talk to him alone."

Nate looked up from a row of boxes, frowning. "Why?"

"Because if he sees you, it'll change everything. Who knows how he'll react to you? He won't know me, but he'll know you. I want the truth, and I have the best shot of getting it if I'm alone."

He didn't answer but turned back to the mailboxes. In a few moments, he tapped one. "Got it. J. Munson, unit 335. That's probably building three, third floor, unit five."

"Okay. Wait here for me." She started off, but he snagged her elbow.

"Liza." He turned her. "What's your plan?"

"Besides brilliant?" She gave him her most dazzling smile. "I'm going to dangle money in front of him."

He slid his sunglasses off, his look stern. "Let me assure you from personal experience, that is not a smart thing to do. A blackmailer never goes away, ever. They get their teeth in you and will suck you dry."

"Blackmail?" She laughed softly. "I'm so much more creative than that." She tried to ease her arm out of his grasp, but he held tight. "What is it, Nate?"

"I don't know," he admitted. "But…" He swallowed and took a slow breath. "I guess I was starting to get used to the idea."

"Of Dylan? You'd be disappointed if Dylan wasn't yours?" She couldn't keep the shock out of her voice. "I'd think you'd jump for joy."

A little war waged behind his eyes, tawny brown darkening to something deeper and quite powerful. "I don't like the idea of you going up to this guy's apartment alone."

But that wasn't what was bothering him, was it? She didn't want to argue, though. "Then stay close by but out of sight. I'll text you if I'm in trouble." She managed to slip out of his grasp, but he got her other shoulder and pulled her close.

For a moment, she was certain he was going to kiss her. She stayed still, looking at him, waiting for it, but he just shook his head. "Be careful."

"I will be." She stepped away and darted toward building three, not turning but knowing Nate wasn't far behind. Up the open stairs that led to each floor, Liza tried to forget him and remember the plan she'd hatched when they were talking with the waitress. She'd gotten enough clues about this guy to feel certain this would work.

At the top landing, a sign pointed left to units four and five, so she turned the corner, following the wall on her left and the railing open to the courtyard below on her right. She rounded the bend, smacking right into a man hustling the other way.

"Oh, shit, damn." Papers—mail, it looked like—went flying, along with more curses.

"I'm so sorry," Liza said, as the man bent over to grab some envelopes. "Really, sorry."

She helped, glancing at the return address as she scooped up what had fluttered away. *J.B. Munson.* Bingo. And with a middle initial to add credibility, too.

Glancing at him from behind a lock of hair that covered her eyes, she got an eyeful of hair and tattoos and faded khakis hanging off sun-weathered skin.

"My bad, sir," she said, straightening and smiling innocently.

He nodded, finally seeing her. And giving her a chance to see his face and any resemblance to Dylan. Brown eyes, yes, and maybe the mouth, but...

She realized he was checking her out, too. "We forgive pretty girls around here. Apartment policy."

"Thanks and, um, listen, you wouldn't happen to know where I could find a Mr. Jeffrey B. Munson, do you?"

He frowned slightly, shaking back some long, streaked hair. "You're looking at him. Why?"

"Really? That's fortunate." She slipped her hand into the side pocket of her purse where she kept her business cards and handed him one. "My name is Liza Lemanski, and I work for the County Clerk in Collier County as head of the public records department, and we've been looking for you."

"County Clerk. Shit." He refused the card, all friendliness gone. "Parking ticket? Moving violation? Don't tell me I owe freaking back taxes, lady. Call my lawyer."

"None of the above, sir. A deceased citizen of Collier County has named you a beneficiary in her will, and we have to complete some paperwork and identification in order to expedite the payment."

His eyes widened. "Seriously? How much?"

She gave him a tight, professional smile. "Most people usually ask the name of the deceased."

"Oh, yeah." He brushed back some hair. "Who croaked? Aunt Thelma from...I don't know where the hell Collier County is."

"The woman's name was..." She took a chance. "Bailey Banks."

His jaw unhinged, color draining from his face. "She's dead?"

At least there was a hint of remorse in his tone, but if this was going to work, there had to be none in hers. "I'm afraid so, and her estate attorney is trying to locate all of the beneficiaries to get copies of the will, but you—"

"How did she die?"

No emotion, Liza. None. "I believe it was a car accident. And it was instant." Oh, why did she add that? A county courier wouldn't know that. "Anyway, I have a few questions for you, and then we'll get the paperwork mailed out."

He looked at her, but she could tell he was thinking about Carrie—Bailey—and not her questions. Which made it a good time to ask them.

"Can you confirm the date she left Key West?"

He frowned, pulled back to the moment, maybe not smart enough to wonder why that question would matter to an estate attorney. She hoped.

"Um, I'd have to check something—no, no. Of course I know. It was my birthday, well the day after. We'd had a party, and shit got pretty real, you know, and she didn't like it. She just...took off."

"And that day was..."

"June 13, however many years ago. Four? Five? I guess five years ago."

Exactly the week Carrie had come into the County Clerk's office. They'd always celebrated June 20 as their "friend anniversary." She tilted her chin up, willing herself not to show any reaction.

"And she was alone when she left?"

"Yeah, as far as I...well, yeah. Sort of." He looked away for a second, his wiry frame tense.

"Mr. Munson? Was she alone?"

He blew out a breath. "More or less."

"What does that mean?"

"Well, listen..." He threaded his fingers though his hair, then kept his palm on his unshaved face, rubbing it while he looked at her. "Does that will really call her Bailey Banks?"

The way he asked the question made perfect sense if he knew her real name. And Liza had seen her Social Security card. She knew her friend's legal name. "Actually, that's what we call an aka. Her legal name was Careen Cassidy, but they are one and the same."

He nodded, all doubt erased from his features as if she'd given him a verbal password and could be trusted. "Yeah, she liked to use that Bailey name. She thought it sounded prettier or..." He shook his head slowly as the facts hit him. "But, wow, so she died. Man, that's sad."

"Very."

"Did she, um, have any other beneficiaries in that will?"

Just Dylan, her *son*. She hedged her bets with a nonanswer. "Her parents passed away."

"I know that. I went to their funeral."

Did he? Because Carrie's journal said Nate had accompanied her there. *Oh, Carrie, why did you leave behind this mess? Why couldn't you tell me the truth?* "Then who do you mean?"

"Like, did she have any...a kid?" He croaked the last word.

"I'm not at liberty to say, Mr. Munson. Why do you need to know?"

"Because..." Another puff of air, this one loud and slow. "'Cause when she left..." He looked to the side, embarrassed. "She was pregnant."

Here we go. She took a wee breath of fortitude and looked him straight in the eye. "Are you the father?" she asked bluntly, willing every muscle in her face to stay in the act of impartial third party and not someone who loved that child with her whole heart.

"Well, technically, yeah, but..."

"Technically? You are or you aren't, sir." Her heart punched her ribs so hard it had to be leaving bruises.

"Would it change me getting any money?" he asked. "I mean, I hate to be crass and all, but we did some...you know...paperwork."

A slow heat rose up from her belly, threatening her stability. "What kind of paperwork, Mr. Munson?"

"I signed a piece of paper. Something called a terminal...rights termination or—"

"Termination of Parental Rights?"

"You know what that is?"

"I do." He'd signed a TPR already? "And if you could just show me a copy of that paper, Mr. Munson, and your legal ID, then I can"—*adopt Dylan*—"get on my way. Do you have it?"

"Somewhere. How much money do I get?"

Nothing. "As a courier, I'm not given that information, but an attorney will contact you after I get a picture of that form. Can I see it?" Please, *please.*

"Yeah, yeah. Gimme a sec." He turned and walked a few feet to the door of unit five. "Just wait out here. The place is a hellhole."

"Okay." She crossed her arms and leaned against the railing, looking out to the courtyard and fountain below. All the while, she willed her heart rate to slow and the questions to stop. She had plenty of time to ask questions...like *why*? Why had Carrie worried about his father, or his father's "powerful family," taking Dylan if she'd already had that signed paper? Carrie had known who the father was all along, but...why was she scared of "his family" coming to take him?

"Beneficiary of a will?" The whisper made her gasp and step back to see Nate hiding around the corner. "That's good, Wonder Woman."

"What are you doing here?" she mouthed.

"*He's* the father?" He sounded purely disgusted.

Liza felt the same way but couldn't deal with those thoughts right now. She had to get that paper.

"I guess I'll know in a minute. Get out of here."

The door clicked, and she flashed a look at Nate and used her fingers to zip her mouth in warning. When she turned, she saw Jeff coming down the hall holding a legal-size document.

She hustled forward to meet him, praying Nate stayed out of sight.

"I can't believe I found this, but here you go."

Forcing her hand to be steady, she reached for the document, recognizing it instantly, along with the authentic seal of the State of Florida. She touched legal papers like this a hundred times a week and knew this was the real deal.

The *signed* real deal.

"Hang on," she said, grabbing her phone. Aware of his gaze on her, she channeled her inner professional. "If you'll just hold that for me so I can get a picture, Mr. Munson, I'll be on my way."

"I signed it because I was pissed at her," he mumbled.

She clicked a photo of the signatures on the top page, not answering.

"But I still, you know, cared about her."

She snapped the midsection full of legalese, the most important part. "I'm sure you did, Mr. Munson."

"She was just so messed up, living in a dream world half the time, writing these ridiculous stories about meeting movie stars and shit." His voice rose with frustration. "It was so stupid. She thought she was going to be some kind of famous author, and she made up these stories. Once she even…"

She lowered the camera and met his gaze. "Once she even what?"

"She liked to make up stuff that would make me jealous. And when that didn't work, then she'd…do stuff to make me jealous."

Like sleep with famous billionaires in limousines. "Such as?" she prodded, hoping he didn't realize that no one in her position would ever ask that question.

"She cheated on me," he said gruffly. "And made sure I knew it."

She had to ask. *Had* to. "Then how are you absolutely certain this child"—she tapped the paper he held—"is really yours?"

"Oh, I'm certain of that," he said.

"How?"

He snorted. "You think I'd sign a paper without knowing?"

She gave him another quick, professional smile and tucked her phone away. "Well, thank you, Mr. Munson."

"So, you sure you don't know how much I get?"

"I honestly don't know." She took a step back, ready to end the conversation, but he came with her.

"Wanna have a drink to celebrate?"

"Celebrate?" Was he serious? "A woman is dead. A woman who you say was the mother of your child. What's to celebrate?"

All that doubt came back into his eyes as they narrowed at her. "Who the hell did you say you were again? What's your name?" Doubt shifted to something more menacing.

"My name—"

"Give me your card." He came too close, right in her face, forcing her back. He didn't stop, inches from her now, slowly lifting a hand as if he was going to grab her.

"I told you I'm with the county."

"Where's this will? Where's your proof?" He slammed a hand on her shoulder, squeezing. "Who are you, lady?"

"I'm with the—"

"Back off!" Nate shot forward from around the corner, reaching the man in three long strides, shoving him off Liza. "Get away from her."

The legal document fluttered into the air.

Jeff's eyes flashed, fear for a second, then anger. "What the hell is going on here? Who are you?"

"Just leave her alone or—"

"You can't have that picture." Jeff lunged at Liza. "Gimme your phone!"

Nate knocked him away, but Jeff reached out and got in a swing. He missed the punch, but rocked Nate's sunglasses halfway over his face and flipped his baseball cap off his head.

"Nate!" Liza shrieked.

Stumbling backward, Jeff sputtered in shock, his long hair caught between his lips.

"Let's go, Liza," Nate said, scooping up his hat but keeping his eyes on Jeff.

The other man stared at him, chest heaving, eyes squinting. "Wait a second."

Nate pulled Liza closer. "Let's go."

With no hesitation, he guided her away, fast, almost running, but Jeff flew forward again, throwing his whole body on Nate to try to pull him to the ground. Nate swung around to shake him off, but the guy gave a fight.

Liza stepped back, hands to her mouth, watching in horror as Nate lifted the smaller man off him and slammed him against the wall.

"Don't make me hurt you." Nate ground out the words, lifting the other man a few inches off the ground.

"I know you!" Jeff's face was red, his eyes furious as he stared at Nate. "You're in the tape! You're the one! You're the guy Bailey fu—"

"Shut up." Nate shook him, veins popping in his neck with the effort to hold the guy still.

"No," he said. "No, I won't shut up. I know everything. I know everything."

Very slowly, Nate released his grip on the guy's shoulders, taking one step backward. "Leave us alone," he said. "We don't have any more business here."

"I got shit on you, man. I got shit." His feet hit the floor, but Jeff shook his head with an ugly smile. "I could do some damage, too."

Nate held out his hands in something remotely resembling a truce. "Just let it go, pal. No harm, no foul."

"Or you could give me some cash for my trouble."

Nate's whole body visibly bristled. "Shut up."

"I can." He brushed his T-shirt, confidence building again. "For a fee."

Nate leaned right back into his face. "What part of 'shut up' don't you understand?"

He shrugged. "Say, ten grand."

Nate puffed a breath of pure repugnance, stepping farther away. "Scum."

"What did you call me?"

Liza and Nate shared a look and silent agreement. Wordlessly, they started walking.

"What did you call me, you dickhead?"

"Just keep going," Nate whispered under his breath, a hand on her back to usher her forward.

"'Cause I can make your life a living hell!"

"Move," he ordered, nearly breaking into a jog just as Jeff fired his parting shot.

"You'll pay, motherfucker! You will pay for what you did to me!"

Chapter Nine

L iza didn't breathe easy until Nate snagged them a cab and they were finally off the streets of Key West, headed back to the yacht. But as the taxi made its way through a warren of palm-lined streets with pastel houses and coconut palms, Nate stayed stone silent.

"I'm sorry," she said to break the uncomfortable quiet.

He didn't answer, his jaw clenched as he stared out the window.

"I feel like now I have what I want"—she patted her phone, safely tucked into her bag—"and you have a big fat problem."

He still didn't reply, making her heart sink.

"And I'm still in shock that I could be such a poor judge of character, because Carrie fooled me. I mean, she did have a great imagination. I used to laugh at the bedtime stories she made up for Dylan…"

He swallowed, visibly fighting some inner demons.

Liza took a chance and put her hand on his thigh. "I wish you'd talk to me."

When he turned, the fury and frustration in his eyes were clear. "If he has that tape, he'll release it now."

"You can't be sure of that. First of all, that's a big if from five years ago. Second, what does he have to gain?"

He snorted. "Revenge."

"If he wanted revenge on you for sleeping with his girlfriend, he'd have sold that tape years ago."

"We stirred a hornet's nest."

And Nate got stung. "Will it make you feel better if I say I'll take the job?"

He almost smiled. "Yeah. We're a good team."

"I outsmart them and then you beat the crap out of them?"

"I didn't beat the crap out of him," he said with a dry laugh, the first in hours. "I could have. Should have. You did outsmart him, though, with the whole beneficiary of the will thing." He put his hand over hers, the tender touch surprising her. "I'm glad you have what you wanted from the very beginning."

She studied the angles of his jaw and strong cheekbones, the warmth in his eyes, and the softness of his mouth. Without consciously thinking about it, she inched slightly closer. "The cost was high."

"Don't worry, I won't pay him."

"What if there's a sex tape released? Isn't that exactly the kind of thing you're trying to get away from? Won't that set you back with your family, and your grandfather, the Colonel?"

"He won't like it," he acknowledged, his tone showing just how much of an understatement that was. "And it won't help the image of the new baseball team, especially now when we're still looking for investors so we don't have to sink so much of our money into it. Yeah, it would suck all around. Especially if it somehow has Dylan's name attached to it."

"I doubt it will, but I appreciate you thinking about that aspect." She lifted their joined hands, surprising both of them by bringing his knuckles to her lips. "And fighting to protect me."

He turned his hand so he could cup her jaw. "You're worth protecting." He rubbed his thumb lightly, grazing her skin. "And I'm reminded once again how little I'm worth."

She rolled her eyes, giving her head a shake of disbelief.

"And I don't mean money," he said. "Just the shit that is my past."

"At the risk of sounding like a page from a self-help book, Nate, you are not the sum total of your past. People change. Look at Carrie. Whatever she was in Key West, she showed up in my office contrite and reformed. I loved her for what I thought she was. Finding out that she had a messy past and a nasty boyfriend and a weakness for rich playboys doesn't make me love her less. She changed."

"I bet you helped her and didn't even realize it."

The compliment, even in the face of the other sweet things he was saying, squeezed a band around her chest. "I don't know," she admitted. "I wish she hadn't felt it necessary to lie to me."

"Maybe she thought you'd judge her. I know I..." His voice trailed off.

"You know you what?"

He smiled, finally releasing her jaw but still holding her hand. "When I come face to face with someone like you, it's humbling."

Was he serious? "Nate, I am the most unremarkable person alive. I work in the County Clerk's office. I live with my mom. I drive a Ford Focus with sixty thousand miles on it. The last thing I am is humbling to a..a..." Did she have to say it again? He was a gorgeous, famous *billionaire*. "A person like you."

"You should see yourself the way I see you." He searched her eyes, as close as he could get without kissing her. "You're resourceful. You're caring. You're beautiful. You're...*damn*."

Damn? Damn *what*? She waited, but the list had come to an end. "Um, don't stop now."

He smiled and gently brought his mouth to hers, the first contact featherlight, almost making her shudder at the sweetness of it.

He sighed into the kiss, adding some pressure but still showing incredible restraint.

"Bottom line, Liza." He broke the kiss just as the cab pulled into the harbor. "You're too damn good for me."

She inched back, trying—and failing—to wrap her head around that statement. But there were so many levels of confounding. Like the fact that he even thought about her in terms of...him.

Unless... "You mean for the job you're offering?"

"No. For me."

After he situated Liza in his sister's favorite stateroom and showed her that she had everything she needed to shower, relax, and change for dinner once they were underway for the return trip, Nate retreated to his own suite to think.

Except, somewhere in Key West, he'd stopped *thinking* and started *feeling*. Feeling something he was not familiar with: inadequacy.

No woman ever made him feel that way. Of course, he'd spent his life with women who were exactly like he was—cocky, arrogant, draped in the trappings of wealth, which covered a multitude of sins.

Sins that he so badly wanted to erase. So what did this little sojourn down to the Keys do? Magnify them. Increase the likelihood of more of those transgressions coming to light. Make him even more ashamed of how he'd lived, what he'd done, and what stupid, dumb decisions he'd made in the past.

When Liza saw that sex tape—which he had no doubt that little prick would find and sell to the highest bidder—she'd be disgusted by him. And for the love of all that was holy, he did not understand why that bothered him so much, but it did.

Almost as much as what he had to do next. But he had no choice. There was a way of doing things in his family—the Ivory way—and he knew exactly what had to be done. Scandals, problems, issues, and any kind of thing the Colonel called "whitewater" had to be dealt with inside so they presented a unified front to the outside. There was no getting around that.

Even just dialing the number made him feel better, getting this off his chest, and into the hands of a person who would know what to do.

The butler answered the phone, as he always had and always would. "Colonel and Mrs. Ivory's residence, how may I assist you?"

"Greetings, Emile. It's Nate."

"Hello, Mr. Ivory. How can I direct your call?"

"I need to speak with the Colonel, please. Is he available?"

"Let me check, sir."

Of course, the old man kept him on hold for nearly three minutes, giving Nate enough time to rehearse what he was going to say. How he'd cushion the blow and try to minimize the damage control.

God knew, it wasn't the first time they'd had a call like this.

But he so badly wanted it to be the last.

"Did you change your mind? Are you coming to dinner tomorrow night?"

Nate sighed into the phone, and all his cushioning and control evaporated. With the Colonel, there was only the truth. "I got a problem, sir. I need to give you a heads-up on something."

He heard the grunt of disgust and disapproval on the other end. Or maybe that was the old man settling into his leather chair, bracing for his grandson's latest debacle. Either way, Nate told him everything. Including his deep-seated suspicions that Jeff Munson might not be telling the truth...about *anything*.

Liza turned in front of the full-length mirror in a walk-in closet the size of her bedroom at home and admired the final results. She might feel like she didn't belong in the queen's velvet and marble stateroom, but she had to admit, she looked the part.

Of course, there were no "everyday" clothes to be found. No simple skirt or T-shirt or casual white pants. And almost everything looked brand new, some still bearing a silk ribbon with a designer's name signed in ink.

Which meant…the closet was full of original couture.

The least-formal thing she found was a sleeveless white sundress that fell to her ankles in soft waves of linen and lace, fitting a little tightly in the bodice, but loose over her hips and waist. She'd dipped into the cosmetics drawer in the bathroom, applying some makeup to accentuate her eyes because…well, face it, because Nate obviously liked her eyes.

In fact, based on that kiss in the cab, he liked more than that.

The thought stilled her, making her nibble on her lip and consider what that meant. It meant a dizzying amount of female hormones rushed through her, which was pathetic but undeniable. And it meant that—

"Liza?"

The tap on her stateroom door made her abandon her thoughts to pad barefoot across the creamy carpet to open the door. And somehow manage not too swoon.

"A tux?"

He grinned. "For dinner on *N'Vidrio* with a gorgeous woman?"

"You look"—*unfairly hot*—"formal."

"I'm sure I'll take the jacket off and lose the tie after dinner." He stepped back and took a moment to look her up and down, smiling in approval. "You're stunning, Liza."

Self-conscious, she brushed the soft fabric. "Please thank your sister for letting me borrow her dress." She leaned forward to playfully whisper, "I think it was made expressly for her."

"Then it's a shame you look better in it. In fact, keep it. She'll never miss it, and you look amazing."

Liza held out her bare foot. "We don't wear the same size shoe, and I couldn't bear to ruin this pretty dress with those sandals I had on all day. I feel a little…underdressed."

"No need." He toed off the black loafers he wore and slipped off his socks to reveal his own bare feet. Which were as ridiculously attractive as the rest of him. *Oh, Liza. This is bad.*

"Now we're even." He kicked the shoes into the room, then took her hand, tucking her closer.

"You feeling okay?" he asked as they followed a teak-floored hallway to the other side of the yacht.

"I'm fine," she said. "How about you?"

He gave her a wide, unexpected smile. "I'm really good."

"Not worried anymore?"

He lifted a shoulder. "What does worry get me? I'd rather enjoy this trip home with you. Here we go."

He opened the door to a private dining room with a small table set for two surrounded by rich mahogany and gleaming glass and about fifty flickering candles all around the room.

"At the risk of repeating myself...wow."

"This is where I eat when I'm alone."

She glanced up at him. "And how often is that?"

"Lately? More often than you think. Come on and enjoy the view."

The sliding doors were open to a spacious side deck, looking right out to the sea. The sun had set, leaving the sky a haunting shade of violet and the water near-black. The longer she looked up, the more stars she saw in the heavens, along with a nearly full moon that bathed them in soft white light.

"Pretty romantic setting," she mused as they walked to the railing.

"I have it on good authority that it'll be raining in a few hours, so we should take advantage of the clear skies. What would you like to drink?"

"Surprise me."

He stepped away and picked up a phone in the dining room, spoke softly, then came back outside, standing right behind her.

"I want to ask you a question, Liza." His voice was low and close to her ear, giving her chills.

"Okay."

He ran his hands up her bare arms. "Are you cold?"

"No. Is that the question?"

He laughed softly. "No." With his hands on her shoulders, he slowly turned her from the stunning view to face him. Which was another stunning view. "Are you satisfied with what we found out today?"

She frowned. "Satisfied?"

"Do you believe that I'm not Dylan's father?"

"Yes," she said. "After thinking about it for the past two hours, I believe that Carrie must have had one hell of an imagination and maybe tried to make her boyfriend jealous or...I don't know. Don't you?"

"I want to put it behind us."

Us. The word made her whole body feel light. "So I can work for you and this issue won't always be there?" Because surely that's what he meant.

"Yeah," he agreed. "And so when I kiss you tonight, you won't be thinking about my past, especially with her."

She didn't know what made her dizzier—the fact that he was going to kiss her or the fact that he had no doubt he was going to kiss her. She lifted a brow. "Will you?"

"Kiss you or think about her?" He pulled her closer. "I'll answer one of those questions easily." He kissed her on the mouth, a steady, strong, serious kiss that was somehow different from what they'd shared in the cab.

"Nate?" she whispered into his mouth.

"Hmm?"

"Is kissing you going to be part of this job you're offering?"

"Actually, we have a strict kissing-is-allowed policy, so..." He kissed her on the nose, lightly. "Yes."

Before she could answer, a steward tapped on the dining room door. "Hold that thought," Nate said, stepping away.

She leaned on the railing, facing the twilight sky and navy blue water, her lips still tingling from the contact. Her whole body, in fact, was humming pretty hard from her head down to her bare toes.

Nate came up behind her again, reaching around to offer a crystal martini glass with clear liquid. With the dimming light behind it, she could see every cut in the glass, which refracted the light like a diamond.

"Another house special?" she asked.

"Just a simple dry martini, but the glass is a family secret."

She took the drink, a little surprised at how heavy the crystal was. "I thought Ivory Glass was the tempered stuff that went into skyscrapers."

He gestured toward a wide leather sofa. "That's true and certainly how my grandfather made the fortune. But we also have some very small and exclusive lines of glass and crystal that are really more for personal use and to give as gifts. There's actual diamond dust blown into the glass." He toasted her. "And you may keep yours."

She laughed. "Thank you. It's like I get to keep everything I touch on this yacht." Except him. She couldn't keep him. She had to remember that all this was a dreamy fantasy, and not reality. Not Liza Lemanski's reality, anyway.

"Cheers." He tapped her glass and sipped, holding her gaze over the rim.

"You seem much more relaxed than when we left town," she observed without taking her own drink.

"I am. I talked to my grandfather."

She inched back in surprise. "You did? You told him...about the tape?"

He nodded. "It's how we roll in the family. No surprises, no matter how bad they might be."

"What did he say?"

He blew out a slow breath. "Some choice words, but, you know..."

"No," she admitted. "I don't know."

"He knows my history and believes in my future."

She smiled, the words a lovely echo of what she'd told him earlier. "Yes. I like that. I do, too."

He leaned closer and kissed her lightly. "You haven't tasted the house special yet."

She answered by intensifying the kiss. Parting her lips, she let their tongues touch, tasting lemon and dry vermouth and the sweetness of a man who'd finally come to terms with his demons.

"I just did," she whispered into the kiss. "And he tastes great."

Chapter Ten

All the parties, all the women, all the noise and chaos and music and wasted nights on this yacht, and Nate simply couldn't remember one night he enjoyed more than his dinner date with Liza Lemanski.

Fresh off the best and most honest conversation he'd had in years—maybe ever—with his grandfather, Nate's mood soared as they laughed, held hands, sipped martinis, and talked about everything and nothing until the twilight turned to complete darkness.

Eventually, they moved into the dining room for lobster and salad, chocolate mousse and dessert wine. With the rain still holding off, and the sea breeze warm and strong, they took a long walk around the deck. The stewards and staff did exactly what he paid them to do—disappeared when he wanted them to—adding to the sensation that they were utterly alone, which was all he wanted to be.

They reached the upper deck with not a soul in sight. He guided her to the oversized leather sun bed at the far end of the yacht.

"We must be getting close to Naples," she said, eyeing the distant lights of the mainland on the port side. "If I see lights, we've passed the Everglades."

"We are, but there's no reason to dock tonight if you want to stay at sea."

"I have a reason. His name is Dylan." She gave him a light elbow. "Trust me, kids change everything."

"I trust you." He ushered her to the sun bed, moving a few tufted pillows to make room for both of them. "But we still have time for a dip in the pool or drink in the spa if you like."

"Hmm." She considered that as she settled next to him, letting him snuggle her under his arm. Her body fit perfectly against his, curvy and soft and feminine. He already itched to touch more skin, to feel her under him and on top of him. He satisfied himself with stroking her bare arm and watching her eyes shutter closed, telling him she wanted the same thing. "I'd have to borrow a bathing suit from your sister."

"Or…not."

She laughed softly. "Don't tell me. You have a strict skinny-dipping-for-all policy that you personally enforce for every employee of your new company."

"I like the way you think, Ms. Lemanski. Ideas like that will have you promoted in no time."

"Promoted to what?"

Very slowly, very carefully, he tucked his arms under her and eased her on top of him. "Over me." Perfect. Her slender legs slid right over his, her hips slipping right where he wanted her.

"Is that my promotion or position?"

"Both."

As she settled against his chest, he was only slightly surprised to feel her heart beat steady and strong and a little fast. He stroked her back, up and down, sliding into the dip of her waist, then inching over the rise of her backside, getting the tiniest whimper in response.

Pressing a kiss on her hair, inhaling the sweet floral scent of her, he let his hips rock once. She looked down at him, nibbling that lower lip.

"So what's the company policy on making out?" she asked.

"Not required, but always…encouraged."

She smiled and offered her mouth, their first kiss warm and full of promise. When it ended, she pulled back and looked into his eyes. "Don't you have more questions about my qualifications and background?"

"Your qualifications are obvious—you proved yourself in the field today. Background?" He considered what he really wanted to know about her. "Yeah. Why don't you have a boyfriend?"

"What makes you think I don't?"

"You're here on this lounge with me. You're not the type of girl to do that if you were involved with someone."

She smiled. "So true. Well, I'm involved with a guy who stands forty inches tall and has a weakness for chocolate milk and purple dinosaurs. What's your excuse?"

"Honestly? I can't commit, have questionable taste, and don't trust anyone who might be after things other than true love."

The response made her bow her back as she lifted her body in surprise. "Really? Is all of that true?"

More or less. "I have to be careful, for obvious reasons. And I have been known to choose unwisely when it comes to women. And commitment? Let's just say it's eluded me. I haven't met the right girl yet."

"I understand. I haven't met the right guy yet."

He brushed some hairs off her face and took another long trip in the beauty of her eyes. What would it be like to be the "right guy" for a woman like her? "So where does that leave us, Liza?"

"Us? I guess...boss and employee?"

"Nothing more?"

She gave him a slow smile. "What exactly are you suggesting?"

"I'd like...to know you better. Nothing official, nothing committed, just better."

She drew in a breath, regarding him. "In other words...almost-not-quite anything."

"Depends on your perspective."

"Right now," she whispered, closing her eyes, "I feel like I'm too close to have perspective."

"But close enough for this." He pulled her in for a long, slow, deep kiss, sliding his tongue between her lips to part them. Her body felt boneless and limp in his arms, sweet and soft and womanly as she intensified the kiss. Their legs meshed, their hips rocked, and their mouths began exploring everything they could taste.

Blood thrummed hot in his veins, swelling him against her, making him move in a natural rhythm that she met with each strained breath.

He moved his hands up and down her back, one settling on the lovely curve of her backside, the other tunneling into silky hair. He angled her head and curled one leg around hers, somehow making them fit as though they were made for each other.

She tasted like chocolate and peppermint, smelled like roses and salt air, and felt like...heaven.

"You're as good at this as everything else," he whispered, tipping her chin up so he could plant tiny kisses on her throat.

"Not from too much experience," she said. "Certainly not with billionaires on megayachts."

"I don't want to be a billionaire on a megayacht."

She laughed. "Hate to break the bad news, but you am what you am, baby."

But he wanted to be more. Different. Better. "Forget that, Liza," he whispered gruffly.

She answered with a slight whimper when he found a sweet spot right above her collarbone.

"Forget who and what I was," he whispered.

"Naughty Nate?" she teased. "How could I?"

"I hate that name." His voice was thick with repugnance.

"Then don't be...naughty." She kissed his mouth, his cheek, his forehead and went back to his mouth for more, making it impossible for him to be anything but.

His hand touched her warm, smooth thigh, lightly stroking her skin, sending another explosion of response through his already electrified body.

"Kiss me again, Liza."

She did, arching her back, giving him the chance to plant kisses on her throat and in the V-neck of the dress, inhaling the feminine scent and licking the delicious skin. Unable to resist, he dragged one hand up her side and curled around to brush her breast, getting a soft sigh of pleasure in response.

And a splat of rain on his face. And another hit his hand where it rested on her thigh.

"There's the rain," she said, turning to look up at the charcoal sky, the moon well hidden by thick clouds. "I guess Mother Nature's giving us a message. Time to stop."

"Here's what I say to Mother Nature." He reached down to the side of the chaise, patting the leather for the button. "There we go."

A low electric hum preceded the awning, which rose from behind them, as if by magic. Liza lifted her head to follow the navy blue canvas as it flattened out over them.

"Are you kidding me?" She laughed.

"We're on a sun bed, Liza. Sometimes people want shade. Or rain protection."

She sat up, straddling him, the white skirt bunched around her thighs, her hair falling back as she looked up at the awning in wonder. "That is…oh my God, *so cool.*"

She looked beautiful in the newly formed shadows, her hair tumbling over her shoulders, a smile of pure joy across her face, her slender body wrapped around him.

"You hiding any other tricks, Nate?"

"Well, in case there are any mosquitoes…" He pressed the second button on the panel below him, and sheer gauze netting rolled down from all four sides.

That got another sweet squeal of delight. "Amazing!"

"So are you," he said gruffly, reaching up to pull her down against him, then eased her on her side so they were lined up on the sun bed.

For a few minutes, they stayed very still, looking at each other in the dim light, the steady drumbeat of the rain matching the one in his chest as he let himself be transfixed by her.

A breeze fluttered the netting, making her shudder.

"Are you cold?"

She shook her head. "I'm scared."

"Of what? I promise, I swear…" He lifted one hand as if to show her how safe he was. "We can lie here and listen to the rain. I promise, I'm good."

She closed her eyes as if the words physically affected her. "Yes, you are. You're so…" She searched for a word, clearly frustrated. "You're not going to like this."

He lifted a little from the headrest, concerned. "Tell me anyway."

"You're not naughty."

He snorted softly. "Stupid word, but tell that to the rest of the world. Anyway, I earned it."

"Well, you're not anymore. Not with me. Not now. Not most of the time. You're…nice."

That made him laugh. "First time I've ever been called that. But I guess you bring out the nice in me." Which was weird. "I don't know why or how."

She smiled. "It's okay to be nice. And it's okay to be…" She rolled a little closer, snuggling into him and looking up. "A little not nice, too."

He took the cue and kissed her, slow and soft and, oh, hell, not *nice*. He plunged his tongue and curled it around hers, coaxing a moan from her throat.

"Nice and deep," he whispered between breaths.

She melted into him. "Very nice."

He stroked her side, lightly brushing her breast with his thumb. "Nice and tender." He barely touched her but felt her harden under his thumb.

Dipping his head, he suckled her jaw and throat, kissing his way to her earlobe, licking it. "Nice and wet."

"Ohhh." Her sigh was pure pleasure, the sound and feel of it on his cheek making his whole body tense.

He flicked his tongue all the way down her throat and over her breastbone, suckling her skin for a taste. He filled his hands with her curves, dragging them over her hips to carefully gather her skirt, inching it up so he could touch her skin.

When his hand pressed her taut thigh, she eased her body back on top of his, as if neither one of them could resist the temptation to press against each other.

"Nice and..." He slid his hand higher and higher, their hips rolling in rhythm as he reached the dip where her cheek met her thigh. "Sweet."

"Mmm. Nate..."

He stilled his hand. "Too nice for you?"

She looked up at him, chaos in her eyes. "I'm dying here."

He curled his hand around her bare behind, finding the silky string of a thong, tracing the line of it right...between...her...legs. She was soft and slippery, making him hard and hot.

"Too nice," she whispered. "So nice. Oh my God, Nate, don't stop."

He wouldn't. Turning her for a better position, he looked at her all mussed from his hands, her lips pink from his kisses. Her eyes lost all their blue-green to the dark, dark promise of arousal. "Let me, Liza. Let me show you how nice I can be. Let me..."

She nodded, her breath coming so hard and fast now, she couldn't talk. He wanted to see what pleasure did to her. He wanted to give her everything and take nothing. He didn't stop to analyze that but caressed her and kissed her with all the tenderness and passion he had.

She let out a tiny cry, jerking once into his hand, then biting her lip as she looked at him.

"Come on, Wonder Woman," he urged. The rain drummed harder overhead, loud enough to drown out her sweet moans of gratification, strong enough to wrap them in a cocoon of water and silk and secret, stolen kisses.

"Nate…" She shuddered again, gripping his arms, digging her fingers into his muscles as he slid his finger all the way into her, stroking the wet, warm skin, finally teasing an orgasm from her quivering, out-of-control body.

It took a minute for her to catch her breath and release her grip, long enough for him to quell his own arousal because he knew—he just knew—they weren't going any further.

"Okay," she finally whispered. "I'll do it."

Or maybe they were going further? "You will?" He couldn't stop the smile. "I'd have been willing to wait, but…"

"I'll work for you."

He blinked, surprise and disappointment colliding. Then he laughed, rocking into her so she could feel how hard that disappointment was. "Probably a good time to make your salary demands, too."

"I only have one demand."

At her serious tone, his smile evaporated. "Yeah?"

"Well, two. Dylan can be in the children's program at the resort."

"Done. Easy. What else?"

"We can't…I can't…" She closed her eyes. "This sounds really selfish considering the pleasure you just gave me, but I'm not ready for…everything."

He didn't answer right away, waiting to hear if there would be a time limit on that one. There wasn't.

"Ever?" He wanted to show restraint, and had, but if they worked together, that might be impossible.

She sighed and cupped her hand on his jaw. "I need some time to forget some things."

"Things in your past?"

"No, yours."

He frowned, then figured out what she meant. "Carrie?"

"I can't fall into bed with a guy she…" She shook her head. "I have to know you for you, not the man she made up in that journal, not the guy in the media, and not what I thought you were. Who you really are. And then…"

So he had one more person to prove his worth to. "I like that plan. Start Monday. The sooner you know me, the sooner we'll finish what we just started."

She smiled, kissing him and wrapping her arms around his neck.

"Will do, boss. Now hold me and tell me something I don't know about you."

He cuddled her closer, smoothing her dress and adjusting himself to let the desire abate. "Something you don't know about me. Let me think."

"And it can't be anything that I'd read in the paper. A secret."

"Okay." He pressed a kiss on her head and confessed, "I've never done that before."

She looked up at him, eyes wide. "You're lying."

"No, I'm not. I've never completely given someone...that. Not without expecting everything in return."

She smiled slowly. "You're right. I bring out the nice in you."

Holding that thought, they stayed under the awning until the rain showers passed, kissing, whispering, laughing, sharing secrets and, finally, sleeping in each other's arms until the yacht docked in Naples and they had to say good night.

Chapter Eleven

Liza put the caller on hold and looked over at Nate, lying on the sofa, one leg bent, his head propped on his arm, reading a legal document he had resting on his chest. It would be so easy to climb over the desk that separated them and cuddle up next to him and do what they both wanted to do ever since they set up a temporary office in Acacia, the spacious beachfront villa he'd taken over for the business.

So far, they'd resisted. But...

Heat, familiar and constant and always strong, curled through her at the thought. Of course, she said the only thing she could. "Nate, it's the county commissioner's office on line one."

He turned his head to smile at her. "Calling to say the agenda is finalized?"

"And to invite you to attend the meeting as an honored guest."

"Probably to thank me for the donation of forty-six new live oak trees for the Naples Parks and Rec Department." He rolled up, still grinning at her. "Genius idea, Wonder Woman."

She angled her head, still not quite used to his compliments on her work, even though he'd been doling them out for almost three weeks. "Hey, you wrote the check."

"But the gesture got us slipped into the County Commissioners' meeting three months ahead of schedule."

"I know county weaknesses, it's true." She shrugged, indicating the flashing light on the phone bank. "Take the call, do your thing, and when you're done we can go over the access-road permits."

He wiggled his eyebrows playfully. "The fun never ends."

She laughed. "This *is* fun. Aren't you having fun?"

He leaned closer. "There's a beach twenty yards away, a pool in the back of this villa, and a bed the size of a small country in the master suite. All screaming for *fun*."

"Hey. We have a deal." She pointed a finger at his face.

"And I've been upholding my end of that deal for twenty days...and nights."

The fact that he counted did crazy, stupid things to her insides. The wait was nearly over, and she knew it. Longing looks, purposeful touches, and a couple of smoking-hot kisses after-hours and Liza was fairly certain where this "work relationship" was headed.

And she couldn't think of a single reason not to say yes. "Access-road permits are fun."

"Okay," he relented. "And then?"

And then she'd have to pick up Dylan after the children's program ended. Sighing, she glanced at the clock on her desk. "Take the call, Nate, before they shove us clear into the June meeting."

He didn't move, staring so hard it felt like he could see right through to her soul. "You know that middle color in the rainbow?"

She tried to come up with a quip but failed, shaking her head instead, no clue where this was going, only that it would be...*nice*.

"That kind of magical mix of turquoise and emerald, not quite one, not the other, but still precious and inviting?" He almost closed the space between them, inches away now, the soapy, masculine scent of him tormenting her.

"Yeah?" she managed.

"That's the color of your eyes." Closer still. "I could look at them for hours."

She closed them for a second, almost unable to take the assault when he flirted like that. Was he teasing? Was he serious? Three weeks into the job, and she still couldn't tell. Nor could she even remember the mundane and dreary existence that was the County Clerk's office.

Still, she dug for the professionalism he so loved to tear away. "Take the call, Nate. And remember the county commissioner is named Sandra Hutchings, and she has an inflated ego, a tiny attention span, and a fiery temper."

"Good to know. God, I'd be lost without you."

She laughed. "Oh, and she would like to have her picture with you in *The Mimosa Times*. Don't keep her waiting."

"I won't." When he turned into the hall to go to the master suite he used to take calls, he stopped and looked back at her. "No one likes to wait too long." With a wink, he disappeared.

For a moment, she rested her chin on her hands, staring at a half-dozen stacks of papers and two neatly arranged files, all labeled and sorted and ready to be tackled. A sensation of pure satisfaction rolled over her. She *loved* this job. And she…loved…okay, she was pretty damn *fond* of her boss, too.

Taking their attraction to each other up a notch—or *six*—wasn't a matter of *if*, it was a matter of *when*. And where…and how. Oh, she knew how. She'd fantasized about how every day and night since they'd docked his yacht in Naples. First, they'd—

The soft hum of an electric golf cart and the sweet sound of Dylan's laughter pulled her from her reverie. Having him so close by during the day was certainly a blessing…and a curse. She was never sure when he'd be cruising by on some seashell-gathering adventure or field trip to the gardens. Still, a smile she couldn't hide broke across her face as she rose from her desk to go to the door.

Late afternoon sunshine poured in, warming her as much as the sight of the boy she loved dearly.

"Aunt Liza!" He practically tumbled out of the cart, followed by his platinum-blond best buddy, Edward Browning. Eddie's mother, Tessa, the resort gardener, was at the wheel, climbing down with one hand on a slightly distended belly.

They'd met a few times—enough to know Tessa was the glowingest pregnant woman in history.

"We come bearing requests," Tessa said in greeting.

"S-L-E-E-P!" Dylan spelled, jumping up and down. He wanted to go to sleep?

"O-V-E-R!" cried his little friend.

Liza laughed, mostly at their high-fiving on the spelling, coming around to greet Tessa. "What's this about?" she asked.

Tessa's dark eyes danced as she eyed the two boys. "They've cooked up an idea, but we need your permission."

"A sleepover?" Her skepticism must have been evident because Dylan immediately jumped into a "Please, Aunt Liza" litany that Edward joined until they were both shushed. "You've never gone to a sleepover," she said to Dylan.

"And I've never hosted one," Tessa admitted. "But Emma's been invited to a birthday party, so I'm down one child and these two…" She smiled at the boys, shaking her head. "They are inseparable. My husband and I don't live far, in town, and I assure you we'll have them in the sack by eight—"

A chorus of "awws" interrupted her.

"Or nine," she added with a laugh. "But we'll take care of him, I promise."

"I'm not worried about his care, it's just…" She put her hand on Dylan's head. "It's a first for him."

"We'll make it special."

"Okay—"

"Woo hoo!" Dylan and Edward were jumping again, but that wasn't enough celebration, so they started running in circles around the golf cart.

"What's all the ruckus out here?" They all turned to see Nate standing in the doorway, trying to look stern, but a smile grew as he watched the whirling dervishes. Dylan came to an instant stop, his face brightening like he'd been handed two scoops of ice cream.

"N-A-T-E!" He tore toward Nate, arms outstretched, getting hoisted in the air upon arrival. "I'm going to my first sleepover!"

"You are?" He made a surprised face, then looked over Dylan's shoulder to Liza, his expression changing from surprise to something else. Something that made her whole body tingle in anticipation. "Then we'll have to…"

Have a sleepover, too?

He lowered Dylan to the ground. "Make sure you have a great time."

Her heart tumbled around because she knew he was thinking of the great time they'd have. "And maybe I can take your Aunt Liza out for dinner," he added.

They hadn't had dinner since the night on the yacht, and she'd kind of ached for another night like that. But Nate had been following the rules and her lead since the day she started working for him.

"Oh, you should get a reservation at Junonia tonight," Tessa said, referring to the resort's fine restaurant, run by her chef husband. "Ian's special tonight is veal chops, and they're to die for. And sweet potatoes right from my garden."

"Perfect. It's a date." Nate ruffled Dylan's hair, but his eyes were hot on Liza. "As soon as we finish the access-road permits."

When he went back inside, Tessa's smile was amused and all-knowing. Were they that obvious?

"This is perfect," Tessa said.

"Completely," Liza agreed, barely aware that her voice held a sigh of dreaminess to it.

"So the rumor mill is true," Tessa mused. "There's more than Bucks business going on in Acacia."

Liza felt her cheeks warm. "No, no…he's my boss." She glanced at the closed door. "We just work together."

Tessa laughed brightly. "That's what I thought about Ian at one time, too. Now I love his children as my own, and we have another on the way."

Liza drew back, surprised. "Edward and Emma are…"

"Ian's from a previous marriage, but they're all mine now. And this one on the way." She rubbed her belly, and her eyes twinkled. "I'm living proof that anything is possible. In fact, here on Barefoot Bay, we're starting to think *everything* is possible."

Was it? Could normal, ordinary, not-quite-anything-special Liza Lemanski win the heart of a world-famous billionaire who'd already stolen hers? "That's a lovely sentiment."

"It's true!" she insisted and leaned closer to whisper, "And it's obvious he has feelings for you."

"It is?" She felt like an eighth-grade girl, but the only person she had to discuss this with was her mother, who couldn't see straight on the subject of Nathaniel Ivory. She'd practically embroidered the towels with their adjoining initials already.

Tessa started to round up the boys but took a moment to continue the girl talk. "He seems like a really nice guy in person. Nothing like his public image."

"He is different from what you'd expect."

"I know you're not asking for it, but my advice? Don't fight whatever's in the air down here. Sometimes the most unlikely people make a great team."

A great team. Nate called them that at least twice a day. Could they be? Right now, they were almost…quite…not anything official. But something told Liza that was about to change.

After they exchanged phone numbers and Liza kissed Dylan a few dozen times, they drove off, with the two boys sitting on the back of the golf cart, waving like lunatics. Liza stood and watched them rumble away.

"Hey, Wonder Woman."

A shiver of anticipation worked its way through her body at the low and sexy tone of his voice. She didn't turn, instead taking a steadying breath and trying to consciously hold the moment in her hand. "Yeah?"

"It's time."

Yes, it was. Very slowly, she turned to see him standing in the doorway, holding up some papers. "Access permits."

Smiling, she took a few steps closer, holding his smoldering gaze, aware of each pulse beat in her throat, each strained breath, each spark of electricity arcing through the air.

"Access"—she took the papers with one hand and pressed his chest with the other, pushing him back into the villa— "no longer denied."

He answered with a slow, deep, hungry kiss as she let the papers flutter to the floor.

"It's about time," Nate murmured into the kiss that had them both breathless in under a minute. Liza didn't answer, tunneling her hands into his hair and gripping his head to press their lips harder.

She heard Nate kick the door closed and then inhaled sharply when he backed her right into the mahogany frame, blocking her with a body that was as hard as the door behind her.

"You're not going to wait for a dinner date, are you?" she asked with a half laugh.

"Oh, we'll have dinner. Later." He pinned her arms over her head with one hand, annihilating her mouth and throat with hot kisses. "Much later."

He already had her sweater halfway up her torso.

"Nate. Here?" If he hadn't been holding her, she'd have probably melted to the floor.

"Anywhere you want." He got the sweater over her head, tossing it to the side and making her laugh. But nothing was funny to him. His face was raw intensity, his hands already all over her breasts, his erection slamming mightily into her stomach, making her want to…ride.

"C'mon." Still kissing and unsnapping her bra, he walked her across the room, flipping lace and satin strips in the air.

He stopped, holding her back to look at her half-naked body, his eyes shuttering as he took her in. "Gorgeous. *Gorgeous*."

She tried to laugh, but the chill of desire and air-conditioning made her quiver and reach for his warmth. "We're never going to make it to the bedroom."

"Not this time." He closed his hand over her bare breast, dipping his head to kiss and lick, and she automatically bowed her back to offer him everything, dizzy and disoriented. He stepped her backward, and her backside hit a piece of furniture. Some papers shifted. The stapler fell. And the next thing she knew, he had her flat on her desk.

A pile of file folders dumped to the ground. "Oh, there went the capital expenditures analysis." She bit her lip and rolled against the crazy hardness of him.

He sat up enough to unbutton his shirt and flatten her with another fierce look. "Sorry." He shook off his shirt, his broad chest heaving with the next breath.

"No, you're not."

He flashed a grin and rocked his hips against her, then came back down for more kissing, more touching and exploring, and something slammed to the floor. "And the zoning surveys hit the dirt."

Laughing, he unzipped her jeans. "As they should. Take these off, Liza."

She lifted her hips and let him help her slide them down, his head following the route so he could kiss her belly. Squirming on the desk, she gripped his shoulders, digging her fingers in and lifting her head to enjoy the view of him nibbling at her panties.

He looked up and caught her eye.

"Careful," she said, nodding to the last pile of folders next to his legs. "The investor presentation handouts are about to eat it."

He didn't look away as he pulled her panties down her thighs. "So am I." He practically growled the sexy promise.

She fought a scream when his tongue slid into her, making her flatten both hands on the desk and send her to-do list flying.

She didn't care. The only thing she had to do was...this. Pleasure careened through her, tightening every muscle and firing every nerve ending. Her fingernails dug into her desk blotter as she rose to meet every stroke of his tongue, fast and furious, then slow and deep.

Suddenly, he stood, making her open her eyes in a panic. He couldn't stop. But he was yanking off his jeans, pushing down a pair of boxer-briefs and, oh…my.

She pushed herself up to appreciate the sight of his manhood. Opening her mouth to speak, she stared. And ached for him—*all* of him—inside her.

"Nate," she finally whispered, reaching to touch him. "I want you."

"You got me." Before she could close her fist over him, he slapped his hands on the desk, forcing her back again. "I mean that."

Falling back, ignoring a pen cap that jabbed her shoulder blade and the ring of the phone a few inches from her head, she stared up at him, absolutely certain there was more to that statement than sex.

"You got me," he repeated, coming closer like he was going to kiss her. But he inched to the side and put his mouth right over her ear. "You got my attention." His breath tickled and teased. "You got my interest. And, Liza, sweetheart, you got my heart."

The phone went silent, and so did her head. No quips, no jokes, no comebacks. She had his heart?

Neither one of them moved, despite the heat of his hard-on throbbing between her legs, the stickiness of bare chests pressed against each other, and the matching drumbeats in their chests.

"What are you saying?" she finally asked, her voice little more than air.

"I'm saying…" He lifted up enough to look at her. "That this isn't…" He struggled for the word, and she didn't begin to try and fill in the blanks. "That this is…" He swallowed, searching her eyes, holding her gaze. "That we are…"

Finally, she smiled. "I get it. We're a good team."

He closed his eyes and returned to the safer place next to her ear, denying her the chance to appreciate the raw honesty in his eyes. "You make me a better man, Liza."

She closed her eyes against the sting.

"Nate, I…" *Love you.* Could she admit that now? Was it the kiss of death or—

"Open the door! I know you're in there!"

They both bolted upright at the shock of intrusion, Liza letting out a little cry of surprise.

Who could that be? One of his friends? Someone on staff? Who would—

A fist—or something wooden—smacked against the door, and the handle jiggled furiously. "Open up, Nathaniel Ivory! I have the DNA tests!"

What? Liza put both hands over her mouth. Jeff Munson? Was he here to make good on his promise to hurt Nate? Fear and confusion collided, nearly blinding her as she blinked in shock.

"Holy shit," Nate muttered, leaping off her and frantically looking for clothes in the mess.

Liza rolled off the desk, smashing her hands over her breasts in case whoever it was broke down the door, because they sounded mad enough to do just that.

"Let me in!"

"All right, all right!" Nate hollered. "Hang on."

"Who is it?" she demanded, scooping up his shirt to slide her arms into it for protection. "What is he talking about?"

He looked at her, and for the first time, she noticed he'd gone pale...and silent.

"Who is it, Nate?"

"My grandfather." He stepped into his jeans and gave her a nudge. "Go hide in the bedroom."

Her jaw dropped so hard it nearly hit her chest. "Your—"

"I will shoot the damn lock, young man."

"Go! You don't want to meet him like this."

No, she didn't. But... "Did he say he has the—"

"Liza!" He barked the word, stunning her into silence. "Go back there."

She froze, vaguely aware of the door handle shaking hard again but fully aware that she stood naked but for Nate's shirt over her shoulders.

"Please," he added. "This might get ugly."

Get ugly? It was already pretty damn unattractive from where she stood. Closing her eyes, she pivoted, stepped over a sea of papers and underwear, then walked around the corner to the bedroom, her head buzzing and her heart still slamming her chest.

But she didn't close the door. Instead, she stood stone still and listened as Nate opened the door.

"What are you doing here?"

"Demanding to take what is mine." It was easy to hear now that it was the voice of a much-older man, accompanied by heavy, uneven footsteps into the room. She cringed, thinking about what he saw. How would she ever—

"Where is he?"

She put her hand on the doorjamb, frowning. *Where is who?*

"Listen, Colonel—"

"No, you listen to me. You were right to send me that test. One hundred percent right. That boy is an Ivory through and through, and there is only one thing to do. We take him home, son. Damn the torpedoes! We take him home."

All around her, the world grew darker, shakier, and completely airless. What was he saying? What was he...

The question faded, replaced by the obvious answer. Nothing made sense. *Nothing.* Except her worst fears had been realized.

The Ivory family was going to take Dylan away from her.

Chapter Twelve

"**W**hat?" It was the best Nate could manage under the circumstances. The intrusion, the news, the plummet from a sexual high to a disaster. "What the hell are you talking about?"

The Colonel powered into the room, waving his cane like a scepter, his steel-gray eyes taking in the hot mess, then settling on Nate's barely dressed state. "You call this work?"

"I call it...*private*." Which was unheard of in the Colonel's eyes. "What do you mean that boy is an Ivory?"

"You called it!" he bellowed, leaning heavily on his cane as he looked down at a jumble of papers. And clothes. He used the end of the cane to lift a pale pink bra by one strap and let it dangle in front of Nate's face. "Is this what you call being a changed man?"

Nate closed his eyes and ignored the taunt. "Please tell me what you found out." Except, he already knew. He'd known when he impulsively sent the DNA kit Liza had left on his smaller boat up to his grandfather for private testing.

When he left Jeff Munson in Key West, he simply hadn't been as satisfied with the man's signed paper. He'd tried to put it out of his mind, but every time he saw Dylan, he wondered. Sending the DNA test to his grandfather was really to prove the truth to both of them, since the Colonel had already talked about forcing the issue himself.

"I found a match right down to the cell matter, son. This young man is part of our family, and we will raise him as ours."

Oh, God. His? Dylan was *his*.

Nate stole a glance over his shoulder. He couldn't see the bedroom door from where he stood. Could Liza hear this whole conversation?

Would she come barreling out here any minute to fight tooth and nail for the child she considered her own?

Even though that child was *his*?

Nate stabbed his fingers into his hair, swiping it back with a deep sigh. "Look, Colonel, I will handle this."

"Like hell you will." Using his cane, he flipped the bra into the air, sending it flying to land on Liza's desk.

Nate bristled, swamped by frustration, compounded by an intense and unfamiliar coldness. Because he'd been yanked from sex with a woman he deeply cared about? Or was his grandfather's disapproval leaving Nate cold?

"I will handle it," he repeated, keeping his tone low and calm. "Liza has full guardianship—"

"Pay her off, get her signature, and..." He looked around, surveying the oversized living room that doubled as a main office. "Where is the boy? I thought he was on the premises."

"He's not here. And you can't pay a person for her child, like—"

"He's *not* her child." The older man pounded his cane, drawing his bushy eyebrows together, deepening the crevice between his eyes. "Nathaniel, you can pay a person for anything, and you know it. She'll have a price. When can I see him? I'd like a look at him and so would Mimsy. She's resting right next door at the little villa called Saffron. Nice place, by the way. I like this re—"

"No, you can't." He ground out the words, the effort to balance his seething temper with a lifetime of compliance to everything this man wanted. "You can't give someone money and expect them to accept that in exchange for a living, breathing child."

"Nathaniel." The Colonel's tone showed he knew what kind of battle was brewing inside his grandson. "I'm disappointed in you."

Nate waited for the words to hit their target and make him feel like a failure. But that sensation didn't take hold in his heart. Something else did.

A deep, profound, wholly alien feeling that made him want to protect, defend, and support Liza Lemanski...over *anyone*, including the Colonel.

"I don't care if you're disappointed in me." The words surprised him as much as his grandfather.

An old gray eyebrow launched north, rising above silver-rimmed glasses. "Excuse me?"

"I don't," he said, the reality picking up steam inside him. "I don't care if you withhold your almighty approval or tie up your purse strings or cut me off from family dinners on Sunday night. *I don't care*."

The words were so liberating, he almost laughed out loud.

"Did you hear that?" Nate asked, raising his voice so someone not in the room had to hear it. "I don't care what you say or do or threaten, *Grandfather*, because I will not let you hurt Liza or have her...my"—*our*—"son."

"I hear you," the Colonel said, pushing himself off the cane. "And, by the way, a young man from Key West sent me a package in the mail. I was going to throw it away, but I think it might be of interest to some of the private investors you're trying to interest in this little baseball project of yours."

His jaw dropped as he stared at a man he thought he loved, a man he thought ruled a family with a velvet fist. But what he saw was a man he didn't want to be like at all.

"I'm not afraid of a scandal, Colonel," he said. "But I will fight to the death if you try to take Dylan from Liza." He swallowed. "And me."

"I wouldn't care if you wanted to raise him, but"—he waved the cane over the chaos of papers and clothes—"you are clearly not the changed man you claim to be, and I would worry for the boy."

"I don't need your worry or your care." Nate closed his eyes and took a deep breath. "I really don't need your approval. So, if you don't mind, you can leave now."

The Colonel stared him down, eyes narrowed, jaw clenched. "Nathaniel, I—"

"You can leave now."

A slow, sly smile pulled at the older man's face as he made his way across the room to the door, his slightly lame gait more pronounced than Nate remembered.. "Well, son of a bitch, I never thought I'd see the day."

"What day?" he asked. "The day I really changed?"

The Colonel put his hand on the door and opened it, standing to face the sunshine for a brief moment. "The day you fell in love."

Maybe they both happened on the same day.

The Colonel stepped outside, and Nate opened his mouth to argue, then shut it again, along with the door. Inside, alone, Nate stood for one second, letting the adrenaline dump through him.

Holy hell, he'd stood up to his grandfather, and won. He'd broken that debilitating need for the Colonel's approval, and he could breathe. He'd proved to Liza what he'd been trying to tell her: that he really was a better man.

Hadn't she heard?

He turned, expecting her to come darting out of the hall, eyes bright with pride, arms extended, her heart soaring like his was. Now they would make love. And talk about Dylan and how they would...

But all he heard was silence.

"Liza?" He walked toward the bedroom, his pulse ratcheting up. "Liza, did you hear that?"

He stepped into the room to see the sliding glass doors that led to the back wide open, the sheer curtain fluttering with the beach breeze.

She hadn't heard enough of it, because she was gone.

Liza darted across the Casa Blanca parking lot, clutching the too-large sweat pants she'd found draped over a chair in the bedroom. Nate's shirt was buttoned all wrong, so the right side of the collar kept tapping her in the chin, and stones and shells jabbed her bare feet as she ran toward the sanctuary of her little blue Ford Focus. She shouldered her bag, eternally grateful she'd been in the habit of hanging it in the bedroom closet. Who knew she'd have to make an emergency getaway out the back door one day?

Twenty more feet. Just twenty more feet and—

"Liza!"

She froze, recognizing Nate's voice even from across the resort property. Fisting her hands with a grunt, she used everything she had not to turn and look and melt and forgive. Because what he'd done was unforgivable.

"Liza, wait!"

She powered on to her car, already digging in her bag for keys.

"Liza, damn it, don't leave!"

With one hand on the door handle and one grasping the sweats that were threatening to eliminate any possible chance of a dignified escape, she turned toward the sound of his voice. He was running full-out, still bare-chested and wearing jeans and no shoes.

He seemed to move in slow motion, calling her name, holding out his hand, desperation pouring out of him.

"Liza, please wait." He slowed down when he got close enough to stop yelling, catching his breath from the sprint.

She shook her head and held up one hand. "Don't, Nate. Don't come at me with explanations and rationalization. You lied to me. You went behind my back and had that test done. And you called in your biggest artillery to get what you want." She squared her shoulders and pointed her finger at his face. "You think some rich old Marine and his brood are going to take my child away from me?"

He let out a slow breath, his chest rising and falling. "He's my child."

Anger and fear ricocheted through her as she whipped all the way around. "You bastard! You would play that card?"

"I'm not playing anything, and I'm not a bastard." He tunneled his fingers into his hair, shoving it back. "I had to know."

"And not share that with me?"

"I had to know," he repeated, his voice taut. "I was going to tell you the test results."

"But you decided it made more sense to bring your grandfather in and, in fact, to have him control the test, which really makes me question its validity and...and...*why* would you do that?" She nearly sobbed out the question, but it didn't matter. She was hurt and confused and furious and sick at heart. No use trying to hide all that.

"Because my family always comes first. Always *came* first," he corrected. "That's how it is, that's how we stay together."

"No, that's how you all stay under the control of one old man who has fed the monster with billions of dollars." She huffed out a breath. "What did you do, send him the swab I gave you?"

His only answer was a pained expression. "I thought—"

"I don't care what you thought!" she fired back. "You could have told me. You could have trusted me. You could have"—*not made me care about you*—"shown your true colors and been an asshole for the last three weeks."

"I *have* trusted you. And I have shown my true colors." With each word, he came closer, rounding the last car in the lot that separated them. She backed into her car, not wanting the assault of his apologies or kisses or that big bare chest that covered a black heart.

346

"How long did you stay and listen to that conversation?" he asked.

"When he asked for Dylan, I left. Oh, maybe I heard the part about paying me off." She choked her sarcasm. "From the king of 'we never pay anyone to get what we want.'"

"You should have stayed longer. I sent him away."

"Well, he'll be back. No doubt with a legion of lawyers and a bottomless checkbook."

"I made him leave, and I won't let him use lawyers or dollars or anything to hurt you. I won't," he insisted. "Not you and not Dylan. I swear."

She regarded him for a long time, mesmerized by the pain and sincerity in his eyes. "I've seen that look, Nate. That same look in your eyes."

"What look?"

"The one that says you're real and you mean this."

"I am, and I do." Encouraged, he closed the space between them, inches away now. "When did you see that look?"

She tipped her head. "Back there, in the villa."

"Because that was real, and I meant what I said."

"And you were five seconds and two inches from fu—"

He put his finger on her lips, silencing the ugly word. "No."

"Um, *yes.*" She jerked to the side to escape the burn of his touch, but it didn't work. Her lips were still warm. "Unless you want to give it another name, Nate. All I was about to be was another girl. A notch on your bedpost. Or desk. Or...*limo.*"

He flinched, and she waited for a jolt of satisfaction, but felt nothing like it. Only sadness.

"You're wrong," he said. "I know what it looks like on the surface, but you're as wrong as my grandfather for making assumptions about me. I wish you would give me a chance." He reached out his hand, palm up, the peace offering obvious.

If only she could. "Your family is never going away."

"And neither is the fact that Dylan is my son, but," he added quickly when he saw the look on her face, "you are his mother in every other way. And that, Liza Lemanski..." He leaned forward and whispered in her ear, "Makes us family, too."

Her chest squeezed so hard she didn't bother trying to breathe. Instead, she reached into her purse and pulled out her keys, turning to the car. Without saying a word, she opened the door and slid into the driver's seat.

After she turned on the ignition, she tried to pull the door closed, but he held it open. So she looked up at him, right into his eyes.

"You have to answer one question," she said.

"Anything."

"Which family matters more to you?"

He hesitated one second. Just one millisecond, and she knew the answer. Getting a hold of the door, she yanked it closed with a loud bang and backed out of the parking lot to go get Dylan.

They'd been so close. So, so close to...love. Almost-but-not-quite love.

Chapter Thirteen

Nate put his signature on the final document and checked the clock. He still had twenty minutes to finish before Zeke and Becker showed up and another ten before the reporter came.

Grabbing the next file from the pile, he opened to find all the documents labeled and in chronological order. He pushed thoughts of the woman who'd made his life so organized out of his mind. She'd been gone long enough that he knew he had to find another assistant, but he still clung to the hope that every time that door opened, she'd be standing there, blue-green eyes sparkling, both arms out bearing his second chance.

A knock kindled life into that hope, but the sound of his friends' laughter crushed it out. He got up to let them in, checking the time once more.

"We have twenty minutes," he said to Zeke and Becker when he opened the door. "And I need every one of them to get my work finished. Why don't you guys wait on the beach?"

Zeke and Becker did simultaneous double takes at each other.

"I'm sorry," Becker said. "I thought we came to Nate Ivory's villa, not a workaholic's. Who are you?"

"I'm running a damn operation that you're both deeply invested in, so I'd think even a moron like you, Becker, would want me to work."

Becker muscled into the villa. "Give it up and get a damn assistant."

Zeke stayed in the doorway, slightly more sympathetic. "No word from her yet?"

He shook his head. "But my grandfather has completely backed off, so there's that victory." A hard-won battle, too, keeping the old man from tracking down Dylan and demanding to take him away. But the Colonel finally let go and returned to the Ivory Tower with Mimsy.

Behind him, Becker slapped a friendly hand on Nate's shoulder. "You know what you need?"

What he needed was the smart, gorgeous, sexy, amazing woman who was raising his son. "I don't drink when I'm working," he replied. "Which is pretty much twenty hours a day now. But the good news is we can have a groundbreaking very soon."

"That is good news," Zeke said, finally coming in.

"I didn't mean you need booze," Becker finished, undeterred. "You need a grand gesture."

Nate laughed. "I know you like those."

"Not about what I like, my man. This is about exactly how to tell a woman you love her."

He inched out of Becker's touch. "How grand?"

"The bigger the gesture, the harder they fall is my experience." He grinned at Zeke. "And in Mr. Nicholas's, too, if I recall from his not-too-distant past."

"He's right," Zeke said. "You have to show her you mean business. Do something she isn't expecting. Get her attention and keep it."

As the two men settled onto seats in the living room, Nate returned to his chair at the desk that took up most of the middle of the room.

"I bet you can't wait to get out of this villa and into an office on-site," Zeke said.

Nate shrugged. The villa—and this desk, including all the files—was still a connection to Liza. She knew where he was in case she wanted to—

"Hello? Anyone in there?" A woman's voice accompanied a light knock on the door, and Nate hated that his heart actually skipped a freaking beat. But that wasn't Liza.

"She's early," Nate said. "My calendar says noon."

Zeke was already up, shooting him a look. "You better have an attitude adjustment for this interview," he said, keeping his voice low. "I know *The Mimosa Times* isn't *The New York Times*, but we have to make the entire island love us and support this baseball team and stadium. Cultivating a relationship with a local reporter is critical."

"Plus, maybe she'll be hot," Becker—the *moron*—suggested. "And you can hire her to replace the nice girl you scared away."

Nate gave him the finger right before Zeke opened the door. "Ms. Simpson?"

"Yes, hi. I'm Julia Simpson from *The Mimosa Times*."

Becker was right, damn it. She was quite attractive, with long blond hair pulled into a neat clip and cheekbones from here to Sunday. "I know I'm early, but I'm..." She laughed softly. "I'm really excited about interviewing you three for the feature."

She was introduced all around, taking a minute to get their names straight, and let out a few nervous laughs before she accepted a cold glass of water and perched on the edge of a chair. She crossed long, shapely legs at the ankle and daintily tucked them as she opened her notebook on her lap.

Nate tried to see her as the beautiful young woman she was, probably a week out of journalism school and deliciously adventurous in...

No. He wasn't interested in other women. He wanted the one he'd had and lost. The one he'd loved and—

"Would that be possible?" Julia asked breathlessly.

He'd missed the question completely, damn it.

Both of his friends looked at him expectantly. Shit, a business question. Of course, he was off in the clouds thinking about Liza.

"I know it's asking a lot," she said. "But I really have to have something exclusive and different. I need an angle that no one else is going to have about this project. Something that will show our readers and your new neighbors exactly what you guys are made of."

Zeke leaned forward. "We could let you see the blueprints for the owners' box. It's going to be top-notch."

She made a face, clearly not interested in blueprints.

"A sneak peek at some of the ballplayers we're recruiting?" Becker suggested.

"Um, well, the team's a long way off. I was thinking of something about you guys. Something personal." She shifted her gaze to land on Nate. "Your life makes good, you know, publicity." Those angular bones deepened with a blush. "It might be fun to get a little bit deeper in the head of 'Naughty Nate.'"

Becker snorted softly, and Zeke actually laughed, but Nate had a little white light pop inside the very head she wanted to get into. He put his hands on the desk and nodded, unable to fight a smile.

"Honey, I've got a story that will sell newspapers, go viral, and skyrocket your career."

Her eyes lit up. "Really?"

Next to her, Becker sat up straighter, his own grin wide as he pointed to Nate. "Now, that's what I'm talking about, Ivory. Grand. Perfectly *grand.*"

"Excuse me, ma'am, but your little boy…"

Liza whipped around, almost dropping the oversized paper towel package she held when she spied Dylan leaning far out of the shopping cart to pull a stream of about six hundred deli numbers out of the dispenser a foot away.

"Oh!" She tossed the paper towels into the basket and lunged for the five-foot-long trail of paper. "Dylan. No."

"Here, I got that." A man came up next to her, snagging the tickets out of Dylan's grasp.

"Thank you." She looked up at him, meeting a kind smile and friendly blue eyes behind serious horn-rimmed glasses. "I'm really…thank you."

He flipped off the top of the dispenser and spun the wheel so all the numbers rolled right back into place.

"Whee!" Dylan cried out, delighted.

"Tough to shop with kids," he said, maintaining eye contact with every word. "I try to get here before I pick mine up at day care."

"Oh…" He picked up his own kid at day care and did the grocery shopping. Single? "Yeah, it's a challenge," she said, giving her own smile, even though the whole exchange felt foreign and forced.

"I'm Mike." He offered his hand, and she barely touched it, not surprised that contact with a light pole would have conducted more electricity.

"Hi, Mike. Thanks again."

Dylan saved her by reaching for the number roll again. "Whoops, I better get him out of here. Bye." She pushed the cart quickly away, feeling bad about dissing the fine-looking and hopeful man, but he wasn't…

He wasn't Nate.

Blowing out a breath of self-disgust, Liza maneuvered the cart into the express line, absently placing milk and cereal and bananas on the conveyer belt. How long was she going to moon over the guy, and worry…he'd come and claim his son?

So far, for a few weeks anyway, he'd let her be. She'd received a paycheck in the mail after a week, and, thankfully, she got her crappy job back at the County Clerk's office. And every single night, after an evening of bearing pitying looks from her mother, she'd cried herself to sleep, longing for—

"N-A-T-E!"

Oh, God. "Shhh." She closed her hands over Dylan's tiny shoulders and gave his head a kiss. Even he missed Nate.

"N-A-T-E!" He pointed to the right, kicking his legs.

Liza's heart rolled around her chest as she looked toward the door, expecting, hoping, *dreaming* her man would be charging into Publix to save her from a lonely, boring, single existence. Or maybe to take Dylan.

But there was no—

"N-A-T-E!" Dylan started kicking again, and finally Liza followed his finger to the rack of tabloids next to the checkout.

And this time her rolling heart fell into her stomach with a thud. The headline blurred for a moment, forcing her to blink to make sense of it.

Naughty Nate Officially Off The Market: Eligible Billionaire Has Fallen In Love

"What?" She reached her hands out, her gaze moving to a picture of Nate taken right outside the villa, leaning on the wall, arms crossed—so of course his biceps looked huge—a serious look on his face.

"That sound you hear?" The voice came from right behind her, forcing her to glance over her shoulder and see the man named Mike behind her in line. "A million hopeful hearts breaking in pieces."

"Including mine," said the woman behind him. "One less eligible billionaire for us to dream about."

Slowly, Liza pulled the brightly colored newspaper from the rack, and Dylan's squeals reached a higher pitch as Nate's face got closer.

"N-A-T-E! Nate!"

Behind her, Mike cracked up. "Sounds like your son knows your guilty pleasures, Mom."

She barely smiled, trying to muster up the concentration to read the first paragraph, but nothing would come together like a noun, verb, or sentence. Just snippets and phrases like *hit by a lightning bolt* and *love at first sight* and *she brings out the best in me.*

"Who?" she demanded, giving the paper a shake.

Mike laughed some more, clearly amused by her frustration. "No wonder I struck out," he said. "Your bar is too high."

The nosy woman behind him poked her head into the conversation. "The whole story broke in a local paper over on Mimosa Key. And they say one of the tabloids had some old sex tape, but this announcement trumped that news, and they didn't even run it."

"I read that," said the woman right in front of Liza, scooping up the bag of groceries she'd just finished paying for. "She's his administrative assistant. Talk about winning the love lottery!"

Liza stared at the paper again, heat and hope and something she'd never ever felt before exploding in her chest, making every cell feel...alive.

"You know he's living over there in Barefoot Bay," the checker chimed in as she started ringing up Liza's bananas. "In fact, my aunt's going to the baseball groundbreaking thing this afternoon to get a chance to see him." She laughed. "What is it about that guy?"

"He's hot," offered the woman in the back.

"He's loaded," Mike added.

"And he's..." Liza looked at the paper right before she relinquished it to the checker to ring it in. "In *love*." And so, according to her insanely wild heartbeat, was she.

Laughing, the checker took the paper and squinted at the picture. "Let me read that. 'Despite the Ivory Glass billions,'" she read in a newscaster tone, "'Nate says the only family that matters to him is the one in his future with a lady he calls a wonder woman.'" She gave an exaggerated eye roll. "Gag me with the cheese, please."

"I think it's romantic," said the lady in back.

"I think—"

Liza whipped around and stopped whatever joke Mike was going to make. "You'd be wrong. And so would you," she said to the checker. Then she pointed to the woman behind him. "But you're right. He's romantic and hot. And I"—she gave an apologetic look to the cashier—"don't have time to pay for this."

They stared at her, shocked, but she didn't wait around, pushing the cart fast enough to get a gleeful shriek from Dylan. "Aunt Liza! Where are we going?"

"To your daddy," she whispered, scooping him out of the cart. "And we aren't going to almost-quite-not make it there in time."

The crowd around the patch of dirt in the central part of Barefoot Bay was sizable but still full of familiar faces to Nate. Zeke and Mandy stood arm in arm while the mayor made a speech. Becker and Frankie held hands, sharing jokes and teasing looks next to him. Several of the resort staff and townspeople had joined in and, of course, there was Julia Simpson, the reporter from *The Mimosa Times* who'd done such an incredible job with his story, and lots of folks from the local political scene.

But no Liza Lemanski.

After a few minutes, Nate stopped looking and concentrated on his job, which was to keep this little event rolling. He handed the mayor some facts and figures he'd been drawing up for the past week. He provided remarks for the local architect, too, but Clay Walker Jr., who'd also designed Casa Blanca Resort & Spa, spoke extemporaneously about the new project.

As Clay neared the end of his brief speech, Nate mentally checked off what came next, then opened his file for the list of county commissioners' names to thank. Flipping the papers, he didn't see the list. He knew it was in here. He straightened the folder and examined the papers again. Had he forgotten that? Once more, he looked, sensing he had about five seconds before Clay finished and he had to—

"It's right here." Two slender fingers reached into the file folder and slid out the list of names. "I put it right behind the commissioner's letter."

Nate snagged those fingers, squeezing as if they—and their owner—might disappear in a flash of his imagination. But she didn't. Instead, two beautiful blue-green eyes looked up at him, smiling, shining, and incredibly...*real*.

"Liza." He barely breathed the name he'd thought so many times in the last few weeks it felt like the four letters had been tattooed on his heart.

"I read the tabloids," she whispered as if she knew the hundred questions in his head. "You really need to be careful what you say to the media."

A slow smile curled his lips, a smile he felt it all the way down to his gut. "I told the truth."

"You're in love?"

Around him, the world faded away. The sights and sounds and worries evaporated as he gave his entire focus to the one thing that mattered. Could he tell her right here and now?

Could he *not*?

Somewhere, a throat cleared. A woman said, "Aww." And Becker snorted.

Only then did Nate look up and realize that Clay had stopped speaking, and everyone gathered around the soft dirt and oversized groundbreaking shovel was staring at him.

Nate pulled the list the rest of the way out of the folder and turned to Zeke. "Could you read this list and recognize these people? I'm kind of busy right now."

Zeke smiled and walked to the center of the ceremony while Nate closed his eyes with a soft laugh. "Yes," he finally answered her question. "I'm in love."

Her eyes widened along with her mouth, opening to a sweet little O that he desperately wanted to kiss. "What about you, Wonder Woman?"

For a long time, she didn't answer, holding his gaze and letting the air between them crackle with expectation. "I am, too," she whispered.

He couldn't wait any longer. Pulling her into him, he kissed her mouth with all the pent-up certainty that had been in his heart since she drove off and left him shattered.

Huge applause broke out, along with plenty of hoots and hollers. "I have a feeling," he mouthed into the kiss, "that isn't for the county commissioners."

She laughed and folded into him, wrapping her arms around him while they listened to Zeke announce that it was time for the first shovel of dirt. Holding Liza's hand, Nate walked forward and picked up the gold-painted spade, cameras humming and snapping all around.

Holding the shovel over the dirt, he glanced around, then settled on the only face in the crowd that mattered to him—the woman at his side. "I've never been more happier to be part of a great team," he announced.

As he stuck the shovel in the soft dirt, another cheer rose as he tossed the dirt to the side, one voice louder than the rest.

"D-I-G! Dig, dig, dig!"

Dylan's little legs were flying, but Liza's mother had a good grip on him, holding him in the back of the crowd. Nate gestured him over.

"C'mere, buddy!"

Paulette let him go, and Dylan shot through the crowd straight to Nate, falling in the soft dirt the minute he reached it. That caused another eruption of crowd noise and cameras snapping, but all Nate saw was the beautiful face of his child.

Without thinking, he dropped to his knees, and Dylan reached up and threw filthy hands all over him, smearing his white Polo with dirt.

"Dylan!" Liza laughed, kneeling next to both of them.

"N-A-T-E!" he cried, smacking his hands on Nate's chest, making him howl with laughter.

"You know what I have to teach you, kid?"

"Not to rub dirt on nice white shirts?" Liza suggested.

He shook his head. "Another word to spell." He leaned closer to Dylan to whisper. "D-A-D."

Next to him, he heard Liza's sweet sigh of contentment, an echo of everything he felt right then. He put his arm around her and squeezed both of them with everything he had. "It'll go great with M-O-M."

Dylan threw a joyous handful of dirt into the air, letting it rain down all over the new Ivory family.

Books by Roxanne St. Claire

The Billionaires of Barefoot Bay
Secrets on the Sand
Seduction on the Sand
Scandal on the Sand

The Barefoot Bay Series (Contemporary Romance)
Barefoot in the Sand
Barefoot in the Rain
Barefoot in the Sun
Barefoot by the Sea

The Guardian Angelinos (Romantic Suspense)
Edge of Sight
Shiver of Fear
Face of Danger

The Bullet Catchers (Romantic Suspense)
Kill Me Twice
Thrill Me to Death
Take Me Tonight
First You Run
Then You Hide
Now You Die
Hunt Her Down
Make Her Pay
Pick Your Poison (a novella)

Stand-alone Novels (Romance and Suspense)
Space in His Heart
Hit Reply
Tropical Getaway
French Twist
Killer Curves
Don't You Wish (Young Adult)

About The Author

Roxanne St. Claire is a *New York Times* and *USA Today* bestselling author of more than thirty novels of suspense and romance, including three popular series (*The Bullet Catchers*, *The Guardian Angelinos*, and *Barefoot Bay*) and multiple stand-alone books. Her entire backlist, including excerpts and buy links, can be found at www.roxannestclaire.com.

In addition to being a six-time nominee and one-time winner of the prestigious Romance Writers of America RITA Award, Roxanne's novels have won the National Reader's Choice Award for best romantic suspense three times, and the Borders Top Pick in Romance, as well as the Daphne du Maurier Award, the HOLT Medallion, the Maggie, Booksellers Best, Book Buyers Best, the Award of Excellence, and many others. Her books have been translated into dozens of languages and are routinely included as a Doubleday/Rhapsody Book Club Selection of the Month.

Roxanne lives in Florida with her husband and two teens, and can be reached via her website, www.roxannestclaire.com or on her Facebook Reader page, www.facebook.com/roxannestclaire and on Twitter at www.twitter.com/roxannestclaire.